W9-AVJ-788

THE TALE OF
OAT CAKE CRAG

THE COTTAGE TALES OF
BEATRIX POTTER

LT

THE TALE OF
OAT CAKE CRAG

SUSAN WITTIG ALBERT

WHEELER
CHIVERS

This Large Print edition is published by Wheeler Publishing, Waterville, Maine, USA and by AudioGO Ltd, Bath, England.
Wheeler Publishing, a part of Gale, Cengage Learning.

The text of this Large Print edition is unabridged.
Other aspects of the book may vary from the original edition.
Set in 16 pt. Plantin.

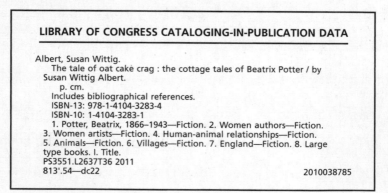

LIBRARY OF CONGRESS CATALOGING-IN-PUBLICATION DATA

Albert, Susan Wittig.
 The tale of oat cake crag : the cottage tales of Beatrix Potter / by Susan Wittig Albert.
  p. cm.
 Includes bibliographical references.
 ISBN-13: 978-1-4104-3283-4
 ISBN-10: 1-4104-3283-1
 1. Potter, Beatrix, 1866–1943—Fiction. 2. Women authors—Fiction. 3. Women artists—Fiction. 4. Human-animal relationships—Fiction. 5. Animals—Fiction. 6. Villages—Fiction. 7. England—Fiction. 8. Large type books. I. Title.
PS3551.L2637T36 2011
813'.54—dc22   2010038785

BRITISH LIBRARY CATALOGUING-IN-PUBLICATION DATA AVAILABLE

Published in 2011 in the U.S. by arrangement with The Berkley Publishing Group, a member of Penguin Group (USA) Inc.
Published in 2011 in the U.K. by arrangement with The Berkley Publishing Group, a division of Penguin Group (USA).

U.K. Hardcover: 978 1 408 49407 3 (Chivers Large Print)
U.K. Softcover: 978 1 408 49408 0 (Camden Large Print)

Printed in the United States of America
1 2 3 4 5 6 7 15 14 13 12 11

*For Dani Greer and my sisters
at the Story Circle Lifewriters' Group who
are always ready with a virtual cup of tea,
a scone, and a cheerful word*

Lake Windermere

Windermere Ferry

Belle Isle

The Ferry Landing

FAR SAWREY

NEAR SAWREY

Wilfin Beck

N

1. Hill Top Farm
2. Tower Bank Arms
3. Tower Bank House
4. High Green Gate
5. Belle Green
6. Post Office
7. Rose Cottage
8. The Vicarage
9. Tidmarsh Manor
10. The Brockery
11. Oat Cake Crag
12. Lakeshore Manor
13. Raven Hall
14. Cockshott Point

CAST OF CHARACTERS

(* indicates an actual historical
person or creature)

PEOPLE OF THE
LAND BETWEEN THE LAKES

Beatrix Potter* is best known for her children's books, beginning with *The Tale of Peter Rabbit* (1901). Miss Potter lives with her parents, **Helen and Rupert Potter,** at Number Two Bolton Gardens, in South Kensington, London. She spends as much time as possible at Hill Top Farm, in the Lake District village of Near Sawrey. **Mr. and Mrs. Jennings** and their children live in the Hill Top farmhouse and manage the farm while Miss Potter is in London.

Will Heelis,* a solicitor, lives in the nearby market town of Hawkshead and is a frequent visitor to Near Sawrey. He and Miss Potter became secretly engaged in *The Tale of Applebeck Orchard.*

9

Winston Churchill,* First Lord of the Admiralty, is an ardent supporter of aeroplane development and a visitor to the aeroplane factory.

Mr. Fred L. Baum, landowner and aeroplane developer, lives at Lakeshore Manor. His partner and pilot, **Oscar Wyatt,** also built the aeroplane. **Paddy Pratt** is a former odd-jobs man at the manor, recently discharged by Mr. Baum.

Captain Miles Woodcock and his new wife, **Margaret Nash Woodcock,** live in Tower Bank House. Mrs. Woodcock is the former headmistress of Sawrey School. Captain Woodcock is the justice of the peace for Sawrey District.

Dimity Woodcock Kittredge, Captain Woodcock's sister, is married to **Major Christopher Kittredge,** the master of Raven Hall. The Kittredges have two small children, **Flora** and **Baby Christopher.**

Vicar Samuel Sackett is the vicar of St. Peter's Church in Far Sawrey. **Mrs. Hazel Thompson** (a cousin of Agnes Llewellyn) keeps house for him.

Mrs. Grace Lythecoe, a widow who lives in Rose Cottage, is the object of Vicar Sackett's affection.

Sarah Barwick operates the Anvil Cottage Bakery in Near Sawrey. She is a Modern

Woman who wears trousers and rides a bicycle to deliver her baked goods.

Jeremy Crosfield, eighteen, has finished his studies at Kelsick and is currently teaching at Sawrey School. He is an artist and amateur botanist.

Deirdre Malone, seventeen, keeps the accounts for **Desmond Sutton**'s veterinary practice and helps **Rose Sutton** manage the eight Sutton children at Courier Cottage.

Caroline Longford, seventeen, a student of music composition at the Royal Academy of London, is visiting her grandmother, **Lady Longford,** at Tidmarsh Manor.

Lester Barrow operates the village pub, the Tower Bank Arms.

George and Mathilda Crook live at Belle Green, where Mrs. Crook takes in boarders. Mr. Crook is the village blacksmith.

Dick and Agnes Llewellyn live next door to Belle Green, at High Green Gate.

Lucy Skead is the village postmistress. She lives with her husband, **Joseph** (the sexton at St. Peter's in Far Sawrey), at Low Green Gate Cottage.

John Braithwaite is the constable for both Near and Far Sawrey. He and his wife, **Hannah,** live at Croft End Cottage with their children.

11

OTHER CREATURES OF THE
LAND BETWEEN THE LAKES

Tabitha Twitchit, president of the Village Cat Council, is a calico cat with an orange-and-white bib, currently residing with Mrs. Lythecoe. **Crumpet** is a handsome gray tabby who covets Tabitha's place on the Council.

Rascal, a Jack Russell terrier, lives with the Crooks at Belle Green but spends his time managing the daily life of the village.

Winston the pony lives at Hill Top Farm and takes Miss Potter wherever she wants to go.

Professor Galileo Newton Owl, D.Phil., is a tawny owl who conducts advanced studies in astronomy and applied natural history from his home in a hollow beech in Cuckoo Brow Wood and his lookout post atop Oat Cake Crag.

Thorvaald, a teenaged dragon, frequently visits his friend **Bailey Badger** at Briar Bank. **Thackery,** a guinea pig, lives there, too.

Hyacinth Badger is in charge of The Brockery, a famous animal hostelry on Holly How. Also in residence: **Bosworth Badger XVII,** retired from his post as holder of the Badge of Authority; Hyacinth's mother,

Primrose, chief housekeeper; and **Parsley,** chef.

1

THE PROFESSOR IS PERPLEXED

In the northwestern corner of England, in the Land Between the Lakes, March is a month of uncertain weather. One day brings snow and sharp frosts, the next offers mild temperatures and misty fog, and then it turns off blustery, wild, and wet. And whilst the distant fells may shiver under snowy shawls and mufflers of winter-brown bracken, the high mountain becks are festooned with frosty icicles, and the wind howls through the rock cairns, the lower dales hold the promise of green, and on the brightest days, the blue lakes and tarns reflect the bluest of blue skies. In fact, it might be said that March is a month of all weathers, occurring altogether at once.

Our story takes place in March 1912. The previous year had brought many changes to England, including the coronation of a new king. George V had been crowned in June, and the twin villages of Near and Far

Sawrey had celebrated the momentous event with a great flower show and a fair. There was a merry-go-round with wooden horses and camels and swans for the children, a concert by the Village Volunteer Band (Lester Barrow on trombone, Lawrence Baldwin on coronet, Tyler Taylor and Clyde Clinder on clarinet, and Sam Stern on the concertina), and a spirited dance exhibition by the Hawkshead Morris Men, kitted out for the occasion in gay vests, ties, sashes, and hats.

After the almost unbearable excitement of this grand event, it had been hard for the village to return to the everyday work of gardening, dairying, haying, and harvesting. But they managed somehow and life went on as usual, more or less. Vicar Sackett performed two marriages in July and August; several new babies were born in September; and in October, three new cottages went up on the outskirts of Far Sawrey, on land that had once been a sheep meadow. New people were moving to the Land Between the Lakes, and some of them brought new ideas and new ways of doing things, which did not sit well with the local folk.

November and December passed without any excitement whatever in the village, although there was plenty going on elsewhere. Captain Miles Woodcock (who serves as justice of the peace for Near and Far Sawrey) read in *The Times* that the Admiralty, now under the direction of Mr. Winston Churchill, was readying itself for military action against the German Navy, should the need arise. Two new super-dreadnoughts had just been commissioned, with four more planned for 1912. The prospect of a German attack against Belgium (which was what the Admiralty seemed to most fear) was unsettling, not the sort of thing one likes to read in one's newspaper at one's breakfast table on a peaceful Monday morning. But the captain was so blissfully happy with his new wife — the former Miss Margaret Nash, head teacher at Sawrey School — that he was able to put his concerns aside, at least for the moment. (If you have not read *The Tale of Applebeck Orchard,* you might put the title on your reading list, for it tells the story of how this confirmed bachelor came to propose — on his knees, amidst pieces of broken crockery and a spreading puddle of tea and milk — to Miss Nash.)

The new year brought storms, and as usual in the winter, the villagers kept to their firesides as much as possible. January, like the previous months, crept by without incident, except that one of the Braithwaite boys slid down Stony Lane on his toboggan, crashed into the stone wall in front of High Green Gate, and broke his nose. In February, the Windermere ferry suffered a boiler breakdown and was closed for repairs for nearly a week, forcing everyone to stay on one side of the lake or the other, or travel all the way down to the south end, across the River Leven on Newby Bridge, and back again. It was very inconvenient, and all were glad when Henry Stubbs got the ferry operating again, especially because February was cold, and Newby Bridge was six long miles away.

Now it is March, and the weather has warmed. The month has so far been mild, with a snowfall that quickly melted away. On days when the sky is not gray with scudding clouds and the air not thick with mist, the sun is pleased to shed a little extra light on the pleasant landscape below, to warm the red-berried hollies and the backs of wooly gray sheep grazing the hillsides. In fact, I think it is fair to say that there is no place on this earth that gives the sun so much pleasure as this lovely green land, with its rambling rock walls, quiet lanes, tranquil waters, and long, sweet silences.

Ah, those silences! We modern folk, who live with the raucous roar of traffic, the ringing of telephones, the blare of radio and television, and the constant company of tiny gadgets that pour words and music into our ears, may find it hard to imagine how silent it was in the country in those long-ago days. Even people who lived at the time in London never failed to remark the superb silences of the countryside, broken only by the most natural of sounds. On any given day in the Lake District village of Near Sawrey, all that could be heard was the cautionary bleating of Tibbie and Queenie (Herdwick ewes-in-chief at Miss Potter's Hill Top Farm), and the gossipy conversations of blue tits and finches, who spend the cold months deep in the hedges, busily doing as little as possible. One might occasionally hear the bell at St. Peter's, or the cheerful ring of George Crook's blacksmith's hammer against the anvil, but these sounds seemed as natural as Tibbie and the blue tits. Indeed, this world was so peaceful and serene that you might think you had stepped into a pastoral painting, where the painter had lovingly recorded the whole lovely landscape, including everything but the sound.

Or perhaps not.

Certainly not if you happen to be Professor Galileo Newton Owl, D. Phil., who has just returned from a lengthy visit with Old Brown. The Professor's cousin lives on an out-of-the way island in Derwentwater (made famous by Miss Beatrix Potter in her book *The Tale of Squirrel Nutkin*), which is cut off from communication. At this moment, dusk is falling, and the owl, his wings folded neatly, is perched atop the spreading oak on Oak Cake Crag, one of his favorite lookout posts. From the crag, a massive stone outcrop overlooking the blue waters of Windermere, he can see the full breadth of this fine lake. He cannot see its full length, however, for even though the Professor has excellent eyesight (especially just at dusk), Windermere is nearly eleven miles long, the longest lake in all England.

But he can certainly see and hear enough to be both greatly annoyed and even more greatly perplexed, although I doubt he would want me to tell you this. Professor Owl likes to believe that he knows everything about everything. When he encounters something he doesn't understand, he becomes highly irritated. (Perhaps you know one or two people who resemble the Professor in this regard.) Just at this moment, he is deeply puzzled, and therefore annoyed and even somewhat frightened, by the enormous lot of noise and commotion produced by an extraordinary winged creature, as big as a boat — no, bigger than a boat, although not quite so big as a barn — that has risen out of the water at a spot near Cockshott Point and is flying up the lake in a northerly direction.

The Professor stared, incredulous. This thing, this ungainly, ungraceful, unbeautiful, boat-like creature, was flying? *Flying?*

Yes, flying. Not just whizzing along just above the surface of the water like a respectable goose or a Whooper swan, or splashing along first on one foot and then the other, as does the blue-footed booby you have seen in pictures. This creature had left the surface of the water on the far side of the lake and had already reached a height nearly level with the Professor's oak tree. And as it turned and came closer, our owl could make out that, whilst the thing lacked a proper tail, it seemed to have two extra wings. There were four — four! — altogether, although as far as the owl could make out, none of the four seemed to flap, as of course, all wings should do.

The sight of this alien creature was startling enough, but there was more. Whereas the well-mannered flying creatures of the

Professor's acquaintance honked or hooted or crowed or croaked or quacked (each according to its nature), this one did none of that. Instead, it emitted an uncivil, earsplitting, high-pitched, frantic drone, like a billion buzzing bees, punctuated by ragged, irregular clattering coughs, quite as if the thing were choking to death.

"Who-who-whoooo?" the Professor muttered in astonishment and fright, opening both his eyes very wide. *"What-what?"*

Then he took a deep breath, summoned his imperial authority, lifted his wings, raised his voice, and demanded loudly, *"Just whoo-oo the devil are yooou, sir, and what dooo yooou think yooou are doooing?"* When the creature paid him no notice, he repeated the question, even more loudly and imperially.

Now, the Professor — a substantial tawny owl with a look of significance about him — is widely acknowledged to be one of the most important birds of the Land Between the Lakes. All of the other creatures are accustomed to answer respectfully when he speaks, and for good reason. It is certainly true that he has earned an international reputation for his scholarship in celestial mechanics (which, if you are not familiar with it, is a study of the motions of astronomical objects such as stars and planets), achieved by years spent in diligent search of the night skies with a telescope from his beech-tree observatory and residence on Claife Heights. Amongst his peers, he is widely respected for his detailed work on celestial navigation.

Locally, however, the Professor is better known for his studies in applied natural history. He takes a special and very personal interest in the mannerisms and tastes of certain feathered, furred, and scaly creatures who live in his territory, which extends across the Land Between the Lakes. Having selected and captured his research subjects, he carries them back to his beech tree, where they are invited to join him for a midnight snack. I think you can see why he is respected and even feared.

But the exotic fixed-wing flying creature the Professor could see on the lake was not as respectful as the natives. In fact, the thing simply ignored his repeated questions — *rudely* ignored them, I am sorry to say. Buzzing and clacking and clattering, it flew very close to Oat Cake Crag, taunting the Professor. Then it cocked its wings, turned sharply (How *did* it do that without a single flap?), and buzzed and clanked and clattered and coughed itself out of sight around a wooded point of land.

The Professor stared incredulously after it. Something ominous had obviously happened whilst he was away on holiday. There had been a breakdown in the natural order of things. An alien flying thing had invaded his territory. If it were permitted to stay, it was very likely to multiply (since it is in the nature of all creatures to reproduce themselves), which would mean that the skies would soon be filled with heaven-knows-how-many impertinent flying things who made a great deal of noise and rudely refused to identify themselves when challenged. To make matters worse, he knew nothing about the origin of this incredible thing, its capacities, and (most of all) its intentions. It might be entirely good-natured and benign, or it might attack. It might bite. And since it was obviously very large, its bite was quite likely to be deadly.

The Professor shuddered. He himself was a strong flyer and could likely evade any tactics that even a much larger enemy — such as this *thing,* which was as large as a thrashing machine — might employ. But what about the smaller birds, especially the water birds? The great crested grebe, the mallards and teals and tufted ducks? The shelduck and the red-breasted merganser and the graylag geese and oh so many others — what of them? A creature of this immense size must have an enormous appetite and require constant feeding. Why, it could decimate Windermere's bird population in no time. And then it might go on to savage the scaled, furred, and feathered creatures who lived on the land. If nothing were done to stop it, many of the owl's research subjects might simply vanish.

Well! This situation obviously required some very careful attention. The Professor thought for a few moments. Then, with a sweep of his powerful wings, he lifted himself and flew away. He was on his way to The Brockery, a short distance away on Holly How, to discuss this dreadful business with his friend Bosworth Badger. Bosworth was always fully informed about everything that went on in the Land Between the Lakes. The owl was confident that, between the two of them, they would be able to come up with a plan.

Normally, the Professor would invite the badger to his beech tree, where they could discuss the matter in greater comfort than the cramped confines of Badger's underground home. But he was feeling urgent, and as it happened (what a lucky coincidence), it was just about teatime, and tea at The Brockery was always quite substantial. The Professor felt that a comforting cuppa would go down a treat, with perhaps a cheering bit of ham and cheese between two slices of buttered bread, and one (or two) scones. Yes, indeed. There was nothing like a bite of something to make a bird fit to tackle whatever challenges might come his way.

I'm sure you would like to follow the Professor and find out what the badger knows about this alien airborne creature. But if you don't mind, we will catch up to the owl later. Instead, we will go over to Hill Top Farm, where Miss Beatrix Potter has just come indoors from an afternoon in the garden and is about to put the kettle on to boil for her own cup of tea.

2
<u>Miss Potter Takes the Case</u>

Beatrix Potter took off her gardening gloves and her woolen jacket and hat and hung them on the peg behind the door, then slipped her feet out of the wooden-soled pattens she wore outdoors and into the softer shoes she commonly wore in the house. The pattens, handmade for her by a cobbler in Hawkshead, were the traditional footwear of farmwives in the Lakes. Beatrix loved to wear them, not just because they were practical, but because they symbolized her commitment to the garden, the farm, and the farmer's way of life.

She had spent the afternoon in the garden, planting lilacs and rhododendrons and a red fuchsia, which she had bought from a nursery in Windermere. The plants should probably have gone into the ground in late fall, but she hadn't been able to get down from London. Her parents — her father was nearly eighty and her mother in her seventies — had a large house there, and required her attention. The more she wanted to get away, the more they found they needed her.

But finally Beatrix had put her foot down. She told her parents that she wanted to spend a few quiet days to herself, in order to work out ideas for her next book, *The Tale of Mr. Tod,* the latest book in a series that had begun some ten years before, with *The Tale of Peter Rabbit.* This was partly true, although she had another reason (a more intensely personal and secret reason) for coming to the farm just now. A reason that —

But never mind: we'll get to that later. Suffice it for now to say that Beatrix *always* loved coming to Hill Top, which she had come to think of as her home in the six years she had owned the farm. It was all very beautiful and dear to her — the green meadows and woodlands and gardens and orchard and house and barn and all the animals — and she longed for it when she had to go back to dirty, sooty, smoky London, where she invariably came down with a stuffy cold the minute she stepped off the train.

Mr. and Mrs. Potter, I am sorry to say, did not happily let their only daughter go, and this departure, like every other one, seemed to precipitate a great crisis. Her mother simply couldn't understand what she saw in the sleepy little village of Near Sawrey. "But there is no *society* there, Beatrix!" Mrs. Potter complained (although "no society" was exactly what Beatrix wanted). And her father thought the farm a silly burden for a woman and the house itself "exceedingly plain and severe," without electric lights or a telephone.

Mr. Potter was very right. Hill Top was plain and severe — and still is, as you can see for yourself when you visit there, for the National Trust (to whom Beatrix donated Hill Top Farm) keeps the old farmhouse just as it was during Beatrix's time. The outside is still plastered with a pebbly mortar and painted with the gray limewash that is traditional in the area. The eight-over-eight windows still march symmetrically across the front of the house, which also features a peaked porch constructed of blue slate from a local quarry. The steep roof is covered with the same blue slate, and the chimneys still wear those peaked slate caps that always reminded Beatrix of schoolboys lined up in a row.

Beatrix herself had made many changes, although none that altered the traditional style of the house and farm. When she bought the place in 1905, it had required quite a lot of fixing. To satisfy the needs of the barnyard animals — cows, pigs, sheep, chickens, and ducks — she repaired the barn, the dairy, and the fences. To accommodate the Jennings family (Mr. and Mrs. Jennings cared for the farm and the garden in her absence), she added on several rooms and a new water system. She also built a detached kitchen at the edge of the garden, where Mrs. Jennings baked and cooked meals for everyone.

In her own part of the house, Beatrix had pulled down a partition in the main room and papered the walls in an airy green print, then laid a sea-grass rug that covered most of the floor and a smaller, shaggy blue one in front of the cast-iron range. Red curtains and a red geranium at the window, the fire on the hearth, and an antique oak cupboard for her collection of dishes delighted her with their hominess. The other rooms suited her, too: the downstairs parlor with its formal marble fireplace and richly paneled walls; her bedroom upstairs, with its window overlooking the farmyard and garden; and the treasure room, where she kept her collection of favorite things. Room by room and altogether, Beatrix felt that the house was perfect in every way. Her heart told her that this was home, and she cherished the quiet days and nights she spent here.

But today had not been nearly as quiet as she had come to expect. In fact, it had been disconcertingly *noisy.* The first disturbance had come early that morning, when the silence was shattered by the dull, hollow boom of a massive explosion. Mr. Jennings said that it must be the gunpowder works at Blackbeck, some ten miles away, near Haverthwaite. When Beatrix took the post to the village post office, Lucy Skead, the postmistress, told her that, yes, indeed, the works had blown up. Tragically, two men were dead and a half-dozen more were seriously hurt. Making gunpowder was a dangerous business, but all the works in England seemed to be gearing up to produce more powder and shells, for fear of war with the Germans. For Beatrix, a longtime pacifist who hated the thought of war, it was altogether unsettling.

Beatrix picked up the kettle and put it on the range, which was built into the fireplace alcove next to the open fire. (If you want to see how this looks, you can find pictures of it in *The Roly-Poly Pudding,* where a kitten named Tom Twitchit narrowly escapes being baked.) She took down a teapot and spooned in loose tea, then spread the red-

31

checked gingham cloth on the table and set
out a loaf of Sarah Barwick's fresh-baked
bread, butter from the morning's churning,
and the pot of blackberry jam Dimity Kittredge had given her. When the kettle
boiled, she made her tea, then ate her bread
and butter and jam with an intense pleasure,
very grateful for the quiet. The aeroplane —
the second loud disturbance that had
marred her day — had thankfully stopped
flying and gone away to its barn or its
hangar or wherever aeroplanes go when they
come down out of the air.

Now, I am sure you have already guessed
that the alien airborne creature that so
perplexed Professor Owl was an aeroplane.
You are, after all, a modern person. You have
seen many aeroplanes in your life and have
most likely flown in quite a few. We live in
an airborne age, and it is as easy for us to
take to the skies as it is to ride in a high-
speed train or drive in our automobiles
across the country.

But I'm also sure that you can forgive the
Professor for mistakenly thinking that the
aeroplane was some sort of bird. He had
never seen a flying machine and did not
even know it existed. And indeed it had not,
until just eight years before. In March 1903,
American bicycle shop owners Orville and

Wilbur Wright assembled one and flew it. The idea took off immediately, so to speak, but it was five years — in 1908 — before the first aeroplane was successfully flown in England. By 1912, at the time of our story, the Admiralty was considering its use as a possible military weapon. City folk were acquainted with aeroplanes, but most people in rural England (let alone most owls!) had never seen one.

Beatrix was not an antiprogressive, and she had no complaint about aeroplanes so long as they kept to the skies above London. With the racket of motor lorries, the hooting of automobile horns, and the clatter of horses' hooves, the city was already so noisy that the aeroplane's buzz could scarcely be heard amidst the din. But here, in the peace of the countryside, the aeroplane's noise was a different matter altogether, and deeply, deeply annoying. Not only did it intrude on her private thoughts, but it reminded her (as did the gunpowder works explosion) that the world — or at least the part of the world that the Admiralty was in charge of — was preparing for war.

She was still thinking of these unsettling matters when she finished her tea, put away the tea things, and got out a pen, ink bottle, and paper. Then she lit the paraffin lamp and settled down to write a letter to her closest friend, Millie Warne.

Millie was Norman's sister — Norman Warne, her own first, sweet love, who had died just a month after their engagement, some six years before. The loss had been devastating, but Beatrix was a practical woman, and although she felt she could never recover, she had gathered up the pieces of her shattered life and gone on. Thanks to Hill Top Farm, which had given her a new challenge to dream about and work for, she had begun to put the loss behind. And thanks to Will Heelis, who had helped to heal her heart and —

But that was another story, not an entirely happy one, and certainly not a story that she was anxious to share with Millie. Not just yet, anyway. She might have to, someday, when she could think of an easy way to tell it. But not today.

So she wrote about the weather (always a safe subject) and the noise. "Today was mild & pleasant — except for two noises." She described the explosion at the gunpowder works, and added: "The other disturbance moved me to bad language. There is a beastly fly-swimming spluttering aeroplane careering up & down over Windermere; it makes a noise like ten million bluebottles."

She dipped her pen in the ink bottle and continued, frowning as she wrote. "It is an irritating noise here, a mile off; it must be horrible in Bowness." (Bowness, if you don't know it, is a picturesque town on the east side of Windermere, quite near to the place where the aeroplane was based.) "It seems to be flying very well; but I am extremely sorry it has succeeded. It will very much spoil the Lake. It has been buzzing up and down for hours today, and it has already caused a horse to bolt & smashed a trades-man's cart."

This was something else she had heard at the post office that morning. The plane — which apparently took off and landed on the water (the reason for the Admiralty's interest, she supposed) — had buzzed low over the ferry landing on the eastern side of the lake. A drowsy old horse pulling a cart piled with empty beer kegs had taken fright and galloped off, smashing the cart to bits against a stone wall and sending cartman and beer kegs bouncing top over teakettle across the grass. (The horse is not to be blamed, certainly. He could not have ex-pected to be attacked by a flying thrashing machine, like a dragon swooping out of the sky. No wonder the poor old fellow bolted.)

Beatrix added a sentence about the shrubs

she had planted in the garden and was signing her initials ("Yours aff HBP"), when someone knocked at the door. When she opened it, she was delighted to see Mrs. Grace Lythecoe, who lived in Rose Cottage, across Kendal Road, on the other side of the village shop. With Mrs. Lythecoe were two of the village cats, Tabitha Twitchit and Crumpet.

"Is this a bad time to call?" Grace asked tentatively. "I haven't interrupted anything, I hope."

"No, of course not," Beatrix said, and stepped aside to welcome her guest. "How very nice to see you, Grace! You've had your tea?"

"I've had a bite to eat, but I wouldn't say no to a cup." Grace stepped into the room and unbuttoned her navy blue coat. Taking it off, she looked down at the two cats who had come inside with her. "Oh, dear. Tabitha is staying with me now — she must have followed me here, and I seem to have let her in. Crumpet, too. Do you mind? Shall I put them out?"

"Oh, please, no, Miss Potter!" cried Tabitha Twitchit, an older calico cat with an orange-and-white bib and fluffy fur and tail. *"My paws are cold, and I'd love to curl up by the hearth."*

"If Miss Potter doesn't mind," said Crumpet sharply, ready as always to correct Tabitha's manners. Crumpet was a handsome gray tabby, sleeker and younger than Tabitha. She wore a gold bell on her red leather collar and lived with Bertha and Henry Stubbs in one of the Lakefield cottages. Bertha, a rather rotund person who enjoyed causing trouble, was one of the village's most colorful characters.

Beatrix laughed. "I don't mind at all. In fact, I'd be glad if the cats would have a look around. They might find a little something in the cupboards to amuse them. I'm sad to say that the Jenningses' cat is an indolent creature who has no interest in patrolling for mice."

"You're certainly right about that," Tabitha remarked in a judgmental tone. *"Felicia Frummety is the laziest cat in the village."* She went to the hearth, where she stretched out full length and basked in the heat.

"Pot calling the kettle black," Crumpet muttered, and went round the table to the open cupboard.

"Seniority, my dear," purred Tabitha smugly, and licked a paw. *"I have killed more mice in my lifetime than you younger cats have seen or smelled. I am entitled to a spot of warm hearth now and then. But feel free to sniff out*

all the mice you like."

Which, from Tabitha's point of view, was a perfectly appropriate response. Having spent many years engaged as Chief Mouser in various homes in the village, she was currently living at Rose Cottage, where Mrs. Lythecoe kept her generously supplied with bread and milk in return for ridding the place of mice. But Tabitha was a clever cat and knew by long experience that a good bargain tasted better than a mouthful of musty mouse. So she had negotiated a quid-pro-quo contract with the Rose Cottage mice. They would pack their furniture and their belongings and take the children and move out to the shed at the foot of the garden, and she would pretend not to notice that they were there. You might call this blackmail, or even extortion, but it does not seem so to Tabitha, or to the mice, for that matter. It is just another gambit in the age-old game of cat and mouse.

"Just listen to those cats carry on," Grace said, hanging up her coat beside Beatrix's. "You'd think they were having a conversation."

"I'm sure they are," Beatrix remarked. She put her writing supplies away and refilled the teapot with hot water from the kettle. "Our tea will be ready in a jiffy," she added.

"Now, sit and catch me up on all the news, Grace. I've only just come down from London the day before yesterday and have been too busy with the farm and the garden to see anyone but Lucy Skead, at the post office."

Grace chuckled. "If you've seen Lucy, you've probably heard most of the news."

She pulled out a chair at the table and sat down. She was a woman of late middle age, dressed in a neat gray skirt, white blouse, and blue knitted jumper, and her dark, silver-streaked hair was twisted into a knot at the back of her head. The widow of the former vicar (that is, the vicar at St. Peter's before Vicar Sackett came there), Grace had lived in the village for a number of years and was much respected by everyone. Well, almost everyone. If you are at all acquainted with villages, you will know that at least one person in every village bears a grudge, sometimes silently, sometimes not.

"Perhaps you could tell me about the aeroplane," Beatrix suggested. "Lucy was interrupted before she could say more than a few words."

"Oh, that aeroplane!" Tabitha exclaimed, and switched her tail. *"Noisy, wretched, ugly machine! Why the Big Folk want to build such ridiculous contraptions is beyond me."*

Tabitha always held decided opinions about everything, but in this case, she was voicing the opinion of all the village animals, who had devoted a great deal of heated discussion to the subject since the contraption had appeared. Mostly, it flew up and down Windermere, but it made occasional sorties over the land. And anyway, the noise was so loud that it could be heard for miles. It echoed off the hills and fells and (especially since the animals were not accustomed to loud mechanical noises) always sounded as if it were directly overhead. At first, the dogs and cats had run for cover, thinking that they were under attack. And the birds . . . well, the poor birds could not for the life of them make any sense of the thing. You know how excitable birds are. They fled for their lives, chirping and screeching, shouting that the awful creature was about to gobble them up.

"Ah, that aeroplane." Grace sighed. "Or rather, hydroplane, as we are supposed to call it, since it lands and takes off from the water. You've heard the beastly thing, then, have you?"

"*Beastly!*" Crumpet growled, coming out of the cupboard. "*Really, Mrs. Lythecoe, I do wish you wouldn't use that word. We beasts have nothing at all to do with that mechanical* monster. It's entirely a man-made invention."

"Heard it?" Beatrix made a wry face. "I couldn't *not* hear it, Grace. I spent the afternoon in the garden, and that infernal buzzing drowned out every other noise. It utterly destroys the peace of the landscape."

"It's even worse for cats than for people, Miss Potter," Tabitha put in. *"Our hearing is remarkably keen, you know. We are terribly sensitive to noise."* To Crumpet, she added, with a superior look, *"I see that you couldn't manage to find a mouse."*

"There's not one to be seen," Crumpet grumbled. *"Maybe Felicity's mended her ways."*

Beatrix eyed the cats, chuckling. "I'm sorry you were disappointed, Crumpet. Perhaps Mrs. Jennings has been setting mousetraps whilst I've been gone. A little milk might make you feel better." Suiting the deed to the word, she put down a saucer and filled it with milk from the jug. "Tabitha, you can share it, too."

"Thank you, Miss Potter," the cats chorused, and settled down to lap up the milk. They had learnt long ago that most of the Big People could not understand what they said. (This does not include young children, of course, who often know exactly what the cats and dogs are talking about.) But Miss

41

Potter was an exception. Whether it was because she had such a long experience of drawing cats and mice and ducks and dogs and foxes for her little books, or because she had some sort of natural affinity for animals and listened carefully when they spoke, she often appeared to know what they were saying. Not the exact words, perhaps, but the gist of it.

Beatrix poured tea into two cups, then set out sugar, milk, and lemon. "That hydroplane — it wasn't flying when I was here last, Grace. How long has this been going on?"

"About three weeks," Grace replied. "It has been flown almost every day, even on Sunday, and during Sunday services. St. Peter's is much nearer the lake, of course, and the pilot has occasionally flown over the church."

"Over the church!" Beatrix exclaimed. "How terribly annoying for everyone. But surely there's something that can be done. Has anyone spoken to Captain Woodcock? As justice of the peace, he ought to be able to put a stop to it."

"Unfortunately, the flights take off and land near the eastern shore of the lake, outside of the captain's jurisdiction." Grace dropped a sugar cube into her tea. "And

I'm afraid that he isn't so opposed to the thing as the rest of us. He's a military man, you know. The hydroplane is said — by its developer, anyway — to have scientific and military importance."

"Scientific," Beatrix muttered darkly. "The science of noise, I suppose. Who is this 'developer'? Someone from London, I suppose, who doesn't care to preserve the serenity of the Lakes."

Grace stirred her tea. "Oddly enough, he's a local gentleman. Fred Baum, whom I think you know. He's a neighbor of Dimity and Christopher Kittredge, at Raven Hall. He's the one who's putting up the money to build and fly the aeroplane."

"Mr. Baum!" Beatrix exclaimed. "I wouldn't have thought it. Yes, we met at Raven Hall after Dimity's marriage to Major Kittredge." She took a sip of tea. "He certainly seemed nice enough, although a little abstracted — and well, rather whimsical. I had no idea that he had any interest in aeroplanes."

"Whimsical." Grace laughed. "Such a tactful way of saying that he's an eccentric, Beatrix. But he hadn't any interest in aeroplanes, or so I understand — until a man named Oscar Wyatt came along with the idea. Mr. Wyatt is a pilot and aeroplane builder. He had the notion, apparently, that it is safer for aeroplanes to take off and land on water, rather than on the ground, and was looking for someone to put up the money. Mr. Baum has invested in the project and seems very enthusiastic about it. They built the plane in Manchester and then brought it here, or rather, to Cockshott Point, across the lake. They've constructed quite a large shed there — they call it a hangar — and are said to be manufacturing a second plane." She made a face. "So there will be two of them flying around."

"Oh, dear," Beatrix said, her eyes widening in alarm. "Cockshott Point is quite a lovely place. It's too bad for it to be used in this way." She set down her cup. "And *two* of the wretched things! What if they both fly at once? And commence flying over the village? However will people manage to shut out the noise?"

"I'm sure I don't know," Grace said. "There's to be a village meeting at the Tower Bank Arms tomorrow evening. I plan to attend — and I understand that Mr. Baum will be there to answer questions. Perhaps you will come?"

"I certainly shall," Beatrix said warmly. She pulled her brows together, thinking. "I wonder if anyone has informed Lady Longford of the meeting. Her opinion carries a great deal of weight in the district. Perhaps she could convince Mr. Baum to fly his hydroplane somewhere else — over the ocean, preferably, where there's no one to be bothered."

"Perhaps," Grace agreed, somewhat dubiously. "If she cared enough to have an opinion. Do you think you might invite her to the meeting, Beatrix? She seems to listen to you." Lady Longford, who lived a rather aloof life at Tidmarsh Manor, was not known for her support of village concerns. More often, she seemed to turn her back on what the villagers wanted, or even go contrary to their wishes, as if she wanted to spite them.

"I'll try," Beatrix said. "I intended to visit her tomorrow, anyway. I understand that Caroline is at home between terms, and I'm hoping to see her." Lady Longford's granddaughter, a favorite of Beatrix's, was studying composition at the Royal Academy of Music.

"Good," Grace said. She put down her cup and leaned forward, her gray eyes somber. "But that's not why I dropped in today, Beatrix. I'm deeply troubled about something — something personal and rather private." She hesitated, biting her lip. "I'm afraid it might require a bit of . . . well, I suppose you might call it detective work."

Now, if this request seems a bit odd, coming out of the blue as it does, perhaps I should remind you that our Miss Potter has been instrumental in solving several village mysteries. The theft of the Constable miniature painting from Anvil Cottage, the mysterious death of poor old Ben Hornby on Holly How, the identity of the baby left in a basket at Hill Top's door, and (most recently) the fires at Applebeck Farm — these are some of the puzzles that have been handily solved by Miss Potter. In fact, in the six years the villagers have known her, she has earned quite a local reputation for her investigative prowess, although I'm sure that she herself wouldn't call it that. If we were to ask, she would only say (quite modestly) that she simply used her eyes and her brain and put two and two together when called upon to do so. Any thoughtful person could have arrived at the same conclusions, if he or she had put half a mind to the task. But even Captain Woodcock had felt compelled to accuse Miss Potter of exercising supernatural powers of observation, and to remark that she was easily the equal of Sherlock Holmes.

"Detective work!" Beatrix exclaimed,

taken seriously aback by the look on her friend's face. "Why, Grace — you look frightened. Whatever is the matter? What can I do?"

"I am frightened, a little," Grace said in a low voice. She looked down. "I suppose I should start by telling you that Vicar Sackett has asked me to marry him."

Tabitha, full of milk and half-dozing by the fire, suddenly woke up. *"You see there, Crumpet?"* she crowed. *"I told you that Mrs. Lythecoe and the vicar are getting married, and you wouldn't believe me."*

"I apologize, Tabitha," Crumpet said. She harrumphed. *"I should have known that you were telling the truth. You're the biggest eavesdropper I've ever seen."*

"I am not an eavesdropper!" Tabitha retorted huffily. *"I was sitting in the very same room when he asked her, warming my paws at the fire."* She sighed. *"It's such a wonderful match, don't you think?"* A sentimental cat, Tabitha had lost her mate many years before and mourned him ever since. *"The vicar is a bit dithery, but he has always been one of my favorite people. And Mrs. Lythecoe is . . . well, there's no one nicer. She is the soul of generosity, especially when it comes to table scraps."*

"They'll make a good team," Crumpet agreed, sitting on her haunches and wiping her milky whiskers with her paw. *"As a former vicar's wife, she certainly knows what she's letting herself in for. And of course, the parish will be pleased."*

I daresay that Crumpet is right. Everyone in Claife Parish agrees that the vicar is a wonderful man who has the very best interests of his parishioners at heart. But they also know that the parish is sorely in want of a vicar's wife, who will bring her woman's touch to their spiritual community. It is, after all, not quite the thing for the vicar to organize the monthly jumble sale, especially when he's not all that well organized himself.

Beatrix clapped her hands delightedly. "The vicar has asked you to marry him? This is exciting news, Grace! I do hope you've said yes. When will the wedding take place?"

"We were planning to marry on April twentieth. The banns have already been read." Grace fished in her jumper pocket for a handkerchief and blew her nose. "But I'm afraid there are . . . complications."

"Complications?" Beatrix studied her friend, frowning. "Vicar Sackett is a wonderful man, Grace. You've known each other

48

for ten years or so, and I'm sure that the two of you would be very happy together. What in the world can you mean by 'complications'? If you love each other and agree that you want to marry, whatever would prevent you?"

There was a note of envy and perhaps even exasperation in Beatrix's voice. She herself had been prevented by her parents from marrying Norman Warne, whom they judged "not good enough" for their daughter. An editor who worked at his family's publishing house and shepherded Beatrix's books into print, Norman belonged to a different social class than the status-conscious Potters — although, of course, that was not their only reason. They intended to keep their only daughter at home, so that she could look after them in their old age, and had been secretly gratified when Norman had suddenly died. So Beatrix had pretty much resigned herself to being a spinster. Hill Top Farm and her children's books had given her some of the freedom she craved, but she feared that she could never marry. Not, at least, as long as her parents were alive. And although they were both old and often in ill health, neither showed signs of a serious illness or any indication of reconsidering their resolve. Even now, when Will

Heelis was pressing her to . . . but there. I've gone too far again. I'm sorry, but that part of our story will just have to wait.

Grace twisted her handkerchief. "I know I can count on you not to speak of this to anyone else," she said. Her voice was now so low that Beatrix could almost not hear her words. "I haven't even told the vicar about . . ." She pulled in her breath. "I've only told him that I think it might be prudent to delay our wedding a little. He would be devastated if he knew the truth."

"Uh-oh," Tabitha said, her eyes very dark.

Crumpet looked up. *"Uh-oh what?"*

Tabitha shook her head. Her tail twitched from side to side. *"I knew that Mrs. Lythecoe was very upset when she got those letters,"* she said in a low voice, *"and now I know why. It's blackmail."*

"If he knew about what?" Beatrix asked. She leaned forward and took her friend's hand. "My dear Grace, surely there is nothing that would keep you and the vicar from —"

"Letters." Grace turned her face away. "Anonymous letters, unsigned. Saying . . . hateful things."

"Anonymous letters?" Crumpet was staring at Tabitha. *"You knew this? You knew about these letters and you didn't tell me?"*

50

"*I don't have to tell you everything, do I?*" Tabitha retorted.

"*But you* knew!" Crumpet wailed disconsolately. "*Why, you probably even know who's writing those letters! And you didn't say a word!*"

Tabitha gave her a cross look. "*If I told you what I know, the story would be all over the village in no time. You'd never be able to keep quiet about something this important.*"

Now, you might be wondering just what Tabitha knows and how she found it out, and so (I confess) am I. But I must remind us that whilst she may be getting on in years, she is still a highly competitive cat who takes every opportunity to gain the upper paw over Crumpet — and all the other village cats, as well. I am really very sorry, but I can't tell you whether what Tabitha said just now — what she implied, actually — remotely resembles the truth. She might know something important. In fact, she might even know who is writing those letters. But then again, she might not. Tabitha is not above telling a very large fib just to make herself look and feel important.

Crumpet, however, took Tabitha at her word. Stung, she sat up on her haunches. "*That's stuff and nonsense,*" she spit. "*I can keep a secret as well as the next cat!*"

51

"Oh, really?" Tabitha snarled. *"Then how did Rascal find out about what happened in the kitchen at Tower Bank House last week? I told you in the strictest confidence. You promised not to tell a soul! And the next thing I knew, all the animals were talking about it. Why, even Max the Manx had heard the story, all the way over in Far Sawrey."*

Crumpet shrilled a laugh. *"What makes you think I'm the one who told? It could have been anybody. It could have been —"*

"Hush!" Beatrix commanded sternly. "If you cats can't be quiet, you're going outdoors." To Grace, she said, "I am so sorry to hear about this, Grace. It must be perfectly dreadful for you. But surely you ought to just ignore the letters and go on about the business of making yourself and the vicar very happy — as I'm sure you will."

"Ignore them?" Grace cried. "How can I ignore them, Beatrix? Anyway, it's not as if I actually believed anything the writer says — although there's nothing very definite, just ugly hints. And of course, there's not a shred of truth in any of it. But that's worse, don't you see? Whoever is writing these things, he's making them up. And if he isn't stopped, he might do something worse. He might spread a rumor, or tell a tale. And you know what villages are like. Once somebody hears a whisper of scandal, it's all over the place in no time. Something like that would hurt the vicar's reputation. Could damage it irretrievably."

Beatrix considered that for a moment. "I suppose you might be right," she said reluctantly. "Although it's hard to believe that anyone who knows you and the vicar could do something like this."

Grace nodded miserably, twisting her handkerchief in her fingers. "That's almost the worst of it, you know. Walking through the village, wondering who it is. Wondering what will come next." She stopped, and her voice became firmer. "That's what I want you to do for me, Beatrix. Find out who's writing these letters and make them stop. Please. You must."

"Now, that's a good idea," Crumpet said approvingly. *"After all, Miss Potter has solved more than one of our local mysteries."*

Tabitha could not disagree with this, for it was true. Miss Potter seemed to have some sort of sixth sense where secrets were concerned.

Beatrix frowned. "Have you discussed this with Captain Woodcock? I'm sure there must be some sort of law against —"

"But I can't, don't you see?" Grace interrupted. "The captain would insist on conducting an investigation, and he couldn't do it privately. Word of it would be sure to get out. I can't take that risk."

"Well, then," Beatrix asked reasonably, "how about talking it over with the vicar? He might have an idea about —"

"Oh, dear, no!" Grace's eyes widened and she gave her head a hard shake. "I could never do that. You know him, Beatrix. Samuel . . . Reverend Sackett is such a gentleman, so tenderhearted. He would be terribly hurt to think that someone — one of his parishioners, most likely — was writing such poisonous letters. He mustn't know, ever."

"But what if —" Beatrix was about to ask what would happen if something the letter writer had said turned out to be true, but Grace put up a hand, stopping her.

"I'm sorry, Beatrix," she said miserably. "I know this is very difficult, and I am so sorry to impose on you in this way. But I can't think of anyone else who can help me — anyone I can trust. Will you?"

"Poor Miss Potter," Crumpet said. *"It sounds like an unsolvable mystery. Where will she even begin?"*

Beatrix sighed. Anonymous letters, poisonous messages, unhappy secrets, a furtive investigation into something ugly and nasty.

It wasn't the sort of thing she wanted to be involved in. But Grace Lythecoe had been kind to her when she needed a friend. Vicar Sackett was a very good man. And of course, Grace was right. Someone who would write poisoned pen letters might be driven to do something that would cause real and lasting harm. That shouldn't be allowed to happen, Beatrix thought bleakly. And if the situation were reversed, if she were in this sort of trouble — in any trouble, really — she knew that Grace would do whatever she could to help.

"Well, I suppose," she said slowly. "Yes, of course, Grace. I'll help."

"Very good!" Crumpet exclaimed. *"So brave of you, Miss Potter!"*

"Our Miss Potter," Tabitha said. *"On the case."*

"But I'll need to see the letters," Beatrix went on. "How many are there? Did you bring them with you?"

Grace shook her head numbly. "There are three. The most recent came just last week. But I didn't think it was wise to carry them around. They're at my house. I've hidden them in a safe place."

"I see," Beatrix said. She straightened her shoulders and added briskly, "Well, then, I suppose I ought to go to Rose Cottage with you and read them, don't you think?"

"Oh, would you?" Grace asked eagerly. "Beatrix, I don't know how I can ever thank you."

"You mustn't expect too much, Grace," Beatrix replied in a cautionary tone. "I may not be able to help at all. And in the end —" She stopped.

"In the end what?" Tabitha asked.

"Yes, what?" Crumpet demanded.

But Beatrix didn't finish the sentence. She had been about to say that in the end, even if she was able to find out who was writing the letters and why, Grace might not have cause to thank her.

Where secrets of the heart were concerned, Beatrix had learnt that the truth — even when it could be uncovered — was not always welcome. Sometimes, it was better not to know.

3

THE PROFESSOR
PUTS HIS FOOT IN IT

Professor Owl did not shilly-shally. Perplexed and uneasy in his mind, he flew straightaway to find his friend Bosworth Badger XVII. Bosworth resided at The Brockery, a very large badger sett at the top of Holly How. He served as the chief badger historian, maintaining the official *History of the Badgers of the Land Between the Lakes* and its companion project, the *Holly How Badger Genealogy.* The badger had always taken his duties as a historian very seriously, recording in detail the various events, episodes, accidents, adventures, misadventures, and other happenstances that occurred throughout the area. The Professor was confident that Bosworth would be able to tell him everything that was known (if indeed anything at all *was* known!) about the rude, impertinent winged creature that had accosted him at Oat Cake Crag.

So upon his arrival at The Brockery's front door, the owl rang the bell as loudly as he could, and shifted from one foot to the other whilst he waited impatiently for someone to open the door and let him in. No one did, at least not right away, so the Professor took a moment to study the Badger Coat of Arms, which was painted on a wooden sign over the door pull. (He was thinking, if you must know, that he himself could do with a coat of arms, and was wondering how he might go about getting it.)

This one, which was quite attractive, bore twin badgers rampant on an azure field, with a shield inscribed in Latin with the badger family motto:

De Parvis, grandis acervus erit.

Which, translated into English, proclaims: *From small things, there will grow a mighty heap,* or, as the local folk put it, *Many littles make a mickle, Many mickles make a mile.* This referred, as the Professor knew, to the badgers' habit of excavating their extensive burrows, each generation adding to the work of preceding generations until there was a mile or more of labyrinthine underground tunnels, with great heaps of dirt piled outside the various entrances and exits. As a result, most badger setts were much too large for individual badgers, and were often used as convenient temporary refuges by animals in search of shelter.

But The Brockery was exceptionally large, even by badger standards, and over the years had gained a wide reputation as an animal hostelry. On any given day, you might go down a hall and discover a fox and a pair of hedgehogs in residence, or a trio of traveling mice and an interesting assortment of spiders, or several squirrels and a variety of voles, or even an itinerant badger from another district, stopping in to catch up on the news. Of course, all animals (including the foxes and stoats who might have an appetite for the mice and voles) had to behave in a civil way toward one another, even — or especially — at the table. Bosworth would not tolerate any animosity or ill-will. "If you can't behave," he had been heard to say, "you can go somewhere else to eat."

The owl rang again, frowning. It was taking longer than usual for someone to open the door, for the simple reason that there was nobody at hand to answer the bell. Flotsam and Jetsam, the twin rabbit housemaids who usually welcomed the guests, had both been sent down to the garden behind the hotel in Far Sawrey to collect a few carrots and turnips for tomorrow's dinner. Parsley, who cooked The Brockery's meals, was visiting her sister near Wilfin Beck. Primrose, the housekeeper, had gone with her, and they hadn't yet returned. Hyacinth (she had recently taken Bosworth's place as the holder of the Badger Badge of Authority and the manager of the hostelry) had gone over to Briar Bank, to invite Bailey Badger and his guinea-pig roommate, Thackeray, to a birthday party. It was Bosworth's birthday and the party was supposed to be a surprise, but the old badger had overheard Hyacinth whispering to Parsley and Primrose about it. He had immediately stopped listening and felt pleased and honored that they would plan such a thing. Now he had something very special to look forward to.

Since everyone else was gone, Bosworth was the only animal left minding the shop, as it were. Glad to be alone for the afternoon, he had spent it in the library, which he had always considered quite the nicest room in The Brockery. The cheery fire cast intriguing shadows on the familiar gilt-framed family portraits that hung on the walls. The comfortable leather chair, spread with Primrose's green-and-brown crocheted afghan, was waiting with open arms beside the fireplace, and the heavy oak table cordially invited him to sit and write. It served as a desk, with his pencils laid out in a neat row, his knife ready to sharpen the pencils, and his inkpot and pen and blotting paper at hand, all very nice for a badger who especially fancied his work as a historian. For whilst Hyacinth had assumed the physically demanding work of managing The Brockery, Bosworth — who was getting on in years and glad to put that part of his life behind him — still maintained the *History* and the *Genealogy.*

In fact, just a few moments ago, the badger had completed a current-events entry in the *History* and had returned the leather-bound volume to its place on the shelf. The place was so quiet (underground houses are very quiet indeed, with a way of swallowing up any loud noises) and the leather chair beside the fire so perfectly inviting, and the fire itself such a lovely sort of warm. So he settled into the chair, pulled the afghan close around him, put his feet on the fender to warm his toes, and dozed off. And why not? There were no animals around to hinder him, nothing he was required to do (he was, after all, semiretired), and a nap before tea was the very nicest thing he could think of.

Bosworth was sleeping quite happily when he dreamed that there was some sort of emergency — a fire, perhaps. Yes, most certainly a fire, for someone was ringing the fire bell with great urgency, *clang-clang-clang.* The badger woke with a start, hoisted himself out of the chair, and made for the closet, where a bucket of water — painted red and clearly marked FIRE BUCKET — was always kept ready to be used in case of a fire emergency. He had the bucket in hand and was making his way down the hall when he realized that the bell he had heard (was still hearing, in fact) was not a fire bell at all.

It was the doorbell. Whoever was pulling the bell pull was doing so with a great deal of fervor.

Bosworth put down the bucket. *"Jetsam!"* he called. *"Get the door, will you?"* He paused, waiting. Then he called, louder, *"Flotsam! Where are you? Someone wants to come in!"*

But then he remembered that both Flotsam and Jetsam — and Parsley and Primrose and Hyacinth, as well — had gone out for the afternoon, and he was alone. So it was up to him to answer the doorbell, which continued to peal furiously.

So he picked up the bucket, stumped crossly to the door, and opened it. He did so with caution, of course, remembering the Seventh Badger Rule of Thumb (Rules of Thumbs are maxims according to which badgers govern themselves): *Even if one hopes for friends at the door, one is well advised to anticipate enemies.* Badgers were vulnerable even in their underground homes, for badger-diggers and their fierce dogs regularly roamed the countryside. More than one unfortunate badger had been forcibly removed from his home in the Land Between the Lakes. It was well to be wary.

But the animal on the other side of the door was not an enemy. It was his old friend Galileo.

"Oh, hullo, Owl," said the badger cordially. *"So it's you. Good to see you, old chap."*

To tell the truth, Bosworth was a little surprised to find the owl on his doorstep. The Professor regularly entertained his friends and colleagues in his beech-tree home, and had even installed a ladder for the convenience of those who were not by nature tree-climbers or fliers. But when it came to invitations from acquaintances who resided underground, the owl usually declined — politely, of course. He much preferred the open reaches of sky, where he could stretch his wings to the winds. He was known to feel that there was something a bit cramped and claustrophobic underground, where if he so much as lifted a wing, he was apt to knock a book off a table or a picture from a wall. Whatever the reason for his call, Bosworth knew, it must be urgent, or the owl would not be here.

"Yes, it's me," the Professor said in an irritable tone. *"It's been me fooor quite some time, ringing this bell. It's rather chilly on this hillside, yooou know."*

"I'm afraid everyone is out. Everyone but me," Bosworth added apologetically, since he was very clearly not out. *"I was having a nap. But do come in, Owl. You'll catch cold standing there."*

The owl came in. *"If everyone's out,"* he said, *"what are yooou doooing about tea?"* He looked down at the bucket. *"And why are yooou carrying that fire bucket?"*

"Because I thought there was a fire," said the badger. *"I dreamt that somebody was ringing the fire bell."*

"There is definitely nooo fire," the Professor pronounced professorially. *"But it would certainly be goood if someone would kindly offer some tea. And a sandwich or twooo,"* he

added, in a more thoughtful tone. *"Ham, if you happen to have it. Or cheese. And a scooone, perhaps."*

The badger put the bucket down. *"Well, come on then, Owl. I expect we can find a little bit of something or other."*

And with that, he led the way down the dusky hall and through the cavernous dining room, which contained a very long wooden table and enough chairs to accommodate the two dozen or more animals who frequently appeared for dinner. The Fifth Badger Rule of Thumb makes it clear that, since badgers often inherit dwellings that are much too large for them, they are expected to practice hospitality and to welcome any lodger, boarder, or dinner guest who comes their way. (This is related to the Third Rule of Thumb, generally thought of as the Aiding and Abetting Rule: *One must be as helpful as one can, for one never knows when one will require help oneself.*) Every chair at the dining table was often taken, especially during the dark days of winter when many might otherwise go hungry, and Parsley and Primrose were sometimes put to the test as cooks. It had always done Bosworth's heart good to look down the expanse of table and see so many animals eating with as much eagerness as politeness would allow.

But it was too early for supper and the table was empty, except for one hedgehog who had not left after luncheon and was asleep under a chair. The badger and the owl went through the chilly dining hall and into the kitchen. It was cheerfully warmed by a fire in the range, where a kettle was steaming. After a few moments, the two friends were seated at the kitchen worktable, with cups of tea and plates of ham-and-cheese sandwiches.

The owl found that hot tea and cold ham and cheese and Parsley's fresh-baked bread did a great deal to soothe his spirit. But it did not relieve his perplexed concern, so he came right to the point.

"I wonder what you can tell me about the creature that's flying over the lake," he said. *"I shall describe it fooor yooou. It has fooour wings that dooo not flap, and practically nooo tail (except for a piece or twooo sticking up), and it makes a horrid noise. It is enormous and must have an exceptionally large appetite."* He took a bite of his sandwich, and then another. *"I am not afraid for myself, of course,"* he added, with a careless flick of his wing. *"But I dooo fear fooor the smaller birds. The creature might devour them all!"*

"I hardly think so," the badger said in a

consoling tone as he smeared some of Parsley's homemade mustard on his sandwich. *"That is, I hardly think it eats birds. It's a flying boat, you see."*

"A flying boat?" the Professor asked incredulously, opening both eyes very wide. *"A boat that flies?"*

"Yes. Or hydroplane, as some are calling it. It's something the Big Folk are trying. An experiment, to see if aeroplanes can be made to go up and come down on water. They have given this one the name of Water Bird. A ridiculous name for the thing, I grant, but there it is."

"Aeroplanes?" The Professor, who prided himself on being well informed about everything that happened in the Land Between the Lakes, now felt distinctly ignorant and uninformed. *"Water Bird?"*

"An aeroplane is a machine with motor-car engines and wings," the badger explained gently, knowing that the Professor does not like to be told something he feels he should already know. *"I confess that I am not sure just how it works, but the wings do seem to keep the thing up in the air, regardless of how heavy it is, and the motor drives it forward. There is a propeller at the rear, although it goes around so fast that you may not have been able to see it."*

The owl was scowling fiercely as he tried to make sense of what Bosworth was telling him. *"A machine? With a motor-car engine?"*

"Yes. The latest rage, it seems, although I daresay it's only a fad." The badger chuckled wryly. *"You know how Big People are. They'll get over hydroplanes before long and be on to something else."* He paused, then added regretfully, *"Although they seem to have rather an enduring fondness for those wretched motor cars."*

Bosworth had no liking for automobiles. Men drove them very fast (it appeared that women were not allowed to drive them at all), and were utterly unmindful of any hapless dog, cat, chicken, badger, or pig who might have been crossing the road. He himself had recently seen the tragic consequences of such criminal disregard. A young cousin had been flattened a fortnight ago in the vicinity of Hawkshead, by a motor car recklessly careening down the lane after dark. The badger had left a grieving widow and four little ones. Times would be hard for them now.

"Ah, a machine!" exclaimed the owl, suddenly getting the picture. *"Of course!"* He cleared his throat. *"Hydrooooplane,"* he intoned, rolling the word around his tongue. *"Hydrooo, as in water, from the Greek,* ὑδρ.

Tooo wit: hydrooography, hydrooopathy, hydrooometer. An hydrooometer," he added professorially, *"is an instrument designed tooo find the specific gravity of a fluid. And then of course there is hydrooophobia, a symptom of canine madness. When transmitted tooo man or beast, it consists in an aversion tooo water or other liquids, and a difficulty in swallowing them. And hydrooosphere, which is tooo say —"*

"Yes, rather," said the badger hurriedly, for his friend showed every inclination of embarking upon one of the interminable lectures for which he was famous, and which would no doubt go on past bedtime. *"It is an aeroplane designed to fly up from the water. And land on it again, when it's time to come down. It's powered by petrol."*

This temporarily silenced the owl. *"Petroool?"* he repeated, in a tentative tone. *"From the Greek* πέτρσ, *meaning 'rock'? As in petroooglyphs and petrooographics, or —"*

"Exactly," the badger put in hastily, before the Professor could get started again. *"This fuel is something they get out of rocks in the ground. Petroleum is what they call it. It's the same stuff they pour into their motor cars."*

"Ah," said the owl, greatly relieved. *"Well, then. This hydroooplane eats rocks, not birds or other small creatures."* He could stop be-

ing concerned for the health of his research subjects.

"Yes," said the badger, fully understanding. He added, *"But no matter what the thing eats, it's still a dangerous threat. On the day before yesterday, it flew very low over the ferry, on which Mr. Paulson was conveying several Herdwick sheep. An old ewe took fright at the noise and leapt into the water. Mr. Paulson jumped in to save her. If Henry Stubbs hadn't thrown a rope, Mr. Paulson and the ewe might both have drowned. What's more, the Coniston coach was also on the ferry. The coach horses were contained, with difficulty. If they had bolted, the ferry might well have capsized."*

"Ah," said the owl wisely. *"A threat to life and limb."*

"Exactly." The badger looked very serious. *"All the animals are up in arms about it, of course. They say that something has to be done. The villagers are concerned as well, although they seem to be complaining chiefly about the noise."*

The Professor helped himself to a scone from the plate the badger had put on the table. *"It is certainly a noisy machine. And there is the danger of its falling out of the sky and landing on someone's head."* He looked

70

around. *"I don't suppose yoooou have any honey."*

"I'm sure I can find some," the badger replied, getting up. But he was still rummaging in the cupboard a few minutes later, when Parsley came into the kitchen and showed him where it was. Parsley had worked and lived at The Brockery for quite a few years, and her ample pantry was one reason that all the seats at the dinner table were usually taken.

"The Professor and I were just discussing the flying boat," Bosworth explained when Parsley had fetched the honey pot and a spoon. *"He got a close look at it when he was up on Oat Cake Crag this afternoon."*

"Oat Cake Crag," Parsley said in a musing tone. She poured herself a cup of tea and sat down. *"That's a lovely place. I suppose you know how it got its name?"*

"I do, indeed," replied Bosworth. *"I've read it in the* History, *where it is noted in several passages. It seems that a small band of Scottish soldiers, on their way to London with Bonnie Prince Charles in November of 1745, were sent to the highest point on the western side of Windermere to set up a lookout. They climbed the crag, and whilst they were there, built a fire and cooked a meal of oat cakes."*

He paused. *"Unfortunately, one of them fell from the crag and died of his injuries."*

"I've heard that," Parsley replied with interest. *"I've also heard that the soldier's ghost has been seen from time to time — a large, dark shadow falling from the crag."*

"Oooh," said the owl thoughtfully. *"I wooonder . . ."* But whatever he wondered, he did not go on with it.

"As a matter of fact," Parsley went on, *"you can still see the blackened stones where the soldiers baked their cakes. When my children were small, we used those same stones. We picnicked there, and the little ones always demanded oat cakes, just like the ones the soldiers made."* Her smile was reminiscent. *"It's a grand view of the lake — you can see for such a distance. And so very quiet. You can hear every lovely bird song."*

"Not sooo quiet toooday," muttered the owl darkly. *"Entirely spoilt by that extremely noisy hydroooplane."*

"Oh, dear me, yes," Parsley said. *"It is certainly much too loud."* To Bosworth, she added, *"The Big Folks are having a meeting tomorrow night to try and find a way to keep it from flying. Major Kittredge is especially opposed, of course, since Raven Hall is so near the lake. The Kittredge children can't take*

72

their naps, and poor Mrs. Kittredge gets a headache every time the thing flies." (Mrs. Kittredge, as you may recall from earlier books, is the former Dimity Woodcock, Captain Woodcock's sister.)

Bosworth shook his head. *"It's a mystery to me why Mr. Baum decided to invest his money in that scheme,"* he said thoughtfully. *"It's not like him."*

The owl blinked. *"Mr. Baum invested money? Mr. Baum — of Lakeshore Manor?"*

Parsley laughed dryly. *"It sounds contradictory, doesn't it? He's always been such an old skinflint. But maybe he thinks he can make money from it somehow."*

"Parsley," Bosworth said, gently reprimanding. The badger practiced the Sixth Rule of Thumb, sometimes called the "To-Each-His-Own" rule. It suggests that a courteous animal did not criticize other animals' choices, whether the subject is living arrangements, relationships, economic practices, or diet. Under this rule, ice cream and earthworms are both recognized as equally delicious, depending on what sort of animal you are and how you live. And however you spend your money (or not, as the case may be), it's your choice.

But Parsley had always been an outspoken badger and was apt to call a spade a spade, regardless of who might be offended. *"Mr. Baum is a skinflint,"* she said hotly. *"He refused to contribute to the school roof fund and he's never given so much as tuppence to help the parish old folks, even though the vicar practically begs him every year. And now he's investing in an aeroplane? No wonder people are angry at him!"*

Now, you may think it odd that a badger would dare to venture an opinion about a gentleman's reputation or his behavior. But if you pause to consider for a moment, perhaps you'll see that it isn't strange at all. Animals — whether they are cats and dogs and canaries who live in our houses, or cows and pigs and chickens in the barnyard, or birds and badgers and owls and voles in the meadows and woods — all know a great deal more about their fellow creatures (including humans) than we give them credit for. We may not notice them, but they're often around, watching and listening, silent witnesses to our idiosyncrasies, faults, and foibles. (How many times have you smashed your thumb with a hammer and said a few words in front of your dog or cat that you would never have said in front of your children?) We may not know what our animals are saying, but they gossip about us behind our backs and under our

74

tables. They have a right to their opinions every bit as much as we do.

"People blame Mr. Baum for the aeroplane?" Bosworth asked, frowning.

Parsley nodded vigorously. *"My nephew was prowling around the back of the Tower Bank Arms night before last and overheard some of the pub conversation. Henry Stubbs promised to punch Mr. Baum in the nose and someone else thought he ought to be flogged. If I were Mr. Baum, I'd be worried."*

"Oh, surely not," Bosworth said gently. *"I doubt that anyone would harm* him, *no matter how people feel about the aeroplane."*

"Don't be too sure," Parsley muttered.

The owl thought it was time to change the subject, and besides, he had something on his mind. *"I was admiring the family coat of arms over your bell pull,"* he remarked, *"and wondered how one might gooo about getting such a thing fooor oneself. If one's family does not already have one, that is."* His family, while distinguished in its own right, had never seen the need for a coat of arms.

"I don't suppose it's all that difficult," Bosworth replied. *"Why don't you choose a motto and have someone draw up an emblem for you?"*

The owl frowned. *"An emblem?"*

"A picture. In your case, probably an owl. Perhaps an owl on a branch." He thought for a moment. *"Perhaps an owl on a branch with a scroll in his claw, signifying great learning. Or a scroll in one claw, and a telescope in the other."*

"And a laurel wreath on his head," suggested Parsley, *"suggesting honor. With perhaps the moon and some stars over his shoulder."* She said this kindly, but with a hint of a smile. Parsley never took the Professor as seriously as the Professor took himself.

Not seeing her smile, the owl brightened, for the idea had possibilities. *"Admirable suggestions, my friends, admirable. I shall have tooo give this matter some urgent attention."* He finished his scone, peered onto the plate to make sure it was empty, and coughed politely. *"I believe I shall gooo hooome and begin attending tooo it right now,"* he said, although what he was really thinking about, now that he had had his tea, was dinner. A largish mouse would do rather nicely, if he happened to meet one on the way. *"Thank yoooou very much for the tea."*

"Shall I see you out with a candle?" Bosworth asked. *"The hallway is rather dark."*

The owl smiled condescendingly. *"Yoooou forget that I am an owl, my friend. I am at my*

76

best in the dark." And with that, he took his leave.

But he wasn't gone long. Parsley was pouring another cup of tea and Bosworth had moved his chair closer to the fire when they heard a clatter and a loud barrage of very unprofessorial words. A moment later, the owl appeared in the kitchen doorway. His belly feathers were dripping.

"I fear I must trouble yooou for a towel," he said.

Parsley's eyes were round. *"Of course,"* she said, opening a drawer and taking out a large one. *"But what happened, Professor? However did you manage to get so wet?"*

But the badger knew exactly what had happened. *"I'm sorry, Owl,"* he said humbly. *"It's entirely my fault. I should have been more careful."*

He had left the fire bucket sitting out in the middle of the hall. The Professor (who might be able to see in the dark but had forgotten to look) had put his foot in it.

4
SPLASH AND SIZZLE

I shall begin this chapter by giving you fair warning. We are about to meet a dragon.

Now, this may matter not one whit to people who are accustomed to encountering a great many unusual things in this world and are not very much put out by odd situations that they happen to trip over, or fall into, or are struck by, or read about in books. On the other hand, there are people who are able to accept the idea of badgers and owls having tea and cats and dogs carrying on civil conversations, but who draw the line at dragons.

"Owls and badgers and cats and dogs exist," such a person might say. "I myself have seen them, and it isn't much of a stretch to imagine them talking to one another. But I have never seen a dragon. Surely, if there were such things, somebody would have caught one, the way people catch elephants and tigers and such, and put it in a circus."

Well, perhaps. I certainly see the point. But dragons are smarter than elephants and tigers and such, when it comes to getting caught, and that is probably why there are no dragons in circuses. And anyway, it is in the nature of dragons to fly and spout fire, two characteristics which would tend to make dragons less attractive to circus owners, who might worry that they would either fly away with the tent or burn it down. Elephants and tigers have better manners.

And if you continue to say, "Oh, come now, this whole argument is totally ridiculous, and the whole thing is impossible, for there simply are no dragons," I shall have to reply that of course it is possible, for this is a dragon tale, and how can we have a dragon tale if there are no dragons?

Well. I can see by the look on your face that you have already come to a conclusion. So I recommend to you that, if you have decided there are no dragons, you should put in a bookmark, close the book, and go and make yourself a cup of tea. If you change your mind, you can always come back later.

On the other hand, if you are open-minded on the subject, you are invited to come along with me, for we are beginning the story of the dragon.

■ ■ ■ ■

A few pages ago, I mentioned that Hyacinth — Bosworth's successor as the manager of The Brockery and the new (and first female!) holder of the Badger Badge of Authority — had gone off to Briar Bank to invite Bailey Badger and his roommate, Thackeray, to a surprise birthday party for Uncle Bosworth, to be held later in the week. (He is not really her uncle, but that is neither here nor there, for she loves him just as much as if he were.) This was the first major celebration she had organized, if you don't count Christmas, which is always Parsley's special event, and Hyacinth especially wanted it to be a success. She was personally inviting everyone, and — since the party was to be a surprise — made certain to ask them not to mention it in Uncle Bosworth's hearing.

But she didn't actually have to go as far as Briar Bank, because before she got there, she ran into Bailey and Thackeray fishing in Moss Eccles Tarn. This beautiful little five-acre man-made lake lies about a mile above the village of Near Sawrey, and when you visit the area, you really must put it on your list of places to see. Miss Potter dearly loved to fish and kept a rowboat there, available for others to borrow when she wasn't using it. (You may be interested in knowing that what was left of her boat was discovered in 1976. It has been restored and is now on display at the Windermere Station Museum.)

This afternoon, the badger and the guinea pig had borrowed Miss Potter's boat, rowed it out into the lake, and were fishing from it. This was something they did frequently, even during cold weather (unless the surface was frozen), for they were both very fond of fish, and the tarn was very full of brown trout. When Hyacinth hailed them from the bank, they quickly rowed in to the shore. Bailey did the rowing, since he is much bigger and stronger than Thackeray and has no trouble at all managing Miss Potter's oars. And since the fish were biting that evening, they insisted that Hyacinth climb into the boat with them and take up the extra rod and reel.

"Look here!" Bailey said proudly, and held up a string of three fat, wriggling brown trout. *"Come out with us, Hyacinth, and see how many you can catch. I'm sure Parsley would be glad to cook them for you."*

As you may remember, Bailey is Bosworth's second cousin, twice removed. He lives on the western side of Briar Bank, in a large sett with many empty tunnels and chambers, dating back to the earliest settlements in the Land Between the Lakes — all the way back to the days of the Vikings, in fact. For most of his life, Bailey preferred to live alone in this labyrinthine place, so that he could spend as much uninterrupted time as possible reading and reflecting in the quite remarkable library he had inherited from his badger forebears. This library contains an enormous number of volumes on nearly every subject you might want to explore — except, perhaps, for modern mysteries (such as Sherlock Holmes) and romances, which the badgers have always thought of as frivolous. The Briar Bank badgers have a reputation as being a rather dour lot.

And Bailey lived up to this family reputation. He was a satirical, unsociable creature who chose to live in a spartan manner. He paid little attention to food, unlike most other badgers, who have very good appetites and are always on the lookout for something tasty from the garden. In fact, when Bosworth visited his cousin, he avoided arriving at teatime, for Bailey's larder was always embarrassingly bare. A hungry guest might be offered a slice of dry bread, a bit of cheese, a swallow of sour dandelion wine, and if he was lucky, a stale digestive biscuit.

This was not a very appetizing prospect, as I'm sure you'll agree. It was no wonder that Bailey almost never entertained company. And when he did, he was often surly and almost always managed to fall asleep before his guests (who by that time had given up all hope of getting a bite to eat) had gone home. Bailey could discourse at length on the book he was currently reading, but he was not what you would call a hospitable host.

But that is all in the past, I am happy to say, for Bailey Badger has entirely put aside his old ways. He is a changed animal. This remarkable transformation occurred when he discovered, quite by accident and much to his amazement, that he had for years been hosting an unknown guest, in the distant and unvisited regions of Briar Bank.

One momentous day, he opened a hidden door behind a floor-to-ceiling bookshelf in one of the library chambers, and discovered a dragon.

Yes, exactly: a dragon. (You can see why the skeptical were invited to go have a cup of tea.)

And whilst this creature was (for a dragon)

on the smallish side and seemed to be safely asleep, he had all the ordinary accoutrements of a dragon — green scales and long toenails and smoke coming out of his nostrils, that sort of thing. There was no mistaking who and what he was.

Bailey stared, thunderstruck at the idea that a dragon was sleeping in his back bedroom. He could see the translucent scales of the dragon's belly glowing with the banked fire that burned inside and hear the growling, wheezy noise that came from within as the dragon's breath rose and fell. The beast was snoring, and with every snore, little white puffs of smoke came out of his nose and rose into perfectly round white *O*s over his head.

Now, Bailey, like every other badger, had been tutored from birth in the Eleventh Badger Rule of Thumb, which is horrifyingly explicit: *Never wake a sleeping dragon, for your flesh is firm and fat and tastes good grilled.* His mother had reminded him of this over and over, and as he stared at the dragon in speechless horror, her words echoed ominously in his mind: *"Your flesh is FIRM and FAT, my very dear son, and tastes good GRILLED — tastes good, that is, to the dragon, for there is nothing that a dragon likes better than a plump young badger. And believe me, dear boy, dragons are much faster than badgers."*

Grilled! It was an appalling thought. But Bailey didn't have time to mull this over, because just at that moment, the sleeping dragon woke up. He stared at Bailey, then opened his dragon mouth as wide as he could and —

Well. This is a fascinating story, but I fear it would take too long to retell the whole thing here. (If you haven't read it yet, I recommend *The Tale of Briar Bank,* where this story is told in its entirety.) To boil it down to just a sentence or two, the dragon (he was young, as dragons go, and went by the name of Thorvaald) woke up and discovered that his treasure — the Viking gold hoard he had been assigned to guard for the past nine or ten centuries — had been burgled. He got into some very serious trouble with the Grand Assembly of Dragons, to whom he was supposed to report. He still is in trouble with the Assembly, it seems, although we'll get to that later.

Anyway, it took quite a while to get all this sorted out, for the affairs of dragons (as you might guess) are terribly tangled. Over the next few days and weeks, Bailey discovered that there are certain advantages to living with a dragon, such as not having to build a fire in one's fireplace as long as there is a warm-bellied dragon upon whom one might rest one's chilly paws or against whom one might cuddle on a blustery night, when the howling wind wants to blow down the chimney and make itself at home in one's living room. And in the evenings, he found that he would rather put aside his book and listen as Thorvaald told dramatic tales of derring-do in which the dragon (who in his version was always the hero, not the villain) valiantly dispatched the errant knight with the knight's very own sword, or roasted a drove of dwarves by whuffing on them until they were toasted to a crisp.

Those early days were gone now, and Thorvaald was no longer a permanent resident at Briar Bank. He came back to visit occasionally, but true to his dragon nature, he spent his time exploring the Back of the North Wind or flying around the Cape of Good Hope, every so often taking the trouble to mail a penny postcard back to Briar Bank so that Bailey would know that he was safe and well. Bailey worried, of course, because Thorvaald was still a teenager, a bit reckless and of an uncertain temperament. But you know how teenagers are — they almost never listen to those who are older and wiser. And you can imagine why, after being cooped up in a dark badger burrow for centuries, the dragon was anxious to get out, stretch his wings, and fly around the world. There was nothing Bailey could do to keep him at Briar Bank.

Bailey, for his part, had gotten so accustomed to entertaining company (and being entertained by it) that he now found living alone to be very lonely. Luckily for him, a guinea pig named Thackeray was in the market for a new home. Miss Potter, you see, had brought the little fellow from London to live with Caroline Longford at Tidmarsh Manor. But he hadn't liked it there (who would?) and had run away at the very first chance. Bailey and Thackeray met at The Brockery and quickly struck up an unlikely friendship. The next thing anybody knew, Thackeray had been invited to move in with Bailey at Briar Bank.

An odd couple? Well, yes, I suppose so. But as it turned out, the two had a great deal in common, for both Bailey and Thackeray (named for the famous novelist, William Makepeace Thackeray, author of *Vanity Fair*) were devoted bibliophiles who believed that "a book a day kept the world at bay," as Thackeray was fond of saying. Bailey was the offspring of generations of badgers who insisted that "Reader" was the most rewarding vocation to which a virtuous badger might be called and who gauged their week's anticipated pleasure by the height of their to-be-read piles. (Perhaps you know people like this. I do.)

Thackeray, whose favorite book was the first volume of Gibbon's six-volume *The Decline and Fall of the Roman Empire,* was beside himself with joy at the thought of living in a library, surrounded by more books than he could possibly read in a dozen lifetimes. The two friends found themselves reading and discussing books at breakfast, luncheon, and dinner. And instead of listening to dragon tales in the evenings, they took turns reading to each other. This month, they were entirely engrossed in the pages of *Framley Parsonage,* the fourth book in Anthony Trollope's *Chronicles of Barsetshire.* (I mention this because of something they found there. You will shortly learn what it is. Please be patient.)

For the next half-hour, Hyacinth and her two friends fished and chatted, chatted and fished. Hyacinth caught two fat, wriggly trout. They talked about the weather (which had on the whole been mild and pleasant), and about the cataloging project (which Bailey had begun before the dragon came into his life and which he and Thackeray were carrying on together). And about the note Bailey had received the previous week from Thorvaald, who was currently in Scotland on an assignment from the Grand Assembly of Dragons, attempting to confirm rumors of some sort of monster lurking in the very deep waters of Loch Ness. It was said to be a snakelike creature with humps and a long, sinuous neck, rather like a seagoing dragon. Thorvaald was supposed to contact this monster and learn whether he or she should be included in the Centenary Census of Dragons, the means by which the Grand Assembly monitors the global dragon population. Dragons have a disconcerting tendency to move from place to place without leaving a forwarding address. The Assembly would very much like to keep track of them, although this is probably not realistic.

"He didn't have to fly all the way to Scotland to look for a monster," Thackeray remarked dryly. *"He could have found one right here at home."*

The afternoon breeze ruffled the guinea pig's long hair, which was so long that it trailed around him like a cloak and covered both ends of him so completely that it was sometimes hard to know whether he was coming or going. He had always been quite the elegant creature and was unfortunately rather vain, forever combing himself with an ivory comb and studying the result in a scrap of mirror that he kept in his pocket along with his pipe and reading glasses. Since coming to the country, however, he spent less time grooming himself and more time enjoying the world around him. I am glad to tell you that his fur was somewhat matted, and that he didn't seem to care.

"You're talking about that hydroplane, I suppose," Hyacinth replied in a rueful tone. She had to raise her voice because, even though it was nearly dusk, the thing was flying again, its loud mechanical drone like a million angry thunder-flies buzzing along the lake on the other side of Claife Heights. *"Everybody hates it. We all wish it would go away. Not crash,"* she added hastily. *"Just go away. It's not so bad underground, but when you go outside, the noise is extremely annoying."*

"It's a monster, all right," agreed the guinea pig. *"But no, I'm talking about the* real *Windermere monster. The one Bailey and I learnt about last week."*

"A monster in Windermere?" Hyacinth asked doubtfully. *"I don't recall any mention of that in the* History." When she assumed her new position as holder of the Badge,

she had spent several months reading through the pages of the *History of the Badgers of the Land Between the Lakes.* These volumes were supposed to be the most accurate reporting of the events that had occurred since record-keeping began. *"I suppose I might have missed it, but —"*

"I'm not sure that this particular sighting is noted in the History*,"* put in Bailey. He reeled in his lure and rested his rod against the side of the boat. *"It seems that my great-great-grandfather saw something very strange in Windermere one late-winter evening. A creature — snakelike and about as long as the ferry boat — swimming through the water. It had three humps, he said. He made a note of what he had seen and stuck it between the pages of* Framley Parsonage, *which he appears to have been reading at the time."* (There. Thank you for your patience.)

"I see," said Hyacinth. *"Well, if you don't mind, I should like to copy the note into the* History. *It sounds important — the sort of thing that should be included, even after the fact. In case anyone sees anything like that again,"* she added, *"and wants corroboration."*

"Of course you may," replied the badger. *"I'll bring it when we come to the birthday party. Although I must say,"* he added cau-

tiously, *"that I'm not sure that you ought to put a lot of faith in my great-great-grandfather's observations. He seems to have been a thoughtful fellow, but a bit nearsighted. It's possible that he didn't really see —"*

But whatever it was that the badger's ancestor might or might not have seen, it was lost in a loud *FLAP-FLAP-FLAP,* like the sound of sheets snapping on the clothesline. This was immediately followed by a great shout, *"LOOK OUT BELOOOOW!"* and a mighty splash, as something hurtled out of the sky and into the waters of the tarn, heaving the little boat up on the shoulders of a giant swell.

Hyacinth screamed and grabbed the gunwales, holding on for dear life. The boat took on water, and the guinea pig bounced onto the bottom. Sputtering and choking, he clung to Bailey's ankle to keep from being swept overboard. Bailey wiped the water out of his eyes.

"Thorvaald!" He flung up his arms in joyful greeting. *"Thorvaald, you're back! You've come home!"*

"Szso sszsorry," the dragon hissed. *"I miscalculated the deszscent."* He began paddling anxiously along beside the boat, bobbing up and down in the waves. *"Isszs*

everyone all right? Did I get anyone wet?"

"You got us ALL wet, you big oaf," said the guinea pig crossly, climbing up onto the seat and shaking himself. Water drops flew everywhere. "Why can't you be more careful? Hurtling down out of the sky like an out-of-control thunderbolt. Put on the brakes before you land!"

"I really am dreadfully sszsorry," the dragon said humbly. The water boiled around him and tendrils of steam curled out of his ears.

"We're not all that wet," Hyacinth said in a comforting tone. "It was mostly the not-knowing that was frightening. What was happening, I mean. We didn't know it was you."

"Exactly." Thackeray took a handful of his dripping fur and began to wring it out. "You might have been Halley's Comet, come back again." The comet had appeared — memorably — in 1910, giving everyone something to talk about for months. "Or that hydroplane, about to crash. One never knows what might fall out of the sky these days."

Bailey picked up the oars. "Let's all go to Briar Bank and discuss things over tea."

"Here — let me give you a tow," the dragon said helpfully. Without a by-your-leave, he grabbed the painter between his teeth and began swimming strongly toward the bank.

But he swam so fast and so hard that the bow of the rowboat dove under the surface and water poured over the sides.

"No!" the two badgers cried in unison, and grabbed at the gunwales. *"Stop, Thorvaald! Please stop!"*

The dragon flipped over on his back, still swimming. *"Am I doing szsomething wrong?"* he asked. His tail hit the boat and knocked it violently to one side. An instant later, his tail struck the boat again, slamming it to the other side.

"You're going to sink us!" screamed Thackeray as the boat rocked back and forth. *"Let go the rope, you dim-witted dragon!"*

"Oh," muttered the dragon as he saw what was happening. He dropped the painter. The boat settled back in the water, the badger picked up the oars, and in a few moments they were safely on dry land again.

"We are very glad to have you home, old chap," Bailey said sternly. *"But next time, let's not be quite so dramatic about it, shall we? Falling out of the sky and grabbing painters and all that. It's enough to give your friends fits."*

"Yesszszsir," the dragon said, hanging his head. *"I'm sszsorry, szsir. I'll try to do better next time."*

"There'd better not be a next time," muttered Thackeray, shaking himself.

"Very good," said Bailey, beaming. *"Now, shall we all go home and have a cup of tea? We can cook our fish and Thorvaald can tell us all about the Loch Ness monster and his adventures in Scotland. Hyacinth, you come, too. There's always room for one more at the table."*

I'm sure you're thinking what I'm thinking: that this is quite a change from the earlier Bailey, who often refused to answer the door when company knocked — a change for the better, or so it seems to me. Briar Bank may be more crowded, but our badger is much less likely to be lonely.

"Thank you," Hyacinth said, taking up her fish, *"but I'd better get back to The Brockery. They'll be having tea without me."* She smiled at Thorvaald. *"You'll come to Uncle Bosworth's surprise birthday party, I hope."*

"If there'szs room for me," said the dragon. He looked down at himself. His belly was so warm that drops of water sizzled on it. *"I am small for a dragon, but rather large for a gueszst. And I do have a tendency to scorch thingszs."*

"You need to learn to bank that fire," Thackeray said, not unkindly.

95

"Dragonszs can't bank their fireszs," said Thorvaald with great dignity. *"It's against their natureszs."*

"I hope you'll come," Hyacinth said. *"Uncle Bosworth will be so glad to see you. If you do, we'll make room."* And with that, she took her leave.

And so will we, for something very important is about to happen in the village and I want to be there when it does.

I'm sure you do, too.

5
In Which We Learn About Secret Lives

When Beatrix returned from Rose Cottage with the letters that Grace Lythecoe gave her, she went upstairs immediately and put them into the bottom drawer of her dresser, under her stockings. She hadn't been eager to bring them home, but she wanted to read them again and study them. Not right away, though. She was already regretting that she had agreed to try to find out who had sent them and why. Her first look at the letters had told her that this was not going to be an easy task.

Still puzzling over this mystery, she went downstairs and lit the paraffin lamp, punched up the fire, and began to deal with supper. Mrs. Jennings had made potato and sausage soup earlier in the day. There was a pot of it on the back of the range, and in the cupboard, bread and creamy yellow butter, a large chunk of yellow cheese, and some gingerbread. She had just put things on the table and was ladling soup into a blue bowl when she heard a sharp rap at the door.

"Oh, bother," she muttered under her breath, for she was not expecting company and had looked forward to spending the evening alone. But when she opened the door, she changed her mind on the spot, for the person who had knocked was Mr. Will Heelis, holding his brown bowler hat in his hand.

"It's not too late, is it?" he asked. "I've just got back from Kendal. I intended to be earlier, but the ferry was overdue. As usual," he added with a crooked smile, for the ferry was notorious for its lack of punctuality. Everyone who had to cross from one side of the lake to the other had long ago learnt to live with the situation.

Beatrix stepped back and invited him inside. "No, of course it's not too late," she said happily, taking his coat and hat and hanging them on the peg next to hers. "I wasn't expecting you at all, Will. What a nice surprise!"

"I wasn't expecting you to expect me." He put both hands on her shoulders. "Hello, my dear," he said softly. "Welcome back. I am so very glad to see you." And with that, he bent (for he was very tall and she was rather short), and kissed her.

Well! I expect you want to know what's going on, don't you? Here is a strange gentleman, appearing unannounced at the door of our Beatrix's cottage after dark, and *kissing* her! What's more, she is kissing him back, if I'm not mistaken. At least, it looks very much as if that's what's happening.

Oh, dear. If Mrs. Potter saw what we have just seen, she would be horrified and take to her bed immediately with a sick head-ache, likely requiring a visit from the doctor. Mr. Potter would be apoplectic. He would turn turkey-red and stamp all about the library, blustering and bellowing. And since he is a barrister and presumably knows his way around a court of law, he might even threaten to sue the gentleman in question for taking liberties with his daughter.

But if you have read the previous book in this series (that would be *The Tale of Apple-beck Farm*), you know something that Mr. and Mrs. Potter do not know — not yet, anyway. This gentleman is no stranger, but Beatrix's friend of several years. More importantly, he is her fiancé. They are engaged to be married.

And if you have not read the earlier book, I hope you will not be too scandalized to learn that the very proper Miss Potter is actually leading a secret life up here in the country, far from London and her parents' prying and censorious eyes. A *very* secret life.

Now, to understand this extraordinary situation, you must first know something about Mr. Will Heelis, this bold fellow who has kissed Miss Potter once and is now kissing her for the second time, between whispers of how glad he is to see her and how much he has missed her since the last time they were together. But to tell the truth, Will Heelis is not in the least bold. In fact, by nature he is very shy. Painfully shy, according to his friends, especially with the fairer sex, and certainly not a man for whispering sweet nothings into a lady's ear, even if they are engaged to be married. But Will has discovered that he is very much in love, and love lends boldness to even the shyest of persons, and so he is probably saying and doing things that he couldn't possibly have imagined himself saying and doing if he weren't in love. I'm sure you understand this, if you have ever been in love yourself.

Beatrix's fiancé is a tall, trim, fit-looking man, broad-shouldered and slim-hipped, with fine eyes, a strong jaw, and a shock of thick brown hair that falls boyishly across his forehead. He is the son of Esther Heelis and the Reverend John Heelis, who was the rector of Dufton and later of Kirby Thore (a village on the main road between Appleby and Penrith). Unlike Beatrix, who had only one brother, Bertram, Will grew up in a family of nine brothers and sisters, four lively girls and five boisterous boys. They were close-knit and fun-loving, delighting in picnics and folk dances and frivolous games (none of which, of course, were permitted in Beatrix's much more staid and status-conscious family). The five brothers went shooting and fishing together and played cricket and tennis and golf. Will was especially fond of swimming and bowling and billiards, and naturally good at every sport to which he turned his hand.

But Will had a sober side, as well. He served his articles of apprenticeship in London, was admitted a solicitor in 1899, and joined the family law firm, which had an office in Bump or Bend Cottage in Hawkshead, the small market town just two miles from New Sawrey. (The cottage is called Bump or Bend because you must duck as you walk past, for fear of hitting your head on a protruding part of the building. When you go there, you will see Will's office, which looks pretty much as he left it, with his desk and chair and files and such, and many of Beatrix's paintings, for the place is now a gallery.)

The firm of Heelis and Heelis, Solicitors, handled all kinds of legal affairs, but Will spent most of his time on property matters, so when Miss Potter began buying property in the area, it was natural for her to consult him. He knew when a certain piece of land was coming up for sale, what its boundaries were, what price it ought to sell for, and what it was worth. He could offer reliable, trustworthy advice to a lady from London who lacked experience in such matters but had her own money to spend (the royalties from her books) and was very willing to spend it on the right piece of land.

The land — that's where it began. Beatrix and Will began looking at properties that came up for sale, walking across the hills and dales together, discussing the land and the buildings and the timber and the meadows and the livestock. They discovered that they both thought that the land should be left as it was, home to sheep and shepherds and small farms, and they worried that the growing demand from developers for holiday houses, bungalows, and villas would destroy not only the picturesque landscape but the traditional hill-country farms and commons. When Beatrix went back to London, Will wrote often to her, keeping her informed about possible purchases and about things that needed to be done or repaired or looked after, first at Hill Top Farm and then at Castle Farm, which she bought (on his advice) in 1909.

Their partnership began in that business-like way not long after she arrived in the village and over the next few years, it ripened into a strong friendship. This was how Beatrix's romance had begun with Norman, who had been her editor on the Little Books, and so it felt right to her. And since Will suffered from such shyness with the ladies, it might have been the only way he could have stumbled into love. And then — to their mutual astonishment — they became engaged.

If you will forgive me, I think I must retell this part of the story, which is told in *The Tale of Applebeck Farm.* It happened, you see, on the same night that the Applebeck dairy burnt, a year and a half before. This was a wildly exciting night for the villagers, who got out of their beds and ran to join the bucket brigade to try and put the fire out. It was also an exciting night for Will. He and Beatrix had gone for a walk in the moonlight, and he had at last been able to muster the courage to tell her what had been hiding in his heart for some time.

This is how he began: "I care for you, Miss Potter. I care deeply. I don't suppose this is any secret to you — I am sure it has been increasingly apparent each time we've been together this last year, and perhaps even before."

It had indeed become apparent, and Beatrix had observed it with growing uneasiness. It was not that she did not have warm feelings of her own. Oh, no, not at all! She knew how she felt and she was fully aware of the danger of it, for those warm feelings for Will Heelis were complicated by equally warm feelings of loyalty to Norman Warne and his family. (Norman's sister Millie would surely be hurt if she found out that Beatrix was beginning to care for someone else.) And her parents —

Oh, dear. Well, that, of course, was the most significant complication, for Beatrix knew that her mother and father would oppose her relationship with Will Heelis in exactly the way they had opposed her engagement to Norman, and for exactly the same reasons. They would say that Will (who was, after all, just a country solicitor, the son of a country parson and his country wife) was not "the right sort of person" to marry their daughter. In fact, they still did not intend that their daughter should marry anyone at all, ever, but should stay with them at Bolton Gardens and look after them in their old age. And Beatrix (who was very modern in some ways and very old-fashioned in others) could not imagine marrying without her parents' consent.

Well, you can see the dilemma she was in. So it was no wonder that Beatrix was uneasy, and that she would really much rather that Will had never found whatever had been hiding in his heart. She wanted to make him stop, but she couldn't, for he hadn't yet finished.

"Please do believe me when I say," he was going on, "that I am not insensible to your feelings for Mr. Warne, nor to your difficulties with your parents. But I must tell you truly, and from my heart, that if your circumstances change —"

At that point, he had paused. Beatrix was not putting her fingers in her ears (that would have been terribly rude) but he could see by the look on her face that she did not want to hear what he had to say. Having opened the subject, however, he could not see any comfortable way to close it, and so he had taken a deep breath and stumbled on.

"I know your parents believe me unworthy. It is true — I *am* unworthy, and I should never wish to cause you a single moment's unhappiness on my account. But if . . . if your circumstances can ever permit you to consider having me, Miss Potter, my heart . . . my heart is yours. Truly, honestly, and eternally yours."

I don't know about you, but if I had been Miss Potter and Mr. Heelis had offered to give me his heart, truly, honestly, and eternally, I should not have hesitated one instant. I should have said, "Yes! Oh, yes, yes, yes!" on the spot. But our Beatrix (who had the foresight to see that matters were coming to a head) had already practiced her "no." And so she delivered it, firmly and compactly.

"I do care for you, but our friendship must remain a friendship. I still have an enduring fondness for Norman, and my parents present a substantial obstacle to my living my life as I would choose to live it."

Now, Will could have accepted Beatrix's rejection and gone on about his business, as any well-mannered Victorian gentleman should have done. (I am perfectly aware that Queen Victoria had by this time been dead for a decade, but that doesn't change the fact that Will and Beatrix are thoroughgoing Victorians, just as proper as you please. Neither would have liked being called "Edwardian," for King Edward, while he was a very good king, had a very bad reputation for playing fast and loose with the ladies.) Will's heart would, of course, have been completely broken, but humans are resilient, and it takes more than a romantic rebuff to do us in. I daresay our Will would not have mourned his loss forever.

But while this man may be very shy, he is also very stubborn, and upon due consideration, he did not find it convenient to take Beatrix's "no" for an answer. Instead, he kept on pressing the subject, and after a little while, Beatrix found herself saying what was truly in her heart: that she cared for him very deeply, and that if her circumstances were different, her answer would be different. Her "no" might become a "yes."

That was what he was waiting for. "Well, then," he said (and I do think that we must forgive him that little bit of triumph in his tone), "if you would choose to marry me under other circumstances, I will be content to wait. Until your circumstances change," he added firmly, "however long that may be. All I ask is a promise, Beatrix. As long as I have your promise, I can wait."

A promise? Beatrix was utterly taken aback. She had said she cared for him, but she couldn't marry him unless things were different. She had given the man an inch, and now he wanted a mile. This was entirely unexpected. She had assumed that he would accept her "no" and that would be that. They could go on as friends, being together when they could, enjoying each other's company, just as before. But here he was, boldly demanding a promise! What in the world could she say that would satisfy him, be true to her own heart's desire, and still protect her obligations? It was a challenge. A conundrum. A lesser woman would have been completely flummoxed.

But our Beatrix was no lesser woman. She raised her eyes to his and said, sweetly and softly, "Well, then, I shall promise not to marry anyone but you, Will. That is my promise, and I freely give it. Will it do?" When he seemed to hesitate, she pounced. "You see?" she said triumphantly. "I *knew* you wanted something more from me. Well, that's all you are going to get. You are free to take back your proposal."

Which, of course, he had not. Her promise was not exactly what he wanted, but he knew that Beatrix Potter was a woman of her word. She would marry him, or she would not marry anyone, and with that he had to be content. Well, he was — at least, on that night, at that moment. They were engaged to be married (someday), and even though it had to be secret, just between the two of them, that would do. It would have to, wouldn't it? And at that moment, it did.

Beatrix had been able to get back to the farm only a half-dozen times since that fateful night. They had not been together often or long, but often and long enough to assure both of them that their feelings had not changed. They had exchanged quite a few letters, although Beatrix (who was in a great state of consternation about this secret engagement into which she had inadvertently entered) had the sense that even letter writing was dangerous. Her mother knew that Mr. Heelis had helped her purchase Castle Farm, so letters bearing his return address might therefore be assumed to be confined to business matters. On the other hand, if her mother caught her blushing over the letters (and Beatrix had an embarrassing tendency to blush), she might suspect that something more than business was in the wind. So Beatrix, who hated fusses and rows more than anything in the world, hid the letters, just as she had hidden Norman's, and of course, said nothing at all about her engagement to Mr. Heelis. Her *secret* engagement.

There it is: the story behind our story, and I hope you don't think I've gone on too long about it. But while I've been telling it, Will and Beatrix have been enjoying, undisturbed, their first private moment together in some months. I'm sure they don't want a flock of curious people peering over their shoulders, wondering how Miss Potter feels to be kissed by this tall, fine-looking man, or how Mr. Heelis feels to be holding his dearest love at last in his arms. So we will stand off to one side and be very quiet. Perhaps you wouldn't even mind holding your breath.

Thank you. We can breathe again, for the moment has passed. Will has lifted his hand to Beatrix's cheek and touched it tenderly, and she has taken his fingertips and put them to her lips. Both laugh a little, shakily, then move apart, but not too far apart, toward the fire.

"It's getting chilly outside," Will said, spreading his hands to the warmth and speaking in what he hoped was a normal tone. However, he had just held his fiancée (*his fiancée!*) close enough to be made a little giddy by the scent of her lavender soap. He didn't feel normal at all. "I shouldn't be a bit surprised to see frost in the next day or two."

"I shouldn't either," Beatrix said, trying for something that sounded like her usual voice but didn't, of course, because she had just been kissed by the man she loved (*yes, loved!*). "Have you eaten? There's soup on the stove. And bread and cheese. Oh, and gingerbread."

"Ah." Will brightened, and things began to feel a little more normal. "Soup. And gingerbread. Why, no, I haven't, actually. I'd be rather glad of a little something, if you're sure there's enough. My dear," he added shyly.

And in another five minutes, Beatrix found herself sitting with the greatest happiness you can possibly imagine across the table from Will, thinking that it was just as if they were married, sharing a simple supper of soup and bread and cheese and afterward, a piece of gingerbread and a cup of steaming coffee. Outside, the March wind was rising, but indoors, all was warm and cheerful and delightfully comfortable, so comfortable that neither could imagine a better, sweeter, happier place to be, not if they searched the whole wide world. They talked about the noisy hydroplane and about a rumor that Will had heard about a possible aeroplane route between Bowness and Grasmere, at the north end of the lake, to be established by the aeroplane's owners. They talked about Castle Farm, and about Will's business (he had been in Kendal, settling a property dispute), and about Beatrix's parents and her brother, Bertram, who at the present time was visiting in London.

"Although," Beatrix added, "my parents seem never to be overjoyed to see him, and of course he is never very glad to come. They all do it out of duty."

It was the story of her family, she thought. Everything they did, they did out of a sense of obligation or duty, and none of it ever seemed to bring them any enjoyment. As Will described the Heelis family, on the other hand, he made them sound very much like Norman's brothers and sisters, full of fun and laughter and happy silliness.

"And he's not yet told them about his secret marriage?" Will asked, pushing away his empty plate and looking straight at Beatrix.

This was a provocative question. The fact of the matter, you see, was that Beatrix's brother Bertram (younger than she by some five years) had been secretly married for over a decade. His wife's name was Mary, and they had met when she was working as a serving girl in her aunt's hostelry. They lived together on the farm Bertram had bought in Scotland (they had no children), but he had still not told his father and mother. Bertram's secret life loomed large between Will and Beatrix. For even though they had not yet discussed it with each other, it had crossed both their minds that *they* might be secretly married. And why not? They were adults and pledged, weren't they? They had had several months to think it over, and neither of them could imagine marrying anyone else. So the possibility of a secret marriage might be a way out of their dilemma.

But Will was a straightforward, honest man who disliked the thought of clandestine dealings. He longed to let the whole world know that Miss Potter had agreed to become Mrs. Heelis and in fact, in a moment of sheer, delirious happiness, had actually told his cousin, who was also his partner in the family law firm. (He had, of course, sworn the cousin to secrecy.)

For her part, Beatrix had been horrified when she learnt of her brother's secret arrangement. She was deeply sympathetic to his desire to live with the woman he loved. But if he loved Mary enough to marry her, he ought to be brave enough to tell his father and mother. And on a practical level, she knew that she could never keep so important a secret as marriage from her parents. They would know in an instant that she had been up to something. Her face would give her away, and in a moment or two, they would have the whole story.

So she reached for a change of subject, snatching at the first thing that came into her mind. "Speaking of marriage," she said, picking up her coffee cup, "I've just been with Grace Lythecoe. She has received several nasty letters from some anonymous person who doesn't want her to marry the vicar. It's making her terribly unhappy."

Beatrix knew the minute she spoke that she had betrayed a confidence. But the cat was out of the bag now, and when Will, surprised, wanted to know what it was all about, she had to tell him, adding, "But really, I shouldn't have mentioned it. Please don't tell anyone else."

"Of course not," Will said firmly. "But this is serious, Beatrix. What is Mrs. Lythecoe going to do?"

"She's asked me to help her find out who is writing them," Beatrix said, and put down her cup. "But I've seen the letters, and I'm afraid they don't give any clues."

Will frowned. "Do you suppose she would let me see them? I've lived in the district for a very long time, and I know a great many people, town and country. I might be able to recognize the handwriting, or see something else that might give us an idea of who wrote them."

Beatrix hesitated, but only for a moment. Will was right. He was acquainted with far more people than she was. He might be able to recognize the sender immediately. The matter could be dealt with, Grace's worries and fears laid to rest, and she could stop thinking about it. She pushed back her chair.

"As it happens," she said, "I have the letters. Mrs. Lythecoe knows you and trusts you. I don't think she would object to my sharing them with you. Perhaps you can tell her who wrote them."

But when Beatrix spread the letters on the table and moved the lamp closer so he could read them, Will had to admit that he could see no clues to the identity of the sender.

"How did she get them?" he asked.

"They came over the course of the past month," Beatrix said, "each in a different way. The first was put through the slot in the front door. The second was dropped over the back fence. The third, which arrived only a few days ago, was sent through the post. But as you can see, the postmark is so badly smeared that it is impossible to tell where it was mailed."

Will nodded. "Too bad there's no bloody thumbprint," he said with a wry chuckle. "If so, we might enlist Sherlock Holmes to help solve the mystery."

Beatrix, too, had read Mr. Doyle's story, "The Adventure of the Norwood Builder," and knew what Will was talking about. Holmes had identified the suspect by comparing a print of his thumb to a bloody print on a whitewashed wall at the scene of the crime. She had to smile a little when she thought about this, for the astute Holmes had also proved that the thumbprint on the wall had been cleverly fabricated by the real villain, and the owner of the thumb, the suspect, was an innocent man.

But even the incomparable Holmes could have found no clues in these letters. The envelopes were entirely unremarkable, and the messages were printed in crude block letters, in pencil, on unlined sheets of plain paper of the sort that could be purchased cheaply at any stationer's shop. The only possible clue was that the paper on which the third message was written was smaller by half and had a rough edge, as though it had been folded once or twice and then torn from another piece of paper.

The first said, simply, "Marry Samuel Sackett and you will be sorry."

The second repeated this warning, with this addition: "He has a terrible sin on his conscience."

The third, most ominously, said, "Cancel the wedding, or the whole parish will know what he has done."

"Sin?" Will was incredulous. "The vicar? What terrible sin could he have possibly committed? He is one of the mildest men I have ever met."

Beatrix had asked herself the same question. But when she inquired (as delicately as she knew how), Mrs. Lythecoe had tearfully insisted that she had no idea what it might be — and what was more, she didn't believe there was any such thing. It was nothing but a lie, she insisted. The anonymous letter writer was making it up.

Beatrix wanted to agree with her friend, of course. It was hard to imagine Vicar Sackett committing even a small sin, unless one counted dithering, of which the poor vicar was endlessly guilty. He always saw all sides of a question, both the positive and the negative, and could never quite make up his mind which way he ought to come down. Some of the villagers saw this as a character flaw, since a man of God surely ought to know the difference between good and bad and be able to tell everyone else exactly what it was. But a "terrible" sin? How could that be? He just wasn't that sort of person.

Still, Beatrix couldn't help wondering. Perhaps the vicar (who had already put his fiftieth birthday behind him) was not the same man now that he had always been. To put it another way, he might have been a different sort of person in his youth, before he became vicar of St. Peter's. People changed, and young men often sowed vast fields of wild oats. Beatrix knew this of her own experience, because she was well acquainted with her brother's various misdemeanors over the years — his failing in school, his gambling, even (sadly) his excessive drinking. Was it possible that the vicar, as a younger person, had done things he now regretted? Had once led a life that he now kept secret?

But that wasn't the real question, and Beatrix knew it. Whatever the vicar had or had not done, the *real* question was whether the letter writer would dare to spread an ugly tale, true or false, around the parish. And whether Grace Lythecoe — a sensible woman, a kind woman and thoughtful, but a woman who cared a great deal about her position in the little community — had the courage to marry her vicar in spite of such malicious threats. Listening to Grace worry and fret out loud about the letters, Beatrix had begun to fear that she did not. She couldn't be blamed, of course. To marry in defiance of others took an extraordinary courage, as Beatrix well knew. She could scarcely criticize her friend for failure of heart, when she herself was in a similar situation.

And now, thinking further about the situation, she was very sorry that she had agreed to help. It was true that the village was small and that everyone knew everyone else's business — which meant that somebody might have seen the person who put the first letter through Grace's door or tossed the second letter over the fence. But it was also true that in order to find out who knew what, she should have to ask questions. And *that* might cause even more trouble for Grace and the vicar. Whoever was writing these letters might not be willing to stop — or worse, might not be willing to stop with the simple act of writing letters.

"I'm sorry," Will said ruefully. "I wish I could be of more help. But I'll keep my eyes and ears open. I may be able to learn something." He folded the letters carefully and handed them back to Beatrix. "Keep them in a safe place," he said, standing.

"You're going?" Beatrix asked, feeling a wrench. It seemed as if he had just arrived.

Reaching for his coat, Will smiled crookedly. "I must, or the Jenningses will talk. And then Mrs. Stubbs will talk, and Agnes Llewellyn and Mathilda Crook, and everybody else." He bent and kissed her. "You know what gossips these villagers are."

Beatrix knew. Bertram might be able to keep his secret safe, on an isolated farm in the wilds of the Scottish border country. It was much harder to lead a secret life in Near Sawrey, where prying eyes were everywhere and the tongues never stopped rattling.

Which was exactly why the vicar and Mrs. Lythecoe were in such danger.

6

"WELCOME BACK, MISS POTTER!"

The following afternoon was misty and quite chill, but Beatrix, who intended to pay a visit to Lady Longford at Tidmarsh Manor, was not one to mind a little damp. She asked Mr. Jennings to harness Winston the pony to the red-painted pony cart and bring it round to the door. Then she filled a small stoneware crock with some of Mrs. Jennings' yellow butter and put it in a basket, along with a loaf of Sarah Barwick's oatmeal bread. Mrs. Jennings' butter was very good, although Beatrix felt that at least some of the credit ought to be given to Kitchen, the Galway cow, whose milk was extraordinarily rich.

When Mr. Jennings knocked at the door to tell her that the pony was ready, Beatrix put on her coat and blue knitted hat, fetched an umbrella and the basket, and went out to the cart, where she found Rascal, the fawn-colored Jack Russell terrier who lived with George and Mathilda Crook. Rascal was a great admirer of Miss Potter, and when she was in the village, he always spent as much time with her as he could.

"Good afternoon, Miss Potter!" he cried, leaping around her in joyful excitement. (Rascal knew better than to leap upon her, for she was very particular about muddy paws on her tweed skirt.) *"Welcome back to the village. We've missed you!"*

"Hello, Rascal," Beatrix exclaimed, bending over to pet him between the ears and feeling that, after all, life with animals was far less complicated than life with people, and infinitely more entertaining. "It's lovely to see you, too. Winston and I are driving to Tidmarsh Manor. Would you like to go with us?"

"Oh, I would!" Rascal barked. He spun around in a circle. *"I would! I would!"*

She frowned down at him and her voice grew stern. "But I must remind you that you shall have to be civil to Dudley. If you can't promise to behave yourself, you must stay behind." Dudley was Lady Longford's fat, indolent spaniel, who did nothing all day but lie around and beg for treats. As far as Rascal was concerned, he was a poor excuse for a dog and should be reprimanded for his unhealthy habits.

But Rascal would agree to anything if it would mean that he could go along with his favorite person. He leapt into the cart. *Of course I'll promise.* He sniffed at the basket Miss Potter had stowed under the seat. *"But I hope Dudley doesn't get any of this nice bread and butter. That fat fellow ought to lose a few pounds. He can barely waddle."*

Beatrix went round to the pony and stroked his brown nose. "Hello, Winston. You're looking very fit today."

"Thank you, Miss Potter," Winston whinnied, and tossed his brown mane. *"Welcome back to Hill Top. So it's Tidmarsh Manor today, is it?"*

"Yes, and after that, Raven Hall, to call on Mrs. Kittredge," Beatrix said with a smile.

"Naaay!" Winston cried plaintively, stamping his neat hoof. *"Please, Miss Potter! Not Raaaven Hall!"*

Beatrix chuckled. Winston was never happy about taking her to visit Dimity Kittredge, because of the very steep hill along the way. "You can stop worrying, Winston," she said, climbing into the cart. "I'm just teasing you. We're not going to Raven Hall. At least, not today."

To Rascal, she added, in a tone loud enough for Winston to hear, "You know,

Rascal, it is always a delight to drive a willing pony. Some ponies make a terrible fuss about every little bump in the road, or shy at the sight of a mouse in the lane." She picked up the reins. "But not our Winston. Oh, no! He is surely the steadiest, most trustworthy pony in the village. And because he is so cheerful and cooperative, he'll find carrots in his manger when he gets back home."

If you are thinking that Winston ought not to be taken in by such compliments — well, I suppose you're right. But I don't imagine that Farmer Jennings, who is a rather matter-of-fact fellow, is any too free with his praise. Winston is probably quite hungry for a compliment, whilst a carrot or two can never go amiss. And Miss Potter, over the years, has had the misfortune to drive ponies who were not cooperative or cheerful as hc, and who threatened to run off and overturn the cart whenever anything unusual crossed their path. She knows a good pony when she meets one, and is not at all sparing with her compliments.

So if Winston pranced a little more proudly as they began their drive through the village, I think you can understand why. It was nice to know that Miss Potter considered him not only the steadiest of ponies, but cheerful and cooperative, as well. And if Miss Potter smiled, it was because she knew that Winston would do his very best to get them to Tidmarsh Manor and back again safely, a sentiment you will certainly understand if you have ever had a pony run away with your pony cart.

Beatrix, Winston, and Rascal had not driven far when they met a young woman coming down the lane in their direction. It was Deirdre Malone, the Irish girl (now seventeen) who keeps the account books for Mr. Sutton, the village veterinarian, and helps Mrs. Sutton with the eight young Suttons, all of whom live rather cozily in Courier Cottage. If you didn't already know that Deirdre was Irish, you might guess it from her bright green eyes, the freckles dusted generously across her nose, and the carroty tendrils escaping from under her gray cap, knitted from the handspun fleece of Miss Potter's Herdwick ewes. In one hand she held a bundle of the Courier Cottage post, for she was coming from the post office. The other held the hand of one of the multitudinous younger Suttons, who held to the hand of another young Sutton, who held to the hand of a third and then a fourth — a veritable crocodile of little Suttons.

"Hello, Miss Potter!" Deidre called. "Welcome back to the village!" To the children, she said, "Boys and girls, say 'welcome' to Miss Potter."

"Welcome, Mith Potter!" dutifully lisped the crocodile in chorus. Several of the Suttons were missing their front teeth, owing to their age.

"Thank you, children," Beatrix said. She had a warm affection for the young Suttons and kept them supplied with books. She also had a great admiration for Deirdre, a resourceful and energetic young person. Not long ago, the girl had discovered that Mr. Sutton's veterinary practice was losing money faster than he could earn it, because of Mrs. Sutton's failure to insist on payment when service was rendered. She had come up with a plan to collect the overdue money (and thereby keep Courier Cottage from being foreclosed by the bank), and Miss Potter had helped her to carry it out. Between the two of them (although Miss Potter always said that the credit belonged entirely to Deirdre), the Suttons had been saved. Now, Deirdre managed the office for the doctor and made sure that arrangements for payment were made before the client and his or her animal friend had left the surgery.

"You're looking very happy, Deirdre," Beatrix said. She gave her young friend a closer glance. Deirdre had not been an attractive child — a rowdy hoyden, she had been gangly and awkward — but she was becoming a beautiful young woman. Her eyes were sparkling and her smile seemed to hold a delicious secret, as if she knew something marvelous.

"Yes, you are," yipped Rascal. He had seen Deirdre wearing her secretive smile for several weeks. *"You're keeping something from us, aren't you? Do you have a beau?"*

"Oh, I am happy, Miss Potter!" Deirdre burst out, and — rather like her old schoolgirl self — gave a little skip. "I'm about to burst with happiness and fly into a million little pieces, like a balloon that's been blown too full of air." She sobered a little. "I'm dyin' to tell you all about it, when I can. Will you be here in the village for a while? May I come to see you in a few days?"

"Of course you may," Beatrix said warmly. She smiled down at the little Suttons. "Bring the children with you, too. I'm sure Jemima Puddle-duck would love to see them. They can play in the barnyard while we talk." Several young Suttons had been present when Jemima hatched a nest of eggs that turned out not to be ducklings at all, but rather —

But perhaps you haven't read *The Tale of Hawthorn House,* so I shan't spoil it for you. You must go and read it for yourself and find out what it was that Jemima hatched. You will be surprised, I'm sure. I was.

"Thank you," Deirdre said. "I can't do it tomorrow, but perhaps the next? Around teatime?"

"Lovely, my dear," said Beatrix, and they said goodbye.

"I wish I knew what sort of secret she's keeping," Rascal said, half to himself, as Deirdre led the crocodile of small Suttons in the direction of Courier Cottage.

Miss Potter lifted the reins. "Well, whatever her secret, I'm sure it's a pleasant one," she remarked. "She looks so very happy. Come on, now, Winston. Let's be on our way."

At the top of Stony Lane, Beatrix paused to look toward Castle Farm, which she had bought some little while ago. The cottage and gardens were currently let to Dick Llewellyn's sister Rachel (the Llewellyns, Dick and Agnes, lived down the lane at High Green Gate). Beatrix had had the barn and fences repaired and pastured cows and sheep on the farm — Herdwick sheep, of which she was very fond, even though they

128

were considered old-fashioned. Her purchase had pleased some of the villagers, those who were glad that the land had not been sold to off-comers and the old buildings torn down and replaced with modern cottages. It had also annoyed others, who felt that Miss Potter was turning into a land-grabber. But Beatrix paid no attention. Will Heelis had advised her to buy Castle Farm. It had been the right thing to do, whatever the villagers thought.

She lifted the reins and Winston started up the hill again (this is not so steep a hill as the one to Raven Hall). But they had barely gotten under way when here came Sarah Barwick, flying down the hill on her bicycle. She had been out making deliveries of the bread and pastries for which she was becoming quite well known (Sarah is the owner of the Anvil Cottage Bakery), and was wearing her usual biking costume, a pair of green corduroy trousers (cut full for maximum comfort), and a green wool coat, with a brown muffler wrapped round her neck. Her cheeks were reddened by the wind.

"Well, hullo there, Bea!" she cried, braking to a stop. "Welcome back to the village."

"It's good to be here," Beatrix replied, thinking how ironic it was that when she returned to London, nobody ever said, "Welcome back," in quite the same way that the villagers did. At most, her mother might ask, in a complaining voice, "Why must you always stay away so long, Beatrix? You were needed here."

Sarah steadied her bicycle with one foot. "Will you be with us for a while this visit?"

Sarah had arrived in the village at the same time Beatrix bought Hill Top, but the neighborhood men still professed themselves scandalized every time they saw her on her bicycle, and Agnes Llewellyn had been heard to quote the verses in Deuteronomy that said that women who dressed in men's clothing were an abomination before the Lord. What really bothered people, of course, was the idea that women who rode bicycles could go anywhere they liked, which meant that they were independent, wherein lurked all manner of menace. Why, a wife might ride her bicycle all the way over to Outgate to see her sister and not arrive back home in time to make her husband's tea, poor man, and him bone-weary and needin' a bite after a day's hard labor. And her gaddin' out and about in the world, goin' who-knows-where, and none at home to scrub his floors and wash his shirts! I don't wonder that Sarah Barwick was viewed as a "dangerous" woman.

"I'll be here a week or so," Beatrix replied in answer to Sarah's question. She sighed, not liking to think of going back to London.

"Only a week?" Rascal cried. *"I was hoping you'd stay for a fortnight, at least!"*

Sarah fished in her pocket and took out a cigarette and a match. (This was another "dangerous" thing. Older women in the countryside sometimes smoked tobacco in clay pipes, but cigarettes were generally thought "fast." The ladies — if that's what they were — of King Edward's set smoked cigarettes, and actresses, and women who fancied themselves artistic or modern.)

"I suppose you've heard that there's a meeting at the pub tonight." Sarah drew on her cigarette and blew out a stream of smoke. "About the hydroplane, that is. According to Mr. Llewellyn, Mr. Baum has agreed to come and listen to what people say." She grinned roguishly. "Ought to make for an exciting evening, I'd say. You're coming, are you?"

"I'll be there," Rascal promised. *"Wouldn't miss it for the world."*

"Shush, Rascal," Beatrix said. To Sarah, she replied, "I'm planning to come. Right now, I'm on my way to Tidmarsh Manor to see Caroline Longford. I thought I would invite Lady Longford."

"Splendid idea, Bea!" Sarah said enthusiastically. "If Mr. Baum listens to anybody, it'ud be her ladyship — not that he will," she added in a more somber tone. "That man! I've never seen anyone so determined to upset so many people by doing exactly what he wants to do." She blew out another puff of smoke. "Although it's not just him who's doing it, of course. It's that pilot of his. Oscar Wyatt. He's the one who built the wretched machine. Flies it, too. Takes people for rides, if they pay him." She scowled. "Can't imagine why anybody 'ud want to go, much less pay for the trip. If God had wanted us to fly, he would've given us wings."

"Rides!" Rascal barked excitedly. *"I should love to ride in that aeroplane! Why, from way up there, I could keep an eye on everything."* Rascal's goal in life was to see and take charge of all that happened. Jack Russell terriers are born organizers, as you know if you've ever lived with one.

"Oscar Wyatt?" Beatrix frowned. "Is he from this area? I don't think I know him."

"From Manchester. That's where they built the blasted thing." She made a face. "Wish it had stayed there, too."

And just at that moment, they heard it:

the loud, insistent drone of the aeroplane, punctuated with an occasional sputter and hiccup, as if the motor might be threatening to quit.

"Hear that?" Sarah asked, rolling her eyes. "Every now and then the wretched thing just seems to want to stop running and fall out of the sky. And of course the thought of that makes me listen all the harder, and hope a little. Not that I want anyone to get hurt," she added hastily. "I just want that racket to go away."

But it didn't go away. The noise followed Beatrix all the way up Stony Lane, across Wilfin Beck, and over to Tidmarsh Manor. When she got there, she found that Lady Longford was taking her afternoon nap. This gave Beatrix and Caroline a chance to sit down for a quiet cup of tea and conversation about Caroline's work at the Royal Academy of Music, where she had been studying since the beginning of term.

"Do you like the Academy?" Beatrix asked. "Are you learning? Enjoying yourself?" She herself was not a great admirer of formal education, for she had been educated by governesses who for the most part allowed her to follow her own interests in her studies. She had always thought that school would have squeezed all the creativity right out of her. But Caroline — who at seventeen was grown up and entirely lovely — was not of that opinion.

"Oh, Miss Potter, I love it!" she cried enthusiastically. "My teachers say I'm doing well, and I'm learning so much about so many things — not just about music, of course, although that's terribly important to me. And I am ever so grateful to you for making it happen! Why, if it weren't for you, I'd still be living here with Grandmama, instead of going to school in London."

"Oh, no," Beatrix objected. "I had very little to do with it, really."

From one point of view, this was perfectly true, since all Beatrix had done was to drop a few well-chosen words into a conversation the previous summer. But those few words (which had to do with the money Caroline had inherited from her father and which Lady Longford had intended to conceal as long as possible) had forced her ladyship to alter her position. From opposing her orphaned granddaughter's studying in London, she changed her tune and accepted the idea. Now, of course, she insisted that it had been *her* idea in the first place. Whenever possible, she boasted that her enormously gifted granddaughter had been accepted to the Royal Academy of Music, and that *she* was the one who had made it all possible.

From Caroline's studies, the conversation wandered to her old friends in the village, to Deirdre Malone, who worked for the Suttons, and Jeremy Crosfield, who was teaching this year at the village school, taking a year from his studies before entering university. Beatrix mentioned the evening's meeting at the pub, and said that she thought Jeremy might be there. At that point, she asked about Caroline's plans for the future.

"What do you want to do in the next few years?" Beatrix asked. It was a serious question, and Caroline answered it seriously — or seemed to.

She hoped, she said, to take a trip to Europe when her studies were completed, and then perhaps to America, and after that, New Zealand, to visit the sheep station where she had lived as a little girl. And then return home and settle down to composing, which was her dearest love. At Beatrix's request, she went to the piano and played one of her compositions, which immediately brought Lady Longford downstairs. Listening to Caroline play, of course (and occasionally criticizing her playing), was much more pleasant than lying upstairs alone.

Beatrix was glad, because it gave her the

opportunity, when Caroline had finished playing, to invite her ladyship to the evening's meeting. "It will be held in the Tower Bank Arms," she concluded, after explaining the reason for the assembly. "The villagers will all be there to express their views about the hydroplane. Mr. Baum will be there, too. You are especially invited, because —"

"Nonsense," Lady Longford interrupted peevishly. "You know I don't go out at night, Miss Potter, especially in chilly weather. I don't know why you should trouble to ask me. Caroline, pour me a cup of tea."

Her ladyship (who rarely said "please" and "thank you" and *never* begged anyone's pardon when she interrupted them) was a tall, formidable-looking person with thin black brows and thin black hair, which she wore twisted into a fist-sized knob at the back of her head. Her husband had been dead for over a decade, but she continued to dress in black. It was a fashion dictated by Queen Victoria, who mourned Prince Albert for forty long years and set the style for every widow in the entire British Empire.

Lady Longford had softened somewhat (but not very much) in the time Beatrix had known her, partly owing to the presence of young Caroline in the house. The girl was the only daughter of Lady Longford's only son, who had wriggled out from under his mother's thumb and escaped to New Zealand, where he married the love of his life and would have lived happily ever after, if he had not unfortunately died in a train accident. Heartbroken, Caroline's mother had died not long after. Reluctantly (and only after being reminded by Vicar Sackett and Mr. Heelis of her familial duty), Lady Longford took her orphaned granddaughter into her care. Now she was glad, but she didn't dare show it for fear of being thought sentimental — which at heart, of course, she was. That is often the way of sentimental people: they are compelled to pretend to be extremely hard on the outside, chiefly because they are soft on the inside.

Caroline handed her grandmother a cup of tea. "But Grandmama," she said gently, "tonight's meeting is about the aeroplane. It's noisy. Miss Potter says that the villagers are going to ask Mr. Baum to stop flying it over the lake."

Lady Longford took the cup. "Well, they won't succeed," she said darkly. "I've known Fred Baum for years. He's silly and eccentric, but when he takes it into his head to do something, he is as stubborn as an old cart horse. That aeroplane is a horrible nuisance, but he will pursue it, no matter what anyone says."

Beatrix cleared her throat. "The villagers believe that if Mr. Baum will listen to anyone, he'll listen to you."

Lady Longford pursed her lips. "I doubt it. Fred Baum thinks too highly of his own opinion."

"Nevertheless," Beatrix went on, "they believe that you are the only one who can persuade him to take his aeroplane elsewhere. It's dangerous to fly it here, where it harms people and animals. What's more, I understand that Mr. Baum and his partner are thinking of starting an aeroplane route between Bowness and Grasmere. They seem to view it as a profit-making opportunity. If they're successful —"

"An aeroplane route!" Lady Longford exclaimed. She narrowed her eyes. "Fred Baum actually thinks he can make money from that flying contraption?"

"Apparently he does," Beatrix said. "I really hope that you'll come to the meeting, Lady Longford. It would be an opportunity for you to let Mr. Baum know —"

"Ridiculous," her ladyship snapped. "As I said, I do *not* go out at night. Night air is bad for the lungs. Especially cold night air.

And this is March, after all, the worst month for colds and fevers. It doesn't matter how I feel about that aeroplane."

"Well, *I've* decided to go, Grandmama," Caroline said with a toss of her head. "Mr. Beever can drive me. And I have met Mr. Baum several times, as you may remember. I shall be glad to tell him your opinion. Perhaps you would like me to invite him here, where you can tell him for yourself."

"Nonsense, Caroline," her ladyship snapped. "Young ladies *never* go out at night alone, especially to a meeting in the village pub. Why should you want to do such a ridiculous thing? It's unthinkable!"

Caroline wrinkled her nose and laughed sweetly. "My very dear Grandmama, you are so old-fashioned! Why, I am practically grown up. And it's not at all unthinkable, you know. Someone from Tidmarsh Manor really ought to be at the meeting. After all, it's *our* village, too. What goes on in the district should concern us. Grandpapa took an interest in village affairs, didn't he? *He* would have gone to the meeting, wouldn't he?"

Caroline's questions took her ladyship quite aback. It was true that the late Lord Longford had been a staunch supporter of village projects and had always rather enjoyed playing the role of the village squire. Her glance went to his portrait, still draped with a black ribbon (just as the Queen had draped all of Prince Albert's photographs), then back to Caroline, who — it must be admitted — certainly did look grown up, and very shapely and pretty with her long, light hair pinned on the top of her head.

In fact, her ladyship thought, with a sharp, sudden pang, that Caroline looked at that moment exactly like her father, who had been sitting in that very same brown velvet-covered chair when he refused to marry the young lady she had picked out for him — a perfect match, it would have been, too. But when she insisted, her son had stamped out of the room and left Tidmarsh Manor the next morning, and she had never seen him again. If she were honest with herself, she should have to say that it was the one thing in her life that she most regretted. She should not have been so insistent. She really should have been more sensitive to —

Beatrix put her teacup down on the table. "I plan to be at the meeting," she said. To Caroline, she added, "If you would prefer to drive to the village with me this afternoon, Caroline, I should be delighted to have you stay all night at Hill Top."

Caroline smiled. "That's very nice of you,

Miss Potter. I'd like that very much."

"Good," Beatrix said. "And you won't have to trouble your grandmother to send Mr. Beever for you in the morning. Mr. Jennings can bring you home."

Lady Longford put down her cup. "I have changed my mind. I shall go to the meeting after all. I find that I wish to talk to Mr. Baum." She snorted. "Hydroplanes, indeed! What an idea! Caroline, you may tell Beever that we shall want the carriage this evening."

Beatrix did not go directly back to Winston, Rascal, and the pony cart. Carrying her bag with the butter and the loaf of bread, she went around to the back of the house and knocked at the kitchen door. It was opened by Mrs. Beever, a stout person in a gray dress, white apron, and white ruffled cap, somewhat askew on her fuzzy hair.

"Why, if it isn't Miss Potter from Lonnon," Mrs. Beever exclaimed happily, "come round to my kitchen her very ownse'f! Welcome back to t' village, Miss Potter. Do come in an' have a cup o' tea an' a bite of summat."

A smile wreathed her round face. Beatrix had been a favorite of Mrs. Beever's ever since she had helped Lady Longford escape from the sinister clutches of Miss Martine, her ladyship's companion. Mrs. Beever had feared that Miss Martine (who pretended to be French but was about as French as I am, which is to say not at all) was about to seize full command of Tidmarsh Manor, send the staff packing, and install her own hand-picked servants — until Miss Potter came to the rescue.

"I'd be glad of a cup, Mrs. Beever," Beatrix said, although to tell the truth, she had already had all the tea she wanted. It was information she was after just now, and Mrs. Beever, who was always willing to gossip, was sure to be a good source. She held out her bag. "Oh, and I've brought you some bread and some of Mrs. Jennings' butter."

"Won'erful!" Mrs. Beever exclaimed. "Mrs. Jennings makes a verra fine butter."

In a moment, tea was poured and scones and black currant jam were set out. The conversation moved at a lively pace from the weather (previously mild, turning chilly) to Caroline's return from London ("Such a growin' girl!") to the health of Mrs. Beever's sister's daughter, who had a new baby. ("Zora, they named her. Canst tha imagine?")

And then Beatrix remarked, rather casually, "I understand that Mrs. Lythecoe and the vicar are to be married next month. What do you think of it, Mrs. Beever?"

Mrs. Beever's grin showed a broken tooth. " 'Tis a verra fine match, in my opinion." She added slyly, "Although I'd wager that t' vicar has made t' better part of t' bargain."

"Oh, really?"

Mrs. Beever nodded vigorously. "Mappen that Mrs. Lythecoe will take a firm hand in t' vicarage, which is sorely needed, if tha asks me. Not to speak ill o' Mrs. Thompson," she added in a pitying voice (although of course that was exactly what she was doing). "But t' poor ol' thing is in over her head, she is." (Please note that Mrs. Thompson is no older than Mrs. Beever.) "That big house, managing t' tweeny and all t' cookin' — it's jes' too much for her, it is," she added with exaggerated sadness.

Hazel Thompson was the vicar's resident cook-housekeeper. She had never been known for her prowess in either field of endeavor, but over the past few years, her skills had visibly deteriorated and the tweeny (the girl who worked both upstairs and in the kitchen), told of many lapses. Visitors to the gloomy old vicarage could not help but remark the dust in the corners and the lamentable lack of buttons on the vicar's shirts. Those unfortunate enough to

143

be asked to dinner were distinctly unimpressed by Mrs. Thompson's culinary efforts, to the point where the vicar himself found it necessary to apologize.

"I see," Beatrix said thoughtfully. "Yes, I suppose Mrs. Lythecoe will feel it necessary to make a few changes when she and the vicar are married. I wonder how Mrs. Thompson will feel about her new employer. The new Mrs. Sackett, that is."

"Employer?" Mrs. Beever exclaimed sarcastically. "Hazel Thompson ain't nivver been one to take direction from anyboddy. Even 't' Rev'rend Sackett, poor man. She nivver listens to 'im. Jes' goes on doin' wot she wants to do, allus and betimes, same as if she was mistress of t' house all by her ownse'f."

Beatrix drained her cup and set it down. "Then I don't suppose Mrs. Thompson is entirely pleased that the vicar is getting married."

Mrs. Beever laughed shortly. "Doan't suppose she is, now, do I? Wouldn't surprise me in t' least if t' new Mrs. Vicar finds another cook-housekeeper reet soon after t' weddin', an' pore ol' Hazel finds hersel' out in t' lane w' her satchel." She picked up the pot. "More tea, Miss Potter? Another scone an' jam? Or some of Mrs.

Jennings' butter?"

Beatrix declined, thanked her hostess, and then thanked her again. In fact, she was truly thankful, for Mrs. Beever had given her something important to think about.

Just how unhappy was Mrs. Thompson at the prospect of the vicar's marriage to Mrs. Lythecoe and the potential loss of employment?

And to what lengths would she go to stop that from happening?

7

TALES OF A DISAPPOINTED DRAGON CENSUS-TAKER

As Miss Potter was calling at Tidmarsh Manor, Thorvaald the dragon was happily making himself at home not far away, at Briar Bank, the very old, very large, and mostly abandoned badger sett that was home to Bailey Badger and Thackeray the guinea pig.

Thorvaald wasn't a stranger at Briar Bank, of course. In fact, it had been his official address for centuries before Bailey Badger was born. He had been assigned by the Grand Assembly of Dragons to guard a hoard of Viking gold hidden there, in a distant chamber in the farthest corner of the sett. But please don't assume that this was some stirring adventure, fraught with danger and enlivened by derring-do. It had been an excessively boring assignment and Thorvaald had slept through most of it. Treasure-guarding, as he said, was about as exciting as doing the washing-up.

And then, through a series of tragic-comic misadventures, the dragon had at last been released from his gold-guarding assignment. Or rather, he had released himself from it, by the simple expedient of depositing his priceless Viking gold with the British Museum — by air mail, if you can imagine such a thing. He dropped it at the foot of a bobby, dozing against a lamppost just outside the museum.

" 'Twere magic, that's wot 'twere," said the incredulous bobby, according to an article in *The Times*. "Just fell out of the sky, it did, in a pair o' leather satchels." (You'll find the full story of the here-and-gone gold hoard in *The Tale of Briar Bank*.)

But if our dragon thought that giving away the gold would free him from his obligations to the Grand Assembly of Dragons, he was wrong. The Assembly felt that the gold did not belong to Thorvaald, and he had no business donating it to the museum. Moreover, the members of the Assembly were greatly annoyed at him for his part in the death of Illva, his fiery supervisor, who had flown into a barn. (Throughout the Land Between the Lakes, the resulting explosion and fire were reported to have been caused by a meteorite.) It was a good thing that the dragons didn't know everything that happened that day. If they had, they would have done more than reprimand Thorvaald. They would probably have canceled his flight permit and put out his fire.

But it was clear to the Assembly that they had to do something to curb Thorvaald's juvenile enthusiasms and instill a greater sense of duty and discipline in the young dragon. So they assigned him to the census, sending him hither and yon, investigating reports of dragons. All of these had proved to be wild-goose chases, or wild-dragon chases, as the case may be, including his trip to Scotland, where he was supposed to discover whether the Loch Ness monster was real or a figment of someone's fertile imagination. Thorvaald's failures to discover and document the whereabouts of dragons had not, I fear, impressed the Assembly, who felt that he probably hadn't worked as hard as he might have done. In fact, one of the senior dragons had been heard to remark that he ought to be hauled home and put to work waiting tables in the dining hall, where the dragon-master could keep an eye on him. He was thoroughly in disfavor — in the doghouse, a modern person might say — and he knew it.

So Thorvaald was taking a few days off to think about how he might reestablish himself in the Assembly's good graces. He should have to do *something* important and soon, or he would forever find himself assigned to fruitless tasks like the census — or worse, waiting tables in the dining hall. There was so much to be accomplished in this world: deeds to be done, wrongs to be righted, knowledge to be gained. Like many young dragons, Thorvaald was an idealist. He earnestly wanted to do his bit, to make his mark. He wanted to create a reputation for himself in the Wide World. But he could do none of these things if he were condemned to the life of a mere census-taker.

While he reflected on these matters, Thorvaald was happily content to serve as a portable stove, warming the parlor at Briar Bank on a chilly night, or to stoke up his steam boiler to heat the tea kettle, or to provide a light for Thackeray's pipe or for the kitchen fire, when it went out. He also served as a foot warmer in the evenings, so that the badger and the guinea pig could keep their toes cozy while Thackeray was reading aloud or Bailey was telling a story.

Bailey enjoyed this very much and often thought that he had missed a great deal in his earlier life, shunning companionship and playing the role of the curmudgeonly bachelor badger. Tonight, as he glanced from

Thackeray to Thorvaald, he was happily reminded of the Seventeenth Rule of Thumb: *Hold a true friend with both paws.* His life was so much more enjoyable now that he could share it with others, although there was sadness, too. Thorvaald was only visiting and would be gone again before many days. *Hold a true friend with both paws,* the Rule said, and went on, *but be willing to let him go when the time comes.* That time was not tonight, however, and Bailey was intent on enjoying his dragon as long as possible.

Thorvaald even added a few tales of his own to the telling, for his census work had taken him to some rather interesting places in search of undocumented dragons. He told about flying across the Pacific to the island of Hawaii to watch Mauna Loa's lava fountains erupt and the rocks glow cherry-red and flow in curling, scarlet ribbons toward the ocean. No dragon there, although the sight of all that molten rock had certainly warmed his soul. Thorvaald had experimented with a few of the rocks to see if he could melt them, but his fire just wasn't hot enough. He would have to leave that sort of business to Mauna Loa, who seemed to be very good at it.

Then he had been sent to Siberia to see

whether there might be a dragon or two in the region of Tunguska, where a few years before (in 1908) witnesses said that a great stream of fire had split the sky from horizon to horizon and that an explosion in the sky had flattened the trees for hundreds of square miles. After a lengthy investigation, Thorvaald determined that the event had been a meteor explosion and reported to the Assembly that no dragons had been involved. A few of the dragons had grumbled about this, for they had been very sure that the Tunguska explosion had been a dragon-caused event and wanted to take credit for it.

Thorvaald's third assignment was in America, where he was supposed to scout out Yellowstone National Park. This evidence harbored a great many geysers — evidence, the dragons hoped, of a large dragon colony, or at the least, a small outpost. Extensive exploration, unfortunately, had turned up no dragons, but the sight of Old Faithful in the moonlight, its fountain of water and steam like boiling silver, had been astonishing. Thorvaald was glad he went.

"You must have been disappointed when you didn't find what you were looking for," Thackeray remarked. *"You've invested quite*

a lot of time and effort in those trips."

"That's what the Aszsembly said," Thor-vaald replied sadly. *"They thought I should have been able to find something to add to the censuszs. But you can't count a dragon that isn't there."*

"And Loch Ness?" Bailey prodded. *"Tell us about the monster."*

This tale was also a story of disappointment, for Thorvaald had not found any evidence that the monster existed, much less that it was actually a seagoing dragon, as the Assembly had hoped. *"I patrolled the loch for several nightszs,"* he said. *"I flew the entire sixty-mile length, from Invernesszs in the north to Fort William in the south."* He sighed gustily, and Bailey moved out of the way of his steamy breath. *"All I sszsaw was a patch of disturbed water and a shadow that may or may not have been the monszster. Of course, it was night, and the moon was only a sliver, and I couldn't szsee very much. That's what comes of being a dragon and having to go about after dark, for fear of attracting too much of the wrong kind of attention."* He sighed again. *"If I had been able to fly down closzse to the water during the daytime, I might have actually caught the monszster in operation."*

"We all have our limitations," Thackeray

remarked sarcastically.

Bailey gave the guinea pig a stern look. Thackeray was not exactly jealous of the dragon, but there might be a bit of competition going on there, Bailey thought. He shifted the subject slightly by mentioning the note from his great-great-grandfather that he and Thackeray had found in the pages of Trollope's novel *Framley Parsonage.*

"An eyewitness account of a monszster in Windermere?" the dragon asked eagerly, and his belly glowed with excitement. *"I don't think the dragonszs have heard about thiszs, or they would no doubt have asked me to look into it. Have you szseen the creature yourself, Bailey?"*

"No, I haven't," Bailey replied. *"Thackeray and I just found the note a few nights ago. Anyway, I'm not sure you can trust my great-great-grandfather's report. He was a truthful old badger, but a bit nearsighted, I am told."* Nevertheless, he got out the note and showed it to Thorvaald. *"A snakelike creature with three humps and a long neck,"* the old badger had written, *"about the length of the ferry boat. Saw it from Oat Cake Crag, swimming between the shore and Belle Isle."* After it was read, Bailey folded up the paper and

put it with his hat, to take to Hyacinth for recording in the *History.*

"Three humpszs and a long neck!" the dragon exclaimed with a hiss of steamy enthusiasm. *"Why, that's exactly what the Loch Ness monster was supposzsed to look like. Perhapszs the two are related!"*

"Perhaps," said Thackeray dryly, *"they both came out of the same bottle of Scotch."*

"My great-great-grandfather did not drink," Bailey said, a little offended. *"He was a teetotaler."* He added, thoughtfully, *"Of course, Windermere is very deep — over two hundred feet at the northern end. It was originally known by the Norse name of Vinandr's Mere.* Mere *is the Old English word for 'lake.'"*

"Perhaps the Norseman Vinandr dropped a baby dragon into his lake." Thackeray snorted a laugh. *"And it's been growing ever since. Imagine that, if you will!"*

"It's more likely to be a very large pike," Bailey replied. *"Some of them do grow to be quite large."*

The dragon ignored him. *"Your great-great-grandfather said he saw this monster from Oat Cake Crag, Bailey. Where iszs that?"*

So then Bailey had to tell the story about the Scottish soldiers who had camped on

154

the crag and cooked their oat cakes there and found it a very fine lookout, until one of their number stepped over the edge and fell to his death on the rocks below. *"The story has passed into legend,"* said the badger. *"I have heard it renewed lately, for there have been a few sightings of a dark, ghost-like shadow falling from the top of the crag — the ghost of the Scottish soldier, it is said."*

"Most likely an owl," remarked Thackeray, who didn't believe in ghosts. However, he had not previously believed in dragons, either, so you may discount his remark if you wish.

"But if your great-great-grandfather saw the monszster from that point," the dragon said, now very enthusiastic, *"it standszs to reason that it would be a good place for me to szset up a lookout."*

"I'm not so sure about that," Bailey said dubiously. *"It's a rather exposed crag. On a moonlit night, someone might look up and see you. You are large, you know. And you do glow."*

The dragon looked down at his belly. *"I can try to turn it off."*

"No, you can't," said the guinea pig. *"Turn off your fire and you won't be a dragon anymore. You'll just be a large green lizard with a*

long tail." He grinned. *"Get used to it, Thorvaald. You are what you are."*

The dragon heaved a huge sigh. *"But I've got to find some way to redeem myself in the eyes of the Grand Aszsembley!"* he moaned. *"Otherwise, I'll be doing the census forever. Or worse, I'll be waiting tableszs in the dining hall."*

"You'll find it," comforted Bailey. *"I'm just not sure you'll find it in Lake Windermere, that's all."*

As things turned out, the badger was wrong. But that's another part of the story. We'll get to it when the time comes. Now, we have a meeting to attend.

8
AT THE TOWER BANK ARMS

But before the meeting, we shall make a stop at Tower Bank House, the home of Captain and Mrs. Miles Woodcock.

I am afraid that there is certain amount of muddle about these two names — Tower Bank House and the Tower Bank Arms. It is the same sort of confusion that people often feel about the names of Near and Far Sawrey, for Far Sawrey is nearer Windermere and the ferry, when approached from the east, and Near Sawrey is farther away. Why is Far Sawrey not called Near? people often ask. And why is Near Sawrey not called Far?

This seemingly illogical bit can be very simply explained, but you have to come at it from the other direction: that is, from the west. (Illogical things often clear themselves up when you turn them upside down, or wrong side front, or inside out.) Then you will see that Near Sawrey is nearer the market town of Hawkshead, while Far Sawrey is farther away by a half mile or so. If you are still muddled, you might want to glance at the map at the front of this book, which may help to unmuddle you.

The confusion in names came about many years ago, when Tower Bank House was home to the village squire, who imagined himself somewhat grander than he was. It happened that the pub — known for many years as The Blue Pig — was put up for sale, and since the price was reasonable, the squire thought he would buy it. However, upon reflection, it seemed to him that owning a "Blue Pig" was a notch or so beneath him, and that he would rather own a "Tower Bank Arms," which sounded a good deal more impressive. The villagers found this funny (they still called the pub The Blue Pig) but off-comers were terribly confused. Some who wanted a bed at the Tower Bank Arms found themselves ringing the squire's door bell, whilst those who had business at Tower Bank House ended up with a half-pint at the pub.

The squire is dead and gone, but the names have lived on. Now, Tower Bank House is the home of Captain and Mrs. Miles Woodcock. Captain Woodcock — a fine-looking, capable gentleman, respected by all who know him — is retired from His Majesty's Army and serves as the justice of the peace for Claife Parish. This position requires him to hear complaints, witness documents, certify deaths, deal with disturbances of the peace, and the like, so that the captain finds himself involved in a great many aspects of village life and feels entitled to hold a general opinion about all of it (even those parts that are none of his business).

The new Mrs. Woodcock (the former Margaret Nash) retired from her position as headmistress of Sawrey School upon the announcement of her engagement to the captain. They were married by the vicar at St. Peter's in a ceremony that was attended by everyone in the parish, and afterward feted at a lovely garden reception at Raven Hall (Mrs. Kittredge of Raven Hall is the captain's sister). Mrs. Woodcock misses her work with the children, although she is very happy with her new position as mistress of Tower Bank House. It took a little while, but she and Elsa Grape (the captain's cook-housekeeper) have come to an understanding about who is to make the menus and oversee the tweeny. Now that the duties have been equitably divided (at least from Elsa's point of view), the household is humming along quite peaceably.

Tonight, the captain and his wife are entertaining the captain's closest friend, Mr. Will Heelis, at dinner. They would have invited Miss Potter as well, if they had known of the secret engagement. But since it is still a secret and nobody knows, they didn't — and anyway, Mrs. Woodcock had not yet heard that Miss Potter had arrived from London and was in residence at Hill Top. So to make four, they invited Jeremy Crosfield, a favorite former student of Mrs. Woodcock's and a recent graduate of Kelsick Grammar School in Ambleside.

Jeremy (whom I'm sure you remember from earlier books in the series) is now eighteen, tall and stalwart, with reddish-brown hair, wide-spaced gray eyes, and fine, regular features. He has taken Mrs. Woodcock's place as teacher of the junior class at Sawrey School, where the young boys in the class particularly benefit from his teaching and his example. He might have gone on to university (with the help of Major and Mrs. Kittredge, who offered), but he decided to spend this year practicing the botanical illustrations that are his passion, which I think is a very good idea. He is already quite a competent naturalist, and the time away from formal studies will give him the opportunity to develop his art, for which he has a true gift.

The fish and soup had already been removed and the company was enjoying lamb cutlets, carrots and cauliflower, and Pommes de Terre Duchesse. (Mrs. Woodcock had got the recipe out of Mrs. Beeton's, but it was nothing more, Elsa said with a sniff, than fried potato cakes dressed up with a fancy French name). Jeremy was young enough not to be intimidated by formal dinner-table rules and enlivened the conversation with his funny tales of the doings of the schoolchildren. Mrs. Woodcock smiled at his stories, but she was a bit misty-eyed, since she missed her charges and was sometimes sorry that she could not go back to teaching.

From there, the talk turned to the subject of the evening's meeting at the pub: Fred Baum's hydroplane. As it turned out, the captain had a definite opinion about this flying machine, and it was not in agreement with Mr. Heelis' position, or anybody else's at the table — or in the village, for that matter. He was very much in support of the thing.

"I am sorry, my dear," he said in response to his wife's complaint about the hours she had spent with cotton stuffed in her ears.

"But I am afraid we shall just have to learn to live with the noise — at least while the machine is under development here in the area. In fact, we should applaud it. The hydroplane is progress. It is necessary to our national defense."

Mrs. Woodcock looked unconvinced.

"Our national defense?" Mr. Heelis asked mildly, picking up a slice of bread. "And why is that, Woodcock?"

The captain waved his fork. "Why, everyone knows the Germans are arming, Heelis. Just look at all the dreadnoughts they are building. And I read in *The Times* that the German Military Aviation Commission has set a prize for the development of new aircraft. If we don't build an aeroplane suitable for combat, they will. And then where will we be?"

"Indeed," replied Mr. Heelis steadily. "The Germans are building one dreadnought for every one of ours. Once we start building aeroplanes for combat, they will, too." His face was sober. "It is a race that neither side can win. And once entered into it, there's no getting out — in my opinion, anyway."

"I can't agree with your premise," said the captain firmly, who as a former military man was entirely convinced that his opinion about armaments was all that counted. "We must enter, and we shall win." His voice rose. "Of course we shall win, and handily, at that. But we shall need aeroplanes, and plenty of them. Losses are likely to be high."

"Because they crash so often, I suppose," Jeremy put in. Even as a child, he had not learnt to hold his tongue and got into all sorts of trouble for talking back to his teachers. Now that he was a grownup, he enjoyed speaking up even more.

"Ah," said Mr. Heelis approvingly. "Yes, Jeremy, indeed they do crash. Which is not to say that we should not have them," he added. "Just that it would be better to fly them over the Channel, say, where, in case of a crash, people and animals on the ground are not injured. *Not*," he said emphatically, "in the Lakes. Over our villages."

The captain ignored both of them. "And some of those aeroplanes ought to be hydroplanes," he went on, "so as to take off and land on water when necessary."

"And is that why we must have that hydroplane flying over our heads from sunrise to sunset?" asked Mrs. Woodcock wearily. "Really, my dear, there ought to be a *limit*. Say, no flying between the hours of two and four, when the village children are having their naps. Otherwise, it is very inconvenient for their mothers. I wish you would tell that to Mr. Baum this evening."

But Mrs. Woodcock spoke gently, so as not to be seen as disagreeing with her husband. She found that she adored him so amazingly that she could not bring herself to contradict him on even the slightest thing, even when she knew in her heart that he was wrong (as in this case). And since they had no children — not yet, at least — it was a matter of inconvenience chiefly to herself.

Her husband chuckled in a loving way. "Yes, of course I shall tell him, my dear, although I doubt he will comply. Baum is still testing his machine, you see, so it must be flown frequently and in all sorts of weather. It is still very experimental. The scientists are keen on learning all they can from every flight."

Jeremy looked up from his cutlet. "Is that why Mr. Wyatt takes paying passengers?" he put in, somewhat ironically. "To test the machine?"

"Who is Mr. Wyatt?" Mrs. Woodcock inquired.

"The pilot," Jeremy told her. "Oscar Wyatt. The machine was all his idea. Designed and built it. Mr. Baum put up the money, but he doesn't know anything about aeroplanes."

"Paying passengers?" the captain asked, frowning.

"Why, yes," Mr. Heelis said. "Didn't you know? People are lining up at the hangar where the hydroplane is kept, hoping for a ride. Wyatt charges them five shillings for thirty minutes in the air."

"Five shillings!" Mrs. Woodcock asked, shocked. "Why, that's outrageous! It's half a week's wages for most people."

"It does seem rather excessive," said the captain slowly. "But of course, there's the fuel cost and —"

"I have heard from a reliable source," Mr. Heelis said, "that Wyatt has it in mind to establish an aeroplane route between Bowness and Grasmere. It might be used to transport passengers, as well as the mail." He looked straight at the captain. "I know that it seems hardly feasible, at least at this stage of the machine's development. But who knows what advancements will be made in the next year or two." He paused. "If commercial development is behind this project, would you support it?"

"An aeroplane route!" exclaimed Mrs. Woodcock, wide-eyed. "But that means that we shall *never* be rid of the wretched thing."

The captain was somewhat flustered. "I

was under the impression that this venture was created for the purpose of national defense. If there is a commercial aspect —" He stopped.

"If there is," persisted Mr. Heelis, "would you support it? Bearing in mind," he added, "that there was so much public opposition to building a railroad into the Lake District that the project failed. It would seem to me that there might be just as much opposition to an aeroplane route, and for some of the same reasons."

Many had opposed the expansion of the railroad into the mountainous areas of the Lake District when it was proposed some years earlier, not only because of the noise and soot from the trains, but because they feared that increased tourism and commercial development would spoil the scenic landscape. On the other side of the issue, many argued that the railroad would be an economic boon to a struggling region, and that jobs were more important than landscapes any day of the week.

"I suppose I shall have to ask Baum to tell us what he has in mind," the captain replied stiffly, now on his dignity. "I shall do that this evening."

"Well, then," Mr. Heelis said, "I think we can count on an interesting meeting. Assuming," he added thoughtfully, "that Baum actually tells us what he and Wyatt are planning. I am not at all sure that he will. This aeroplane of theirs is surely a long way from any commercial use, but neither of them will want word of a possible air route to get out. Some other aeroplane developer might come along and trump them — or attempt to buy them out. Or people might start organizing an opposition."

The captain did not reply to this. Instead, he looked down the table at his wife. "My dear, will you ring for Mrs. Grape? I believe we are ready for our dessert. What are we having?"

"A Charlotte Russe," said Mrs. Woodcock proudly, having also got that recipe from Mrs. Beeton. In case you don't know, this is an elaborate dessert in which a mold is made of ladyfingers, filled with a vanilla custard and decorated with fruit, berries, and whipped cream. Some say that it was created by the French Chef Marie-Antoine Carême and named in honor of his Russian employer, Czar Alexander, others that it took its name from Queen Charlotte, wife of George III. Mrs. Woodcock, being British, inclined to the latter view.

After the dessert was handed round and they had all begun to eat it, Mr. Heelis remarked, as if quite casually, "I understand that the vicar and Mrs. Lythecoe have set their wedding date."

"Yes," Mrs. Woodcock said happily. "It is to be on April twentieth. Not quite a month away." Now that she is married, she feels it the most blessed state in the world and wishes that everyone else could enter into it, too.

"Seems like a good match to me," Mr. Heelis commented. "I suppose everyone in the village is delighted."

"Universally," agreed Mrs. Woodcock.

"Not quite," said Captain Woodcock.

"How so?" asked Mr. Heelis, all ears. (You can probably guess that he, like Miss Potter, is playing detective.)

"I've heard it said," the captain replied slowly, "that a few people object on the ground that Mrs. Lythecoe was married to the former vicar. Apparently, it seems a bit . . . well, incestuous. Or something equally ridiculous."

"Miles!" exclaimed Mrs. Woodcock, scandalized. She framed the word *incestuous* with her lips, but could not bring herself to say it aloud.

"But the two vicars were not related, were they?" Jeremy asked curiously.

"Cousins, as it turns out," the captain replied.

"Is that right?" Mr. Heelis raised an eyebrow. "I'd never heard that."

"First cousins," said the captain. "Reverend Sackett was appointed to the living after the death of Reverend Lythecoe, who was his mother's sister's oldest son. I heard this," he added, "from the vicar himself, several years ago. At the time, it was not widely known, I believe."

"And it is now?" Mr. Heelis asked, frowning.

"Well, I don't know about 'widely,' " the captain said. "But I've heard talk of it, yes. As I said, a few seem to disapprove."

"But who?" Mrs. Woodcock persisted.

"And why?" Jeremy asked, frowning. "I mean, what business is it of theirs who anybody marries?" There was a tone in his voice that suggested a deeper sort of interest, perhaps personal. This makes me a little curious, and I wonder if there's something in Jeremy's life that we don't know about. We shall have to look into it, I think. Perhaps it is part of our story.

"What business?" The captain gave a short laugh. "Why, nobody's business, of course. The marriage violates no laws. But that doesn't keep people from objecting. Specifically," he added, in answer to his wife's question, "I overheard Henry Stubbs and George Crook discussing the matter at the pub."

"Which probably means that it is their wives who object," Mrs. Woodcock said darkly. "I shall have to ask Elsa. Bertha Stubbs and Mathilda Crook spend far too many afternoons with her in our kitchen, gossiping." It was an activity she had been longing to curtail but had not thought it prudent whilst she and Elsa were negotiating more important matters, such as authority over the menu. (The captain's sister, Dimity, who had charge of her brother's household until her marriage to Major Kittredge, had not been courageous enough to challenge Elsa, who over the years had assumed full control in the kitchen.)

Mr. Heelis made a mental note to ask Mrs. Woodcock how her inquiry turned out. Aloud, he said, "Please also tell Mrs. Grape, from me, that her Charlotte Russe is delicious."

Mrs. Woodcock brightened. "Elsa will be very glad to hear that." She looked around the table. "Now, then. Would you like to have coffee before you go?"

I said that we were going to a meeting this

evening, and so we are. But unfortunately for us, and for all those in attendance at the Tower Bank Arms, Mr. Baum failed to put in an appearance, so everyone went home disappointed and more than a little disgruntled.

The disappointment did not dawn for some time, however. It had clouded up before sunset, and by the appointed hour, an intermittent March rain was falling. This did not reduce the attendance, and as the hour grew near, more and more villagers — both men and women, because the women had very strong opinions on this subject — streamed into the main room of the pub. The space is not large, as you will know if you have visited the place, and it wasn't long before the room was packed so tightly that not another person could have squeezed in. The air was thick with tobacco smoke and the familiar fragrances of garlic, onions, and wet wool and filled with the buzz of voices and the music of Sam Stem's merry concertina.

At last, pub owner Lester Barrow sent his oldest son to stand by the door and tell people that they could not come in until someone went out, and to hold the door open in order to bring in a breath of cooler, rain-washed air. Lester did this with some regret, naturally, for the more people who packed themselves into his pub, the more half-pints of ale he would sell in the course of the evening. He was enough of a business-man not to miss this chance.

Some of the people crowding the pub were villagers whose names and faces are familiar to us. Lady Longford (as you know, she changed her mind and decided to come) had arrived early and was seated at a table in the front of the room, with her grand-daughter, Caroline. Jeremy, seeing Caroline (who had been his friend during their days together at the village school), made straight for the table and sat down beside her. Within a moment, the two were deep in conversation.

Beside the bar stood Major Kittredge, master of Raven Hall. The major had lost an arm and an eye fighting with the Boers in South Africa, but those losses only seemed to add to his stature in the district, especially since his marriage to Captain Woodcock's sister, Dimity, a match that everyone had heartily approved. The major, wearing his customary black eye-patch, was chatting with Roger Dowling, the village joiner. Joseph Skead (the sexton at St. Peter's) and his wife, Lucy, the village postmistress, sat at a nearby table. In the corner sat George Crook, the blacksmith, and his wife, Mathilda, as well as Constable Braithwaite, who was not wearing his blue serge uniform, since he was not on duty. Mr. Sutton, the veterinarian, was there, and the Jenningses as well (Miss Potter's farmer and his wife). Oh, and Miss Potter herself, seated in a chair near the fireplace. With a smile and a warm greeting (but not as warm as he would have liked to make it, since this was a public place), Mr. Heelis joined her, as Captain Woodcock motioned to Sam Stem to stop playing his concertina, stepped up on a bench, and convened the meeting.

Of course, the minute everyone grew quiet and began to look around, they saw that Mr. Baum had not yet arrived. Major Kittredge made a motion to wait for fifteen minutes, and Lester Barrow happily seconded it, giving latecomers a chance to throng the bar and get their half-pints. But in fifteen minutes, the absent man had still not arrived, and people had begun to whisper that he had deliberately stayed away — an insult, of course, to Lady Longford, who had made a special effort to come.

Scowling, Captain Woodcock waited another ten minutes, then called the meeting to order, saying that even if Mr. Baum wasn't there to hear it, everyone ought to have a chance to speak. He requested that speakers limit themselves to three minutes each, and set his pocket watch on the bar, where he could see it.

He invited Lady Longford to speak first (an acknowledgment of her importance in the village). She, however, declined to speak at all, since Mr. Baum was not there to listen. She was clearly irritated, glaring at the captain as if it were his fault that Mr. Baum had not arrived and was heard to mutter that she was sorry she had come out on such a night, on a fool's errand.

The captain next invited Major Kittredge to speak. The major summed up the problem in a few terse words: "The issue is whether we are to lead our accustomed quiet lives here, or be bombarded daily with an infernal noise. I hereby move that we form a committee to discuss this matter with Mr. Baum, and present our views forcefully. Woodcock, I suggest that you chair it."

"Second the motion!" Roger Dowling shouted. "But Major Kittredge ought to be on the committee, too."

"Moved and seconded," the captain announced. "Is there any discussion?"

There was, and plenty of it. One after one, the village men stood up and said what was on their minds. They were irritated and angry at the noise, concerned for the health and safety of their animals, and offended at the idea that the absent Mr. Baum — someone they knew, one of their neighbors — would so blatantly disregard their safety and comfort.

And as it sometimes happens in meetings like this, the more people stood up to speak, the angrier everyone became, and by the time the last person had spoken, the room was crackling with rage. These wrathful fires continued to burn as the captain adjourned the meeting and people began to leave the pub.

A group of men came out of the door and paused in front of the pub, heads together, hands in pockets, shoulders hunched against the mist.

"I'm givin' that fool Baum a piece o' my mind when I see him," growled the normally staid Roger Dowling. " 'Twere reet bad-mannered o' 'im to agree to talk wi' us tonight an' then stay away."

"Ought to give 'im a good smack on t' head wi' a big board," avowed George Crook. He grinned darkly. "That 'ud set 'im straight."

"Mappen that's wot I'll do next time he gets on me ferry," said Henry Stubbs, the ferryman.

"Smack Baum on t' head an' then throw *him* overboard," laughed Lester Barrow, who had come out just then. He had a great deal to laugh about. His ale kegs were empty and his till was full. "That'd put an end to t' aeroplane business."

"Mebbee sumbody's a'reddy done that," suggested Roger Dowling slyly, "an' that's why he's not here."

The men looked from one to another, a trifle uneasily, then Lester Barrow laughed again, scoffing this time. "Doan't be silly, Roger. Baum stayed away 'coz he already knew wot he'd hear an' he had no intention o' listenin'. Anyway, if Baum decided not to go on wi' the project, that pilot o' his — Oscar Wyatt — he'd find a way. That aeroplane is here to stay, like it or not." Barrow turned and went back into the pub to count the cash in his overflowing till.

But Roger Dowling wasn't finished. "Wotever may be up wi' Baum," he growled, "that aeroplane ain't here to stay. We canna have machines buzzin' in t' air over our heads, scarin' animals and frayin' nerves. We're goin' to fix it, we are."

"Aye?" George Crook asked skeptically. He and Roger had been friends for a long time — his blacksmith's forge was next door to Roger's joinery — but he was a careful man who hated to go out on a limb. "Wot dusta mean by 'fix'?"

"An' who is 'we'?" Henry Stubbs asked. "I hate that flyin' machine as much as th' next 'un, but —" He stopped, looking wary. Henry was full enough of talk, but wasn't always willing to put his muscle where his mouth was.

Roger looked over his shoulder to make sure that no one was listening. "I'll tell thi wot I heard from Baum's odd-jobs man. Baum sacked 'im last week and he's mad enough to chew horseshoe nails. T' fella says mebbe we woan't have to listen to that aeroplane much longer."

"That 'ud be auld Paddy Pratt, now, wouldn't it?" asked Henry. Paddy was a well-known village character who hired himself out at the homes of the local gentry, doing repairs, lending a hand with the garden, running errands. He was generally liked but not much trusted, at least by those who knew him well. "Paddy Pratt is nivver up to awt good. Goosey, he is. Dunno as I'd trust any bright ideas that started wi' him."

"Jes' hear me out," Roger said. "But afore I tell thi wot's afoot, tha'll have to swear not to tell nawt to noboddy."

"I'll listen," George said. "And I'll promise. If Paddy's got a way to scotch that aeroplane, I'm all fer it." And with that, the three of them faded into the dark.

At that moment, Captain Woodcock, Mr. Heelis, and Miss Potter came out of the pub together.

"It's too bad Baum wasn't here to listen to village opinion," Mr. Heelis said regretfully.

"Yes, indeed," Miss Potter agreed. "Why do you suppose he stayed away?"

"Kittredge and I shall find out when we speak to him tomorrow," promised the captain. He smiled at Miss Potter. "Now that you're back in the village, I do hope you'll join Mrs. Woodcock and me for tea one afternoon."

Miss Potter returned the smile. "Why, thank you, Captain. I should be glad to."

When the captain had gone, Will Heelis leaned closer and lowered his voice. "Earlier this evening, I heard from Captain Woodcock that Bertha Stubbs and Mathilda Crooke are opposed to Mrs. Lythecoe's marriage to Reverend Sackett. It seems that they are offended because she was previously married to the vicar's cousin. It crossed my mind that this might have something to do with those letters."

"Well, if that's their objection, it's very

silly," Beatrix replied. "Thank you, Mr. Heelis. I'll see what I can find out." She held out her hand, quite properly. "Good night."

He pressed her fingers with a quite improper passion, then raised his hat and smiled. "Good night, my dear Miss Potter. Good night." (You and I know that these two are engaged, but I doubt if anyone looking on would have suspected a thing — and their secret is safe with us.)

Beside the road, Jeremy Crosfield was handing Caroline into her grandmother's carriage. "I should like to come and see you in a day or two," he said as she settled her skirts. "It's been a long time since we've had a chance to talk."

Lady Longford frowned. "I do not see the need —"

"Of course you may come, Jeremy," Caroline said, smiling warmly. "Grandmama, Jeremy and I will go out into the garden, so as not to disturb you. I'm sure it won't be too cold."

"Thank you," Jeremy said, avoiding Lady Longford's barbed glance. "Day after tomorrow, then? At four? I'm finished with school by that time."

"Day after tomorrow," Caroline promised happily. "At four."

"Harumph," her ladyship said, and raised her voice. "Drive on, Beever!"

Jeremy stood in the dark and watched the carriage drive off, the lantern swinging on its hook, casting swaying shadows through the dark. He was thinking — what is he thinking? He is surely remembering Caroline when they were both students at the village school: she a leggy, lonely young girl, longing for her native New Zealand; he shy and awkward and conscious that she was the granddaughter of the wealthiest woman in the district.

Or perhaps he has forgotten their shared past (how long ago? five years, six?) and is thinking only of the present, reflecting that this grownup young lady, with her clear gray eyes and sweet smile, her fair hair pinned up on her head, is the most charming girl he has ever seen, charming and utterly, utterly desirable.

He has asked permission to call — I wonder: is it just a friendly visit, for old times' sake? Or is he actually imagining that he might court this lovely and accomplished young lady? After all, he now has a paid position. He is a teacher, which is a situation of some honor and standing in the village, especially when it is held by a man, even a young man. There is no reason why, if he chooses, he might not advance to headmaster, at Sawrey School or Hawkshead, or somewhere nearby.

But I am sure you are aware that Jeremy has no status at all in the eyes of Lady Longford, who still thinks of him as that runny-nosed urchin whose aunt resides in one of her farm cottages and earns a poor living spinning and weaving. No, not in the eyes of Lady Longford. If Jeremy has courtship in mind, I foresee complications.

But our young friend does not seem to be troubling himself with the thought of complications, at least not at this moment. Whistling softly, his hat pushed back at a jaunty angle on his head, Jeremy pushes his hands into his pockets and, with a little skip, turns to go across Kendal Road and up Market Street. He has been boarding with Mr. and Mrs. Llewellyn at High Green Gate since the beginning of the school year, for it is not nearly so far to walk from there to the school as it is from the outlying cottage at Holly How Farm, where his aunt lives. He enjoys boarding with the Llewellyns. Mrs. Llewellyn is rather a sourpuss and fault-finder, but Mr. Llewellyn is always cheerful. He allows Jeremy to do the milking before school — a chore Jeremy enjoys — in exchange for his board and room.

Ah, Jeremy, young Jeremy. What are your dreams? Are you reaching above yourself?

And yes, I do think this is part of our story, and an important part, I believe — although I wasn't sure of it until just now.

9
A BADGER MAKES
A CHILLING DISCOVERY

The villagers were not the only ones in attendance at the meeting. Throughout the evening, Rascal was stretched out on the floor beneath Lady Longford's table. He was pretending to be asleep, but he kept one eye half-open, watching the door for Mr. Baum's arrival. Tabitha Twitchit and Felicity Frummety, taking mental notes of all that was said, were crouched together on the hearth near Miss Potter's feet. Crumpet had a better view from her place on the bar, where she kept an eye on the captain's pocket watch, flicking the tip of her tail faster and faster as the speakers approached their three-minute limit. (The captain noticed this, and said to his wife when he got home, "The oddest thing, my dear. There was a gray tabby cat with a red collar on the bar, and she actually seemed to be keeping time with her tail.")

Other creatures were present, too, although they were occupied with their own business and paid no attention to the people in the room, who, of course, paid no attention to *them*. There was a large family of mice gathering crumbs under the floor, silly and scatterbrained as mice always are, running off in all directions and forgetting where they were going before they got there. A small brown spider was dreamily spinning a new web in the corner. And another animal was present as well, nearly as large as Rascal, but heavier, dark, and handsomely striped. But she was outside, poking around under the window, where (because people were angry and talked in very loud voices) she could overhear every word that was said. After the meeting was finished, she went round the back to visit the few turnips that still lived in Mrs. Barrow's wintry patch of garden. She was digging one up when she met Rascal and the three cats, who came out the back door.

"Well, hello, Hyacinth," Tabitha said cheerily. *"We haven't seen you for a while."*

You have probably already guessed that this forager amongst the turnips is Hyacinth, the young female badger who now holds the Badge of Authority at Holly How. She and Bosworth had talked it over and decided that one of them should attend tonight's meeting and learn what the Big People were going to do about the flying boat. Since Bosworth didn't venture far from Holly How these days, Hyacinth had volunteered.

"Although I don't think there was much to be learnt tonight," she added, when she had told the animals why she was there. *"Too bad that Mr. Baum couldn't hear what people had to say. He might have changed his mind and decided to fly his aeroplane somewhere else."*

"It's very strange," remarked Rascal, cocking his head with a puzzled look. *"He was planning to come."* After he and Miss Potter had returned from Tidmarsh Manor that afternoon, Rascal had happened to meet the brewer's drayman on Kendal Road. Having nothing else to do, the little dog hopped on the brewery wagon for a ride down to the ferry, then rode back at teatime with Dr. Butters, who was returning from a call on the eastern side of Windermere. The doctor, one of Rascal's many friends, always invited him to ride in his gig. The doctor's horse was very fast and Rascal was delighted to accept, since he loved the feeling of the wind blowing his ears.

"And just how do you know?" asked Crumpet.

"I was at the landing this afternoon, when

Mr. Baum got off the ferry. He had crossed over from Cockshott Point, where he keeps his aeroplane. I heard him tell Mr. Wyatt — they had been on the ferry together — that he intended to go to the meeting."

"You don't suppose something happened to him, do you?" Tabitha asked, frowning.

Crumpet giggled. "You mean, like an aeroplane crash? His own medicine, going down the wrong way?" She elbowed Felicity Frummety, proud of her clever little joke. "Get it? Going down the wrong way?"

Felicity (the ginger cat who lives with Mr. and Mrs. Jennings) ignored Crumpet's elbow. "If his aeroplane had crashed, I'm sure we'd have heard about it." She shuddered. "Some of the Big People who spoke tonight were very angry. You don't suppose somebody's koshed him over the head, do you?" Felicity enjoyed both a delicate constitution and a vivid imagination, and loved to frighten herself by conjuring up the worst, whereupon she fled to the nearest corner and covered her eyes with her paws until the danger was past. Crumpet liked to say that Felicity gave new meaning to the term scaredy-cat.

"I suppose he never intended to come at all," put in Crumpet, who is a very skeptical cat. "Big Folks lie all the time."

186

"Personally, I do not suppose at all," Rascal said in a definitive tone. *"There is never any point in supposing — at least for more than a minute or two. It is far better to find out the facts."*

"Oh, right," said Crumpet, with a sharply sarcastic meow. *"And just how far will you go to find out the facts? Where does Mr. Baum live?"* She answered her own questions. *"He lives at Lakeshore Manor, that's where. On the far side of Raven Hall, on the lake shore below Oat Cake Crag. I make it"* — she squinted, calculating — *"well over a mile away."*

"Which is why I had better be going," said Rascal, getting to his feet. *"Major Kittredge must be ready to leave for home. I'm sure he won't mind if I ride along with him as far as Raven Hall. From there, I can take the path through the woods. Won't be far at all."*

"Not far to go, maybe," Crumpet said ironically. *"Plenty far to come back."* Crumpet wasn't lazy, but she did like to conserve energy.

Rascal ignored her. *"Anybody want to go with me?"* he asked, looking around the little group. *"Tabitha?"*

"Not I," said Tabitha firmly. *"I have a date with a vole in the Anvil Cottage garden."*

"You won't find out a thing," Crumpet remarked cattily. She smoothed her whiskers. *"Waste of time."*

Felicity shook her head. *"I don't go beyond the village at night."* She shivered. *"One never knows what beasts one might encounter."*

"Well, then, it'll have to be just me," Rascal said bravely. *"I'll let you know what I find out."* It wasn't that he was afraid, of course. Jack Russell terriers are never afraid of anything. Or rather, they never admit to being afraid — which is not quite the same thing.

"I'd love to go with you," Hyacinth offered. Unlike the village cats, who are domesticated creatures with a preference for staying close to home, badgers are adventuresome animals, always eager for new experiences. *"But I doubt that the major would offer* me *a ride,"* she added, *"and I don't think I can run as fast as the major's horse."* Most Big Folks in the Land Between the Lakes are prejudiced against badgers, whom they think of as pests who raid gardens and chicken coops. Granted, badgers do a certain amount of this, for they have to eat, too. If badgers have set up housekeeping in your neighborhood, you would do well to fence your turnips (Mrs. Barrow has not) and install a strong clasp on your chicken

coop door.

"He probably wouldn't offer," Rascal agreed with a grin. *"But the gig he's driving has an empty wooden box on the back, for carrying bundles and such. I'll distract him and give you time to jump into it. He'll never know you're there."* Rascal was happy to have Hyacinth along, because badgers have very strong claws and are fierce fighters, particularly when they are cornered. He knew he could count on Hyacinth to back him up if they ran into something unexpected and . . . well, dangerous. In that event, the cats wouldn't be any help at all. It was just as well they stayed home.

So Rascal ran to Major Kittredge's gig and barked and jumped and begged with a great deal of excited energy, and the major, who knew the little dog, immediately invited him to sit on the driver's seat. Whilst this was going on, Hyacinth climbed into the box and shut the lid. As it turned out, the box wasn't completely empty. It contained (in addition to one badger) a dozen eggs that the major was taking home to his wife, as well as a parcel of biscuits that Mrs. Woodcock had baked for her sister-in-law's tea. Showing great restraint, Hyacinth touched neither the eggs nor the biscuits, feeling that since she was getting a free ride, so to speak, she ought not to take advantage. A less well-mannered badger might have enjoyed supper en route and arrived fully fed.

The horse was fast and they reached Raven Hall expeditiously. Rascal made a big show of thanking the major whilst Hyacinth climbed out of the box and hid in the shrubbery. The two met a few moments later and made their way to the footpath that led through the trees of Claife Woods. The nearly full moon was rising over the lake and cast a silvery light, more than enough to see the narrow path that wound through the still-leafless trees. And since both the badger and the dog are accustomed to going about the countryside after dark, they had no trouble at all in finding their way to Lakeshore Manor, where Mr. Baum lived.

The two-story, early Victorian manor house, built of brick and topped with a slate roof, was set on a bluff above the waters of Windermere. Before it, a grassy park sloped steeply to the lake's edge, where the moon painted a wide swath of silver across the water. Behind it towered the high cliff of Oat Cake Crag. The house was dark and seemed (so Rascal thought) to wear an almost frightened look, as if it were waiting for something.

"No lights," Hyacinth whispered. *"P'rhaps Mr. Baum has already gone to bed."*

"Or he's gone out and hasn't returned," Rascal replied. But where had he gone? Not to the pub, certainly. And they hadn't met him on the road to the village, or on the path from Raven Hall.

At that moment, there was a stir in a tree on the crag, followed by the ominous crack of a twig. A dark triangular shadow swooped with frightening suddenness down the face of the cliff, exactly like the shape of a falling man.

Hyacinth ducked under a bush, remembering Parsley's tale about the ghost of a Scottish soldier who had fallen to his death from the crag. Was it the ghost? But Rascal (who had a pretty good idea what was going on) bravely stood his ground.

Without a sound, not even a rustle of wings, the shadow settled in the top of a nearby tree. *"Whooo?"* inquired the owl's commanding voice. The great head swiveled from side to side, the amber eyes glaring. *"Whooo goooes there, I say! Halt, and identify yourselves!"*

"Good evening, Professor," said the dog in a deferential tone. All of the local animals know that it is well to speak respectfully to the owl, who is quite large and formidable.

191

"It's Rascal, from the village. And Hyacinth, from Holly How. We hope we haven't disturbed you."

"Yooou have not," the owl said in a kindlier tone, and settled his feathers. To tell the truth, he was rather glad to see Rascal, who had a nose for news and often carried interesting bits of village tattle. *"A bit far from home, I'd say. What brings yooou here at this hour of the night?"*

"We rode with Major Kittredge," the dog explained. *"Mr. Baum was supposed to come to the meeting at the pub tonight, so people could tell him how they feel about his aeroplane. But he didn't, and everyone is wondering why. Hyacinth and I thought we would try to find out."*

"That is commendable," replied the owl. *"But I doubt that yooou'll learn anything. There's nooobody at hooome. There's been nooobody at hooome all evening. At least,"* he amended, *"since I have been here."* He raised his round eyes to the moon. *"Which (according tooo the stars, whoooose passage I have been observing from my vantage point atop the crag) has been a considerable while. Three hours at least, I shoooould say. Venus is now past ten degrees from its meridian and Jupiter has nearly reached its zenith, which is tooo say —"*

"Nobody at home?" Hyacinth interrupted, coming out from under the bush. She had never felt it necessary to defer to the owl, whom she viewed as rather a stick-in-the-mud. She was always polite, though, because the Professor was Uncle Bosworth's friend and, as an older animal, deserving of respect. She was also quite aware that once he had well and truly launched into a lecture on the movement of the stars, they were likely to be here all night.

"That's odd," she went on, before the owl could get his second wind. *"If Mr. Baum didn't come to the meeting and he's not here, where is he?"*

The Professor had not liked the idea that a female badger might hold the Holly How Badge of Authority, and when Bosworth had first mentioned the possibility, the owl had opposed the appointment vigorously. He was in fundamental agreement with the French novelist Guy de Maupassant, who said, "The experience of centuries has proved to us that females are, without exception, incapable of any true artistic or scientific work." The owl believed, as he had said to his friend Bosworth, that females suffered from *"certain innate and irremediable intellectual deficiencies"* and should not be allowed to hold positions of authority.

However, since the owl was an owl and not a badger, his opinion regarding the Badge of Authority had not been considered. After a grueling test that proved to Bosworth that she suffered from no deficiencies of any sort, Hyacinth had been named to the post. Which did not mean that the owl had to like it. Moreover, he did not like to be interrupted when he was discussing the stars. In fact, he did not like to be interrupted at all.

He turned a severe gaze on Hyacinth. *"Perhaps Mr. Baum met with an accident on the way tooo the village,"* he suggested in an icy tone. He lifted his wings, shook them, and resettled them. *"An unfortunate possibility, but a possibility nooonetheless. The horse runs away, the cart is overturned, the driver is throoown out and killed. It's a possibility that must be considered."* Having settled the matter, he took a deep breath and went on. *"Now, as I was saying about Jupiter —"*

This time it was Rascal who interrupted, since they really had to get on with the discussion and not be sidetracked by an academic dissertation on the stars. *"But we came by the road, Professor, and we didn't see anything of Mr. Baum. So I don't think there's been an accident."*

"We didn't come by the road the whole way,

194

though," Hyacinth reminded him. *"We only came by the road as far as Raven Hall, with Major Kittredge. After that, we followed the path through the woods."*

"Yes, of course," Rascal said, seeing immediately that Hyacinth was right. *"So we need to go back by the road and see if there's any sign of —"*

"Wait a minute," Hyacinth said, holding up her paw. *"What's that?"*

Rascal looked around. *"What's what?"* he asked nervously.

"That noise," Hyacinth hissed. *"Listen!"*

The animals fell silent. For a moment, they heard nothing — nothing except the companionable conversation of the wind in the trees, the soft *slush-hush-slush* of the lake waters lapping against the shore below, and far away, the inquisitive *crawk?* of a night heron.

"Really," said the Professor, still irritated at Hyacinth. *"I dooo not think —"*

"Shush!" said Hyacinth.

And then all three of them heard it at the same time: a long, low moan. Then one word, low, weak, quavery.

"Heellllp!"

It seemed to come from somewhere behind them, at the foot of the cliff.

"Whooo?" cried the owl, lifting his wings

and turning his head from side to side to peer into the darkness all around. *"Who-who-whooo?"*

"Where?" barked Rascal sharply, turning around several times. *"Where? Where are you?"*

But Hyacinth wasted no time in asking questions. With her nose to the ground and her ears tuned for any sound, she made off into the dark, moving silently and skillfully in the way of a badger who knows what she's looking for. It didn't take her long to find it, either, in a thorny tangle of bushes growing out of a heap of fallen stones at the foot of the cliff, some thirty yards away. That's where she made her chilling discovery.

For a moment, all she could do was stare. Then she raised her voice. *"Over here!"* she cried urgently. *"Rascal! Professor! Over here!"*

When the others reached Hyacinth, they found her crouched beside the sprawled figure of a man. His arms were flung out wide, his legs at odd angles, his head bleeding badly.

"Whooo?" asked the owl somberly. *"Whoooooo?"*

Rascal didn't have to look twice. Hyacinth and I have already guessed, and I'm sure you have, too. But since the owl has asked . . .

"*It's Mr. Baum,*" Rascal replied.

10
"Is He Dead?"

With a frightened cry, the injured man struggled to push himself up, looking wildly at the three animals clustered around him. Then, coughing weakly, he fell back against the rocks and lay very still, as still as death. He was a heavyset fellow, of a substantial size and girth. His eyes were closed, and in the moonlight, his round face was pasty-white. A trickle of blood oozed out of the corner of his mouth.

"Is he dead?" the owl inquired anxiously, peering down.

Hyacinth bent closer, checking the man's breathing. *"No,"* she said, *"at least, not yet. But he's very badly hurt."* She looked up at the crag looming above them. *"He must have fallen from up there, wouldn't you say? He needs a doctor. But how can we —"*

"There are servants in the house," the owl said. (He always had an answer for everything.) *"We must rouse them. Rascal,*

gooo and bark at the windows."

"But there aren't any servants," Rascal replied grimly. *"At the ferry today, I heard Mr. Baum tell Mr. Wyatt that he had to let them go. He said he had put all his money into that aeroplane and couldn't afford to pay them."*

The man moaned again, but very faintly, and closed his eyes. *"We have to get help,"* Hyacinth said. *"Quickly!"*

Rascal turned to the owl. *"Raven Hall is not too far away. You could fly there and bring someone back, Professor. Fly fast!"*

"No." Hyacinth shook her head. *"That won't help, Rascal. No offense, Professor, but nobody will pay attention to an owl."*

"Oooh, cooome now!" the Professor exclaimed, deeply affronted. Still, while he would never admit it, he knew that the badger had spoken sensibly. Big Folks are clever. Some are even clever enough to construct machines that fly. But they simply do not have what it takes to understand animal language, particularly the languages of wild creatures. Some amongst them might interpret his calls as an omen of death, but the more enlightened — Major Kittredge, for instance — would view that as mere superstition. As far as the major was concerned, his alarm cries would be just so much night noise.

"*Well, they certainly won't listen to me, either,*" Hyacinth said in a practical tone. "*In fact, somebody would probably shoot me. Rascal, that just leaves you. You'll have to go and get help. Hurry.*"

"*I'll do my best,*" Rascal said without hesitation, and set off. Racing through the night, he followed the path through the woods, back to Raven Hall. When he reached it, he saw that most of the windows were dark and guessed that the residents had gone to bed. By moonlight, the house looked even more commanding than it did during the day: an imposing example of baronial Gothic, a Victorian version of a medieval castle, with crow-stepped gables and turrets topped with candle-snuffer caps and battlements. Rascal could almost imagine that defenders were stationed behind those battlements, ready to pour boiling tar upon the head of any intrepid trespasser.

But Rascal was undeterred. There was a light burning on the main floor, and he knew that the major was at home. So he ran around the house to the main entrance and raced up the wide stone steps. The bell pull was out of his reach (no one imagines that a small dog will have need of a door bell), which meant that he had to jump up on his hind legs to yank at it with his teeth. He jumped and yanked and jumped and yanked several times, then began barking and yelping and pawing frantically at the door.

At last, it opened and an elderly manservant, his sparse gray hair in a muddle all over his head, peered out. He was wearing a dressing gown and carried a candle. (A candle? Yes. The major has installed an electrical generator that provides a reading light in the library and two lights in the kitchen, but the rest of the huge, sprawling house is lit by paraffin lamps and candles. It's very romantic and certainly in keeping with the idea of the medieval castle, but a little hard on the eyes, I should think.)

"What's all this noise?" the butler demanded, for that's who this was. "What do you want?" Not seeing anyone, he opened the door wider, holding up the candle and putting out his head to look around. "Who's there?" he called loudly.

"It's me!" Rascal barked. *"I've come to get Major Kittredge! We have an emergency."*

The old man looked down. "Why, it's only a little terrier!" His voice hardened. He was a butler and accustomed to giving orders to underlings, who were expected to follow his orders. "What are you doing here, dog?" he barked. (I'm sorry, but this is the only way of describing his tone.) "Where's your master?"

Of course, the butler didn't expect an answer to his questions. He was simply expressing his displeasure at being summoned to the door after he'd already gone to bed — and by a dog. A mere *dog,* for pity's sake.

"I'm here about Mr. Baum!" Rascal barked. He pawed the air, dancing around in a circle. *"He's hurt! He may be dying! The major must come and help! Hurry!"*

It was an urgent message, delivered urgently and succinctly, and if it had been you or me or Miss Potter, I am sure that we would have understood that something important was being said and that we should have to pay attention. But all that the servant could hear was a flurry of barks and yelps, and all that he could see was a pesky little dog, bouncing up and down on his hind legs, waving his forepaws in the air.

"Go away," the old man growled. By now he was feeling extremely out of sorts. "Go home, cur. Whatever it is that you want, we don't have any of it here." And with that, he put out his foot and gave our Rascal a very hard kick.

Now, I understand that it is late and the butler wants to go back to bed and has no patience with a noisy little dog, barking and yelping at the front door and threatening to rouse the whole household. But even so, I hardly see the necessity for calling Rascal a cur, do you? And giving him a *kick?* That really is going too far. All the man had to do was shut the door in the dog's face, and that would have been the end of that. (Although probably not, for Rascal is a determined fellow and would have raced right around to the kitchen and got in that way.)

But Jack Russells do not like to be kicked, and they especially do not like to be addressed as "cur." When Rascal heard that offensive word and felt that sharp toe in his ribs, he did something he had never before considered doing, for he is by nature an accommodating, polite little dog. That is, he is accommodating and polite in ordinary circumstances. But this was an extraordinary circumstance, so he responded in an extraordinary way.

He bit the butler's ankle.

"Yowch!" cried the old man, grabbing his ankle and jumping up and down. "Mad dog! He bit me! There's a mad dog on the loose! Get a gun!"

Now, you may feel differently about this, but I am of the opinion that a man (no mat-tcr his age) who kicks a dog ought to get something in return for his effort. So I don't have a problem with Rascal's giving him a generous nip. Tit for tat, I say. Perhaps this person will think twice before he kicks another animal.

Then, whilst the butler was assessing the damage to his person, Rascal took the opportunity to dash between his legs and through the open doorway, and thence into the wide baronial hall, arriving just in time to meet Major Kittredge, who had been sitting up reading under the electric light in the library and was still fully dressed. The major had heard the racket and wanted to know what was going on.

"Why, it's Rascal," he said in surprise when he saw the dog. "What's all the noise, old chap?"

"That beast must be shot!" the butler cried. By now he had worked himself into a frenzy. "He bit me! I'm bleeding! Mad dog!"

The major stepped forward, bent over, and inspected the butler's ankle. "I don't see any blood, Frederick." He put a gentle finger on a spot where the skin was bruised. "Is this what all the fuss is about?"

The butler looked down, frowning. "P'rhaps it's . . . it's not as bad as I thought 'twas," he muttered. He glared at the dog.

"But I still say he ought to be shot."

"I didn't intend to hurt you," Rascal barked defensively. *"But nobody likes to be kicked."* He could still feel that toe in his ribs.

"I'm sure the bite must have startled you, Frederick," the major said diplomatically. "Why don't you wake Mrs. Durham and see if she has a salve for it?"

"Yes, Major Kittredge," the butler said, although he knew very well that if he waked Mrs. Durham, she would take his head off. Putting on an exaggerated limp, he went off down the hall.

The major turned to the dog, frowning. "Now, then, Rascal. What's going on here?"

"It's your neighbor, Mr. Baum." Rascal sat down on his haunches and put up an earnest paw. *"He fell from Oat Cake Crag. He's badly hurt. He needs a doctor! Please —"*

"What is it, Christopher?" Mrs. Kittredge leaned over the stairs, looking down. She was wearing a dressing gown and a lace-trimmed sleeping cap. "What is all that barking? It'll wake the children." And then she, too, saw the little dog. "Why, it's Rascal!" she said. "George Crook's dog, from the village. Whatever is he doing here, at this time of night?"

"I am trying to tell you," Rascal exclaimed. *"Mr. Baum is hurt. He may be dying. You must*

come!" And with that, he jumped up, seized the hem of the major's jacket in his teeth, and began tugging him toward the door.

Now, Jack Russells are not very large dogs. But when they have a job to do, they are exceedingly diligent about doing it. In fact, as you undoubtedly know if you have ever been acquainted with a Jack Russell, once they have accepted an assignment, it is virtually impossible to keep them from carrying it out. I daresay that the only way to deter Rascal from this task would have been to chain him to a tree, which the major was not inclined to do.

"Why, how very strange," the major exclaimed, trying unsuccessfully to disengage himself. "He's acting as if he wants to take me somewhere."

Mrs. Kittredge spoke decidedly. "Christopher, I have the feeling that something is the matter. Perhaps there's a cart upset on the road, or a fire. You'd better take a couple of the servants and go and see."

Rascal stopped tugging long enough to say, *"Yes, oh yes! Come on — let's go!"* and then began tugging again.

The major sighed. It was late, he was tired, and he was not happy at the prospect of going out in the cold to look for somebody's upset cart. But his wife was pushing him from one direction and Rascal was pulling from the other, so he (prudently) yielded. He reached for a bell on the wall, and rang it. When a young man appeared, he said, "Fetch Richard and bring several lanterns around to the front. We're going out."

"Where, sir?" the young man asked.

"How the devil should I know?" the major said helplessly. He pointed to the dog, who by now was standing beside the door, waiting. "We're following him."

And that is how Rascal managed to summon the major and a pair of stout, husky young men to the place where Mr. Baum lay. Hyacinth and the Professor wisely stayed out of sight, knowing that there would be no explaining this odd collection of animals around the injured man.

"Is he dead?" Richard asked, bending over the injured man.

Major Kittredge knelt down and put an ear to Mr. Baum's chest. "No, but he's in bad shape. Go to the manor house, quickly, and bring the servants. We'll get him to his bed and summon the doctor."

When the house proved to be completely empty, Major Kittredge instructed his servants to hitch a wagon to a horse they found in the manor stable. With difficulty (Mr. Baum really was a very stout person, weighing well over fifteen stone), thcy got the injured man into the wagon and conveyed him to Raven Hall, where he was carried upstairs (with even more difficulty) and put to bed in one of the many guest bedrooms. Another servant rode off on the major's fleetest horse to fetch Dr. Butters from Hawkshead.

But since the market town was some three miles away and the doctor had to be rousted out of a sound sleep, it was over an hour before he arrived. Meanwhile, the major paced the floor, wishing that he could have simply rung the doctor up. Telephones were everywhere in London. Even towns as small as Kendal, on the eastern side of Windermere, now had them. There was no service on this side of the lake, though, and not likely to be for some time to come.

And of course, he was also thinking about the irony of the whole thing. For whilst the villagers were muttering about Baum's absence from the meeting that night, the poor fellow was lying, injured and unconscious, upon the rocks at the foot of Oat Cake Crag. The major had come to the same conclusion that Hyacinth had reached: Mr. Baum had climbed Oat Cake Crag and then fallen. Why had he gone up there? The major couldn't hazard a guess. He was relieved when the doctor finally arrived and took charge of the situation, as the best doctors do.

Doctor Butters has put on a little weight around the middle since his marriage to Miss Mason, whom he met during those odd events and confusions of identities at Briar Bank House, and to whom he has been happily married ever since. But he still has the same reddish hair and gingery mustache, the same engaging (if somewhat caustic) manner, and he is still beloved by all in the district, who consider him the very best doctor in the world. Now, having set Mr. Baum's broken arm and leg and tended to his unconscious patient's other visible injuries, he wore a look of deep concern.

"This is a bad business," he told the major, who had helped him to set the broken limbs. (During his wartime service, the major had been often called upon to do much more than this, and was as competent as any nurse.) "The fractures will mend in time, of course. But there may be some internal bleeding. And with a head injury of this sort —" He frowned. "Well, it's simply unpredictable, that's all. I've seen some wake up the next morning and demand coffee and *The Times*. I've seen others spend the rest of their lives in a coma. There is just no telling how this will end. With that in mind, I should think he would be more comfortable at Lakeshore Manor, where his people can take care of him."

"Poor fellow," the major said sympathetically. "But he can't be taken home, I'm afraid. There's no one to look after him. No servants, I mean. I was there tonight. The place is empty — and I don't mean that they're simply out for the evening or a day or two. Looks like they've all cleared out."

"Oh, dear!" It was Mrs. Kittredge, still in her dressing gown and ruffled cap. She had come into the room at that moment and heard her husband's words. "Well, then, Mr. Baum must stay with us. We'll take care of him until he is up and about."

The major gave her a frowning look. "Dr. Butters says that it may take some time, my dear. The fellow has a serious head injury. There's no predicting how long he will —"

"That does not matter in the slightest, Christopher," Mrs. Kittredge said decidedly. "The poor man is our neighbor. We must do all we can to help."

"That's very kind of you, Mrs. Kittredge," the doctor said, although he was thinking that the dear lady had no idea what she might be letting herself in for. Baum might lie there in that bed for weeks. For months.

Forever.

Mrs. Kittredge smiled. "Thank you, Doctor." To her husband, she said, "I'll just go and wake Ellen, dear. She can come and sit with him for the next few hours." With that, she left the room.

The doctor rolled down his shirtsleeves. "What happened, Kittredge, do you know? A vehicle accident, I suppose." It was a logical guess, since many of the injuries the doctor treated were caused when a wagon or cart overturned.

The major shook his head. "It seems to have been a fall. My men and I found him at the foot of Oat Cake Crag a couple of hours ago, just before we summoned you. I have no idea how or when he might have fallen, though. For all I know, he could have lain on those rocks for a day or more. Lucky for him that the weather's been mild."

"Well, I can tell you that it had to have happened more recently than that," the doctor replied, fastening his cuffs. "He was on the ferry this afternoon, coming across the lake. He was having an argument with that partner of his. Oscar Wyatt. The fellow who built the aeroplane." He pulled his gingery brows together and pursed his lips. "Now, there's an obnoxious character if I ever met one. Wyatt, I mean. He was telling Baum that he needed more money for this and that — all having to do with the aeroplane, of course. Baum said he didn't have any more money to put into the project. Said he'd even had to let his servants go."

"Ah," said the major thoughtfully. "So that's why the house is empty."

"Apparently." The doctor closed his black bag, nodding. "But Wyatt wouldn't leave it at that. The fellow kept after Baum unmercifully. Money for fuel, for repairs, for more work on the motor, on the hangar. One thing after another — money, money, money. Quite importunate, he was. Didn't care who heard him, either. Rude and annoying, I thought. Baum seemed quite put out about it, although it was a public place and he is a gentleman, so he didn't respond." He shook his head. "If you ask me, I'd say that Baum is heartily sorry that he's gotten involved with that aeroplane business. He's looking for a way out."

"Ah, yes. That aeroplane," the major said. He glanced at the doctor. "You knew about the meeting tonight?"

Butters nodded. "I would have been there, but I was called to deliver Mrs. Tall's latest boy — which makes seven, if I've counted right." He grinned crookedly. "Imagine. Seven boys under the age of ten. Poor woman, and her with no girls to help with the laundry." He paused. "What did I miss? At the meeting, I mean."

"Not much," Kittredge replied with a small shrug. "Everyone in the village is against it, as far as I can tell — except for Woodcock. He thinks aeroplanes are necessary for defense."

"Which they just might be," the doctor replied soberly. "I suppose we shall all have to get used to the noise." He snapped his bag shut. "Had you heard that Churchill is coming to have a look at the thing?"

Kittredge pressed his lips together. "I hadn't, but I can't say I'm surprised. Churchill likes to be seen to have his hand in everything, on the off chance that some of it might work." He gave a sour chuckle. "When is he coming?"

"No idea. Baum and Wyatt were talking about it. Churchill apparently has it in mind to establish a Royal Flying Corp. I got the idea that Baum was reluctant, though. Seemed to feel that the aeroplane was not yet ready for official scrutiny. Wyatt, on the other hand, was brimming with enthusiasm for the visit. Gave him another reason to ask for money — and show off his machine, of course." He picked up his bag. "Wyatt may be a crack aeroplane pilot, but his dealings with people leave something to be desired. Inconsiderate, I'd say. Churlish."

Kittredge frowned. "What should be said if he shows up here, wanting to see Baum?"

Butters glanced back at the motionless man on the bed. "It might be a good idea not to let him in. The two men did not part company on the best of terms this afternoon, or so it seemed to me. Tell Wyatt that there are to be no visitors. Doctor's orders."

"Agreed," said the major.

The doctor opened the door. "I understand that Wyatt is staying at the Sawrey Hotel. I'll stop there on my way back to Hawkshead and leave a message for him, telling him what has happened. If no one's awake, I can put it through the door." He sighed. "I suppose I'd better let Woodcock know, as well. He may want to send the constable over to talk with you."

The major nodded. "I'll see you out," he said, and they went downstairs.

A moment later, as they were saying good night on the broad stone steps outside Raven Hall, the doctor turned for one last word. "You say you found Baum just a couple of hours ago? After dark? Lucky for him, but it's curious. How did you happen to discover him?"

"It *is* curious," the major agreed. "I was

just ready to go to bed when George Crook's little dog — Rascal, he's called — appeared at the door. Bit the butler, which got my attention."

"Ah, Rascal. Yes. He rode from the ferry with me this afternoon." The doctor chuckled. "Bit the butler, you say? That's rather dramatic. Should I have a look?"

"Not necessary. He didn't break the skin. But he did insist quite urgently that I accompany him. I brought along two of my fellows, and he took us straight to where Baum lay."

"Remarkable," the doctor said. He put on his hat. "You never know about animals, do you? I'm often glad that my horse can't talk." He chuckled again. "Might tell Mrs. Butters where I've been and what I've been up to."

But the doctor's horse (a bay gelding named Phoenix) can talk, and very well. He and Rascal, as well as Hyacinth and the Professor, had been having a conversation as they waited for the doctor to come out. Phoenix had already invited Rascal to ride back to the village, and the little dog had said good night to his friends and settled himself in the buggy, as the doctor discovered when he climbed in.

"Hello again," Rascal said.

The doctor picked up the reins. "I hear you bit the butler," he said, scowling down at the dog.

"He kicked me," Rascal replied in a defensive tone. *"And it wasn't much of a bite. If I had really wanted to, I could have taken his foot off."*

"Well, don't try it with me," the doctor warned dryly. "I'll bite you back." He clucked to his horse. "Let's go, Phoenix."

Their next stop was at the Sawrey Hotel. Late as it was, the hotel was dark, so the doctor merely scribbled a note on a piece of paper, folded it, and wrote Oscar Wyatt's name on the outside, then put it through the mail slot in the front door. Then they were off again. When they got to the village, Rascal barked his thanks to the doctor, jumped out of the buggy, and trotted up the street in the direction of Belle Green, feeling that he had done his duty for that night.

I think you will agree that he had, and more. It is entirely possible that Mr. Baum owes the little dog his life.

11

MISS POTTER INVESTIGATES: AT ROSE COTTAGE AND THE POST OFFICE

The next morning, Miss Potter worked for an hour or two on her current book, *The Tale of Mr. Tod.* If you haven't read it, you might. It's short, and won't take more than ten or fifteen minutes, depending on how fast you read — although I hope you'll take time to linger over the drawings, because they show how carefully Beatrix observed the wild animals of the Land Between the Lakes. Which is why, I suppose, the animals felt that she understood their language.

The main characters are a pair of rather unpleasant creatures. "I have made many books about well-behaved people," the tale begins. "Now, for a change, I am going to make a story about two disagreeable people, called Tommy Brock and Mr. Tod." Tommy Brock is a fat, curmudgeonly badger who is "not nice in his habits" and "waddled about by moonlight, digging things up." He sleeps in the daytime, and goes to bed in his boots.

(*Brock,* of course, is the common country name for "badger," as you can see by the name our Holly How badgers have chosen for their animal hostel: The Brockery.) Mr. Tod (*Tod* being the country name for "fox") is a cunning character, too tricky by half. He has a distinctive odor, is of a "wandering habit," and has foxy whiskers.

Miss Potter's story involves a sackful of baby rabbits whom Tommy Brock (in no way related to the friendly, helpful badgers who live at The Brockery and in Briar Bank) has kidnapped and shut up in the oven in his kitchen, preparatory to putting them into a rabbit pie — a dish that I am sure Parsley would never in the world consider adding to her menu. But Benjamin Bunny (the rabbit babies' father) and his cousin Peter rescue the little ones by taking advantage of a fearsome fight between the fox and the badger. They carry their charges safely home to the babies' mother, Flopsy, and (although they are "rather tumbled and very hungry") recover completely after dinner and a good night's sleep. Unfortunately, Peter and Benjamin do not linger long enough to witness the outcome of the fierce battle between Mr. Tod and Tommy Brock, so we are left to guess who won. Personally, I think it was the badger, because foxes, whilst they are tricky, are more apt to give up quickly and run away. But really, it is a very exciting tale. I hope you will read it.

Unfortunately, Miss Potter's editor (Harold Warne, who would have been her brother-in-law, had she and Norman married) was not very enthusiastic about *Mr. Tod.* Although he was always after her to produce more and more books (to the point where she was beginning to rebel), this one did not suit him. He seems to have feared that mothers and grandmothers, who buy a great many books for birthday and Christmas gifts and sometimes tell their children what they ought to read, might be shocked by the ill-mannered and churlish villains, and he wrote to the author with several suggestions for changes.

But Beatrix would have none of it. "If it were not impertinent to lecture one's publishers," she wrote impertinently, "you are a great deal too much afraid of the public; for whom I have never cared one tuppenny-button. I am sure that it is that attitude of mind which has enabled me to keep up the series. Most people, after one success, are so cringingly afraid of doing less well that they rub all the edge off their subsequent work."

It *is* impertinent, isn't it? But it is also

exactly the right answer. I daresay Mr. Warne was quite taken aback — at least, I hope that he was. I am glad to see our Beatrix making such a spirited defense of her work in the face of opposition from a staid and stuffy gentleman who thinks more of propriety and how many copies the book might sell. (This is very odd, when you consider what will happen a few years hence, when it emerges that the outwardly respectable Mr. Warne is a crook. Yes, a crook! He had been secretly taking money from Beatrix's royalty accounts instead of paying it over to her, and was convicted and remanded to gaol on charges of embezzlement. So much for propriety.)

And although Beatrix might not have cared so much for the mothers and grandmothers who bought her books, she cared a very great deal for the little children who read and cherished them, and who were surely breathless as they read about the scoundrelly fox and the rascally badger who slept in his boots and Benjamin's and Peter's daring rescue of the about-to-be-roasted bunnies. And the disagreeable villains didn't hurt book sales one little bit (so much for *you,* Harold Warne!). Over the next few years, *The Tale of Mr. Tod* appeared in three printings, for a total of 45,000 copies, which was an astronomical number of books in those days. Which just goes to show that if you have an idea for a story, even if it does involve a shocking villain or two, you should stick to your guns and tell it exactly as you please, for it is your story and no one else's.

And now we must get on with ours. Beatrix rose at her accustomed early hour and worked on the narrative, which she was writing out in ink in an exercise book. She had done one or two of the drawings (just to get the idea of them) and thought to leave the rest until the story was finished and she had decided which scenes to illustrate. But as she worked, she couldn't help thinking about what Mr. Heelis had said the night before, regarding Mathilda Crook and Bertha Stubbs and the unfavorable opinion they had expressed about Mrs. Lythecoe's marriage to the vicar.

Unfavorable? It was more than that, wasn't it? It was downright hostile.

In fact, Beatrix was so distracted that at length she put down her pen and gave the problem her full attention. Was it possible that one or both of the women were upset enough to write those ugly letters? She knew the pair of them, and found this hard to believe. But she had been surprised before

221

by the depth of people's cunning (like the fox) and churlishness (like the badger) and understood that, under certain circumstances, almost anyone can be driven to almost anything.

She sat back in her chair, thinking. Mr. Heelis had said that his information was secondhand, and it was possible that it was exaggerated, or an outright untruth. She thought she really ought to confirm it, although she felt that neither Mathilda nor Bertha would willingly tell her what they had said to each other in private. How to find out?

Now, Beatrix has learnt from long experience with her mother that when something needs to be done, it is sometimes better to go at the task indirectly. Not that Beatrix herself is devious — no, not in the least. She is a very straightforward person (sometimes blunt, in fact) and much prefers to look at things squarely. It is her mother who is devious, to a degree that Beatrix finds appallingly frustrating. To get things done in the Potter household, she often finds it necessary to adopt her mother's scheming ways.

In this case, Beatrix knew Mathilda Crook fairly well, since she had boarded with the Crooks whilst the farmhouse at Hill Top was being expanded to accommodate both herself and the Jennings family. Mathilda was every bit as stubborn and opinionated as Mrs. Potter, and it occurred to Beatrix that she might be able to learn what was really going on if she practiced the same sort of subtleties upon Mathilda that she had to practice at home.

So she got up from her work and went to the dresser drawer where she kept her kitchen linens. Mathilda took in sewing, and since Beatrix's favorite red-and-white-checked tablecloth needed darning, that would be her excuse. She wrapped the tablecloth in a brown-paper parcel, gathered up the letters that needed to go in the post, and put on her coat and woolen hat. Then she walked up the street toward Belle Green, where the Crooks lived. But on the way, she stopped at Rose Cottage for a quick word with Mrs. Lythecoe. She wouldn't stay long, but she felt she needed to be sure of the facts of the case.

Caruso, Mrs. Lythecoe's canary, was singing loudly when she knocked at the door. His cage hung in the front window of the cottage, and he always sang when people walked past or dropped in. This morning, he was singing so exuberantly that Grace had to throw a cover on his cage so that she and Beatrix could sit in the front parlor and talk. (Of course, Caruso didn't stop singing. He merely reduced the volume, contenting himself with a quiet little warble.)

"Good morning, Miss Potter," said Tabitha Twitchit, coming into the room and rubbing against Miss Potter's ankles. She was feeling quite cheerful this morning, having just seen a new generation of village cats into this world. Her niece, Treacle, who lived across the lane at High Green Gate, had given birth to six kittens. Treacle had named the eldest — the finest of the lot — Tabitha. Fitting, Tabitha thought.

"Good morning, Tabitha," Beatrix said. She took off her coat, said "No, thank you," to the offer of a cup of tea, and went right to her question, happy that she could be her own straightforward self with Grace Lythecoe.

"I have heard that one or two of the villagers have expressed some concern about your marriage to the vicar because you were once married to his cousin," she said. "I hope you are not offended, Grace, but I thought I should ask. Is it true? Was your first husband a cousin of Reverend Sackett? Or is this just another of those village rumors?"

Beatrix knew all about rumors, for the village had once had her practically married to Captain Woodcock and installed as his wife at Tower Bank Arms, whilst everyone had been absolutely sure that Mr. Heelis was going to ask Dimity Woodcock to be his bride — and when Dimity had surprised everyone by agreeing to become Mrs. Kittredge, he was supposed to have asked Sarah Barwick. And when it was clear that Mr. Heelis was not courting Miss Barwick, the villagers had decided that the honor of marrying Mr. Heelis (who was quite a catch) would go to Margaret Nash. She, however, had astonished the village by becoming Mrs. Woodcock.

The village almost never got it right, you see, but that didn't stop them from enjoying the game. It was a miracle that no one had yet connected her to Mr. Heelis, for which she was terribly grateful. Her parents lived in London, but they often took holiday houses in the neighborhood and had local connections. If they thought she might be interested in someone, they would move heaven and earth to put an end to the relationship.

"Of course it's true, Beatrix." Grace did not appear to take offense. "I met Samuel — Reverend Sackett — at a family gathering the year before my husband died. That

225

was a very long time ago. Nearly ten years, as a matter of fact."

Tabitha sniffed. *"Ten years is a long time. Why are you asking about this, Miss Potter? Does it have to do with the letters?"* Tabitha knew about those letters because she lived with Mrs. Lythecoe and had seen how dreadfully upset she was when they arrived. She had also been present when Mrs. Lythecoe asked Miss Potter to find out who had written them.

"Your husband and his cousin — were they acquainted?" Beatrix asked.

Grace frowned. "Not intimately. At the time, Reverend Sackett was serving in the south of England. My husband and I were here, in the vicarage, of course," she added, smiling reminiscently. "Mrs. Belcher kept house for us."

Tabitha brightened. *"Ah, Mrs. Belcher. She lived here in the village for a time, in one of the Lakeside cottages. A generous, good-hearted person, always ready to put down a saucer of something nice."*

"A splendid job she made of it, too," Grace continued. "Mrs. Belcher, that is. I understand that she's available again. I'd love to have her back."

Beatrix paused, remembering what Mrs. Beever had told her the day before. "The vicar already has a housekeeper, doesn't he?" she ventured, although, of course, she knew the answer. She had met the lady in question a time or two.

Grace shifted uncomfortably. "Well, yes. Mrs. Thompson. Hazel Thompson. Samuel has had her for years. But he's . . . well, he's not happy with her, I'm sorry to say. She is not a very good cook and her housekeeping isn't the best. Worse, she listens at doors. He has been aware of this for some time. But you know our dear vicar." She smiled a little. "He doesn't like confrontations, so I'm afraid it will be left to me to deal with her."

"I see," Beatrix said. "So you'll be hiring Mrs. Belcher."

"A very good plan," Tabitha said with an approving mew. *"A splendid plan."* She had not yet decided whether she would leave the village and move to the vicarage with Mrs. Lythecoe. But perhaps, if Mrs. Belcher was coming to cook, it would be a good idea.

Grace nodded. "I've already spoken to her about the possibility. But not, of course, to Mrs. Thompson. The vicar will give her notice when the time comes — but not just yet. And certainly not until this business about the letters is settled and we can go forward with our plans." She leaned forward. "Tell me who's talking about this cousin thing, Beatrix."

"I could tell you, if you asked me," Tabitha said slyly, examining one of her claws.

I am not in the least surprised by this, for both Mathilda Crook and Bertha Stubbs are quite well known to all the village cats. In fact, the cats have probably been in the room when Mathilda and Bertha were discussing the matter. And now that the matter has come up, I find myself wondering whether Tabitha knows anything about those letters, as well. Is it possible that she could tell us who's writing them?

But Beatrix had to answer Grace's question. "I'd rather not say, if you don't mind," she replied. "The information came to me indirectly. I need to look into it." She got up. "I must be going, Grace. I'll let you know if I learn anything."

As she left, she heard Caruso singing again, now very loudly. She smiled a little to herself, thinking that Grace must have taken off his cover so he could see out the window again. She remembered that one of the letters had come through the mail slot in the door. It wouldn't be at all surprising if the canary had seen who put it there. It was too bad he couldn't tell them

228

what he knew.

Beatrix wanted to be sure that her letter to Millie went out with the morning post, so instead of going straight up to the Crooks' house, she made a detour to the post office, in Low Green Gate Cottage, on the eastern side of the village. She had once borrowed the green-painted cottage door with its fanlight for a scene in *The Tale of the Pie and the Patty-Pan,* thrilling Lucy Skead, the village postmistress, who bragged to everyone that Miss Potter had made hers the most famous door in the village.

The short, plump, round-faced postmistress was standing behind the tall counter on the wooden box that her husband, Joseph, had made for her. It was widely known that Lucy, an incorrigible and unrepentant snoop, could be counted on to read the addresses of all the letters and cards and packages that came and went through the post, and thus to know the names of everyone's friends and relations and how often they kept in touch — or didn't, as the case might be. A few of the villagers objected to her surveillance, but it did them no good, for Lucy could no more refrain from noticing and remembering names and relationships than her customers could keep themselves from their breakfast, dinner, and tea tables.

They were lucky that she went no further than the outside of the envelope.

"Good morning, Miss Potter," Lucy said briskly. "Tha hast two letters." (Lucy always knew, without looking, exactly how many pieces of post were waiting.) She got down from her box and went to the tier of wooden post boxes built against the wall. She found the one marked HILL TOP and took out two pieces of mail. "One comes from thi publisher, t' other from thi brother." She handed them over. "Mr. Bertram Potter's in London, I see, stayin' wi' thi mum and dad. He'll be goin' back to Scotland soon, will 'ee?"

"Thank you." Beatrix took the letters without answering the question. She was a private person, and was not at all happy with the idea that Lucy Skead (whose tongue wagged at both ends and was loose in the middle) knew so much of her business. She was very glad to see the letter from Warne, which was supposed to contain the cheque for the royalties she had earned in the last half-year — at least, she hoped it did. It seemed that there were perennial accounting problems at the publishing house, and it was not always easy to get the money that was due to her. She was not anxious to read the letter from Bertram, however. She was afraid he might be writing to ask her to return home, for some urgent reason or another — and she had just got here!

She put the letters into the pocket of her coat, handed over her post, and was turning to go when Lucy spoke, with the air of someone making a very important announcement, "I suppose tha'st already heard about poor Mr. Baum."

"Mr. Baum?" Beatrix turned back. "Why, no. That is, I know that he wasn't at the meeting last night, but —"

"He wasn't there b'cuz he was layin' up on t' rocks under Oat Cake Crag wi' a cracked head," Lucy said, speaking with a regrettable relish. It is often said that nobody likes to be the bearer of bad news, but this was not true of Lucy. The more terrible the tale, the greater her pleasure in telling it. "He's got a broke leg an' a broke arm, too. Still hasn't woke up, neither." Lucy shook her head mournfully. "Dr. Butters says there's no tellin' whether he'll ever wake up, poor man."

"Oh, dear," Beatrix exclaimed, genuinely distressed. "What happened, do you know?"

Of course Lucy knew. She always did, although what she knew was not always the exact truth. "He tumbled down t' face of Oat Cake Crag," she said. "Jus' like t' poor

Scottish soldier, all those years ago." She leaned forward. "People are sayin' that it's a punishment for that aeroplane. If t' good Lord had've wanted folks to fly, he'd've give us wings." She lowered her voice confidentially, although there was no one else in the post office. "T' question I want to know is wot he was doin' up there on t' crag in t' first place. An' whether somebody helped him down. A strong, healthy man in his reet mind doan't just take it into his head to step off a rock when 'tis forty feet to t' bottom." She narrowed her eyes. "If tha take'st my meanin', Miss Potter."

Beatrix did. What's more, she supposed that everyone who came into the post office this morning would take Lucy's meaning, too, which meant that by the time the village sat down to tea, everyone would be speculating about whether someone pushed Fred Baum off the top of Oat Cake Crag, or whether he was not in his "reet mind" and went up there in order to jump. It was all very mysterious.

And there was nothing that the village loved more than a mystery — unless it was a romance.

12

MISS POTTER INVESTIGATES: AT BELLE GREEN

Beatrix didn't linger to discuss these shocking possibilities with Lucy Skead. She did take a moment to open the letter from Warne, and was happy to find the overdue cheque enclosed. She didn't open the other, though. She was anxious to get on with what she had decided to do. So she walked on up the hill to Belle Green, where Mathilda Crook, wearing a white apron over her gray dress and a smudge of flour on her cheek, opened the door and invited her into the kitchen.

"I'm jus' doin' a little bread-bakin', Miss Potter, so if tha dustn't mind, tha cans't sit at t' table wi' a cup of tea whilst I finish kneadin'." She poured the tea, then attacked the mound of white dough, turning it deftly and pummeling it once again. "It's me mum's soda bread recipe, which she always baked plain. But I like to put in a few dried herbs from the garden. Needs no risin', which makes it quick."

"I've always enjoyed your bread, Mrs. Crook," Beatrix said with a smile, adding, "I've told my mother how very good it is."

Now, it was true that Mrs. Crook's soda bread with herbs was very good, although Beatrix had not thought to mention it to her mother, who would not in any case have been impressed. Mrs. Potter had never baked a loaf of bread in her life — or cooked a meal, for that matter. Cooking and baking were best left to the cook one hired for that purpose. I hope you'll forgive Beatrix's little fib, for it didn't hurt anyone and certainly pleased Mathilda Crook to no end, which was exactly Beatrix's intent, of course.

"Hast thi, then?" Mathilda beamed. "Well, now, that's nice, Miss Potter. And how are they? Thi mum and dad, that is." She turned and pummeled and pummeled and turned (but gently, for soda bread does not require a great deal of kneading), then shaped the dough into a large round loaf.

"As well as can be expected, for their ages, thank you," Beatrix replied. "I'll let them know you've inquired."

Mathilda was by now mightily pleased. Mr. and Mrs. Potter had rented a summer house not far from the village some years ago, and had brought their servants, their horses, their coach, and their coachman. Their well-staffed holidays were still spoken of with something like awe in the village. She felt deeply complimented at the thought that she would be mentioned to them.

"Well, if it isn't Miss Potter!" exclaimed Rascal, dancing through the door. He had slept in that morning in his bed in the pantry, worn out with the excitement of Mr. Baum's accident the night before. *"So good to see you!"*

"Good morning, Rascal." Beatrix leaned over to pet the little dog. "Oh, by the way, Mrs. Crook, I wonder if you might be willing to do some mending for me." She put her parcel on the table and opened it. "My favorite tablecloth needs darning, and I've always admired your almost invisible work. What do you think?"

"Let me jus' finish this, and I'll have a look," Mathilda said. She placed the round loaf on a greased and floured baking tray, patted it back into shape, cut a deep cross on the top, then put it into the oven. She wiped her hands and sat down at the table. "Now, let's see." She bent over the tablecloth. "Oh, my goodness, yes. An easy job." She reconsidered quickly. "Well, easy enough, p'rhaps, but cert'nly it'll take some time."

"I'll bc glad to pay you whatever you think is right," Beatrix said. She sat back in the chair. "Now, catch me up on the village news, Mrs. Crook. I've been away too long."

"Have you heard about Mr. Baum?" Rascal asked excitedly. *"He fell off Oat Cake Crag last night!"*

Mathilda frowned down at the dog. "If tha'st goin' to bark, Rascal, tha can'st go out t' door," she said sternly. "We doan't need thi noise in t' house."

With a sigh, Rascal went under Miss Potter's chair. Mathilda poured herself a cup of tea and sat down at the table. She was very glad to oblige with news, although since she had not yet been to the post office, she had not heard about Mr. Baum. Rascal knew it was pointless to try to make himself understood. And Beatrix didn't bring up the subject, either, but contented herself with sipping her tea and listening to Mathilda carry on about a dozen trivial things, from the sore throats that were plaguing the village schoolchildren to the performance of Jeremy Crosfield as the new junior teacher and the new Mrs. Woodcock's difficulties (now smoothed over) with the longtime Tower Bank housekeeper, Elsa Grape.

At last, Mathilda ran out of steam. "That's

about all I know," she concluded, picking up the teapot. "More tea, Miss Potter?"

"I believe I shall," said Beatrix. She did not really want more tea, but they had not yet got to the question she had come to ask. Whilst Mathilda poured, she added, "But you've said nothing at all about Mrs. Lythecoe's marriage to the vicar, Mrs. Crook. Everyone in the village must be delighted to know that Mrs. Lythecoe will be back in the vicarage again." She paused. "She lived there earlier, I've been told. When her first husband was the vicar at St. Peter's."

Of course, this was all said very sweetly and innocently as Beatrix stirred sugar into her tea and declined milk and lemon. Mathilda, however, was frowning.

"Oh, aye," she said darkly. "She lived at the vicarage years ago. When she was married to t' vicar's cousin, on his mother's side. Reverend Lythecoe."

"I didn't know that," Beatrix said with interest. "Cousins? How very nice for Mrs. Lythecoe — to already be acquainted with Reverend Sackett's family, that is."

"Nice!" Mathilda exclaimed hotly. "I doan't call it 'nice' mese'f. I call it disgraceful. Against t' law, too. T' pair of 'em ought to know better, old as they are."

"Against the law?" Beatrix opened her

eyes wide. "Why, whocvcr told you that, Mrs. Crook! Marriage between first cousins is discouraged, but there is nothing said against a woman marrying her deceased husband's cousin. Or a man marrying his deceased cousin's widow."

Mathilda gave her an uncertain look. "But Bertha said . . ."

Beatrix laughed lightly. "Oh, this is Mrs. Stubbs' notion, is it?" She rolled her eyes. "Well, you know Bertha Stubbs. She doesn't always get things right."

Beatrix was being kind, for it was widely known across the village that Bertha Stubbs got almost everything wrong. What was worse, once she got something into her head, it was almost impossible to get it out, however mistaken it might be.

"I s'pose," Mathilda acknowledged doubtfully. "But dustn't thi think it's a little . . . well, close? Bein' married to two cousins, I mean, one after t' other."

"I don't think it's close at all," Beatrix said firmly. "I think it is splendid that Reverend Sackett is about to find true happiness." She gave Mathilda a direct look, by now certain of her ground. "I very much hope you will not help Bertha Stubbs spread this dreadful misinformation amongst the villagers. You won't, will you, Mrs. Crook?"

Feeling cornered, Mathilda dropped her eyes. "Well, now —"

"Oh, good," Beatrix said with evident relief. "I knew I could count on you. You are always so fair-minded and concerned for the welfare of others." This assertion was patently untrue, for Mathilda Crook was not at all fair-minded and rarely exhibited any special concern for others. But Beatrix saw no harm in appealing to her better nature. She paused, looking straight at Mathilda. "I don't suppose you know anything about the letters, do you?"

"Letters?" Mathilda asked. By now she was thoroughly irritated that Bertha had led her down the wrong path with that silly business about cousins. She would set Bertha straight the next time she saw her. "Wot letters?"

Beneath Miss Potter's chair, Rascal stirred. *"Letters,"* he said thoughtfully. *"You wouldn't be talking about —"*

"Hush, Rascal," Mathilda commanded. "Wot letters, Miss Potter?"

"The letters Mrs. Lythecoe has been receiving," Rascal muttered. Well, naturally. If the cats know about the letters, all the other village animals are likely to know, too. Tabitha was right when she said that Crumpet could never keep a secret, and she isn't much bet-

ter. And then, of course, there's Caruso, who sings so loudly that he can be heard up and down the street. Who knows what secrets he's spilling into the air?

"Oh, nothing," Beatrix said, glad to drop the subject. She knew Mathilda well enough to tell from her expression that she was completely in the dark. She sniffed the air. "That's not your bread burning, is it?"

"S'cuse me whilst I check," Mathilda said. Going to the oven gave her a chance to slightly recover herself, and she returned to the table and her guest, this time with a new — and entirely unexpected — topic of conversation. "We've been talkin' about Mrs. Lythecoe and t' vicar gettin' married, but I understand that we'll soon be able to congratulate thi an' Mr. Heelis, Miss Potter."

Beatrix's stomach knotted. "Congratulate . . . me?"

"Aye." Mathilda smiled coyly, feeling that she had the upper hand over her guest, which was much more pleasant than being on the defensive. "It's still s'posed to be a secret, is it?" The smile broadened into a chuckle. "Well, thi knowst our village, Miss Potter. 'Tis impossible to keep a secret, especially when it's got to do with a weddin'!"

Now it was Beatrix's turn to deny. "I have no idea what you're talking about." She spoke with great outward firmness, although within, she felt a great confusion. "There is to be no wedding." This much, at least, was true, for while she was secretly engaged, there had never been any talk of a wedding — not one word. However much she and Mr. Heelis might desire it, both of them knew that marriage simply was not possible, in the circumstance.

"No wedding just yet, perhaps," Rascal amended, putting his muzzle on the guest's foot. *"But we're on your side, dear Miss Potter."* Rascal and his friends the cats knew all about Miss Potter and Mr. Heelis, of course, and were entirely in support of the engagement. *"We hope it can happen, soon."*

"No weddin'?" Mathilda asked, disappointed. Miss Potter, who was known to be honest and straightforward, had spoken with an exceedingly firm tone. "You're sure 'bout that?"

"No wedding," Beatrix repeated. "Of course I'm sure. I should know, shouldn't I?" She frowned sternly. "And I'll thank you to say as much to anyone else who repeats such a wicked tale."

"Aye. I'll be sure to say jus' that." Mathilda raised an arch eyebrow. " 'Miss Potter

241

says there's to be no weddin','" she said, and smiled with the air of one who has triumphed over an unwary opponent. " 'And she's asked me to say as much.' Them'll be my words, Miss Potter. My very words. You can count on me to set 'em straight."

The knot in Beatrix's stomach tightened. The fat was in the fire now. Mathilda would say that there would be no wedding, with a wink and a nod that implied exactly the opposite, and before long, everyone would be talking about it — if they weren't already, that is.

Her heart sank. She would have to tell Will that their secret was out of the bag. And then what? If people were already talking about it behind their backs, it wouldn't be long before they were asked point-blank about it. Should they deny it? How long could they deny it? And what would happen if the rumor spread beyond the village? What would happen if her parents heard it?

Beatrix was swept by a sudden panic. She could not stay another minute. "I must be going," she said. She stood, adding, "Please let me know when you've finished the tablecloth, Mrs. Crook."

"Oh, aye," Mathilda said, beaming. Her equanimity was entirely restored, now that she had the upper hand. She was thinking that as soon as her guest was out of sight, she would rush right next door to tell Agnes Llewellyn what Miss Potter had just said.

Rascal, who knew Big People as well as they knew themselves (which sometimes isn't saying much), understood exactly what Mrs. Crook had in mind and sensed Miss Potter's dismay. *"I'll walk down the hill with you, Miss Potter,"* he said, feeling that she needed a friend.

Which is why Rascal was with Beatrix a few minutes later, when she took her brother's letter out of her pocket and opened it. She had read only a few words when he heard her sudden exclamation of shock and alarm. "Oh, no! Oh, *no!*" She stopped stock still in the middle of the lane to read the rest of the letter.

"What is it, Miss Potter?" he cried, looking up at her. *"Is someone sick? Has someone died?"*

No. No one was sick, and no one had died. But Bertram's news really couldn't be worse. The very same scrap of village rumor that Mathilda Crook had just repeated so triumphantly to Miss Potter had already reached the ears of her parents.

My very dear Beatrix,

You will not be happy to learn what I am about to tell you, but I'm afraid there's no way around it, so I shall simply jump right into the very unpleasant middle.

Our parents have heard from a certain Mr. Morrow in Hawkshead (a solicitor, I understand) that you and Mr. Heelis are secretly engaged. I am sure that you can guess their reactions. Mama has been put to bed by the doctor after a fit of screaming hysterics, and Papa is stamping around the drawing room like an enraged hippopotamus. Really, the idea of your being married is quite preposterous, and they should know that you have no such silly scheme in mind. I must tell you that this business is making my visit exceedingly unpleasant, and if I could, I would leave this instant for Scotland. But someone must hold the fort until your return, and I suppose it must be me, for which I am sorry, but there it is.

I am not writing to ask you to come straight home. I regret to say this (for my usual unabashedly selfish reasons), but I believe it would be wise for you to remain at Hill Top until Papa and Mama are calmer. This may take several days. I do, however, hope that you will write to them as soon as you receive this letter. Tell them in no uncertain terms that you do not intend to be married (what an absurd idea!), and that they really must not allow themselves to be troubled with idle rumors spread by uninformed and possibly malicious persons. They will no doubt feel better when they hear from you, and that will make the situation here a bit more bearable for

Yr much-beleaguered brother,

Bertram

Beatrix was horrified. She couldn't help being annoyed at Bertram's tone of immature self-pity ("Someone must hold the fort," "yr much-beleaguered brother," and the like), but her exasperation was swept aside by the appalling news that her parents had learnt her secret — long before she was ready to tell them herself. Under other circumstances, she might have smiled at the image of her father stamping around like an "enraged hippopotamus" (very apt), or shaken her head at her mother's "screaming hysterics," but neither of these were at all amusing, in the circumstance.

She folded her brother's letter and put it back in her pocket, biting her lip in consternation. What should she do? Write and tell them that it was just village gossip and didn't bear repeating? They would likely believe her, for even her brother thought that she was too old, too unattractive, and too confirmed a spinster to win a husband ("The idea of your being married is quite preposterous"). She narrowed her eyes. It would serve Bertram right if she wrote to the family and told them that it was all quite true. Whoever this Mr. Morris was, his facts were accurate. She was engaged to Mr. Heelis and they would be married — someday, when it was convenient — and everyone would just have to get used to the idea.

She sighed heavily. But what would be the point of such a letter? It could only cause another family row, even worse than the one over her engagement to Norman. She could not imagine a time when her parents would agree that it was "convenient" for her to marry anybody, let alone a country lawyer who had no standing in the London society in which they moved.

But she also could not imagine writing them a letter in which she denied her engagement. She hated lying and dissembling and pretending that everything was one way, when it was another way altogether. But that's what her life in London had become, hadn't it? Nothing but pretense and make-believe. Sometimes it seemed that she could be her own true self only in this little village. If only she could stay here forever, hidden away from the rest of the ugly world!

But she couldn't. This was only a respite, a temporary retreat — and now that the villagers had got wind of her engagement, it wasn't even that. She sighed again and thrust her hands into her pockets. "Come on, Rascal," she said, and picked up the pace.

"I'm coming," the little dog said, hurrying to keep up with her. *"But where are we going?"* For Miss Potter had now turned aside from the way back to Hill Top. They were headed in quite a different direction, along a path that struck off cross-country, in the direction of Claife Heights.

For a moment, Beatrix did not answer. And then she said, partly to herself and partly to her companion, "I am in the mood to take a long walk this morning."

Beatrix loved to tramp through the fields and woodlands of the Land Between the Lakes, and walking had always helped her to solve her problems. But this time, her dilemma seemed too immense, too irresolvable. She doubted she could ever find an answer.

13
MR. HEELIS AND CAPTAIN WOODCOCK INVESTIGATE

Will Heelis arrived at Tower Bank House not long after breakfast. He found the captain, in his official capacity as justice of the peace for Claife Parish, conferring with Constable Braithwaite in the library. The constable wore his usual blue serge uniform with the polished brass buttons, and both men wore very serious expressions.

"It's Baum," the captain said to Will. "He fell off Oat Cake Crag. He's at Raven Hall just now, in a very bad way. Dr. Butters saw him last night, and woke me on his way back to Hawkshead to tell me about it." With that, he related the story, as the doctor had told it to him and as he had just told it to the constable.

"So that's why he wasn't at the meeting last night," Will said. "Any idea how he happened to fall off that crag? Or what the devil he was doing up there in the first place?" In his frequent rambles around the countryside, Will himself had climbed the lookout often. But he was fit and lean. Fred Baum was an extremely stout fellow who preferred to ride rather than walk, and the cigars he smoked gave him an incessant wheeze. In Will's opinion, he wasn't in any kind of trim to go climbing up the rocks.

The constable, baffled, echoed his thought. "Surprises me that Mr. Baum would want to climb t' crag," he said. "He wud've been huffin' an' puffin'. Must've had a ver' good reason to go up there."

The captain agreed. "Braithwaite and I are going to Lakeshore Manor to talk to the servants, Will. On the way, we'll stop at Raven Hall to see if Baum is awake and able to tell us anything. We're taking my motor car. It's an official visit, but perhaps you would care to come along."

"I would indeed," Will replied, and they set off.

Captain Woodcock's teal-blue Rolls-Royce had caused quite a sensation in the village when he first began driving it some four years before. Some of the villagers had been thrilled, but others had grumbled that the captain's motor was only the first of many to come. Their narrow lanes would soon be jammed with those fast, noisy, *dangerous* vehicles, frightening the horses, raising the dust, and rattling the windows. There wouldn't be a scrap of peace or a patch of safety left in the world.

They were right about the traffic. It wasn't long before motor cars had begun coming across on the ferry, and down from Ambleside and up from Newby Bridge, lumbering through Near and Far Sawrey at the incredible speed of ten miles an hour, trailing a cloud of thick dust and an appalling clatter that sent dogs and cats and chickens and children flying in panic. In fact, it wasn't at all unusual to see as many as five or six motor cars in a single day, and one or two more idled beside the road with a punctured tyre or a broken water hose.

Now, Will sat in the front seat beside the captain whilst the constable sat in the back, holding his tall blue hat in his lap lest the wind blow it off. They rattled along the road to Far Sawrey, then turned up the lane that zigged and zagged through the trees to the top of Claife Heights, to that medieval-looking fortress, Raven Hall.

Major Kittredge, hearing the sound of the motor car, came out on the broad stone steps to greet them. "I'm afraid it's no good trying to question Baum," he told the captain when he had heard the reason for their official visit. "He's still unconscious.

The doctor says he has no idea when — or if — he'll come out of it. Oh, and it's no good wanting to question the servants at Lakeshore Manor, either. Baum let them all go, I'm told. He's been putting every cent into that aeroplane venture of his."

The captain frowned. "No servants, eh? That's interesting." He paused. "I understand from Butters that you discovered the accident last night. What can you tell us about it?"

"Not much," Kittredge replied. "It was late, and I wouldn't have gone out if Dimity hadn't urged me. It was George Crook's dog, you see." When that part of the story had been told, he added, "I suppose you would like to see the spot where we found Baum?"

"We would," the captain said. So Will climbed into the backseat with the constable, and Major Kittredge rode up front with the captain, and they all drove round the road (no taking the woodland path this time) to Lakeshore Manor, which sat, alone and silent and deserted, on the slope above the lake.

The captain parked the motor car and they all got out. "We found him back here," said the major, and led them to the spot beneath the crag, where they could clearly sec broken brush and scuffed soil at the spot where Mr. Baum had been discovered.

Kittredge pointed up. "You can also see where a few of the smaller trees and bushes snapped off as he fell. As to what the fellow was doing up top, I can't even hazard a guess."

"I believe I'll go up," Will said. "Coming?"

The captain frowned at him. "You're not going to climb up the face of that cliff, are you, Heelis?"

Will chuckled. "Of course not. There's a path. It's steep — I wonder that Baum, heavy as he was, would undertake the climb. But I've done it often. There's quite a view from the top."

Constable Braithwaite sucked in his own rather substantial belly. "I'll go wi' thi, sir," he said bravely. "We might find a clue as to wot happened up there. How t' pore gentleman come to fall down, I mean."

"Well, then," Captain Woodcock said with a sigh, "I suppose I should go as well."

"Count me in," said the major cheerfully. "I climbed it often, when I was a boy."

So fifteen minutes later, winded and breathless in different degrees, all four men stood on the top of Oat Cake Crag. It was a wide, flat, bare rock, some twelve by fifteen feet, surrounded by bushes and trees. If they had been looking for signs of an accident or any evidence that might explain Baum's fall, they would have been disappointed, for nothing of the sort was readily apparent. But there was plenty else to see. The lake spread out in front of them like a wide blue ribbon. Below were the roofs and chimneys of Lakeshore Manor, and its wide, grassy park sloping down to the water. Off to the right steamed the ferry, just leaving from Ferry Nab on the eastern side and sailing in their direction, as lopsided as always, since the steam boiler was on the starboard side, giving it a heavy list. The blue water was dotted with sailboats, for the day was mild and the wind favorable.

"You're right, it's quite a spectacular view," said the captain admiringly, looking around. "I'm sorry to say it, but in all the years I've lived in the district, this is the first time I've been up here."

"My brother and I used to climb up here often when we were youngsters," Major Kittredge said reminiscently. "We would bring our spyglass and watch the lake birds or spy on the ferry. It's amazing what you can see from here with the right kind of aid." He stepped to the lip and looked down, then stepped quickly back. "Poor Baum," he said, shaking his head. "It's a wonder he wasn't killed outright."

"Speaking of spyglasses," Will said suddenly, "look here." He had been scouting around the lip of the crag. Now, he pointed to a brass telescope. They hadn't seen it at first because it lay half-hidden under a bush that was growing at the very edge, as if it had rolled there. In fact, if it hadn't been prevented by the bush, it might have gone right on over.

"Why, that's an R and J Beck instrument, I do believe," said Major Kittredge in some surprise. He bent down to have a closer look. "The best telescope to be had, bar none. Do you suppose it's Baum's? I didn't know the fellow had an interest in birds."

"I wonder," said Will. He picked up the telescope, put it to his eye, and began to look around, first in one direction, then the other, finally settling on a spot directly opposite the crag. He studied it for a moment, then straightened. "Have a look, Woodcock," he said, handing over the scope.

The captain had a look. "Why, it's the aeroplane hangar," he said in surprise. "You can see it plain as day. And it looks like they're getting ready to take the aeroplane out on the water." He turned to the major. "Did that pilot — Oscar Wyatt — put in an appearance at Raven Hall this morning? The doctor told me he left a note at the Sawrey Hotel, informing Wyatt of Baum's situation."

"He did," the major replied. "He rather insisted on seeing poor Baum, but my wife wouldn't allow it." He grinned at the captain, for (as you no doubt remember) the major has married the captain's sister. "As I'm sure you know, Woodcock, Dimity has a will of iron, when she wants — or doesn't want — something. And in this case, she was bent on following the doctor's orders. No visitors. No exceptions. Wyatt was not amused." His grin turned rueful. "The fellow is very forceful, I must say. Dim stood firm, but I found it necessary to step in myself and make it clear that she and the doctor were to be obeyed."

Will turned the telescope in his hands, studying the gold casing. "Look here," he said, pointing. "Engraved initials. FB. Baum's scope, without a doubt." He put the scope back to his eye. "The aeroplane is getting ready to take off. See how it's dodging the boats in Bowness Harbor. What a disaster that machine is going to be. Shouldn't be allowed on the lake."

"I'll have to agree with you on that score," Major Kittredge said. "But I understand that Churchill has an interest in it, so I suppose there's no use in our opposing it."

"Churchill!" exclaimed Captain Woodcock. "The Admiralty? You don't say!"

"That's according to Dr. Butters," Kittredge replied. "He overheard Baum and
Wyatt talking about it. Seems that Churchill
is coming to have a look at the hydroplane,
with the idea that it may come in handy for
the navy. Has it in mind to set up a Royal
Flying Corps and thinks Baum's aeroplane
might be just the thing. Baum was not
enthusiastic. Didn't feel that the machine
was ready for that kind of attention. Wyatt
felt quite the contrary, according to Butters.
Gave him another reason to ask for money,
apparently."

"Money?" Will asked, lowering the scope.

"Yes. Baum put up the money for this
venture, but apparently it's running out.
The doctor overheard Wyatt trying to
squeeze more out of him — repairs, work
on the hangar, that sort of thing. All in
public, too. The doctor thought it was quite
a rude display. It's his opinion that Baum
rues his bargain and would be glad to be
out of it if he could."

Will raised the scope again. "Looks like
Wyatt is getting ready to take off. He's carrying a passenger, too. Maybe that's how
he's raising the money he needs for repairs.

Charging for a ride." He chuckled wryly. "Dangerous business, that. The riders aren't strapped in — just told to hang on as best they can. Wonder if Churchill has it in mind to send up a man with a rifle on every aeroplane."

"Don't you think it's a little odd that Wyatt is taking up passengers when the government is considering the military possibilities of the thing?" Major Kittredge asked, frowning. "For all anybody knows, those riders might be German spies, aiming to steal the design of the thing."

"Perhaps Baum objected to the practice," Will said. "It sounds as if he had a few disagreements with his pilot. Maybe he came up here with the scope in order to do a little spying of his own — on Wyatt."

He lifted the scope to his eye again, pointing it, this time, toward the house below. "Hullo, who's that, do you suppose?" He was looking at a man who had just come around the house, walking furtively, as if he did not want to be observed. He was carrying a burlap sack slung over one shoulder. "Braithwaite, do you recognize that fellow?" Will handed the telescope to the constable.

"Aye, that I do," the constable said grimly after a moment. "That's Paddy Pratt, that is. Odd-jobs man for Mr. Buchanan."

"Former odd-jobs man," Will muttered. "Wonder what he's doing down there. Didn't you say all the servants had gone, Kittredge?"

"I did indeed," Kittredge said. "Last night, the house was empty. They'd all cleared off. That's why we carried Baum to Raven Hall. There was no one here to look after him. And a little later, the doctor told me that the servants had been given the sack. Baum was short on funds, apparently."

"Whatever Paddy Pratt's up to," the constable said in a dark tone, " 'tis nae good. T' man is not to be trusted, in my opinion."

"Paddy Pratt." The captain frowned. "Isn't he the thief who made off with Mrs. Lytle's rooster a fortnight ago? Let's go and see what he has in that sack, shall we?"

Climbing back down the path took less time than climbing up, but when they reached the bottom of the cliff below the crag, Paddy Pratt and his sack were nowhere to be seen. However, the constable knew where Paddy lived and volunteered to go and have a little talk with him ("Put t' fear o' God in his bones"), so they all climbed back in the captain's motor car and headed for Raven Hall.

"Well, we accomplished something," the

captain said as he drove. "We know that Baum was up there to have a look around — at that aeroplane of his, probably, on the other side of the lake. He was using the telescope, it seems."

"And fell while he was using it, I suppose," Kittredge added. "He was engrossed with whatever he was looking at, took one step too many, and went right on over the edge." He shook his head. "Easy enough to do."

Easy enough, they all agreed. Easy enough.

14

THE PROFESSOR INVESTIGATES: SPY IN THE SKY

As he flew through the night on his way back to Claife Woods after the rescue of Mr. Baum, Professor Galileo Newton Owl reflected, with some chagrin, that he had not exactly covered himself with glory. He had been, in his own estimation, more or less a bystander, doing little more than folding his wings and watching as others did the work. Of course, this was not entirely his fault, he reminded himself. Hyacinth (who had quite a remarkable sense of smell) had discovered the injured man. Rascal (who could more easily communicate with humans) had gone for help. There had been nothing for him to do — nothing, that is, that he *could* do.

But it now occurred to him that there was something he could be doing right now — *should* be doing, actually, for he was feeling peckish. He ought to go shopping for a late supper. Luckily, the meat market was still open, for as he flew over a small clearing in the woods, he looked down and saw a pair of unsuspecting voles searching for mushrooms in the moonlight. It appeared that they had been at the job for some time, for they had already collected a full sack. The Professor swooped down, invited the larger vole to dinner, offered his apologies to the smaller for not having selected *him* (the owl was not wearing his flying vest and had no pocket in which to carry a passenger), and then flew off, with the reluctant guest in one claw and the sack of mushrooms in the other.

The Professor is something of a gourmand, so when he arrived at his beech tree, he flew directly to the kitchen and pulled his mother's recipe for *Vole à la Chateaubriand* out of the recipe file. This dish required a turnip, a large carrot, two onions, a small marrow, thyme, rosemary, parsley, and pepper and salt, all of which he had in his larder. Oh, and of course the vole, who by now was past caring what sort of vegetables would accompany him to table. (If this sounds cruel, I must remind you that everyone has to eat, and that the vole himself had dined on several fat white grubs, a large earthworm, and a tasty mushroom just before the Professor invited him to dinner.) The Professor put both vole and vegetables into a large pot. While this was cooking, he prepared the sauce: fresh mushrooms and shallots sautéed in butter, with white wine, tarragon, and lemon juice. This was one of his favorite dishes, and while it strikes me as a little bit heavy for a late supper, I am not an owl, and have no business criticizing.

The owl laid his table, with a bouquet of winter grasses as a centerpiece. Then, whilst his supper continued to cook, he flew up to his observatory to take a few star-sightings. The observatory door bears this hand-lettered sign, which is both an announcement and a warning to those of the Professor's guests who are taller than he and might get bumped.

OBSREVERTRY
G.N. OWL, D. PHIL.
OBSREVER AT LARGE
MIND YOUR HEAD!

As you may guess by the sign, the Professor (who is really very intelligent) is much better at astronomy than he is at spelling. I hope you will not hold this against him, since I'm sure you have one or two of your own spelling demons.

The Professor's observatory, which has windows on all sides, is equipped with a telescope mounted on a swivel, allowing the observer to see the sky in all directions. It also contains a stool for perching and shelves for star charts, a globe, reference volumes, and the owl's log books, with several writing implements at hand.

The owl spent some time studying various stars through his telescope and carefully noting their positions in his *Obsrever's Notebook,* where he regularly records the details of his celestial research. Then he flew back down to the dining room to enjoy his vole, which he found much enriched by the vegetables and herbs and, of course, the sauce. With his meal, he took a small glass of red wine, a gift from his cousin, Old Brown, who was introduced to young readers by Miss Potter in *The Tale of Squirrel Nutkin.* The Professor had been a little annoyed by the book, for the author had made the silly, pestiferous squirrel into the principal character of the story, when it ought really to have Old Brown, who had shown a great deal of patient forbearance.

After his meal, the Professor retired with a cup of dandelion coffee to his favorite wing chair, where he put his feet on an ottoman and began to ponder the puzzle of the unfortunate Mr. Baum and his flying boat. It had been very good of Bosworth

Badger, the owl reflected, to review the fundamental operating principles behind the aeroplane, at least so far as they were known. And while he himself was more at home with celestial mechanics than with the mechanical details of a man-made machine, he had finally understood. That is, he had grasped the fact that the thing he had seen in flight was not a living creature but a mechanical object, a combination of a boat and a motor car, but designed to take off and land from water and to fly through the air. And like the motor car, it fed on petroleum (petrol for short), which was wrung out of rocks. It did not consume (as he had at first feared) feathered or furred creatures such as the vole he had brought home to supper. This was a distinct relief, for the owl had imagined that such a large competitor would have an enormous appetite and would very quickly clean out the regional larder.

The badger's explanations may have partly satisfied the Professor's curiosity about this Water Bird, as Bosworth had said the thing was called, but they had raised even further concerns in the owl's mind. No matter what Mr. Baum's machine ate or didn't eat, and no matter that it bore such an innocuous (and misleading!) name, it was an undeniable threat to the people and animals around Windermere. The noise of the beastly thing obviously terrified horses and sheep and cows. It was only a matter of time before a horse became so frightened that it lost its head and plunged over a cliff and killed itself and its rider, or the cows refused to give milk, or the ewes abandoned their lambs.

The Professor shuddered at the thought of dead horses and motherless lambs. But there was worse. Motor-car engines were notorious for stopping unexpectedly in the middle of nowhere and not starting again until they were towed to a mechanic who could bully them back into operation. What would happen if the aeroplane's engine stopped when it was high in the air? Why, the thing would come right down, that's what would happen — and it wouldn't come down in a graceful glide, like other respectable birds, landing lightly on the earth, then giving its wings and its tail a shake to settle its feathers.

No.

It would fall straight down.

Fall like a stone.

And whoever was standing beneath it would be smashed flat. If it happened to fall onto a house or a barn or a church, many persons might be smashed flat. And then there would be a great hue-and-cry and letters to *The Times* and threats of lawsuits, none of which would matter in the slightest, of course, to those who were smashed and dead, although the lawsuits might bring some comfort to the living.

The Professor scowled, reminding himself irritably that this sort of thing was exactly what one had come to expect from these presumptuous humans, who had no respect for their place in the Great Chain of Being. If Mother Nature had intended them to fly like owls and angels, she would certainly have given them wings. But Nature had not chosen to do so, and attempts by humans at flight — like that of the legendary wax-winged Icarus — could only end in ignominy, or worse. Flying was a business that ought to be left to the professionals. To himself, for instance.

But Mr. Baum and his pilot obviously intended no such thing. They had loftier goals, and the more the Professor thought about the impertinence of their uninvited, unwelcome invasion of his skies (*his* skies!), the more incensed he became.

How dare they? How *dare* they! Really, something must be done, and the sooner the better.

266

But Mr. Baum had already plummeted (like Icarus) from the lofty heights of Oat Cake Crag and perhaps would not survive the night. Nothing to be done there. Moreover, the owl was rather full of vole (it had been a truly delicious meal), the hour was late, and the wine had put him into that pleasant state which is known to the colonial Australians as half-cocked. And of course, there was absolutely no point in flying across the lake in the middle of the night to do something about the Water Bird, since the creature was clearly not nocturnal and would be sound asleep in its barn until the next day.

Which is why the Professor put up no resistance at all when a nap crept up stealthily behind him and seized him by the scruff of the neck, throwing him bodily down upon his bed and refusing to let him up until the sun had risen above the eastern shore of Windermere, crossed the lake to Claife Heights, and was peering into his windows.

The owl woke from his slumber refreshed and hungry. As he was preparing breakfast (coffee, toast, and a lightly scrambled pigeon's egg with a bit of kipper), he recalled his intention of the night before.

"Yes, indeed. Something must be done

about that Water Bird," he muttered to himself as he tucked his napkin under his chin and sat down to his egg. *"But in order to know what, I shall first have to learn more about the creature's flying habits. I must spy out its strengths and vulnerabilities. I must know something of the man who flies it — who he is and what his purposes are. I shall reconnoiter."* He munched on his toast, giving the matter more consideration. *"But perhaps I should take a sandwich. I might not be back until tea."*

So when breakfast was over and the washing-up done, the owl made a sandwich of thickly sliced ham and onions between slices of buttered bread spread with his favorite Dijon mustard, and wrapped it in brown paper. Then he donned the khaki flying vest that he wore on longer aerial missions and stuck a pad and pencil stub in one pocket, a folded map in another, and the sandwich in a third. He wound a green wool muffler around his neck and put on his daytime flying goggles, the ones with the dark lenses. (As you know, owls' eyes are adapted to night flight, and sunlight is uncomfortable.)

His preparations concluded, the Professor flew up to the top of his beech tree and took off in the direction of the lake. As he flew, he noted with some pride the power of his wings, the way he could change direction with the slightest flick of his tail, and how aerodynamically suited his feathers were to the flow of the air. If his engine failed (he could scarcely comprehend such a thing), he would not fall but would merely swoop down to the nearest treetop. All perfectly natural. All entirely perfect, just as Nature intended. And if you are thinking that perhaps our owl is just a little too smugly self-satisfied, I hope you will reconsider. In his owlness, he embodies everything to which the flying machine's designer and builder might aspire. In my opinion, he has a right to feel smug.

Now, as it happened, the Professor's flight path took him directly over Oat Cake Crag at the very same moment that Mr. Heelis picked up Mr. Baum's spyglass and began looking across the lake. Curious, the owl tilted his wings and circled overhead, wondering what the four men were doing and why they had climbed the crag. It seemed clear that their activity had nothing to do with his mission, however. So the owl left them to their own devices, took a visual sighting, and flew across Belle Isle (the long island in the middle of the lake) to Cockshott Point, where the flying machine lived when it was not in the air.

The lake itself was no more than about three miles wide, so the owl's flight was not a long one. It was, however, quite bouncy, for the breeze was blowing briskly from the north. The Professor was glad he was wearing his vest and woolen muffler, although he wished he had thought to bring some candied ginger. Ginger is a good remedy for airsickness, and after being buffeted and bounced about, the owl was feeling distinctly queasy. If he hadn't been on such an important assignment, he would have turned around and flown home, for it was no sort of weather to be flying for fun. He was relieved when he arrived at his destination.

Cockshott is a grassy point, a favorite of trippers, ramblers, and people who just want to stand and admire the lake, which is certainly one of the loveliest in all England. The pretty finger of land juts out into the water very close to the picturesque, shoreside town of Bowness-on-Windermere. (The novelist Arthur Ransome called this town Rio, in his stories of *Amazons and Swallows,* which you may have read as a child.) When you visit, you will see that the busy little harbor is home to dozens of sailboats and fishing boats as well as the ferry that crosses over to the western side of the lake. It is really quite crowded most of the time, with boats going to and fro and hither and yon, just as it was at the time of our story.

And at the time of our story, Cockshott was also home to the Water Bird. When the flying boat was not in the air or on the water, it took shelter in a large, rickety-looking wooden hangar, with wide doors that opened at both the front and the rear. The hangar was built right at the lake's edge, with a steep wooden slipway that slanted down over the rocks and into the water below. As the owl arrived and took up his observation post on a nearby pine tree, he saw that the machine was just emerging from its hangar and sliding gingerly down the slipway, winched down by ropes and accompanied by several men. This appearance had already attracted an excited crowd of spectators, pushing and jostling along the shore, pointing and shouting as the Water Bird slid clumsily down the ramp. The owl took out his notebook and pencil and began jotting down as much as he could make out of the machine's appearance, construction, and operation, as a good spy should do.

Now, I should like to give you some technical details about this aeroplane that our owl is likely to miss. If you have no interest in the history or mechanical operations of this machine, you might wish to skip the following four paragraphs and go on to the one that begins "But in a few moments . . ." If you do, please be assured that you won't miss any important bits of story, although the description of the machine might help you to understand what is about to happen when Water Bird takes to the air.

Very well, then. If you have ever seen a biplane — that is, a plane with two canvas-covered wings, one stacked on top of the other like two pieces of cardboard held apart by toothpicks — you can easily picture how the Water Bird looked. Or you might want to look for a photograph in a book about early aeroplanes, under its name. I did, and discovered this interesting information: "The Lakes Water Bird is remembered as the first consistently successful British seaplane, developed by the Windermere based Lakes Flying Co, during 1911."

Oh. You thought this aeroplane was something I had made up for the purposes of our story? Oh my dears, oh no, oh not at all! Water Bird was very real, and the way people — and especially Miss Potter — felt about it at the time was just as I have told you. In fact, in its day, the affair of the

272

seaplane was rather a *cause célèbre,* with discussions in Parliament, articles in *The Times,* and a great deal of hullabaloo.

But to go on. This particular aeroplane was built in Manchester, England, and first flown on May 19, 1911. Then it was brought to Windermere, where its wheels were replaced with a pontoon and airbags and where it was flown for the first time on the following November 25. (If you are keeping track, you know that this is just four months before the beginning of our story.) The aeroplane's top wing was forty-two feet long, the bottom thirty-two, and the body just over thirty-six feet long. Unlike most modern planes, this one was known as a "pusher," and had an eight-foot-six-inch propeller mounted in the rear so that it pushed the plane forward, rather than pulling it through the air, as a forward propeller does. The motor (if you care about such things) was a fifty-horsepower Gnome nine-cylinder rotary engine, which is about the size of the motor on your neighbor's outboard motor boat. Since the Water Bird was a hydroplane, it had no wheels, but rather a central mahogany pontoon or float, with a cylindrical airbag (known locally as a "Wakefield sausage") slung under each of the lower wings. When it settled into the water, it was buoyed up by the pontoon and stabilized by the airbags. Like all early planes, Water Bird lacked a cockpit or any sort of enclosed body, and was mostly a matter of wings, a tail, and struts. The pilot sat on the leading edge of the lower wing and managed the motor, rudder, and ailerons. There was a second seat behind the pilot, in case someone wanted to fly along.

And in this case, someone did, as the Professor, still taking notes in his lookout tree, could plainly see. The pilot, a wiry, dark-bearded fellow, sat in front, giving orders to the men who were assisting Water Bird down the ramp. A passenger was perched in the second seat, holding on to the struts with both hands and looking as if he already regretted his wish to go up in the air — and they hadn't even left yet.

But in a few moments, the machine, the pilot, and the passenger were safely bobbing on the water in front of the slipway. Someone gave the propeller a hard turn, and the engine sputtered to life. The spectators cheered and threw their hats in the air and shouted, "Good luck! Stay out of the water!" and "Hope you come back in one piece!"

And then the hydroplane began to move, maneuvering clumsily amongst the crowded moorings and out to the choppy open water of the lake, where the wind was blowing hard — too hard, the owl thought, to make a takeoff possible. But this did not deter the pilot. After a moment, he turned the aeroplane into the wind and speeded up his engine. The propeller turned faster and faster until it was nothing but a blur, and the Water Bird began to bounce and skip across the white-capped waves, its wings tipping first to one side and then the other. The Professor thought it looked for all the world like an ugly, ungainly duckling who wanted to fly but wasn't exactly sure how to get off the water and into the air.

And then, as the owl watched, Water Bird took to the sky, rising just a few feet at first, then higher and higher, until it was twenty, then fifty, then a hundred feet in the air. From the crowd on the shore came a great shout, whether of triumph or disappointment the owl couldn't say. He knew enough about the human temperament to suspect that half of the spectators longed to see the aeroplane fly successfully whilst half longed to see it crash.

But if the owl wanted to find out more about Water Bird's strengths and vulnerabilities in flight, he would have to get closer. He pocketed his pad and pencil, flew out of his tree, and stroking with his powerful wings, easily caught up to the aeroplane, which seemed to be having a bit of a hard go, struggling to gain speed and altitude against the powerful headwind. The owl himself, a much more accomplished flier, did not like flying into such a blustery breeze, but he was on a serious spy mission and now was not the time to worry about a few gusts.

So for a few minutes, the Professor (not wanting to call attention to himself) cruised just behind and below the lower wingtip, out of sight of the pilot and the passenger. He noted that the engine was very, very loud (imagine a motor boat's outboard motor running at top speed not ten feet from your head) and that its violent operation seemed to make the struts hum and vibrate. He saw that the flimsy wings flexed in the air currents, and that the rudder swung from side to side as the pilot steered the machine. He also saw there were clumsy-looking hinged flaps on the trailing edges of the wings, apparently used to maintain or restore the flying balance, and that the pilot operated these by bamboo poles.

"Poles!" the Professor thought scornfully. *"How very primitive."* He flexed his own sturdy wing feathers, which were perfectly configured to do exactly the same thing

without a single conscious thought on his part — and certainly required no bamboo poles. None of his other observations struck him as very significant, though. The machine did not appear to be at all sturdy, and the pilot had to manipulate a great many moving parts, and of course, the engine had to operate continuously to keep it from falling out of the sky. But Water Bird was flying. In fact, it was flying very well.

And then, suddenly, it wasn't. The motor, which had been running more or less smoothly, gave a series of abrupt hiccups, coughed, sputtered, and stopped. In the dead silence, the owl could hear the panicked passenger cry out, "What's happened? Why has it stopped?"

The pilot was working furiously to get the engine started again, but he was unsuccessful, and the aeroplane — which was really very rickety — put its nose down, hesitated for a heartbeat, and then began a perilously steep dive toward the water, some hundred or so feet below. The passenger gave an earsplitting shriek. The Professor, amazed, held his breath. He had never seen such a thing before. Would Water Bird fall into the lake and sink like a stone? Or would it plunge like a loon beneath the waves and come up a little farther on with a fish in the pilot's lap?

It didn't do either. The pilot, still wrestling the controls and with the passenger screaming hysterically in his ear, managed to pull the machine up at the last minute so that it landed on its center pontoon. It hit the water hard, bounced ten feet into the air, then bounced again, and again, one wing up, one wing down. Then one wing-tip airbag caught the surface of the water and spun the machine around. Both men were catapulted out of their seats and into the water, where they clung to the floating aeroplane, which appeared to have crumpled its right wing and broken its tail.

"Help!" the passenger shrieked frantically. "Help, somebody! I can't swim! I don't want to drown!"

"That's enough," commanded the pilot. "Be quiet. You're not going to drown. Hang on. The Bird floats."

And so it did, after a fashion. Since one of the wing airbags was damaged, the aeroplane seemed to be listing heavily. Luckily, however, there was a sailboat not far away and it came to the rescue immediately. The yachtsman dropped the mainsail, furled the jib, and paddled up to the floating plane. He pulled both men into his boat, the pilot obviously chagrined, the passenger clearly angry. "I want my money back," the owl heard the passenger demand loudly. "I wasn't counting on a crash."

It didn't take long for a pair of small boats to rush out from Cockshott Point, attach lines to the floating Water Bird, and tow it back to shore, whilst the pilot directed the operation by shouting instructions from the sailboat. The Professor, curious, followed closely and perched in a nearby tree to watch as the pilot and two other men winched the crippled aeroplane back up the slipway and into the hangar.

The spectators were watching, too, all of them exceedingly well satisfied. They had seen the aeroplane dive into the lake and could go home and tell everyone all about it (with plenty of exaggeration, of course). It wouldn't be long before the entire district knew that the Water Bird's engine had failed and that it had gone down right in the middle of Windermere with a mighty splash. It was only by the grace of God and the extraordinary skill of the pilot (and the lucky fact that a sailboat was nearby) that the lives of the two men aboard were saved.

The passenger, of course, was the brave Hero of the Moment, and made the best of his wetting by telling everyone what a thrilling ride it had been up to the moment the engine quit and how he had escaped death by a hair's-breadth when the machine plunged into the ice-cold water, never saying a word (of course) about his fears of drowning or his frantic cries for help. As for the aeroplane — well! It looked to be a total loss, with one wing torn nearly off and the tail severely damaged. Surely this would be the end of Water Bird, which naturally pleased some (those of the "If God had wanted people to fly" opinion) and distressed others (those who felt that since the Germans were building aeroplanes, the British ought to be sharpish about it). With these and other similar remarks and still discussing the matter excitedly amongst themselves, the crowd dispersed.

By that time, our spy had become more audacious. There was a great deal of commotion and everybody was fully engaged with what was directly in front of them. So the Professor flew into the aeroplane's hangar and perched on one of the rafters, high above in the darkness. He took off his dark goggles, pulled out his notepad and pencil, and (like any good spy) began making notes about what he heard.

He heard plenty. One of the men, a tall blond man whose name was Anderson, walked around the Water Bird, surveying the injured wing and damaged tail section with a grim shake of the head.

"Broken struts, cracked ribs, torn canvas, wrecked airbag — and who knows what went wrong with the motor," he said darkly. "The repairs are going to cost a pretty penny. Baum's not going to like it. You know how he feels, Oscar. He may decide not to pay."

"Baum's in no condition to decide to anything today," said the pilot, Oscar Wyatt — the very man we were hoping to get a close look at. He was thin and wiry, with dark hair and a neatly trimmed dark beard and mustache. "Fellow's laid up with a cracked head and a broken arm and a leg. They've taken him to Raven Hall. I tried to see him this morning, but was prevented." He frowned. "Said it was doctor's orders."

"A cracked head?" a third man asked, startled. "Broken bones? How'd that happen? And when? He was here yesterday afternoon, bustlin' about and getting in the way, as he allus does. 'Tis a pity he's been hurt."

"A great pity," Anderson agreed. He stepped away from the aeroplane and folded his arms. He gave Wyatt a narrow look. "Especially if it means that we're not going to be able to repair the Bird. If Baum's laid up, where's the money coming from?"

"I have good news," Oscar Wyatt said, and laughed roughly. "I've located another potential investor. I'm seeing this person this evening. If I'm successful — well, I'll tell you, boys. This person has enough money to take care of any problem we could encounter, and then some."

"Another investor?" Anderson gave him a narrow look. "Why do we need another investor? Is Mr. Baum pulling out?"

Wyatt didn't answer.

Anderson repeated the question. "Is Baum pulling out? And who's this other investor you've found?"

"Never you mind, Anderson. The person prefers to remain anonymous, and anyway, the deal isn't done yet. But I'm confident enough that it will be that I'm telling you to carry on. Get that wing repaired. Build a new airbag. Patch up the tail. Fix the engine. Do whatever's necessary."

Anderson wouldn't give it up. "But what about Mr. Baum?" he asked insistently. "Does he know about this new 'investor'? Does he want these repairs made?"

Wyatt pulled himself up. "I am telling you, Anderson, to —"

"The thing is," Anderson cut in, "that Mr. Baum told us that he was drawing the line at any more expenditure." He turned to the third man. "You heard him, didn't you, Tommy? You were standing right there when he said he wasn't putting another penny into this machine. It either flies or it doesn't, he said, but he's not —"

"And I'm telling you to stop worrying about Baum!" Wyatt shouted. "That's not for you to bother your head about, d'you hear? My job is to find the money to get this aeroplane into flying condition and take it back up in the air. Your job is to get the repairs done — and bloody quick, too. Churchill and his military men will be here in three days. They'll expect to see the Bird take the air. And we're going to make it happen."

In the rafters, the owl blinked. Churchill? Winston Churchill?

Anderson was even more surprised than the Professor. "Churchill?" he exclaimed, staring. "Churchill, from the Admiralty? He's really coming, then? You're not just larkin'?"

"Right," Wyatt said flatly. "He's really coming, and he says he wants to go up in the Bird — maybe even use her in his Royal Flying Corp. No time for games now, boys. It's a matter of the national defense. So stop your jabberwocky and open up that engine.

I want to know what happened up there. Why the motor quit. It's never done that before."

Tommy cleared his throat. "Could've been the petrol," he offered diffidently. "Water in it, mebbee? That would've made the pistons stop firin'."

"Water in the petrol?" Wyatt asked, his eyes narrowing. "How could that have happened?"

Tommy gave a careless shrug, not quite meeting Wyatt's eyes. "The petrol tank is right outside the door, ain't it? Anybody could've poured water in it, couldn't they?"

Anderson stared at him. "Are you suggesting sabotage, Tommy?" he asked in a disbelieving tone. "You don't really think —"

"Not suggestin' anything," Tom said blandly. "I'm just sayin', is all."

Wyatt's mouth hardened. He turned to Anderson. "I want a twenty-four-hour guard put on this place, Anderson. All day, all night. You got that?"

"A guard!" Anderson whistled. "That'll cost as much as the repairs."

Wyatt slammed his fist against his palm. "I don't care what it costs!" he shouted. "I want that engine repaired, the wing and tail put to rights, and a guard on this place. Nothing more is going to go wrong here.

Do you hear me?"

"Yes, sir," Anderson said mildly, but with more than a hint of sarcasm. "You're the man who's getting the money, so you're the boss."

"As long as you understand that, we'll get along just fine," Wyatt growled in a sour tone. "Now, you get to work."

The Professor watched as Anderson and the man called Tommy busied themselves around the plane, tending to its crumpled wing, opening the engine. Oscar Wyatt lingered for a time, watching, as if he didn't quite trust them to do the job. After a while, he said he was going out to have a talk with the "new investor" and would see them tomorrow, at which point he expected major progress to be made on the repairs. The minute he was gone, Anderson laid down the tool he was holding and shook his head.

"I don't like this, Tommy," he said in a low voice. "I don't like this one bit. Baum said there'd be no more repairs, and now he's laid up and Wyatt's got money from a 'new investor,' whatever that means. And I'm supposed to hire a twenty-four-hour guard."

"I was thinkin' 'bout that," Tom said. "I got a friend who's lookin' for work. He could stand night guard. He'll work cheap."

"Tell him to come by and talk to me," Anderson replied shortly. He was scowling. "You know, I've got half a mind to go over to Raven Hall this evening and see what I can find out from Baum."

"I wouldn't if I were you," cautioned Tom in a practical tone. "I agree that it ain't good, this business, but I can't see as you can do anything about it. Baum's out of the way and Wyatt is runnin' things here. He made it plain. If we want to get paid, we do as he says. That's how I see it, anyway."

Anderson hesitated, then nodded reluctantly. "I suppose you're right," he said, going back to work. "But if you ask me, something's fishy here. I wonder how Baum got that cracked head."

And so, of course, do we. But our spy has begun to feel that there's nothing more to be learned from these two men and has decided to abandon his station — and anyway, he is feeling the pangs of hunger. It has been, all told, a rather long morning. He finishes taking his last note, quietly pockets his pad and pencil, and flies silently out of the hangar, a dark shadow against the darkness of the roof over the crippled Water Bird.

The flight back across the lake doesn't take long. Fifteen minutes later, the Profes-

286

sor has landed in the tall tree at Oat Cake Crag, where he pulls out his ham-and-onion sandwich and begins to eat. While he is eating, he reviews his notes, considering what he has seen and heard over the past several hours. It has been a very busy and eventful several hours, to be sure. His mission has been — at least in the Professor's view — remarkably productive.

Of course, while the owl has been spying, other things have been going on in the area. Mr. Heelis has returned to his solicitor's office in Hawkshead. Captain Woodcock has gone back to Tower Bank House to have luncheon with his loving wife. Mr. Baum continues to lie, white and unmoving, in a guestroom bed at Raven Hall, tended to by Dimity Kittredge, who is hoping that Dr. Butters will be able to stop in during the afternoon to check on his patient.

And while all these things have been happening, Miss Potter has been making her way toward —

But I think perhaps we should start a new chapter.

15
MISS POTTER INVESTIGATES:
AT THE VICARAGE

When we last saw Miss Potter, she was on her way back from Belle Green in the company of her friend Rascal. She had just opened her brother's letter and read that her parents had been told that she was secretly engaged to Will Heelis. This news was startling and dreadfully unwelcome, and it had left her deeply dismayed.

But Beatrix was a staunch person who rarely gave in to darker sorts of feelings. Her philosophy was trusting and uncomplicated: she believed that a great power silently turned all things to good, and that you should behave yourself and never mind the rest. Of course, she wasn't above taking a hand herself when there was something she could do to help. But for the most part, her practical turn of mind encouraged her to behave as though things would turn out well and trust that they would and leave the problem or the challenge or the dilemma to sort itself out. Then she could be surprised and pleased when it did, when what she dreamt of turned out right in the end. And if it didn't — well, it wasn't meant to be, that's all.

It had been that way when she had lost Norman. She had feared, deep in her heart, that she would never again be happy. But she had believed and trusted, and now, to her surprise, just six years later, she found herself busy and content with her books and her farm and her animals here in this little Lake District village. And to her great delight, she had found another man who loved her and whom she could love, perhaps even more deeply and truly than she had loved Norman so long ago. The letter from London was lead in her pocket and the thought of what was happening at Bolton Gardens was an ominous cloud over her head, but she reminded herself that if she could only believe and trust, things would turn out well.

So she resolutely turned her attention away from the letter to the sun-brightened landscape around her. "Isn't the country-side beautiful, Rascal?" she asked, making her voice as light and cheerful as she could. "It's such a wonderful day. I want to go for a long, long walk!" But a few minutes later, to her surprise, she found that she couldn't quite keep her attention from the letter. So she spoke about it to Rascal, and in a few moments, had spilled out the whole story, from the moment of the engagement to her efforts to keep it secret to receiving Bertram's letter. She felt she had to tell someone, and who better than Rascal?

Rascal had been aware of the engagement for some time, of course. Animals always know a great deal more about human affairs than we give them credit for. But he wasn't about to let Miss Potter know that he was already in on the secret.

"I'm delighted," he said firmly, when he had listened to the whole thing. As of course he truly was, for he loved Miss Potter with all his heart and was a great fan of Mr. Heelis, who always seemed to find a bit of biscuit in his pocket for his four-footed friends. *"I'm sorry to hear that your parents have learnt your secret. But it was bound to come out sooner or later, wasn't it?"*

Beatrix sighed. Now that she thought about it, she was surprised that the news of her engagement hadn't leaked out sooner. Villages were horrible places for gossip, and she and Mr. Heelis had been together as often as they could. They pretended that they were just going about the country in search of property, but someone must have seen them and thought otherwise.

"But what am I going to tell my parents?" she wondered aloud. "What *am* I going to tell them?"

"Whatever you decide," Rascal said in a comforting tone, *"I'm sure it will be the right thing. Just trust your heart, and you'll be fine."* He leapt up and nipped gently at her sleeve. *"Now, then, shall we go for our walk? It's such a beautiful morning. I will follow you wherever you like and we will make a grand time of it, just you and I. Lead on, dear Miss Potter. Lead on!"*

So, cheered by the little dog's friendship and encouragement, Beatrix led on. The north wind was blustery and chill, and the trees in Penny Woods and along Claife Heights had not yet put on their springtime dresses. But the sun was bright with the promise of April, not many days away, and the grass was green and sweet-smelling. The new lambs frolicked joyfully around their mothers, who watched with patient forbearance and now and then reminded their young charges not to venture too far. In the hedges, the robins were singing as gaily as if the warm days were already here and it was time to think about mates and babies and blossoms and worms. Spring in the Land

Between the Lakes is a magical time, and it didn't take long for that magic to lift and lighten Beatrix's spirit.

The path that she and Rascal were following led away from the village, eastward across the meadows, to the rocky ford across Wilfin Beck. The name itself says what it is, for the word *wilfin* means "willow" and a beck is a stream. Even though (in the grand scheme of things) it is only an insignificant little beck, Wilfin feels very proud of itself and its willows as it wends its way across the greensward. I don't wonder at that, for small as it may be, the beck is very beautiful. In the winter, it is sometimes frozen and quiet, glassy with ice and sparkling with diamonds of frost. And in the summer, when there is less rain, the water may move slowly, loitering along like a sluggish school-boy. But in the spring, oh, in the early spring the beck brims bank-to-bank with the clearest, purest, sweetest snow-water from the higher fells, some of which are often still white with snow in March, even though the land below is emerald green.

This morning, the beck was in a mood to make sure that all this fresh, lovely water flowed as fast as it could into Windermere, and south right through the lake to the River Leven, under Newby Bridge and past the lovely white cottages of Greenodd and into Morecambe Bay and finally out into the broad, blue Irish Sea, a journey that takes a great deal more time to make than for me to tell you about it. But if you think this lovely adventure has ended when Wilfin's water is lost in the vastness of the salty ocean, you must think again, for the sun on the sea is warm and inviting and pulls the water up to itself, into the highest atmosphere, where each drop lives in the clouds until the perfect moment, when it falls once again onto the higher fells, onto Crinkles Crag and Bow Fell and High Raise, and onto the lower fells, too, onto Latterbarrow and Claife Heights and then into the myriad rivulets that hurry down to Wilfin Beck and its willows and the green grass of the Land Between the Lakes.

Beatrix was reflecting on this wonderful cycle of nature as she lifted her woolen skirt and stepped from rock to mossy rock across the beck, whilst the dippers and wagtails and water-ouzels, splashing and chirping in the shallows, cheered her on. It was comforting, somehow, to know that all the life around her was part of a larger pattern, in which even the smallest drop of water, the least lichen and liverwort, and the slightest water-ouzel had its great and important and even magnificent role to play. It helped her to believe and trust that her own life would turn out as it was meant to do, no matter how dark it might seem at the moment.

It was in this more optimistic frame of mind that Beatrix looked across the meadow and realized that she had reached a fork in the path. One way led north into the higher fells, in the direction of Latterbarrow, where there were no houses and no people, only a great stone cairn standing guard at its lonely post and a splendid western view of the Coniston mountains and the Kentmere fells beyond. Oh, and from Latterbarrow a path went on to Windermere and Wray Castle, that huge, ugly pile of rock where her family had stayed one holiday long ago, when she was sixteen. Should she go that way, and visit Wray, and spend the day poking around her past?

But the other, nearer path led to the vicarage. This, of course, was where Reverend Sackett lived — the same Reverend Sackett who was pledged to marry her friend Grace Lythecoe sometime next month, if nothing intervened. At the distant sight of its gray stone walls, its gables and steeply pitched slate roofs, Beatrix discovered that her question was answered. She had not consciously chosen to come this way, but now that she had, she knew why. She would have a sit-down chat with Mrs. Thompson, the vicar's cook-housekeeper, who was destined to be replaced when the vicar and Mrs. Lythecoe were married. Mrs. Thompson was said to listen at doors. If she knew or suspected that she was facing imminent discharge, she would have a very good reason to wish that the marriage would not take place, and (although one did not like to think of it) the motivation to write those ugly letters.

But although Beatrix had met Mrs. Thompson on one or two occasions, she didn't really know the woman and felt that she couldn't just go barging in on such a slight acquaintance. She needed an excuse for her visit, like the tablecloth she had taken to Matilda Crook for mending. What could it be?

And then, as she asked herself this question, she realized that she was very thirsty, and thought that no excuse could be better than the truth. She looked down at the little dog. "Rascal, do you suppose you could occupy yourself for a while? I am going to drop in on Mrs. Thompson at the vicarage."

"Of course," Rascal agreed cheerily. *"I'll just pop out to the barn and see if Cyril is around."* Cyril was the shaggy old sheepdog who had lived at the vicarage for longer than Rascal

295

could remember. *"The dear fellow is really rather lonely. He doesn't get out much these days, and I like to drop in and bring him up to date on the news whenever I'm in the neighborhood."*

A few minutes later, Beatrix was ringing the bell at the vicarage's tradesman's entrance, around the back of the large house, near the kitchen. The bell was answered by a meek-looking young girl in a white apron and cap. She admitted Beatrix to the downstairs back hall and summoned Mrs. Thompson, a tall, angular woman with sharp elbows, gray hair skinned back in a bun, and dark eyes deep-set in a thin, sallow face. Beatrix always thought of a stork when she saw Mrs. Thompson, not so much because of the way she looked as because of the stiff, ungainly way she moved, as if she were picking her way amongst the reeds along the lake shore.

"It's Miss Potter come callin', mum," said the girl with a quick bob, and vanished.

"Oh, Miss Potter!" cried Mrs. Thompson, wringing her hands in consternation. "My goodness, Miss Potter! Oh, dear, dear, dear, I'm verra sorry — t' vicar is out for t' mornin'. But whyever didn't tha knock at t' front door?"

The real answer was that Beatrix didn't

want to talk to the vicar and was glad that he was out. But she could hardly say that. Instead, she uttered another truth, just as it popped into her mind.

"Because I'm really rather muddy." She looked ruefully down at her brown boots, which were indeed muddy after crossing Wilfin Beck. "I went out for a walk this morning and have come farther than I meant. I'm so thirsty, and when I saw that I was nearby, I thought I would impose upon you for a cup of water. I'm sorry to trouble you, but would you be so kind?"

"Oh, it's no trouble, no trouble at all, Miss Potter!" Mrs. Thompson exclaimed. "I'm glad for t' comp'ny, I am." In fact, her sallow cheeks had become quite pink with pleasure and she was wreathed in smiles. "Dost tha mind t' kitchen? Nay? Then do come in for a bit of a rest, an' we'll have a cup of tea. T' kettle's on. It woan't take a moment. An' p'rhaps tha wudst like a bite, as well? T' scones for t' vicar's tea have just come out of t' oven."

Well. I must admit to being a little surprised, now that we have met Mrs. Thompson. With everything that has been said of her, I have been expecting a dark-featured person, sullen and disagreeable and exceedingly ill-tempered, who might begrudge even so much as a cup of water to a thirsty caller, and who might be capable of writing nasty letters in an attempt to hold on to her employment.

But even though she might not be the best housekeeper and cook in the world, and although she may occasionally apply her ear to a door, it appears that Mrs. Thompson is, after all, a pleasant person. In fact, it is entirely possible that she (like Cyril the sheepdog, out in the barn) is really rather lonely, for the vicarage is out of the way and if she wants to see anyone — her cousin Agnes Llewellyn, for instance, to whom she is very close — it is something of a walk. The vicar is busy about his duties all day and with his books all evening, and the only other persons she is likely to see on a regular basis are the butcher in Far Sawrey, the tweeny and upstairs maid, and old Mr. Biddle, the gardener who comes twice a week. Upon reflection, I am not surprised that she is delighted to see Miss Potter, who is after all the most famous resident of Sawrey, Near and Far — and here she is, come to beg a cup of water!

The vicarage kitchen was quite large, for it had originally been built for a vicar who had a substantial family and quite a few servants to feed. It was located in the basement, as many kitchens were in those days, to keep the smells of cooking from the more delicate noses of those upstairs. It had a stone floor, a high ceiling and tall windows, a monstrous black iron range, a long pine worktable, and heavy oak dressers full of pots and pans and serving dishes. There was a smaller table, spread with a cloth, beside a window. Beatrix, sensing that her visit was rather an occasion for Mrs. Thompson, allowed herself to be seated there. It wasn't long before napkins and china plates and silver were laid and tea was poured and a plate of scones was set out. These proved rather crusty and a challenge to chew (as we have heard, Mrs. Thompson is really not a very good cook), but Beatrix made the effort, even managing, truthfully, to compliment the cook.

"My, these scones are quite something," she said in an admiring tone.

"I'm so glad tha likest them," Mrs. Thompson replied, beaming. "Scones are a specialty o' mine." She paused, obviously hungry for gossip. "Tha'rt in t' village for a time, Miss Potter?"

"I'm not sure," Beatrix said, thinking of the letter in her pocket. "I may need to go back to London on a family matter." But Bertram had said that it would be better for her to stay away until her parents were calmer, and perhaps he was right — she certainly hoped so. "In any event," she added, "I hope to be here for the vicar's wedding." She stepped into her subject bravely, with both feet, watching Mrs. Thompson carefully for any sign of displeasure or vexation. "I'm sure it will be an occasion to be remembered. Don't you agree?"

Mrs. Thompson sighed gustily. "Ah, t' weddin'." She rolled her eyes with exaggerated feeling. " 'Twill not be a fancy weddin', I understand. But t' whole parish has been asked to t' ceremony. And t' reception's to be here at t' vicarage."

"Oh, dear," Beatrix said sympathetically. "I'm sure it will be a great deal of work for you. But I know you will manage."

"Oh, 't won't be me by m'self," Mrs. Thompson said with a wave of her hand. "Sarah Barwick from t' bakery is helpin' out, and Mrs. Kittredge's cook from Raven Hall. T' vicar wanted to be sure that I had plenty of help wi' t' cookin'." Another deep sigh. "Such a kind man, he is."

Beatrix nodded, thinking that the vicar had likely asked Sarah and the Raven Hall cook to help out in order to avoid serving scones like the one on her plate, which she hadn't quite finished. But of course she didn't say that. Instead, she said, "Oh, he is indeed. A very kind man. You must be pleased that he is finding happiness so late in life. And pleased for Mrs. Lythecoe, too." She paused and looked around. "I understand that she lived here in this very house when her first husband was the vicar, many years ago."

"Aye, that she did." Mrs. Thompson picked up the teapot. "An' didst tha know that t' vicar and Mrs. Lythecoe's first husband were cousins?"

"I've heard that," Beatrix said noncommittally.

"O' course, it doan't perturb me none," Mrs. Thompson said pragmatically, "although it be a bodderment to some. Bertha Stubbs is up in arms." She picked up the pot. "Another cuppa?"

"Please," Beatrix said, and held out her cup. "Mrs. Stubbs doesn't like it?"

"Not a whit." Mrs. Thompson poured. "Says it's a sin. Says somebody ought to've said so when t' banns was read out."

Beatrix phrased her question delicately. "Does Mrs. Stubbs plan to do anything to try to prevent it?"

"Oh, I doubt it." Mrs. Thompson put down the pot. "Bertha's a good'un for talk, but when it comes down to doin', mappen not so much." She shook her head. "Anyway, wot could she do? T' weddin's set."

"It would be terrible if something should happen to endanger the vicar's happiness," Beatrix said firmly.

"Oh, aye," Mrs. Thompson replied with genuine feeling. "Truly, Miss Potter, I *am* happy for t' dear, sweet vicar. An' I'm sure Mrs. Lythecoe will do her verra best to make him happy." She gave a mournful sniff. " 'Tis a tragedy that I woan't be here to do for t' two of 'em."

"Won't be here?" Beatrix asked in some surprise. "You're . . . leaving?" Grace had particularly said that (even though she had discussed the matter with Mrs. Belcher) the vicar had not yet given Mrs. Thompson her notice.

"Aye. I'm leavin', and verra sorry to say so." She sighed heavily. " 'Tis mi mum, poor ol' dear. She lives in Ambleside, all by her lone self, an' I'm her only daughter. She's been askin' an' wantin' me to come an' live with her. I've kept puttin' her off and puttin' her off, 'cause I truly love our vicar and felt it was mi duty to stand by him and be sure he was well fed and looked after."

She cast a slantwise look at Beatrix, who murmured, "Very commendable, Mrs. Thompson."

Mrs. Thompson looked gratified. "But I can't put Mum off any longer. She's gettin' on in years an' needs me t' do her cookin' an' laund'rin' an' cleanin'. I'm that worrit about her, truly I am. So I've wrote an' told her I'm comin' to live with her, just as soon as t' weddin' takes place." She lowered her voice, speaking anxiously. "I haven't told t' vicar yet, Miss Potter, so I hope tha woan't go an' say anything to him — or to noboddy else. I made up my mind only this mornin', y'see. Mr. Biddle took t' letter to t' post just before tha knocked at t' door. So it's fresh in mi thoughts."

"Oh, *dear* Mrs. Thompson," Beatrix said, "I am truly sorry to hear about your mother. Of course you must do whatever you feel is right." She smiled a little, thinking of her own situation. "It is not always convenient for daughters to do what their mothers want or feel they need, but there is duty to be considered."

"Ah, duty," said Mrs. Thompson, shaking her head sadly. "I've been a martyr to duty my whole life, Miss Potter. First 'twas Mr. Thompson's mum, and then Mr. Thompson hisself, both in poor health 'til they died. I did my duty by them two, an' then by mi mum for a while, and then I came here when t' dear vicar asked me, near nine years ago. I've loved ev'ry minute of t' work here, an' am that sorry to leave." She bit her lip and the tears welled in her eyes. "But yes, tha'rt right. We must do wot we must, Miss Potter, like it or not."

Deeply touched, Beatrix put her hand over Mrs. Thompson's hand and pressed it. "You are a good daughter, Mrs. Thompson. I'm sure the vicar will miss you dreadfully. And of course, I won't repeat a word of this to him. Not a word. I promise."

She did not promise, however, that she wouldn't say a word to Mrs. Lythecoe. In fact, she had already decided to stop at Rose Cottage on her way back to Hill Top. It would very much relieve Grace's mind to know that there would not be a confrontation over Mrs. Thompson's leaving.

"Thanks," Mrs. Thompson said mistily, and wiped her eyes with the corner of her apron. "I've been wrackin' my poor brain to think of someone t' dear vicar might get on with after I'm gone, an' I think I've thought of someone. Mrs. Lythecoe — that is, Mrs. Sackett-to-be — might like to have her, too, since t' two of 'em know one another quite well."

"Oh, really?" Beatrix asked, hardly daring to hope. "Who?"

"Mrs. Belcher," Mrs. Thompson said.

"Maggie Belcher. She lives over in Kendal now, but she had t' post here at t' vicarage some years back. She's a dear person, an' a verra good housekeeper. Keeps things neat as a pin, she does." She smiled a little. "O' course, her scones aren't quite up to mine an' I can't recommend her steak an' kidney pie, which is t' vicar's favorite. But then —" She gave a rueful shrug, as if to say that one couldn't be all things to all people, and the vicar and his new bride would just have to endure steak and kidney pie and scones of a lesser quality.

Beatrix allowed herself a private smile. Sometimes, if one leaves well enough alone, things really do sort themselves out. It was looking as though there would be no difficulty here at the vicarage. Mrs. Thompson would depart for Ambleside to do her duty, Mrs. Belcher would take her place, and Reverend Sackett and the new Mrs. Sackett would live happily ever after.

Or would they? As Beatrix left, she thought that she rather liked Mrs. Thompson (and so do I, although I am glad I didn't have to eat any of those scones, which look like small brown rocks laid on the plate). She was relieved to know that the housekeeper had nothing to do with the poisoned pen letters, for Mrs. Thompson obviously had no motive to write such things, and her high regard for the vicar would surely not allow her to speak ill of him in any way.

But if Mrs. Thompson didn't write those letters, who did? she wondered.

And how would she ever find out?

16
In Which Bosworth Is Surprised and the Dragon Learns More About the Monster

While Miss Potter is visiting with Mrs. Thompson, Parsley, Hyacinth, and Hyacinth's mother, Primrose, are busy getting ready for a party — and trying to keep their preparations from coming to the attention of the badger who is to be the honored guest. We will not ask Bosworth's age, for that would be impolite. But he has been a part of Miss Potter's story since 1906, and he was already in his middle years at that point. I am told that wild badgers live some twelve or fourteen years, so our badger is getting on, although still in good health and certainly in fine spirits — all the more, perhaps, from having relinquished some of his many duties. He is enjoying the privileges of the senior badger, without the responsibilities.

In the Brockery kitchen, Parsley and Primrose had been cooking and baking at top speed for several days. Parsley had made a honey cake and decorated it with some pretty blue violets that one of the visiting hedgehogs had brought from the woods, as well as the requisite number of blue candles, to match the violets. Primrose had made various kinds of sandwiches and was baking her specialty seed wigs, as well as shortbread and gingersnaps, scones made with dried fruits (raisins, dates, prunes, apricots), cheese scones, and vanilla slices, as well — rich, thick, vanilla custard layered on top of a baked pastry sheet, topped with baked pastry, and then frosted. For the scones and tea biscuits, there were all sorts of jams and jellies: pear and ginger jam, orange marmalade, bramble jelly, rose geranium jelly, and lemon curd. There was popcorn and nuts and bowls of dried berries. And for drinks, nettle beer and ginger beer for the elders, and lemonade for the youngsters. It was going to be a magnificent party.

Early in the afternoon, Bailey took the supposedly unsuspecting Bosworth out for a mushroom-seeking ramble through Penny Woods. This gave Hyacinth, Thackeray, and the rabbit twins the opportunity to decorate the dining hall with balloons and paper streamers and a large hand-painted sign over the mantle that said HAPPY BIRTHDAY, BOSWORTH! The hedgehogs had gathered armloads of early-spring daffodils, violets, and heartsease, and arranged them artfully in thimble vases, with curly fern fronds and pretty green leaves. When everything else was ready, Primrose and Parsley brought in the food and arranged it on the table, buffet-style, with plates and silverware and napkins. It was to be a stand-up party. As the guests arrived — friends, neighbors, and several special guests invited for this special occasion — they stacked their wrapped gifts on the mantle and around the fireplace. And since there were dozens of guests, the stacks of gifts were quite impressive.

As I said earlier, Bosworth had heard whisperings about the party (he might be old, but there was nothing wrong with his hearing), so it wasn't a surprise. He knew that everyone around him was up to something, and tactfully chose to ignore it all. But when he walked into the dining room at two in the afternoon and saw the brightly colored balloons and streamers and the HAPPY BIRTHDAY, BOSWORTH! sign over the mantle, and the towering pile of gifts, and the food and the birthday cake and the candles and the flowers, and above all, the special guests, he was overwhelmed with astonishment. He had expected a birthday party, but not this sort of elaborate birthday party.

"Happy birthday, Bosworth!" rang out a happy shout from all of the guests in unison, at the top of their lungs. The shout was very loud because the room was so full that the guests were standing elbow to elbow, oh, so many of them! There were some whom we know: the Professor, naturally, and Reynard the fox (Jemima Puddle-duck's friend); Fritz the ferret, in the company of his friend Max the Manx; Rascal, Tabitha, and Crumpet from the village; Thackeray and Bailey and Thorvaald. And a great number of other friends and acquaintances, besides: a pair of red squirrels, three brown hares, a prickle of hedgehogs, a bevy of beetles, a voluntary of voles, and a sleuth of spiders. All were happy to be invited, all had brought gifts (even if only an acorn or a berry or a curious rock). And all were on their best behavior.

"Happy birthday, Uncle Bosworth!" came another chorus, and at this, Bosworth had to blink back the tears. For these were the animals he held dearest in all the world, Parsley and Primrose and Hyacinth, and oh my goodness, Thorn and Buttermilk, as well! Thorn, Hyacinth's brother, who had once lived at The Brockery (and whom Bosworth had for a time considered to be next

in line for the Badge), and Buttermilk, his wife, had come all the way from their sett at Brockmoor, near Underbarrow. They had brought with them three cubs from their first litter: Tansy, Turnip, and Rhubarb. The cubs were now a year old and rowdy, but respectful of Uncle Bosworth, who was immensely charmed by them.

"Quite a delightful sight, isn't it?" said Fritz to Max, nodding affectionately at Bosworth, who was surrounded by a babble of little badgers and happy hedgehogs, all of whom were helping him unwrap his presents. It did not, however, make Fritz want to surround himself with little ferrets. An artist, he was a confirmed bachelor. His burrow in the bank of Wilfin Beck was so full of his paintings and sculptures that it was rather like a gallery.

"A delightful sight, indeed," said Max. He was now employed full-time by Major Ragsdale (Ret.) at tiny Teapot Cottage, in Far Sawrey, but the major gave him weekends off, to spend with Fritz. The two had become fast friends, if rather an odd couple. *"Oh, by the way, old chap."* Since he had moved in with Major Ragsdale, Max had begun to sound like a military man. *"Have you heard about the aeroplane crash this morning?"*

"No!" exclaimed the ferret. *"It crashed? What happened? Was anyone hurt? Is it done for? I hope,"* he added. *"Not that I wish anyone ill. It's just that the plane is a wretched nuisance. One can't sleep properly in the day-time."* This was important to the nocturnal ferret, who was making an exception to his no-daytime-outings rule to come to Bosworth's party.

"The pilot and passenger got a good dunking," Max said, *"but the aeroplane isn't permanently damaged. The crew is working on repairs."* Max went on to tell Fritz what he had learnt from the major, who had been waiting for the ferry when the aeroplane nosedived into the water, and had shared the news with a neighbor in earshot of Max.

In another corner of the room, the fox was hearing a similar report from Rascal, who had got it (secondhand) from the Dalmatian who rode on the seat beside the driver of the Coniston coach, who had got it from a passenger who had been among the spectators when the wrecked plane was brought in.

"Do they know why it crashed?" asked the fox curiously.

"The Dalmatian said that the passenger said that somebody heard there might have been water in the petrol," Rascal replied. He

grinned. *"I can think offhand of a couple of dozen Big People who might have put it there. Can't you?"*

"And they call foxes sly," said Reynard with a chuckle. *"I wonder which of the villagers is the culprit."* Now that they mention this, I wonder, too. When we last saw Roger Dowling, in the company of Henry Stubbs and George Crook, it sounded as if he might be hatching a plot — or might know of someone else who was doing so.

In another corner, Bailey and Thorvaald, sipping ginger beer, were observing the scene. The dragon had banked his fire as much as he could and was keeping a close eye on his tail, lest he inadvertently knock a picture off the wall, or disturb the spiders assembled in the corner, where they were not so likely to be trodden upon.

The Professor came up to them. *"And whooo are yooou?"* he asked the dragon. *"I don't believe we've met."*

"Well, I can fix that," Bailey said, and introduced them forthwith. *"You two have something in common, you know,"* he added with a grin.

The owl eyed the dragon. *"Oh? And what is that?"* His tone suggested that he did not think that this large scaly beast was anything like his proudly feathered self.

"Why, you can both fly," said the badger, and went off to wish Bosworth the happiest of birthdays.

The owl and the dragon regarded each other for a moment, pondering this unlikely likeness. The owl widened his eyes and flexed his wing feathers slightly, as if to suggest that there was a basic aerodynamic anomaly here, but the dragon immediately saw the similarity.

"Why, szso we can," he said cheerfully. *"Matter of fact, I've just returned from a little flying trip myszself."*

"And I have just flown back across Windermere," replied the owl. *"Quite bumpy out there this morning, actually."*

To his credit, the dragon did not boast that his "little trip" had been an around-the-world flight that had taken him to America, Hawaii, and Siberia, with only short stops for refueling — a distance that would have been impossible for the owl. Instead, he said, *"I've just been hearing about the posszsibility of some szsort of large creature living in the lake. You wouldn't have szseen it, by any chance?"*

"I believe I have," the owl replied. *"Largish beast, about . . . oooh, about the size of the ferry boat, I'd say. Tail, fooour wings, very*

314

noisy. Is that what yooou're looking for?"

"You've szseen it?" the dragon hissed with great excitement. When the owl nodded, his belly began to glow warmly. "You've actually szseen it! And you say it has four wings and a tail? Four wingszs!" He whooshed out a smoky breath. "The Grand Dragonszs will be astonished when they hear thiszs!"

The owl stepped back, fearing that his feathers might be singed. "Why, yes," he said. "Indeed, I saw it crash, just a few hours ago. Right down intooo the water. Made a gigantic splash, it did. Broke a wing, wrecked the tail, nearly drowned twooo men."

"Oh, my starszs!" breathed the dragon. His words were studded with exclamation points. "Oh, my scaleszs! Perhaps I shall be able to give the Grand Dragons an eyewitneszss report! Even arrange for an interview!" He paused for breath. "Bailey sayszs that one of his relatives saw this creature from Oat Cake Crag. Do you think that would be a good place for me to watch for it? Tonight, perhapszs?"

"You could certainly see it from there," the Professor agreed. "I don't believe, however, that the thing is likely tooo fly again anytime soon. The men have got tooo repair the wing, rebuild the tail, and get the motor working

315

again, yooou see. It might be several days before —"

"The men?" The dragon was staring at him blankly. *"The motor?"*

"Why, the men who are supposed tooo keep the hydroooplane flying, of course."

"The hydroplane?"

"Indeed." The Professor, with some justification, felt himself to be in the company of a backward student. He cleared his throat. *"Hydroooplane."* He uttered the word carefully, to ensure that Thorvaald understood it. *"That is hydrooo, as in water, from the Greek, ὑδσ. Tooo wit: hydrooography, hydrooopathy, hydrooometer. There is also hydrooometer and hydrooophobia and hydrooosphere, which is tooo say —"*

"Excuszse me," broke in the dragon. *"I'm not at all zssure we're talking about the same thing, Professzsor. I am inquiring about a dragon-like creature that swimszs in the water. It may fly from time to time, but —"*

"And I am talking," interrupted the Professor stiffly, *"about a dragonfly-like creature that swims in the water from time tooo time but otherwise flies through the air."*

As you can see, there is some confusion here. I think we should leave Thorvaald and the Professor to sort it out and drop in on one or two other conversations. It is, after all, a party, and the animals are sharing a few other tidbits of local news, some fact, some fiction.

In the corner near the fireplace, Hyacinth was regaling a rapt group of listeners with the true story of what had happened on Oak Cake Crag — Mr. Baum's fall and rescue, as well as the doctor's report that it was impossible to tell when or even whether the injured man would awaken.

"It's a good thing for Mr. Baum that you and the others happened to be there," Thorn said. *"Otherwise, he might have lain there for days and days."*

"Too right," said a brown hare. *"He might never have been found."*

"People never really appreciate all that animals do for them," the second brown hare said. *"They think they do it all themselves."* This was a common lament when animals got together. Humans took them for granted, or abused them, or actively campaigned against them. It hadn't always been that way, of course, but it was now.

"If Mr. Baum is out of the picture," the third brown hare asked, *"does that mean that the aeroplane will go away?"*

"There might not be any aeroplane left," a hedgehog put in excitedly. He had just been listening as Max the Manx and Fritz the

ferret discussed the aeroplane crash, so he began to repeat what he had heard.

But since we already know that story, we'll move on to another corner, where Parsley and the village cats have put their heads together over a subject of great interest — a romantic subject.

"I've just heard," said Parsley excitedly, *"that Miss Potter and Mr. Heelis are secretly engaged to be married. Flotsam and Jetsam went down to the Crooks' garden for carrots around lunchtime, and overheard Mrs. Crook telling Bertha Stubbs all about it. Isn't that lovely news?"*

"Married!" squealed Tabitha and Crumpet in unison. *"Is it true? Married?"* They turned to Rascal, who had just walked up to them. *"Rascal! Mrs. Crook says that Miss Potter is secretly engaged to Mr. Heelis! They're going to be married! What do you think of that?"*

Rascal knew the truth about Miss Potter's engagement, for she had told him herself. But of course, he didn't mention that part of it. What he said was, *"Sorry to disappoint you, ladies, but I heard Miss Potter tell Mrs. Crook explicitly that there's no wedding planned. If Mrs. Crook is saying otherwise, she is deliberately contradicting what Miss Potter told her."*

"You heard it?" Tabitha asked, wide-eyed.

"With my very own ears, in Mrs. Crook's kitchen, where I was sitting under Miss Potter's chair. This morning. No wedding." He looked around the group. *"You might want to tell the others,"* he added. *"There's no point in spreading unfounded rumors."*

"No wedding," Crumpet repeated sadly.

"No wedding," Tabitha moaned.

"No wedding," Parsley said in a disappointed tone. *"I'll tell the rabbits that they're not to say another word to anyone."*

"And that goes for you two, as well," Rascal barked to the cats. *"Not a word. Got it?"*

"Yessir," said Crumpet. Tabitha nodded.

"Well, now!" Parsley said brightly. *"I think it's time to light the candles and sing 'Happy Birthday' to our favorite badger."* She raised her voice. *"Everybody, gather round. We're about to cut the birthday cake!"*

Let's make our exit while everybody is singing. I'm sorry to miss out on Bosworth's birthday cake, but I've just remembered that something important is scheduled for four o'clock at Tidmarsh Manor, and I shouldn't like to miss it.

17
"No Proposals, I Say!"

We must now direct our attention to a part of our story that we have neglected, for the very simple reason that nothing of any consequence has seemed to be taking place. Or if it has, we're not privy to it — which often happens, you know. A story can't include every single detail, or we would be reading forever. By necessity, a great many things are left out because they don't seem immediately important, such as the color of the shirtwaist Miss Potter was wearing when she went out this morning (it was pale green, with a darker green ruffle down the front), or the whereabouts of the vicar when Miss Potter arrived at the vicarage (he had gone to call on Mrs. Taylor, who was ill with pneumonia). What's more, a great many important things (some of them *very* important) are left out for the simple reason that we don't know about them. Much goes on in this busy world that we don't learn about until somebody chooses to let us in on the secret. Maybe they will and maybe they won't. Maybe we'll be in the dark forever.

I think, however, that we are about to witness something important. It is just now getting on to four o'clock, and today is the day that Caroline Longford has agreed to walk with Jeremy Crosfield in the garden at Tidmarsh Manor. Lady Longford, as usual, has not withheld her opinion of this agreement. She has told Caroline, in a sour tone and several times over, that it is not seemly for her to consort with this young village person, who is not of her social class and must not be encouraged to think that he might be permitted to become a suitor. But I suspect — or at least, I hope — that this is just talk, and that her ladyship learnt her lesson when her son left: it is no good trying to make people do what you want them to do.

And Caroline (who I am happy to say has become quite willful now that she has become a young lady and spent some months in London, where all young ladies are by definition quite willful) has told her grandmother very sweetly that she intends to see whomever she likes and that if her grandmama wishes, she may spy on them

321

out the window and see that they are behaving circumspectly.

Now, I am a little puzzled by this, and perhaps you are, too. Earlier, when Caroline told Miss Potter about her plans, she did not mention having a particular inclination toward a certain young man, let alone Jeremy Crosfield. She *said* that she expected to finish her musical studies and then take a trip to Europe and perhaps to America and New Zealand, and then return to Tidmarsh Manor and settle down to pursue her dearest love, musical composition. She is free to do this, and to do whatever else she likes, wherever she chooses to do it, because she is an heiress and will inherit not only her father's small fortune but also her grandmother's much larger one. She will never have to work to get her living, unlike her friend Deirdre Malone, who keeps the accounts for Mr. Sutton's veterinary practice and helps Mrs. Sutton manage the eight Sutton children at Courier Cottage — two big jobs that Deirdre performs very capably, I must say.

But perhaps Caroline didn't mention her feeling to Miss Potter because she wanted to keep it secret. After all, one does not tell one's grownup friends all one's private thoughts, does one? Moreover, she had not seen Jeremy for some time. He had gone off to school and then she had gone off to study music at the Academy, and their paths had not recently crossed. But not seeing him did not keep her from thinking longingly of him, or saving in her scrapbook the few casual cards and notes she had received from him over the years. Or treasuring his photograph, which she herself had taken on the top of Holly How, one splendid afternoon of blue skies and bright sunshine when they were students together at the village school. That photograph, too, was hidden in her scrapbook, and the page was dog-eared and limp from being looked at so often, and touched, and — yes — kissed.

And now you and I have teased out Caroline's secret, which she has never confessed to anyone. She had long ago fallen into love with Jeremy, and had never fallen out. And when they met again at the Tower Bank Arms, where the villagers came to discuss their concerns with Mr. Baum's aeroplane, she fell even more deeply into love with him, and was overjoyed when he asked if he might call.

And why not? Jeremy Crosfield is even handsomer than he was when she took his photograph, tall and well built, with the most appealing of features and the dearest red-brown hair that Caroline has ever seen on a boy. (She has not, I must observe, seen a great many boys, but of course, that's neither here nor there.) He is clearly very intelligent. He did exceedingly well at Kelsick Grammar School and is greatly admired in his current position as teacher of the junior class at Sawrey School, where he is spoken of as a potential headmaster, should he choose to stay on. His botanical drawings are really quite remarkable, and Caroline — who believes that Jeremy has an extraordinary talent (she is, after all, in love with him) — hopes that he will be able to pursue the artistic career for which he is so clearly destined.

In fact, in her romantic dreams, Caroline cannot help picturing herself as Jeremy's loyal patron, her financial support enabling him to draw and paint unfettered by any obligation to earn a living in the ordinary way. From there, it is only a hop-skip-and-a-jump to picturing herself as his beautiful bride, all in white, with an armful of white roses. And then as his loving wife and the mother of his adorable babies, of whom there will certainly be as many as possible, since she will hire a nanny to take care of them.

When she thinks about this, she thinks

that her friend Deirdre Malone would make a splendid nanny, and the two of them together — she and Deirdre — would have such delightful romps with the children. And there would be a nanny's helper and a laundress and a cook to make the nursery milk puddings and a nursery maid to sweep the nursery floors and iron the babies' ribbons and laces, so that they looked sweet and pretty when Deirdre fetched them down for Caroline and Jeremy to give them kisses before bedtime. And again, why not? After all, Jeremy has a great deal of talent and Caroline has (or will have, which amounts to the same thing, at least when you are dreaming) a great deal of money. And since she has grown into a confident and willful young lady who is accustomed to having things her way, she sees no reason why her dreams can't become a reality.

Well, you and I know that this is not always possible, and that the world has a habit of getting in the way of what we would like to do and putting up such road blocks that we are forced to go stumbling around in the dark. But a young girl's fancy turns quite easily to ardent thoughts of love and a husband and babies — even a young girl who is ardently pursuing her own musical interests. And this particular young girl sees no conflict at all between her passion for music and her passion for Jeremy and his passion for drawing. In her imagination, it has already worked itself out, and the third floor of Tidmarsh Manor has already been converted into a nursery, with a sleeping room for Deirdre, so that she can get up with the babies when they cry in the night.

Oh, and an artist's studio has been built for Jeremy in the back garden, with clever curtains at the windows and its own dear little patch of flowers in front, and an awning over a sweet little table where they will take their tea, with the children all in white pinafores and ribbons, pink for the girls, blue for the boys, playing around their feet. She will wear a pale yellow dress the color of daffodils and Jeremy will wear a blue frock coat and one of those wonderfully floppy artist's ties, and he will tell her that he would love to paint her, instead of climbing the fells to paint those rare wild flowers. "You, my sweet," he might say, "are my dearest flower, my very own."

And so it is with a great deal of pleasure and anticipation that Caroline dresses this afternoon in her most stylish blue woolen suit, which has one of those modern ankle-length hobble skirts (so narrow at the hem that walking is an uncomfortable challenge).

She buttons up the close-fitting jacket with its blue velvet piping and clever blue buttons, brushes her hair until it gleams, and tops her pretty head with a pretty blue velvet cloche decorated with a cluster of pretty blue feathers, and pauses to admire herself in the mirror, thinking that she is very glad to be pretty and have enough money to dress attractively and hoping that Jeremy will think she is pretty, too.

And the masculine object of Caroline's unconfessed feminine affections? Jeremy Crosfield? What is *he* thinking as he shuts the door on his classroom at Sawrey School, puts on his Norfolk jacket and tweed cap, and strides purposefully in the direction of Tidmarsh Manor?

I wish we could see into Jeremy's head, but he (because he is a boy, I suppose) is not as transparent as Caroline. We can, however, hear him whistling and see by his jaunty, arm-swinging walk that he is mightily pleased with himself. In fact, he is so pleased that he puts me in mind of Peter Pan, who (when he thinks that he has cleverly reattached his shadow), crows "How clever I am. Oh, the cleverness of me!"

Perhaps Jeremy is feeling pleased because his day in the classroom has gone well. He is, after all — and I say this objectively, and not as one who is romantically smitten — a gifted teacher who is able to inspire in his pupils the same love of learning that so inspires him.

Or perhaps he is whistling because he has just sold (for a guinea! a whole guinea!) a watercolor he has painted of a rare wild orchid, the Dark-red Helleborine, that grows on the remote limestone screes of Coniston Old Man. Or because the collector who bought the painting was quite taken with his work and has assured him that he will look for more of Jeremy's paintings in the future.

Or because — and surely this is the reason — he is thinking of the young lady whom he loves, which should come as no surprise to us. After all, we have seen Jeremy and Caroline together since Miss Potter came to the village and made friends of both of them, Jeremy first and then Caroline. We were there when they first met on Holly How, when Caroline was so desperately unhappy after the deaths of both her parents and her arrival at the gloomy and forbidding Tidmarsh Manor. We went along with Jeremy and Caroline and Deirdre Malone on their fairy-hunting expedition in Cuckoo Brow Wood, where they found fairies and much, much else. We watched them become friends and then fast friends, and speaking for myself, I have wondered if perhaps their friendship might not ripen into something more enduring.

And perhaps it has. I confess to hoping so, for it does seem to be a very good match. Jeremy will not have to struggle to support his wife, for she can support both of them. Caroline's musical talents will be complemented by her husband's creative gifts and the two of them can move together in artistic circles, both in London and in the Lakes. And surely Lady Longford will be reconciled to the match once she understands that these two young people are determined to be together and that nothing she can do will stop them. But now I am being as romantic as Caroline herself, and should rein in my imagination until . . . well, until we see what happens.

Which it is just about to, for Jeremy is ringing the bell at the front door, and Caroline is flying down the stairs (as fast as that ridiculous hobble skirt will allow her to move) so that she can reach the door before the maid. She is opening the door, and Jeremy is taking off his cap and smiling at her, and she is slipping out before her grandmother can raise her voice from the drawing room and tell her not to. And now she is tucking her arm through Jeremy's and leading him off in the direction of the garden, trying not to show how happy she is to be with him at last, and alone, for she doesn't really think that her grandmother will spy on them through the window.

"You are looking very pretty today, Caroline," Jeremy says, which is exactly the right thing for a young man to say when he is alone with a young woman. "That's an attractive suit." He looks down at the skirt and then blurts out the wrong thing. "I say, Caroline, I'm glad we're not climbing Holly How. You'd never make it in that silly skirt. Why do girls wear such things?"

Caroline tosses her head, accepting his compliment and ignoring his rude question. But she forgives him, of course, because she loves him and because she is finding that he is right. The skirt is really very confining. It feels as though she has a rope looped around her ankles. "Thank you, Jeremy," she says sweetly. "And how was school today?"

He tells her — at length and with enormous enthusiasm, for he loves teaching and his pupils, especially the boys, some of whom will be leaving at the end of the year for work in the charcoal pits or the stone quarries or (if they are very lucky) the retail trade. He particularly enjoys teaching drawing, and often takes his young charges on walks through the countryside, drawing the plants they see and then reading about them when they return to the schoolroom.

Then he asks, "How are your studies progressing, Caroline? You're between terms, are you? Are you going back to London soon? Do you like living in the city?"

Now it's her turn. She tells him that she will be going back to the Academy in another few days, and is enjoying the concerts and museums and the theatre in London, but that she plans to return home to Tidmarsh Manor after her studies are complete. She does not tell him that she is thinking of a trip to Europe, America, and perhaps New Zealand because . . . well, because. Perhaps she is hoping that he will want her to come back to the Lakes just as soon as possible, in which case she might decide that Europe, America, and New Zealand are not so enticing after all, and that a husband and babies and a third-floor nursery provide a much more delightful prospect.

Then she asks, in a proper, somewhat proprietary tone, "And what of your art, Jeremy? I very much hope you are spending all your spare time drawing. You are, aren't you?"

Well, he isn't quite, for like any other young man, he has other urgent interests to look after. But with that encouragement, and knowing how much it will please her, he tells her about the sale of his watercolor painting of the Dark-red Helleborine (for a whole guinea!) and the promise of more work to come, and of the other drawings and watercolors he has added to his portfolio, one or two a week, as he has time.

Naturally, she is delighted to hear this, and heaps him with compliments until he blushes quite pink. Then she tells him about the piano concerto she has composed, which is to be performed in a fortnight by one of the Academy's leading pianists. He is very pleased and tells her that she must play at least a part of the concerto for him. He confesses that he does not have a musical ear, but he will be delighted to listen because she plays so beautifully.

By now, arm in arm and keeping up this lively chatter, the two friends have walked all the way to the back of the garden, away from the drawing room windows and behind the shrubbery and the rosebushes, where Lady Longford can't see them, even if she takes the trouble to look. There is a stone bench in a corner there, overseen by a pair of flirtatious stone cherubs and a little stone lamb, and Caroline demurely sits down. Jeremy joins her, and they sit in silence for a moment as the March twilight falls around them. Caroline is content simply to be sitting beside Jeremy, for his presence beside her on the bench is testimony enough to her that he cares for her in the same way that she cares for him.

But he seems uncharacteristically nervous and uncertain. He leans forward with his elbows on his knees, then sits up straight. He starts to say something and then falls silent, then begins again, and again can't quite manage to find the words for which he is so clearly searching. Sensing his unease, Caroline smiles a little to herself and waits. Clearly, she thinks, he wants to tell her that he loves her, but he fears that she will reject him, either because she does not love him or because her grandmother disapproves. Nothing else could account for such an obvious, un-Jeremy-like unease.

At last, visibly gathering his courage, he straightens his shoulders, sucks in his breath, and blurts out, "I say, Caroline, I have something to tell you. Something very important."

She lowers her gaze. "Yes?" she murmurs

expectantly.

"I wanted to write this to you. In fact, I tried, but it didn't really seem to be the sort of thing a fellow says in a letter." He gulps and kneads his fingers together. "I mean, I wrote it down but it didn't sound the way I wanted it to, and I gave it another go but finally decided I needed to say this face to face. So now I really have to tell you, Caroline. That is, I've been wanting to say that I —" He flounders again, and is lost again, and she feels she must help him out.

"Whatever it is, Jeremy," she says gently, putting her hand over his, "you know you can tell me." She glances down and sees that her hand looks delicate and lovely, the nails pink and shaped into ovals, and thinks that soon she may be wearing his ring. By this time, her breath is coming faster, and she is certain that he is going to say that he loves her. That he can't live without her. That he wishes she would not go to London, but if she goes, that she will come back here to the Lakes just as soon as possible, so they can be together. Forever and ever.

"You can tell me anything," she adds encouragingly, and leans toward him with a smile. "Anything in the world, dear Jeremy. It doesn't matter what it is."

"Oh, I am so glad to hear you say that,

Caroline!" He squeezes her hand and lets it go as the words tumble out in a rush. "What a brick you are! I knew you would understand and be as happy for me as I am. You see, I am to be married."

"M-m-married?" She stares at him, not quite believing what she has heard. Her heart seems suddenly frozen in her breast. "Married?"

"Yes!" he exclaims. He jumps up from the bench and begins to pace back and forth on the gravel path. "It happened just a fortnight ago, and I have been bursting to shout it out to the heavens, but I've waited to tell you first of all, since you are my oldest, dearest friend. Except for *her*," he adds tenderly. "Of course."

Stricken, she says, "Of course." She swallows, finding it very hard to breathe. "Except for . . . who? Who is she, Jeremy?"

"Who?" He stops in front of her, blinks. "Why, you don't know? You haven't guessed?"

"No," she says, swallowing a sob. "I haven't . . . I haven't guessed." Her voice quavers and breaks. "Who is she?"

"It's Deirdre, Caroline. Dear, dear, dearest Deirdre." He throws back his head and laughs richly, the image of a young man who is beside himself with delight. "Deirdre has made me the happiest of men. We're to be married in June, right after school is out."

Deirdre? Deirdre Malone? Oh, my goodness! I must confess that I am completely and totally and entirely surprised. I thought . . . that is, I expected . . . Why, I had no idea that Jeremy was going to marry Deirdre! Although there was that little bit about a secret, when Deirdre and the Sutton crocodile met Miss Potter in the lane. Perhaps we should have guessed then that something romantic was afoot, although I don't know how we could have supposed that it had anything to do with Deirdre and *Jeremy.* I still find it very hard to believe.

And so does Caroline. "Deirdre?" Up comes a sob she cannot swallow. "Deirdre Malone? You and Deirdre are to be . . . married?"

At last Jeremy comprehends that something is dreadfully wrong. He pulls off his tweed cap and drops to one knee in front of her as she sits on the bench. He seizes her hand. "Caroline? Caroline, what's amiss? I thought you would be happy for me, and for Deirdre, too! I thought —"

"Then you don't love *me?*" Caroline wails.

Jeremy stares at her, speechless. And then, just as he is beginning to fathom what has happened and attempt to find the words to answer her question (as if it *could* be answered!), he is interrupted.

"Up!" cried a loud, angry voice. "On your feet, young man! There will be no proposals at Tidmarsh Manor! Not as long as I am alive!" It was Lady Longford, fierce as a fiend and all in black, brandishing her ebony cane like a club. "Be gone, churl!"

"But I wasn't —" Jeremy scrambled to his feet, clutching his cap. "I swear, Lady Longford, I didn't —"

"No proposals, I say!" the old lady screeched, advancing on the pair. "Leave, rogue! Out of my sight, you wretched rascal!"

"But, Grandmama —" Caroline wailed disconsolately. "You're wrong. You don't understand! It's not what you think."

"Be gone, scoundrel!" And with that, her ladyship whacked Jeremy smartly across the shoulder blades with her cane, once, twice, three times. She raised her voice. "Beever, I want you. Come and eject this insolent, impertinent rogue from the premises. Immediately, Beever!"

For a moment, Jeremy stood, stunned. And then, understanding that nothing he could say would remedy this terrible situation, he picked up Caroline's hand and kissed it gently. "Thank you for being my friend," he said, and turned on his heel.

Caroline collapsed on the bench and began to cry in earnest, huge, wracking sobs that shook her slight frame.

Lady Longford bent over her, hands on hips, chin thrust out. "And you, you disrespectful, disobedient young miss," she hissed, "you have deliberately deceived me! You knew that I consider this young man entirely unsuitable as a husband, and yet you entertained his suit. You are confined to your room until further notice. I do not want to see your face at table. Do you hear?"

Oh, cruelty heaped upon terrible cruelty! Jeremy's heartless rejection, followed by Lady Longford's spiteful misunderstanding. What a wretched outcome to Caroline's romantic dreams of babies in white smocks and a nanny (Deirdre, of all people!) and a third-floor nursery and an artist's studio in the garden.

Well, all love affairs do not end happily, as perhaps you know from your own experience. Young girls' hearts are as fragile as the most delicate crystal goblet, and no doubt Caroline's will be broken once or twice more before it is safe in the hands of someone who will cherish it and promise never to let it be broken again (which promise will not, of course, be any guarantee, for life itself is utterly unpredictable).

But it does seem appallingly cruel for her to be punished twice in the space of a minute or two: once by the young man who has just told her that he has proposed to and been accepted by another; and then by her grandmother, who wrongly assumes that this same young man is proposing to *her*. And cruel, as well, that this second punishment falls on her at this moment, when her tender spirit and her loving heart are both so broken. Oh, if only Miss Potter were here. I am sure that she could set things to rights! Lady Longford would surely listen to *her*.

But Miss Potter is not here, and Lady Longford is in no mood to listen to anyone. I am afraid that Caroline will just have to linger in limbo until her grandmother learns that she has made a terrible mistake. Which she will, tomorrow, when Mrs. Beever visits her sister-in-law in the village and brings home the latest village news: that Jeremy Crosfield and Deirdre Malone are to be married.

Then her ladyship will realize that she has wronged poor Caroline and will find herself doing something that does not at all come naturally to her. She will confess that she acted hastily. She will beg Caroline's pardon. But will she beg Jeremy's pardon, as well? I very much hope so, although I'm not holding my breath. If it happens, I hope we are present to witness it. It would certainly be something to see.

And there are one or two other things I should like to know about. I should like to know how long Jeremy has been courting Deirdre, how it all came about, and what the Suttons — who stand *in loco parentis* for Deirdre, since she is an orphan — think about it. As I said at the beginning of this chapter, a great many important events are left out of stories for the simple reason that we aren't let in on the secret. What happened between Jeremy and Deirdre was one of those things, and I suppose they had some very good reasons for behaving as they did, and for telling no one, including us.

18
"DO SAY IT'S WONDERFUL!"

Beatrix had just begun getting out the tea things when she heard a knock at the door. She opened it to find Deirdre on the doorstep, pink-cheeked and smiling. She welcomed the girl, then peered over her shoulder. "Where are the little Suttons?" she asked.

"Mrs. Sutton decided that it was too near their teatime to go visiting," Deirdre replied. "So I came by myself."

Beatrix was secretly glad that they would not have to keep an eye on the children playing in the barnyard, where they were bound to annoy the three old hens. Mrs. Boots, Mrs. Shawl, and Mrs. Bonnet did not like their tail feathers pulled. "Well, then," she said cheerily, taking Deirdre's coat and hat, "you and I will have longer to talk. I've been thinking about you since I saw you in the lane. Do sit down, dear, and tell me your news. The kettle's boiling —

tea won't be a minute."

Deirdre sat, looking extraordinarily happy. Her eyes were sparkling and her unruly red curls seemed to dance with sheer delight. Of course, you and I know her secret — the Jeremy part, at least. But Beatrix doesn't, and as she set out bread and butter (she believed in simple teas), she was genuinely puzzled.

"Well," she said finally, "I hope you are going to tell me, and not just sit there looking as pleased as a kitten who's caught her first mouse."

"Oh, Miss Potter, I *am* pleased!" Deirdre exclaimed. "But it's not like catchin' a mouse — oh, no, not at all! Jeremy Crosfield has asked me to marry him, an' I have said yes!"

"Jeremy!" Beatrix exclaimed, astonished and a little dismayed. "Married!" And then she thought that perhaps it was like catching a mouse, after all, except that she wasn't sure whether the mouse was Jeremy and the cat was Deirdre, or the other way around.

But Deirdre did not seem to hear the dismay. "Aye — isn't it wonderful?" she crowed happily. "We're to be wed in t' garden at Courier Cottage in June, when Jeremy's school is out. Mrs. Sutton has promised to help me make my dress, an' there'll be lots of flowers, an' all our friends are invited, especially you!" She clasped her hands under her chin. "Dear Miss Potter, *do* say it's wonderful! Oh, do!"

"Well, my goodness," said Beatrix, by now feeling not just dismayed but envious. First it had been Grace and the vicar, and now Deirdre and Jeremy — free to pledge themselves, to follow their hearts, whilst she herself could not. Still, she managed a smile as she poured their tea. "Why, of course it's wonderful, my dear. How did this all come about? And when?"

And with that encouragement, Deirdre's story spilled out, embellished with girlish giggles and happy asides and enough starry-eyed happiness to soften even the hardest heart. She and Jeremy had realized their attraction to each other long ago, years ago, in fact. But they'd had precious little opportunity to spend any time together until he came back to the village to teach. He boarded at High Green Gate with the Llewellyns, just up the hill from Courier Cottage. This had made it convenient for him to accompany Deirdre and the little Suttons as they walked to Moss Eccles Tarn and along the shore of Esthwaite Water, supplying the children with paper and pencil stubs and showing them how to look at a plant and draw it.

"Drawin' is his passion," Deirdre said. Beatrix already knew this, for the first time she had met Jeremy, he had been drawing a cat, and quite a good one, at that. She had been working on her frog book at the time, and he had shown her where to go to find frogs to draw, so she had named her book *The Tale of Jeremy Fisher.*

It hadn't been long before the hours Deirdre and Jeremy spent together had become the highlight of their days. But it had been a much longer time before they could agree to be married, because, as she said rather shyly, "There was so much to be worked out."

The "so much" was mostly money, Beatrix suspected. Two could not live as cheaply as one — that was a fallacy. Did they think they could manage to live on Jeremy's salary as a teacher, assuming that he would stay on at the village school? But that was an impolite question. Instead, she asked another. "Have you spoken to Mr. and Mrs. Sutton?"

Deirdre, as you may remember, was an orphan, claimed five years before by Rose Sutton (such was the practice at the time) to help with the children, in return for room and board and the privilege of going to school. Sometimes, these arrangements did not work out well, and the orphan was sent back. But not this time. The Sutton children thought of Deirdre as their sister, and the Suttons considered her their daughter. And since she had no real parents, the Suttons would have to speak for her.

"They were a little surprised," Deirdre admitted. "An' they didn't think it was a good thing — in the beginning. They feared I was too young, an' we wouldn't have enough money. But we kept talkin' to 'em and lettin' 'em know we were serious, and they finally agreed, especially after Jeremy was asked to stay on and teach at the school." She grinned engagingly. "The Suttons like Jeremy, o' course. An' they married when they were young, even though Mrs. Sutton's parents didn't approve. And now just look at their fine family."

Indeed, Beatrix thought to herself. It was a fine *large* family. And then she asked the question that was at the top of her mind.

"But what about Jeremy's art? And his university education. I thought . . . that is, I hoped . . ." She stopped. She had understood that Jeremy was simply taking a year to work on his drawing and painting skills before going off to university. After all, Major Kittredge had promised to help support him while he finished his studies. If he were to marry, that avenue would be closed to him. But it was his decision, wasn't it? What rights did she have in the matter? None at all, of course.

Deirdre sobered. "To tell t' truth," she said quietly, "that's why I said no at first, Miss Potter. And kept on sayin' no all t' way through Christmas and t' winter. I thought he ought to go to university, since Major Kittredge is so keen to help, an' I promised to wait an' work an' save as much as I could until he was finished. But he says he would rather draw an' paint than spend his time studyin' in books, and would rather teach an' live in t' village than go off to Cambridge." She colored prettily. "An' marry me, o' course. I told him I thought he was wrong to miss his chance, but he says he knows what he wants."

"And what do *you* want?" Beatrix asked softly. It was the same question she had asked Caroline, who had not told her all the truth.

"Me?" Deirdre met her eyes in an utterly straightforward way. "I want Jeremy to be happy," she said simply. "If livin' here an' teaching at t' school an' bein' married to me makes him happy, that's what I want. I've asked him over an' over, an' that's what he says." She sighed and looked down at her hands, capable hands with blunt fingers and close-trimmed nails. "T' won't be easy, I know. I've promised to help by goin' out to work — Mr. Sutton wants me to stay on at the surgery, at least for a while. An' we've found a cottage in Far Sawrey that will be vacant come June. Slatestone Cottage. Just a little place, but it's clean an' not too far from Jeremy's school an' has a vegetable garden an' even a little shed where he can paint." She smiled a little. "I know you've wanted Jeremy to be an artist, Miss Potter. You've helped him an' encouraged him. I promise not to do anything to stand in the way of his art."

Well, there it is. And I must admit that I cannot help comparing Deirdre's feelings about Jeremy to Caroline's. Caroline was full of romantic dreams of white bridal gowns and babies in ribbons and pinafores (cared for by Deirdre and the nanny's helper) and tea under the awning. In fact, now that I think about it, all her dreams had Caroline herself at the center of them, with husband and children and servants on the periphery, like a young girls' dolls.

Deirdre's dreams, on the other hand, are centered on Jeremy: what he wants, what will make him happy. Some of us might say that perhaps she is too focused on him, at least for our modern sensibility. Where are her own desires? Her own wishes? Isn't there something she wants for herself, not for Jeremy?

But I hope we won't be too judgmental. Deirdre, like Beatrix and Caroline and all the others in this story, are creatures of the time and place in which they live, and we cannot fault them for not seeing beyond the walls of their dwelling. Even Sarah Barwick, that Modern Woman who wears men's trousers and smokes cigarettes, is a person of her time, for if she lived in our day and age, she would surely be aware that while trousers are a good thing, cigarettes are not. In any event, I am glad to see that Deirdre is so clear-eyed and realistic when she speaks about her marriage. When it comes to marriage, realism goes farther than romance, and Deirdre seems prepared to work. And although every marriage is held together by mutual love and respect, work — especially when two people find something they want to work for together — can be a remarkably strong glue.

And so the conversation turned to wedding dresses and curtains for the new cottage. When Beatrix asked Deirdre what she and Jeremy would like for a wedding present, she was quick to say, "Oh, pots an' pans, for sure, or dishes for every day! Nothin' fancy, please, Miss Potter." Then she looked down at Beatrix's blue rug and smiled. "Unless it's a little blue rug, like this one. It's so pretty."

This remark made Beatrix smile, for it was so like Deirdre. She made a mental note to obtain an identical blue rug for the floor of Deirdre's and Jeremy's cottage, and perhaps a nice serving dish, as well. This made her think what sort of wedding presents she would like, if she and Will were to be married — a thought that she immediately pushed away. But not that far. It lingered, like a curious spectator, at the edge of her awareness, as she and Deirdre talked about village matters, about the little Suttons and their father's veterinary practice, and about the aeroplane, which, Deirdre said, had fallen into the lake that morning.

"It did?" Beatrix asked, astonished. "Into the *lake?*"

"You haven't heard? Mr. Alter, one of Mr. Sutton's clients, was waitin' at the landin' to catch the eastbound ferry, when he heard the engine sputter-like and saw the thing go down in the water."

"Was anybody hurt?"

"I don't think so. But they say the wing is

busted, and the tail, too. No tellin' when it'll be flyin' again. Weeks, maybe."

"Well, that will be some relief," Beatrix said. "It's a mercy it didn't fall on someone's house."

After Deirdre had finished her tea and left, Beatrix sat at the table looking out of the window, watching the gray March twilight creep ghostlike across the garden. She was lost in thought, reflecting on the young and innocent love between Deirdre and Jeremy, the recent weddings of her friends, Dimity Woodcock and Margaret Nash, and the happiness that Grace and the vicar had found together later in their lives — if the mystery of the letters could be solved. The world seemed to be full of people who met and fell in love and married. But sadly, it was a world from which she was excluded, because, as Mrs. Thompson had put it so aptly that morning, she was a martyr to duty. "We must do what we must," Mrs. Thompson had said, her voice heavy with resignation, "whether we like it or not." But did that have to exclude any possibility that she and Will might find happiness together?

She sat awhile longer, thinking. Then, when the room darkened, she brought the paraffin lamp to the table and lit the wick, loving as she always did the circle of warm light that fell like a blessing across the red-checked cloth. She poured herself another cup of tea, sat down, and took Bertram's letter out of the pocket of her skirt. She reread it for the dozenth time. Then she got up and went for pen, ink, and paper.

It was time to write a letter to her parents.

19
"READ THIS!"

There is always more than one side to every story — and when the story is a love triangle, there are, by definition, three sides to it. (At least. Life being what it is, sometimes there are more.) We've already heard Caroline's side of this story, and Deirdre's. Now, I think, it must be Jeremy's turn.

Poor Jeremy. He was not physically injured when Lady Longford whacked him so soundly with her cane. He is a tall, strong young man, and it would take more than an old lady's smacks to cause any serious damage. But his spirits were very low, and he was blaming himself for what had happened. It was his fault, he told himself. He should have been more sensitive to Caroline's feelings. He should have known better. He had injured one of his oldest and dearest friends.

Head down, hands in his pocket, Jeremy looks nothing like the self-satisfied boy who started off for Tidmarsh Manor that afternoon with a Peter Pannish air of "How clever I am. Oh, the cleverness of me!" Occupied with his unhappy recriminations, he reached the end of Tidmarsh Lane and turned toward the village. At that moment, a small fawn-colored terrier — full of Bosworth's birthday cake and the good fellowship of his animal friends — scrambled over the stone wall and rushed up to him.

"Hullo, Jeremy!" Rascal barked. *"Nice to see you today! I've been having the most wonderful time at The Brockery."*

Jeremy Crosfield was another of Rascal's favorite people. In Rascal's informed opinion, Jeremy had always been much nicer than the other village boys, who teased small dogs and tied rattles to their tails and were often cruel. Jeremy had made something of himself, too — going away to grammar school (none of the other boys had ever done that!), becoming an artist, and now teaching at the village school. Unfortunately, though, the little dog didn't see much of Jeremy these days. The boy seemed to spend much of his time at Courier Cottage, where the Suttons lived. Rascal didn't like to go with him, because Mr. Sutton had adopted a fierce black dog with huge white teeth, abandoned by a client who did not pay his bill. Rascal, who rarely admitted to being afraid of anything, was more than a little afraid of the fellow.

"Hullo, Rascal," Jeremy said unhappily. "Well, I've put my foot in it this time."

"Uh-oh," Rascal yipped. *"What happened?"*

Jeremy looked down at the dog, who was always so perky and cheerful. He was glad that Rascal had happened along. He needed to give voice to his thoughts, needed someone to talk to — someone who would never tell anybody what he said.

"Well, to start with," Jeremy said, "I never meant to propose to Caroline, and it was wrong of her grandmother to think so."

"You proposed to Caroline?" Rascal barked incredulously. *"You and Caroline Longford are getting* married?"

He knew, of course, that grownup people did this, all the time — people as old as Miss Potter and Mr. Heelis, or the vicar and Mrs. Lythecoe. People were forever falling in love and saying their vows in the church and moving into their own houses and having babies, like Major Kittredge and Miss Woodcock, who was now Mrs. Kittredge and a mother.

But Rascal had never imagined that *Jeremy* might get married. The boy had always seemed to him to be a free spirit, liking nothing better than to ramble through the woods and fells — with Rascal himself by his side — looking for plants and animals to draw. People who got married didn't have time for rambles or drawing pictures. They were too busy fixing things around the house, or taking care of babies, or digging in the garden. And he somehow couldn't imagine Jeremy living happily at Tidmarsh Manor, under the stern gaze of that crepe-hung portrait of old Lord Longford.

Jeremy kicked at a stone. "I feel that I've been tarred by the wrong brush, Rascal," he muttered. "I've always understood who I am, you see. I'm not a gentleman's son. I've always known that Lady Longford would never consider me as a proper suitor for Caroline. Anyway, I didn't think of it because . . . well, because I don't care for Caroline. At least, not in that way."

"Oh, good," Rascal said, much relieved. *"You're* not *getting married. Sorry — I misunderstood."* There would be rambles, after all, and fun. Things would go on as they had in the past, and all would be well.

"And I had no idea — not the remotest sort of a glimmer — that Caroline might care for me."

"She does?" Rascal asked, skipping to keep up. *"Caroline Longford loves you?"* Not that

this was surprising. Jeremy (in Rascal's experience) was an exceedingly lovable person. But Caroline had gone to London. In Rascal's experience, Big People who went into the Great Wide World rarely came back to live in the village, where there was so little excitement.

Jeremy kicked at another stone. He had begun to understand what was behind Caroline's anguished wail, "Then you don't love *me?*" Like her grandmother, Caroline had completely misunderstood his intentions. She must have assumed — perhaps from the moment he had asked to call on her — that he was coming to tell her that he loved her.

"I don't think she really loves me," he went on, talking mostly to himself. "But she thinks she does, which amounts to the same thing." He looked down at Rascal. "Doesn't it?"

"How should I know?" Rascal replied ruefully. *"I don't have any idea what goes on in the minds of ladies. I don't have time for romance."*

This was true. Rascal was fully employed (and then some) as Near Sawrey's Chief Dog. His job was a twenty-four-hour, seven-day-a-week assignment that required him to monitor strangers in the village, settle disagreements among other dogs, and sleep with one eye open on the porch at Belle Green, on guard against trespassers and evildoers. He had his duty, and romance would only get in the way.

"I'm sure she'll get over it," Jeremy said, although he wasn't. He knew that he had never tried to mislead Caroline about his feelings for her. But he also knew Caroline, too, and pretty well. He had perceived, several years before, that she was developing a certain romantic streak, a tendency to dream about the future. It hadn't crossed his mind, though, that her romantic dreams might center on *him.* What a thick-headed clod he had been!

Now, you and I might say that if Jeremy hadn't intentionally led Caroline on, he couldn't be held responsible for her misunderstanding. But that didn't keep him from feeling absolutely rotten about it, and cursing himself for causing her pain. Or (which was even worse, he thought) causing a rift between Caroline and Deirdre. He knew that the two girls didn't see each other very often these days — Caroline had become quite the lady and Deirdre was . . . well, Deirdre, and still as hardworking and down-to-earth as ever. Nobody would ever call her a lady, and she would laugh in their

357

faces if they did. But lady or no, she was a splendid girl. As far as Jeremy was concerned, she was pretty nearly perfect.

"What I really hate," he said out loud, "is the idea that Caroline will be angry at Deirdre, and think that *she* is the cause of it all, when getting married was totally *my* idea, not Deirdre's. She kept saying no, over and over again, until I finally wore her down."

Now, Rascal was really confused. *"You are getting married after all?"* he growled. So that was what was behind all those visits to Courier Cottage! Jeremy had been visiting Deirdre. Fierce black dog or no, he told himself, he should have gone along, to keep an eye on the two of them.

The boy bent over, picked up a stone, and shied it at the hedge. "Happiest day in my life when she said yes," he said and grinned. "Just wish we had a little more money coming in. With the cottage and all — well, it's going to be a near thing." He looked down at the dog and brightened even more. "But if I can sell a painting every fortnight or two, it'll help matters considerably. And if I can just get this awful business with Caroline smoothed out, I'll be happy."

"Well, if you're happy, I'm happy," said the dog. Still, he was doubtful. To him, it seemed like a risky proposition. But he was

just a dog — what did he know?

By this time, they had reached the top of the village. Mrs. Crook was out in the yard at Belle Green, calling for Rascal, so the dog excused himself and trotted home to see what was wanted.

Jeremy himself didn't have far to go, only to the Llewellyns' house next door, where he was boarding. He let himself in at the back, for, like the other homes in the village, High Green Gate was never locked. Inside, it was dim and silent. Mr. Llewellyn had gone to Carlisle two days before to visit his ailing father, and Mrs. Llewellyn was probably out calling. She went out a lot in the late afternoons, and often had tea with her cousin, who was the housekeeper at the vicarage. The two of them seemed to be very close.

Still feeling unhappy about the ugly scene at Tidmarsh Manor, Jeremy wandered through the quiet rooms. High Green Gate was a pleasant house, situated on the shoulder of the hill with a view of the buildings on the other side of the street below, the joinery and the smithy and Rose Cottage and the shop that Miss Potter (in one of her books) had called Ginger and Pickles. But while the house itself was nice enough, even Jeremy, boy that he was, could see that Mrs.

Llewellyn was not a careful housekeeper. The sitting room was littered with newspapers, odd bits of clothing, a plate with a stale slice of bread left on it, and various cats, most of them napping. One, an orange tabby named Treacle, had recently given birth to kittens, and was curled contentedly on a pillow, nursing them. They were being watched by a rather plump calico with an orange-and-white bib. When Jeremy came in, she looked up and meowed.

"I've been waiting for you, Jeremy." It was Tabitha Twitchit.

Jeremy sat down beside her and rubbed her ears. "What are you doing here, Tabitha?" he asked. "You belong across the street at Mrs. Lythecoe's, don't you?" A silly question, that, since the village cats belonged wherever they happened to sit down, which could be anywhere.

"I dropped in on my way home from Bosworth's birthday party to visit Treacle and her new kittens," Tabitha said, purring warmly. *"I brought her a bit of birthday cake."* Indeed she had, for if you looked closely, you could see traces of crumbs on the pillow where Treacle was nursing her babies. The kittens were too young to eat cake, but Treacle had enjoyed it very much.

Jeremy smiled at the mother cat and her

kittens. "Nice," he said. Thinking out loud, he added, "Maybe Mrs. Llewellyn will let Deidre and me have one of those kittens when we're married and living in Slatestone Cottage. I'm sure there will be mice. There always are." He was right, for every cottage in the village was staffed by at least one tribe of mice, and possibly two. A cat was a prudent investment.

"You and Deirdre are getting married!" Tabitha exclaimed. *"Why, that's wonderful news, Jeremy! I'm delighted to hear it."* And she jumped into his lap and began to purr quite loudly, rubbing her face against his arm.

Jeremy chuckled and stroked her. "I guess it's time I thought about getting some tea. Mrs. Llewellyn will probably be home late, and I'm hungry."

At the mention of Mrs. Llewellyn, Tabitha stopped purring. *"I found something a minute ago,"* she said. *"I got up on the table to look out the window, and I saw something. I want you to have a look at it. Please."* And with that, she put out a claw and snagged his sleeve.

Jeremy disengaged the claw. "Silly old Tabitha," he said affectionately. "But now you must excuse me. I'm going to find something to eat."

"Not just yet," Tabitha insisted, and jumped

361

to the floor, planting herself firmly in front of him. *"It's over here, on the table in front of the window."*

Jeremy frowned. It looked as if the cat was trying to get his attention. What was this all about? Was she wanting to show him something? The next minute, she had leapt up on the small writing table that sat in front of the window. She put her paw on a piece of paper. *"This."* Her whiskers twitched briskly. *"Read this."*

Now, it must be admitted that our Tabitha is not much of a reader. Unlike Thackeray the guinea pig and Bailey the badger, she does not live in a library or spend her days and nights with her pretty nose in a book. However, she had been raised from kittenhood by Mrs. Abigail Tolliver, who lived in Anvil Cottage before Sarah Barwick came there. Mrs. Tolliver used to read aloud, and Tabitha loved to sit on her mistress' shoulder and follow the words on the page as Mrs. Tolliver said them. In this way, Tabitha had learnt to read printed words, although her vocabulary was limited to the words that occurred most often. She was especially expert in words like *the* and *and.* So whilst she had an idea of what might be written on this particular paper, she wasn't sure.

"Read this!" she commanded again, louder.

362

"And tell me what it says."

Jeremy frowned. "I don't read people's letters," he said. "That's against all the rules." But his glance strayed to the paper, just the same, because the cat was so insistent, and — now that he looked at it — this one was so odd. It was written in pencil, on a piece of plain paper that had one rough edge, as though it had been creased and torn from a larger piece of paper.

His eyes caught the first words. "What the devil?" he muttered. And then he did something he knew he should not do, should *never* do, in any circumstance.

He read it.

And then he sat dumbfounded, for he didn't know what to do.

20

IN WHICH WE LEARN MORE
ABOUT LETTERS

At Hill Top Farm, Beatrix sat at the table, her pen in her hand, the paper in front of her. She had been a writer all her life, beginning a journal when she was sixteen, writing letters almost every day of the week, crafting the stories in her little books. Words came easily to her, phrases popped unbidden into her mind, graceful, thoughtful phrases that usually flowed readily from her pen onto the paper without any need for revision.

But not today. Not this letter. She had already made several starts, scratching out words, even whole sentences, and once balling up an entire sheet and throwing it into the fire. It wasn't so much that she didn't know what she wanted to say — she had already decided that. The challenge was finding the right words, for she kept thinking of how her father would turn red and sputter and how her mother would wail and

364

take to her bed with smelling salts. And she knew very well what they would say when they wrote back to her, or to her face when she returned to London. That a country solicitor was as far beneath her as a book publisher had been, for she came from an illustrious family of "Bar and Bench." That marriage at her age was out of the question. And that marriage was out of the question in any event, for if she married and moved to the Lakes, who would look after them? The arguments, most of them, would be the same ones that they had raised when she and Norman became engaged — except now, they were older, and the prospect of her leaving would raise even greater fears.

But at last, after many false starts, Beatrix had crafted a letter that satisfied her. Slowly, thoughtfully, she read it out loud to herself. Then she reread it and scratched out a few words.

Dearest Papa and Mama,
Bertram has written to tell me that you have heard that I am engaged to be married, and that the news has ~~greatly~~ upset you. I am deeply sorry for that. I would not have wished it, as I'm sure you know. But now that you have been made aware of the situation, it is only right for me to tell

you all of it.

It is true that I am engaged to William Heelis. The event took place some while ago and the matter is now settled between us. As you know, Mr. Heelis is the solicitor who has arranged for my recent purchases of land and property, and is a well-known and widely respected person here in the Lakes. In fact, I think it is fair to say that there is no more respected person of the law in this whole region than he. Over the past several years, I have become acquainted with him both in the way of business and in a more personal way. We have learnt to value each other's opinions, interests, and experiences and have come to take a great deal of pleasure in each other's company. I am sorry that you have not yet met him, but ~~since you were so ill-disposed to my suggestion about this last summer, I'm afraid that it will have to wait.~~ I hope you will agree to meet him later this year.

Having said that Mr. Heelis and I are engaged, I must also assure you that our marriage is not imminent. No wedding has been planned, no living arrangements have been made, and we have not discussed a date by which we might think to marry. I am fully aware of your needs and

366

expectations, and you must know how completely I am devoted to your care. And if I have all the ordinary longings for a home of my own with the man with whom I wish to spend my life, I fully intend to fulfill my duty to you. I trust this will reassure you and somewhat ease the pain that this unexpected (and I am sure unwelcome) news has caused you.

I am writing this letter to let you know what has happened, what I feel, and what I intend. I wish not to discuss this matter when I return to London, but to consider it a settled thing, and to go on living quietly together. I promise to do all in my power to ensure your health and happiness. Please know that I am now, and shall always remain,

Yr. affectionate and dutiful daughter,
Beatrix

She then recopied the letter, omitting the lined-through words. She read it once more, then put it down and took up her pen again. This time, she wrote to her brother.

My dearest Bertram,
I am enclosing a letter that I hope you will read aloud to Mama and Papa at the earliest opportunity. It informs them that the

news they have heard is correct, and that
Mr. Heelis and I are engaged. I hope it will
also reassure them that I do not intend to
marry in the near future.

I am sorry that they heard this from
someone else, and that you find yourself
in the middle of such an unpleasantness.
But I think perhaps it is better that you are
there, and I am here. By the time I return,
they may have begun to accept the situation, at least so far as is possible. I mean
what I say: that I do not want to discuss
the matter but to consider it a settled thing.
(This is probably a vain hope, but it is my
hope, nonetheless.) Please do what you
can to help them come to terms, as far as
they are able, with my decision.

Yr. loving sister,

Beatrix

Feeling as triumphant as if she had just
signed her own emancipation declaration,
Beatrix folded both letters carefully, one
inside the other, and put them into an
envelope, which she addressed to Bertram,
at Number Two Bolton Gardens. The envelope would go into tomorrow's post and arrive the day after that. Even if her parents
wrote back immediately (as they probably
would, a long letter, full of angry

recriminations), it would take another day for their letter to arrive. It would be four days, most likely, before she heard. Four days before she had to deal with the problem again.

So for now, she would simply put the matter away on a dark shelf in the farthest corner of her mind, where she wouldn't stumble over it inadvertently, and fill the intervening hours and days with something pleasant — garden work, and a walk around the farm. She hoped Will would have time to come by, so she could tell him what she had done. He had been kind enough not to urge her to tell them, but he would certainly be pleased to have it out in the open at last. He would —

Her thoughts were interrupted by a light rap at the door. Her heart leapt. Had thinking of Will conjured him up? But when she opened it, she saw Jeremy Crosfield, standing outside in the darkness. At his heels was Grace Lythecoe's cat, Tabitha Twitchit.

"Oh, hello, Jeremy," she said, trying to keep the disappointment out of her voice.

"Do you have a moment, Miss Potter?" Jeremy asked soberly. "There's something I need to talk to you about."

"And there's something I need to say to *you*," Beatrix replied as he stepped inside.

Tabitha came with him. "I had a visit from Deirdre this afternoon. She tells me that you and she will be married in June. So I must say congratulations, my very dear boy. I am happy for you both."

That brought a wide smile to Jeremy's face. "Thank you. I know that we have some hard times ahead, but we care for each other and we're willing to work."

"Of course you are," Beatrix said, taking his coat. "And of course, you know that I hope very much that you won't neglect your art."

He brightened still more. "Oh, I won't, Miss Potter!" he exclaimed. "I won't!" And he told her about the sale of his painting of the Dark-red Helleborine.

"Why, Jeremy, that's wonderful!" Beatrix replied happily. "There are a great many rare plants and fungi tucked away among the rocks and fells, and all begging to be painted. The land is changing and they may not always be there. I know you will be busy with teaching and your new home, but I hope you will make time for your art."

But even as she said this, she found herself smiling ruefully. In years past, she had always made time for her art, finding it a great solace and an escape from the demands of her parents. But as time went on, she found more creative delight in the work she did on the farm than in the drawings for her little books. Indeed, if she were truthful with herself, she would have to say that it was becoming a chore to settle down to drawing fictional animals, although it was never a chore to pay attention to the real ones. And her publisher's calls for more books and more books had begun to weigh on her almost like a physical burden.

But Jeremy was just at the beginning of his artistic work, she reminded herself, while she had been drawing and painting for many years. It was right that he should make time to pursue his art, and it was good that he would have the support of a wife who had his interests at heart.

"Have you had your tea?" she asked as she hung his coat on the peg behind the door. "I have fresh bread and butter and some new-made cheese." When Jeremy said "yes, please" to the offer of bread, cheese, and tea, she went to pour a cup, and then thought of something else he would like. "Oh, and Mrs. Jennings has left a large apple pudding, made with our own Hill Top apples."

"That sounds wonderful," Jeremy said, smiling. "I usually have tea at the Llewellyns', but they're both out this evening." He sat down at the table, sober-faced again. "I'm afraid that I'm on a serious errand, though. I need to ask your advice about something. Something very important."

"Tea first," Beatrix counseled, thinking that perhaps he wanted to ask her about his upcoming marriage or his art. "Then we'll tackle your serious errand." She looked down at the cat. "And I suppose you would like something too, Tabitha."

"If you please, Miss Potter," Tabitha mewed politely, and happily bent to the saucer of milk that Beatrix put down.

A little later, Jeremy sat back with a sigh. "Thank you," he said, pushing his plate away. "That was a fine tea. Mrs. Jennings' cheese is outstanding."

"It's Kitchen's cheese, too," Beatrix said firmly. "The cheese can never be any better than the milk it begins with, no matter the talents of the cheesemaker."

"And Kitchen's milk is tip-top," Tabitha purred. *"I've sampled the milk of every cow in the village, and I know."*

Beatrix rested her forearms on the table. "Now, are you ready to tell me about your errand?"

"I wish I didn't have to," Jeremy said, shaking his head. "Really, Miss Potter, I don't know what to make of it."

"I do," Tabitha said, getting up from the hearth and pushing her face against Jeremy's ankle. *"I know exactly what to make of it. And so will Miss Potter, when you show it to her. Please do."*

"Make of what?" Beatrix asked curiously.

"This," Jeremy said, and pushed a piece of paper across the table to her. On the paper was written, in Jeremy's hand: "Dear Mrs. Lythecoe, If you don't cancel the wedding by next Monday, you will be very sorry."

Beatrix stared at it, a shiver of apprehension crossing her shoulders. "Where did you get this?" she asked.

"I copied it," Jeremy said. He bit his lip. "I know it was wrong to read the letter, but it was lying right out in plain sight on the table. I couldn't . . . I couldn't help seeing it."

"He couldn't help seeing it because I told him to look at it," Tabitha said proudly. *"He wouldn't be here showing it to you, if it weren't for me."*

"After I read it, I didn't know what to do," Jeremy confessed. "I shouldn't have read it — I know that. But once I had, I had to do something. I couldn't just go away and pretend I hadn't seen it, but I couldn't tear it up, either. So I copied it and left the original where I found it."

Beatrix took a deep breath. "And where was that, Jeremy?"

"At High Green Gate," Jeremy said miserably. "On the table in the Llewellyns' parlor."

The minute he said that, Beatrix understood. Everything fell into place.

"I see," she said softly. "I understand."

"Good," Tabitha said. *"I'd like a little credit, please."*

Jeremy was still staring at the paper. "Can you think of what should be done?" he asked at last.

"I believe so," Beatrix said. "And I'm very glad you've brought this to me, Jeremy. It was wise." She sighed, not wanting to think about what had to come next. "But it's too late this evening to do anything about it. I think you should go back to High Green Gate and pretend that nothing at all has happened. Can you do that?"

He nodded. "I can try, anyway."

"Meee-ow," Tabitha said.

"Good." Beatrix smiled. "And thank you, Jeremy, more than I can say. You've solved a very unhappy mystery that has been troubling Mrs. Lythecoe for some time."

"Me!" Tabitha cried petulantly. *"What about me? Don't I get any credit?"*

374

"I'm sorry about that," Jeremy said. "I'm glad I could help." He looked down at Tabitha, who was curling around his ankles. "We ought to thank Tabitha as well, though. If it hadn't been for her, I wouldn't have looked at the letter."

"Indeed." Miss Potter bent and stroked the cat. "Thank you, Tabitha."

"It's about time," Tabitha said tartly.

21
"A HALF-MAD WIZARD"

When the news of the Water Bird's crash got around the village (which of course it did, and quicker than a dog can wag its tail), everyone was delighted. It was human nature to be glad that the nuisance noise was gone. It was also human nature to speculate about how Mr. Baum had come to take such a tumble from the top of Oat Cake Crag, the night before his aeroplane fell out of the sky. And it was human nature — at least in the village of Near Sawrey — to talk about it, and talk, and talk, and talk.

So early the next afternoon, Bertha Stubbs put on her everyday blue hat with the purple ribbon and a heavy shawl and went up the hill to Tower Bank House, where she sat down for a cup of tea and a fresh-baked raisin scone with her friend, Elsa Grape, the Tower Bank cook-housekeeper. Bertha had heard about the aeroplane crash from her husband, Henry, who had heard about it from his cousin Tommy, who worked on the aeroplane. What's more, Tommy had told Henry that the engine failure occurred because water had got into the petrol barrel. Tommy thought he knew how that happened, but he wouldn't say.

"Dust Henry know who dunnit?" Elsa demanded. "If he does, he ought to tell Captain Woodcock."

"Henry says t' aeroplane hangar is on t' other side of t' lake and not in t' captain's district," Bertha replied. "Anyway, he says Tommy prob'ly done it hisself, an' he's tryin' to cast asparagus on sumbody else."

Elsa shook her head. "Aspersions," she said. "Cast aspersions on sumbody else." Bertha was known for her abuse of the English language.

Bertha sniffed, but rephrased. "Henry says Tommy prob'ly left t' lid off t' petrol barrel an' he's afeard he'll be incinerated."

Elsa looked alarmed. Then she sighed. "I think tha meant to say 'incriminated,' Bertha."

Bertha and Elsa were discussing the meaning of "incinerate" when Hannah Braithwaite dropped in. As the wife of the village constable, Hannah was a valued member of any group of gossipers, because she had a direct route, so to speak, to important village information and generally knew what was going on for miles around.

Hannah had plenty to tell today. Her avid listeners heard that Constable Braithwaite had had a long conversation with Paddy Pratt, Mr. Baum's odd-jobs man — his *former* odd-jobs man, that is, since Mr. Baum had discharged him and the rest of the Lakeshore Manor servants the previous week. Amongst the topics of discussion was a sack of tools taken from the manor barn and discovered by Constable Braithwaite behind a barrel in Paddy Pratt's shed. The tools bore a distinctive mark, identifying them as Lakeshore Manor tools. Paddy was due to explain himself to Captain Woodcock, the justice of the peace, that afternoon. However, as far as Mr. Baum's fall from Oat Cake Crag was concerned, Paddy claimed to have no knowledge of it, and the constable was inclined to believe him, since Paddy was far too fat and lazy to climb to the top of the crag.

Having delivered this news in a breathless sort of way, Hannah remembered that she had promised to drop in and see how Rose Sutton was coming along. Rose was expecting another baby ("Good heavens," said Elsa, "does that make *nine?* However will they all fit into Courier Cottage?") and would soon be losing Deirdre.

"Losin' Deirdre?" Bertha demanded. "Why, where's she goin'?"

"Why, dustna know?" Hannah asked. "Deirdre's marryin' Jeremy Crosfield in June and movin' to Slatestone Cottage. Mr. Braithwaite told me so this mornin'."

Hannah couldn't just drop this bit of tantalizing information into the conversation and then leave, so it was another ten minutes before she walked out the door — ten minutes filled with such ordinary gossip that it does not bear repeating here. When Hannah was gone, Bertha looked up at the clock and remarked that if she didn't go home and put the sausage and taties into the kettle straightaway, Henry wouldn't have any supper and she would be in for it (which isn't true, since it is Bertha who wears the pants in that family).

After Bertha and Hannah had both left, Elsa took off her flower-print apron and put on a thick knitted jumper and pulled a knit cap over her ears. She took up a basket and went through Sarah Barwick's back garden and across the lane to the village shop, which had been called Ginger and Pickles in Miss Potter's book by that name and by almost everybody in the village ever since. Lydia Dowling was happy to sell her a nice piece of lean bacon for thc Woodcocks' breakfast, a thrup'ny twist of tea, and a packet of needles. Both Lydia and her niece Gladys, who helped in the shop on alternate afternoons, were glad to listen (with appropriate exclamations of interest and curiosity) to Elsa's tale about the water in the aeroplane's petrol barrel, the stolen tools the constable had found in Paddy Pratt's shed, and the pending marriage of Deidre Malone and Jeremy Crosfield.

Not to be outdone, Lydia told Elsa that Mr. Baum had still not awakened ("t' poor man is lyin' mute as a stone an' stiff as a dried fish in Dimity Kittredge's guest bedroom") and that heaven only knew whether he would ever in this world awaken, and whether it could possibly be discovered just how he had come to tumble off the top of Oat Cake Crag.

Gladys broke in to confide that it was her personal opinion that Mr. Baum had been pushed off the crag, and the pusher had to be that pilot of his, that loud-mouthed braggart Oscar Wyatt, who was always after Mr. Baum for more money. She knew this for a fact because her friend Pearl (who worked as a chambermaid at the Sawrey Hotel) had heard from her friend Arnold (who worked as the hotel barman) that the two men had

had a jolly loud row ("Pearl says they nearly came to blows!") over drinks in the hotel bar. Mr. Baum said that he was pulling out as an investor in the aeroplane business, and Mr. Wyatt said he was very glad that Mr. Baum felt that way, because he (Mr. Wyatt) was sick and tired of hearing that there wasn't enough money for this or enough money for that and trying to do things the way Mr. Baum wanted them done, when that wasn't the right way at all. To which Mr. Baum replied, well, that was jolly good, because he was jolly sick and tired of having to shell out money and now Mr. Wyatt could do exactly as he jolly well pleased, which was to go to the devil, as far as *he* was concerned.

Lydia added that it was her personal opinion that the bad luck of the aeroplane crash and the worse luck of Mr. Baum's fall both taken together added up (in a manner of speaking) to a windfall of good luck for the village. Now, the aeroplane would surely go away. Everyone could enjoy the silence that the Good Lord had so generously bestowed upon the lakes and fells. The village children could get their naps and their poor mothers would finally get some peace. Happy days were here again.

Elsa and Gladys agreed. All three of them

were happily congratulating one another on the fact that they couldn't hear anything when they heard it. The loud buzzing of the aeroplane's engine, like a hive of demented bees in the garden.

"Oh, no," all three moaned in unhappy unison. And from the bedroom in the back came the disconsolate wail of Gladys' little baby.

The Water Bird was in the air again.

The aeroplane's remarkable recovery was due to the concerted efforts of two men — Anderson and the man called Tommy — who toiled through the night, rebuilding and repairing and replacing broken parts. When Oscar Wyatt came back to the hangar late the next morning, looking relaxed and chipper and ready for anything, the aeroplane's wing, tail, and engine had been repaired.

"I say, now, fellows," Wyatt proclaimed, walking around the aeroplane. "You've done excellent work. First-rate! The Bird looks jolly good. Good as new." He looked at Anderson. "And what went wrong with the engine? Did you figure out why it stopped?"

"We checked the petrol in the outside barrel," Anderson said, wiping his hands on a rag. "Sure enough — there was water in it. It's been replaced now, and the lid on the barrel's been secured." He glanced at Tommy, who ducked his head and shifted from one foot to the other.

Wyatt missed the glance. "Must've been sabotage, then," he muttered sourly. "I suppose it's one of those people around here who are always railing against progress. God knows, there're plenty of 'em. Like ostriches, they are. Got their heads in the sand, wishing they could turn the clock back a century or two. They're even trying to get Parliament involved. Fancy that!" He shook his head. "Well, they'll just have to get used to it. The Bird will be back in the air again. This is progress, men, progress." He thrust his fist into the air. "We're working on behalf of the national defense! Britain needs this aeroplane!"

"And what about Mr. Baum?" Tommy asked, changing the subject. "Any better, is he, Mr. Wyatt?"

Wyatt shrugged. "I called this morning at Raven Hall. Still wasn't allowed to see him." His voice took on a new resonance. "But you can put him out of your mind, boys. Baum or no Baum, we've got plenty of money to keep the Bird flying. It's firm now. I've found another investor. And this one has no problem putting up the money we need. This one is ready to go along with us, all the way."

"Well, now," Anderson drawled, "I think we ought to have a little talk." He put his hands on his hips. "Just who is this person, Mr. Wyatt? I'm asking you because Mr. Baum hired me and made me responsible for the maintenance on this machine. If somebody else is taking his place and will start giving me orders, I have a right to know who it is. And I want to know *now*."

Wyatt's eyes narrowed. "I told you before, Anderson. The person prefers to remain anonymous. However, I can tell you that this is a local individual who —"

Wyatt did not get a chance to finish whatever he had been about to say, because he was interrupted by a shout from the far end of the aeroplane hangar and the appearance of a small group of men. The gentleman in front (clearly a gentleman, from his light gray top hat to his gold watch fob to the polished tips of his black shoes) wore a black wool overcoat, carried a walking stick, and sucked on a huge brown cigar. The other three hung behind until a fifth man, wearing a natty white naval uniform strung with ribbons across his chest, stepped forward.

"I say there!" he shouted at Wyatt, Anderson, and Tommy. "Look sharp, men. The

First Lord of the Admiralty is here to inspect your aeroplane. The Right Honorable Winston Churchill!"

"Churchill!" Anderson exclaimed. He shot a look at Wyatt. "What the devil —"

"Oh, glory!" Wyatt breathed. "I'd no idea he was coming *today*." And he went forward to be introduced.

Well. It looks to me as if the Water Bird has been repaired in the nick of time, for Mr. Churchill, First Lord of the Admiralty, would have been greatly out of temper if he had ridden the railroad train all the way from London to see a crippled aeroplane. But thanks to the diligent overnight work of Anderson and Tommy, the Bird has been fully restored to her former glory and is ready to take to the air.

Mr. Churchill walked all the way around the aeroplane several times, alternately nodding, shaking his head, and scowling. Once he rapped on the wing with his stick, twice he rapped on the tail, and finally he kicked at the center float, all the while muttering to himself or tossing gruff staccato words over his shoulder to a man who walked three paces behind him, making rapid notes in a leather-bound book. Another man was taking photographs, first from one angle and then from another. Wyatt strongly objected to the camera, but the imperious Mr. Churchill brushed his objections aside as if they were flies.

After his third circumnavigation of the Water Bird, Churchill stopped, folded his hands on the head of his walking stick, and swept the aeroplane with his glance from one end to the other.

"Now, then, Mr. Wyatt," he growled, around his cigar, "shall we go up?"

Oscar Wyatt's eyes widened. "You . . . you want to . . . to fly, sir? In the Bird?"

Churchill took his cigar out of his mouth and fixed a stern glance on Wyatt. "I am not wearing wings, am I, Mr. Wyatt?"

Wyatt swallowed. "No, sir, but —"

Churchill pounded his stick on the dirt floor of the hangar. "Well, then, what the devil is the delay? I didn't come here to talk, by Jove. I came to see what your machine can do." He scowled. "Are you trying to tell me she's not in flying condition?"

"Oh, no, sir," Wyatt replied hurriedly. "She'll fly. Pretty as a picture she is in the air, sir. Graceful as a girl. Best little hydroplane you could ever wish for, sir."

"Well, dash it all, then," Churchill barked, "let's fly!"

And that, for the next several hours, was what Winston Churchill, Oscar Wyatt, and

the Water Bird did. They flew. They flew
north toward Ambleside and south toward
Newby Bridge, the Water Bird soaring far
above the waves without a hiccup or a
cough, Wyatt sitting in the pilot's seat, and
Churchill perched in the passenger's seat,
wearing goggles and an aviator's cap, with
his black overcoat billowing out behind him.
I think it is fair to say that he was enjoying
himself, for he thrust his stick into the air
and shouted with an undisguised gusto. He
looked for all the world (said Tommy later,
over a half-pint in the Bowness pub) "like a
half-mad wizard ridin' a bloody dragon."

When the Bird, her pilot, and her illustrious passenger were safely back in the hangar
at Cockshott Point, Mr. Churchill announced gruffly, "Mr. Wyatt, I commend
you. I do, sir. Your seaplane design is first-
rate. Greatly superior to anything we have
seen so far." He looked at his group. "Right,
gentlemen?"

"Right, Mr. Churchill," chorused the men
in unison.

"Right." Churchill turned back to Wyatt.
"Very good, then. I shall shortly send one
or two officers from the Admiralty to discuss
the details of transfer with you."

Wyatt looked blank. "The details of . . . of
what?"

"Why, the transfer of ownership, of course. I am commandeering this project for the purposes of the national defense. Its development and testing will continue under your supervision — for now. However, the site here is vulnerable, and we shall have to secure this aeroplane to protect it from hostile intelligence operations. The Admiralty will compensate the investors, of course." He paused, eyeing Wyatt. "What did you expect?"

Wyatt was entirely taken aback, for he had not thought any further than showing off the aeroplane and had not a clue to what might come after. He gulped. "Why, I expected — That is, I thought — I mean, I —" He sputtered to a stop. "Yessir."

"Excellent," Churchill snarled. "Expect my officers in the next few days. And in the meantime —"

He rapped the aeroplane's wing affectionately with his stick. "In the meantime, I am holding you personally responsible, Wyatt. Don't let anything happen to my Bird."

22
THE DRAGON AND THE OWL
HATCH A SCHEME

The three ladies in the village shop weren't the only ones to hear the hydroplane, like a hoard of angry hornets, buzzing up and down the lake. Miss Potter, cutting rhubarb stalks in her garden at Hill Top Farm, heard it and heaved a heavy sigh.

Out on the lake, Henry Stubbs, piloting the ferry with the Coniston coach and one black-and-white cow on board, heard it — and held his breath while the coachman clung to the bridles of his plunging horses and the cowman grabbed the horns of his terrified cow and hung on to keep her from leaping overboard.

In Bowness, a shopkeeper was so startled by the noise that he dropped an expensive crystal goblet and broke it. When he turned to get the broom, he knocked the matching crystal pitcher from the shelf.

In Ambleside, at the blacksmith's shop, the smith and his helper rushed out to see the plane, leaving a pile of wood shavings too near the forge. The shavings burst into flame and caught a horse blanket, which burnt a timber and then another and finally ended by bringing the roof down.

And down at Newby Bridge, a motorcyclist looked up to see the plane and was so distracted by the sight that he ran into the back of a wagon carrying a load of milk cans bound for the cheese factory, startling the draft horse so that it bolted and flung the wagon, cans and all, into the ditch.

None of these major and minor calamities, however, was visible from Oat Cake Crag, where the owl and the dragon were watching Water Bird as it skimmed up and down the lake with its pilot and its animated passenger. The owl was perched on the limb of a tree, whilst the dragon crouched beneath, disguised as a bush. The dragon had turned nearly purple with astonishment, for he had never before seen a flying object the size of Water Bird — except for other dragons, of course.

Now, the last time we saw the owl and the dragon together (at Bosworth's birthday party), the two of them appeared to be very confused. The dragon had inquired about the Windermere monster whose sighting had been reported by Bailey Badger's great-

great-grandfather. The owl replied with regard to the hydroplane. It was clear that each was laboring under a rather substantial misconception as to the meaning of the other.

But at last the dragon realized that the owl was describing some sort of motorized flying machine, like an oversized mechanical wind-up toy that was somehow capable of getting into the air, and the owl got it through his head that the dragon was looking for a water-dwelling monster, something on the order of an aquatic dragon.

Having sorted out their misunderstanding, the pair discussed the matter at length. They decided to go to Oat Cake Crag, take up a lookout position, and see what they could of the monster, the hydroplane, or both. The owl had packed a light lunch (mutton-and-cheese sandwiches with pickle, cold sliced tongue, deviled eggs with capers, carrot sticks, and frosted ginger cakes). In addition, he had worn his vest and daytime goggles and brought binoculars, a notebook, and a stopwatch. Thus equipped and provisioned, the owl and the dragon had just set up their post when the hangar doors swung wide open and Water Bird skidded down the ramp and splashed into the water.

The dragon watched, open-mouthed, as

the aeroplane wended its way through the moorings of sailboats and rowboats and fishing boats and took off upwind, climbing into the sky. *"Oh, my starsz and scaleszs,"* he hissed incredulously. *"It swimsz and it fliesz. It really doeszs."* He stared at the Bird out of the ragged fringe of fir branches he had tied to his head and shoulders. *"Doesz it dive? Under the water, I mean."*

"It did once, after a fashion," said the owl, watching the aeroplane through his binoculars as it whizzed up the lake in the direction of Ambleside. *"But that was when it stopped flying and crashed intooo the water. I dooo not believe that it dives deliberately. It does not seem tooo be constructed for that purpose."* He frowned, trying to focus on the passenger riding behind the pilot. The previous passenger had clung to the struts, bleating and terrified and repenting his desire to fly. This one, however, was almost demonic, shouting and waving his arms, with his greatcoat streaming behind like a magician's cape. He was obviously enjoying himself.

"And thiszs iszs the thing that haszs been terrorizszsing the neighborhood?" asked the dragon, studying the hydroplane from behind his screen branches. *"Thiszs iszs the*

creature who iszs annoying people and frightening animalszs?"

"This is it," the Professor replied grimly. "But people know what it is and can take account of it. The animals — particularly the not-sooo-bright ones, the cows and silly sheep — are terrified of it, and with gooood cause. They fear it is going tooo eat them, and nooo amount of talking will persuade them otherwise." He put down his binoculars and shook his head gloomily. "The machine is truly a monster," he added, "although not in the sense that you are looooking for."

"Perhapsz it iszsn't," the dragon said regretfully. "I would rather have discovered a dragon that waszs more like the Loch Nesszs monszster, swimming and diving and the rest of it. But I wonder if it won't serve my purposze just as well. And perhaps even better, considering its dire effect on the neighbors."

"Serve the purpose?" The owl looked down from his perch, beginning to feel a niggling sense of suspicion. "Just what purpose dooo you have in mind, Thorvaald?"

Thorvaald shuffled his feet, looking a bit shamefaced. "Well, to tell the truth, I am looking for a way to redeem myszself with the Grand Asszsembly of Dragonsz." He gave a windy sigh, exhaling a stream of smoke and

393

live flame, which sparked a nearby fir branch.

"Don't dooo that!" the owl cried urgently. *"Are you trying tooo start a forest fire?"*

"Szsorry," the dragon muttered, and inhaled, pulling the smoke and flame back into his nostrils, as if he were a vacuum sweeper. *"I am not exactly in the Asszsembly'szs favor, you see. In fact, I shouldn't be at all surpriszsed if they revoked my airworthinesszs certificate and put me to work in the dining hall instead. I flew all around the globe on the Asszsembly expense account. I waszs supposed to be counting dragonszs, but I couldn't find any to count. This thing, though —"*

The Water Bird had made a large loop and was now flying south again, sweeping over Belle Isle and turning eastward in front of them, preparing to make a landing. The engine was buzzing so loudly that the dragon had to raise his voice to be heard above the racket. *"Thiszs flying thing — this mechanical dragon — it isn't just a law-abiding monszster minding its own busineszs in the depths of a very deep lake, where it's a threat to nobody but a few large pike. In fact, this creature is much more dangerouszs. It threatens the lives and happiness of creatures all acroszss this region. Isn't that what you're telling me, Professor?"*

"Indeed," said the owl soberly. He was now beginning to get the picture. *"That's what I'm telling yoooou, Thorvaald. But I don't see that there's anything you can dooo to stop it."*

"Oh, really?" the dragon remarked in a carelessly contemptuous tone. *"I don't suppose you know very much about dragonszs, do you? I am descended from a long and illustriouszs line of warriorszs."* He lifted himself up and his voice rang out. *"I am the son of the magnificent Thunnor, son of the splendid Snurrt, son of the celebrated Sniggle. Our family motto is* Alta pete: *Aim at high thingszs. Our family emblem is two dragonszs rampant on an azure field, with a burning —"*

"Of course, of course," said the owl crossly. He was not accustomed to being addressed in such a tone, and he did not like being reminded that he was the only one amongst his friends who did not have a family motto and emblem. *"But I still say that there's nothing yoooou can dooo. The aeroplane is locked up at night, and there's a guard. Yoooou can't just break in there and expect tooo —"*

"Aim at high things!" cried the dragon in great excitement. His belly was glowing like a hot stove, and sparks flew from his nostrils. *"Don't you see, Owl? It's deszstiny, that's what*

it iszs! I am the one ordained to bring this high-flying monszster to justice and szsave the Land Between the Lakeszs. Aim at high thingszs!"

The owl (who prided himself on aiming at high things with his telescope and felt himself to be much more experienced in such matters than the dragon) gave a derisive snort.

"What?" fumed the dragon. Tendrils of sooty smoke curled out of his nostrils. *"You don't believe me?"*

"I will believe yooou," the owl replied in a lofty tone, *"when I see you actually doooing it."* He paused, frowning. *"Just what are you planning on doooing?"*

"Don't rush me," the dragon said. *"I'm hatching a scheme."* He cast a hopeful look at the owl. *"I wonder — are there any more sandwicheszs?"*

23
MISS POTTER, MR. HEELIS,
AND THE LETTERS

The morning after Jeremy gave her the letter he had copied, Miss Potter sent a note to Mr. Heelis by the early post. By teatime that afternoon, after the aeroplane had finally stopped flying for the day, Will knocked at her door. She was (as I'm sure you can guess) very glad to see him.

I hope you won't object if we step away for a moment to give them a little privacy. Every moment together is precious to them, and onlookers are . . . well, we would just get in the way. So we'll go into the little downstairs parlor, which Beatrix has set out as a small drawing room, with an imposing marble Adam-style chimneypiece, pine-paneled walls, rich mahogany furnishings, and an Oriental-style rug. But we won't be bored. We can spend a few moments studying the silhouettes hanging beside the fireplace; and the Edward VII coronation teapot, in the corner cupboard with the pink crown lid and the colored pictures of Edward and Alexandra; and the Potter coat of arms that hangs to the left of the window. And an Italian red lacquer box on a rosewood worktable and —

And shortly, Will is seated at Beatrix's table with a fresh cup of tea at his elbow and a piece of Mrs. Jennings' rhubarb pie in front of him, and it is safe for us to return.

"So," he said, picking up his fork. "Your note said that you've discovered the identity of the poisoned pen."

"Yes, with the help of Jeremy Crosfield," Beatrix replied. She sat down opposite and told him the whole story, just as she had it from Jeremy, then showed him the copied note. "Agnes Llewellyn is the only person who could've written this," she concluded. "Jeremy found the original letter on the table in her parlor. Her husband, Dick, went to Carlisle some time ago to visit his ailing father, and there's been no one in the house except for Agnes and Jeremy."

Will looked again at the note and shook his head. "It's hard to believe that Agnes Llewellyn would do such a thing. She doesn't strike me as a very happy woman, but — But why, Beatrix? Why would she want to spoil Grace and the vicar's happiness?"

"She's Hazel Thompson's cousin," Beatrix said.

"Hazel Thompson?" Will asked blankly.

"The vicar's cook-housekeeper," Beatrix replied. "Perhaps you've met her, when you were having dinner at the vicarage."

Will thought. "Ah. I remember that she once served a roast lamb that —" He made a face. "But it's best to let bygones be bygones. So you're guessing that Agnes Llewellyn must have expected Mrs. Lythecoe to discharge Mrs. Thompson and bring in her own cook." He smiled crookedly. "Probably not a bad idea, come to think of it. The vicar was terribly embarrassed by that roast lamb, as I recall. And he's complained about Mrs. Thompson listening at doors."

"Yes," Beatrix said. "I think that Agnes Llewellyn wanted to derail the marriage, hoping that might save her cousin's employment."

"It all seems very illogical to me," Will muttered.

"It *is* illogical, entirely," Beatrix replied. "But that's the point, of course. Logic goes out the window when passions run high. And Agnes Llewellyn must have felt passionately that her cousin ought to stay at the vicarage." She paused. "The irony of this is that Mrs. Thompson is planning on handing in her resignation."

"She is?" Will asked in some surprise.

"I spoke to her yesterday. She told me that she had just made up her mind to go to Ambleside to take care of her mother. Once Grace and the vicar are safely married, they will be free to employ whomever they choose." Beatrix paused, glancing at Will. "But now that we know who wrote the letters, Will, what do you think should be done?"

Will chuckled. "I think I know what *you* think should be done, my dear."

She had to smile at that. "Ah. You know me so well that you can read my mind?"

"Rather," he said, and chuckled. "I imagine I'm going to have a talk with Mrs. Llewellyn."

She sobered. "Would you mind, Will? I would be glad to do it, but Agnes Llewellyn will be much more likely to listen to a man than to a woman — and to a man of the law, rather than a neighbor. You can put on your stern solicitor's face and frown your darkest solicitor's frown, and tell her that if Mrs. Lythecoe ever receives another of those 'anonymous' letters, it will go very badly for her."

He smiled affectionately. "Perhaps I

should threaten to haul her before the justice of the peace and get Woodcock to read her the riot act before he turns her loose? And what about the vicar? What should we tell him?"

"I don't believe that having the captain lecture Agnes would accomplish anything useful. But I do think she should be required to beg Mrs. Lythecoe's pardon. Poor Grace has been beside herself these last few weeks, worrying about this business — she deserves to hear Agnes say she's sorry. We can leave the vicar out of it, at least for the moment, since Grace doesn't want him to know. And I don't think it would be well to mention Jeremy, either."

Will nodded. "A wise course of action, my dear. I will go to see Mrs. Llewellyn, and then escort her across the way to Rose Cottage to apologize to Mrs. Lythecoe. It won't be enjoyable, but I'm sure that Mrs. Lythecoe will be glad that the mystery of the letters has been solved."

"Thank you," Beatrix said gratefully. "And now I've something to tell you, Will. I've written my own letter, of a very different sort."

He raised an eyebrow. "Really? What sort?"

She opened the drawer of the table and

took out a piece of paper. "This is a copy of what I wrote to my parents." She laughed ruefully. "Poor Bertram. I can just imagine the scene he will be forced to witness. I'm sure it will not be very pleasant." She pushed the letter across the table and watched his face while he read.

When he was finished, he looked up. The lines of his face had softened, and he was smiling. He stood, went around the table, and kissed her cheek softly. "Thank you, my love," he whispered. He sat down again. "How did they find out?"

"Bertram said that a Mr. Morrow, a solicitor from Hawkshead, told them. Do you know the man?"

"I do," Will said with a sigh. "Morrow's had dealings recently with our law firm. I took the liberty of telling my partner about our engagement a few weeks ago. I'm sure that's how Morrow learned about it." He looked repentant. "I'm sorry, Beatrix. I shouldn't have said anything to anyone."

"I'm not," Beatrix said firmly. "I'm not one bit sorry, Will. Once I got through the difficulty of actually putting the words on the paper, I felt very good about it. It's right that Mama and Papa know, and it was high time that I told them. Secrets are a terrible burden. I was very tired of keeping this one to myself."

Will's face lightened and he reached for her hand. "What a joy it is to hear you say that, my dear." He picked up her hand and kissed it. "My own very dear."

I don't know about you, but I do not especially care to witness Agnes Llewellyn's guilty embarrassment when she learns that her secret has been discovered (Will was able to avoid mentioning Jeremy's role in the matter), and I don't really want to watch her squirm like a beetle on a pin when Mr. Heelis lectures her in his sternest solicitor's manner, or look on as she apologizes, abjectly, to Mrs. Lythecoe (who accepts her apology with graciousness and a great deal of relief). Suffice it to say that when the discovery of her guilt was presented to her by Mr. Heelis, Agnes immediately saw the error of her ways and promised that she would never again do anything so foolish.

So I think we can bring this chapter to a close and with it one of the plots of this book, with special thanks to Jeremy Crosfield, our very own Miss Potter, and her dear Mr. Heelis for solving the mystery of the poisoned pen letters.

Excuse me. I'm sorry — what's that?

Oh. Oh, yes. How could I forget?

And Tabitha Twitchit, too, of course.

24
THE STORM

It was a dark and stormy night.

The dark was the usual sort of dark, only darker and deeper, since the moon and the stars were completely covered with an ominous blanket of storm cloud. The storm, however, was rather stormier than usual, even for March, for it was carried along by a tempestuous north wind. The storm began swirling somewhere in the lap of Lapland, and was then swept south by the wind across the Arctic Circle and Sweden and Norway and the icy North Sea, happily howling and shrieking as it passed over the Orkney Isles and danced down the mountainous spine of Scotland's highlands. The storm was enjoying itself so thoroughly that it didn't feel like stopping at the border (what storm ever does?), but whistled across the western fells and the Pennines and skipped into Wales and on across the Lizard and into the Channel, where it blew itself out before it got to France. It snowed in some places, sleeted in others, and rained in the rest, everywhere hurling lightning bolts as carelessly as a boy throws darts and scattering thunder claps in its noisy wake. Yes, indeed, from the northernmost, rockiest tip of Scotland to the southernmost cities of Falmouth and Dartmouth, it was truly a dark and stormy night.

In the Land Between the Lakes, the little villages of Near and Far Sawrey sat squarely in the storm's path. There, the houses turned their backs against the roguish, high-spirited north wind and huddled as close together as they could get without stepping into the next-door gardens, whilst the barns and sheds locked their doors and shut their windows tight and held on as best they might to the slates and shingles on their roofs.

Inside the barns, the cows and horses and pigs were grateful for the steamy warmth of their friends' and neighbors' bodies. As it always does, the devilish wind wanted to get in where she shouldn't, so she knocked at the door and rattled the window sash, whilst Mesdames Boots, Bonnet, and Shawl pressed close together on their roost, convinced that the wind was going to get inside and pluck out their pretty feathers. Meanwhile, the ducks snuggled the younger ducklings under their wings, quacking and clucking in a comforting way about the other just-as-stormy nights they had managed to live through, just as they would live through this one, too, you wait and see if we don't.

Outside the barns, in the gardens and on the hills around the village, the grass and trees and shrubs had no choice but to yield to the unruly wind as it lashed them from side to side, but they clung fast to the earth and felt very grateful for the roots that pushed down deep and held them in their proper places. This wasn't true for limbs and branches, though, and the trees found that they couldn't hold on to all of them and might as well let the wind have the ones they were no longer quite so attached to. On the distant fells, the ewes sought refuge behind low stone walls, where they sheltered their little lambs from the boisterous, blustery gale, whilst in the rookeries, the rooks clung to tossing branches and wished that the wind would get tired of whipping them around and go somewhere else to play her rowdy games.

Out on Lake Windermere, the storm was having even more fun, for the waves had joined forces with the wind with such a lively, playful rough-and-tumble of foam and froth that you could not tell which was wind and which was wave. Indeed, the lake was having a jolly old time of it, the water sloshing about and the waves dancing gaily from the north to the south, working themselves up into higher and higher crests as they went, so that by the time they reached Newby Bridge, they were as wildly frothy and foamy as they had ever been in the whole life of the lake, which (it must be said) is a very long life indeed. And then they tried to crowd all at once into the narrow mouth of the River Leven, so that there was a grand and glorious and gleeful melee of wild waves, just as there is at a football match when the home side has won and the people all begin to push toward the exits, shoving and shouting happily.

Speaking for myself, I should be quite happy, on such a tumultuous night, to be indoors and out of the wind — beside Miss Potter's glowing hearth at Hill Top Farm, for instance, or in the library at The Brockery, listening to Hyacinth read aloud to Bosworth from the *History,* with a nice glass of elderberry wine at my elbow and a plate of Parsley's tea biscuits on the table.

But that is not where our story takes us. We are going out into the storm on an adventure, so I must ask you to put on your mackintosh and rubbers. I'm afraid an umbrella would do you no good — the wind would have it inside out in an instant, for she loves to flip umbrellas nearly as much as she loves to twist the limbs off trees. However, if you have a rain hat that ties on securely, do bring that, and a muffler might be nice, for the wind likes to go down necks, as well. Of course, you may choose to stay indoors by your own fireside and read about this adventure, but you are likely to miss a great part of the fun of what is about to happen. Wouldn't you rather *be* there?

So. One way or another, we are going up to the top of Oat Cake Crag, where we will join two of our friends: Thorvaald the dragon and Professor Galileo Newton Owl. It is much too stormy for anyone (besides us, that is) to be out looking for dragons, and even if they were, it is very dark, so Thorvaald does not have to disguise himself as a bush. He is sitting on his haunches, studying the opposite side of the lake through the owl's binoculars, whilst the owl hunkers down close beside him, in the shelter of one of his dragon wings. There is no moon, for the storm has blanketed the whole sky with billowing black clouds, but on the other side of the lake, the dragon can see a pinprick of light near the airplane hangar. It bobs around the hangar, disappearing when it goes behind, then reappearing shortly after.

The dragon lowered the binoculars. *"There's a guard. It appears that he is patrolling the aeroplane hangar. He's going around and around is the way it looks."*

"Of course there's a guard," the owl said crossly. *"I told yooou as much. Yooou won't be able to get inside, if that's your plan."*

The dragon sighed. *"I'm afraid I don't really have a plan. Not yet, anyway."*

"Excuse me?" cried the owl, pushing out from under the dragon's sheltering wing. *"If yooou don't have a plan, what are we doooing out here? It is wet and cold and excessively windy. My feathers are about tooo be blown right off my back. If yooou are just going tooo sit on this crag and stare across the lake through those binoculars, I'm going tooo fly back tooo my beech tree and see what there is in the larder."*

"Go right ahead," the dragon said. *"Nobody'szs keeping you. Anyway, I don't know what you're making such a fusszs about. It's a perfectly pleasant evening, if a bit windy."* Of course, it is easy for the dragon to talk. He has a built-in belly-fire to keep himself warm, and his wings and scales are

an impervious cloak against the rain and wind. Sitting on this exposed point, buffeted by the wind and rain, Thorvaald is just as comfy and toasty as if he were basking beside the Briar Bank fire.

The owl seriously considered leaving, for he had (if he remembered correctly) a bit of leftover *Vole à la Chateaubriand* on his shelf. But somehow he felt that he had an investment in whatever sort of scheme the dragon was hatching. He gritted his beak and muttered, *"I'll wait. But don't be toooo long about it."*

"I'll try," said the dragon. He began to hum softly and in a minor key, an odd little melody that coiled and curled around his head like a wisp of smoke until the wind heard it, liked it, and made off with it. After a little while he said, *"I think I have it."*

"Have what?" asked the owl.

"Have a plan. Would you like to ride along?"

The owl was alarmed. *"Ride?"*

"Well, yeszs. Unlesszs you want to fly, that is."

"Fly where?"

The dragon pointed across the lake. *"Why, over there, of course."*

"Over . . . there?" The owl gulped. *"Tonight?"*

Now, the lake at this point — at the foot

of Oat Cake Crag — is less than five miles wide. But the wind was wild and growing wilder, and the owl (while he is certainly large as tawny owls go) was understandably nervous about venturing too far from shore on such a night. Out there, in the unprotected middle of the longest lake in England, the wind could toss him around as easily as if he were a hummingbird or a dragonfly. He was a very brave owl — but not that brave.

"That'szs why I'm offering you a ride," said the dragon in a kindly tone. *"I suggest that you climb aboard and hang on to my neck, and we'll fly acrosszs the lake. It'szs not at all difficult for me, for I am heavy and air-worthy enough to resist being tumbled about by that frisky wind. But I should think it would be a bit breathtaking for you, if you attempted to wing it on your own."*

Frisky was not the word the owl would have chosen to describe the wind. *"But why are we going ooover there?"* he asked, rather desperately. *"What in the world dooo yooou think yoooou can dooo?"*

"Why, deszstroy the aeroplane, of course," said the dragon. *"It iszs an ill wind that blowszs nobody any good."*

The owl was taken aback. *"Destroy the —*

411

But how? The Bird is very large, you know, much larger than yooou are." (The Professor was quite right to say this, for our dragon is only twelve or thirteen centuries old and not very large, as dragons go.) *"The aeroplane is also quite heavy, and anyway, it's probably chained down, so you can't possibly lift it. And if you break intooo the hangar and try tooo damage the plane, I'm sure the guard will stop you. He probably has a gun, not tooo mention —"*

"If you're coming," the dragon interrupted impatiently, *"please climb aboard. I'm ready to take off."* To demonstrate how ready he was, he lifted his wings and puffed smoke out of his nostrils.

The owl was in a quandary. He much preferred to return to his beech tree. But as the senior owl in the district, he had a responsibility to the animals who lived there. If the dragon thought he could rid them of Water Bird, he felt obliged to go along and help. If the dragon couldn't, if he failed — well, somebody ought to be there to document the debacle. And to tell the truth, the owl was becoming rather fond of Thorvaald, who, in spite of his impulsive and somewhat thoughtless nature, was a likable beast. He would be sorry if something happened to Thorvaald and nobody was around to notice.

"All right," the owl replied bravely, although a voice within him (the voice of the not-so-brave owl) was crying, *"This is a terrible mistake!"* Summoning all his courage, he clambered onto the dragon's shoulder, dug in his claws, and threw his wings around the dragon's neck.

"Hang on," said the dragon. With a hiss of live steam, the dragon (don't ask me how he did this, for it is a trade secret known only to dragons) lifted himself off the flat rocky top of the crag and straight up into the air. Once they were airborne, he began to flap his leathery wings. They were off.

The dragon was heavy and airworthy, as he said, but it was clear from the beginning that this was not going to be an ordinary flight. When the wind discovered that some-one other than her wild and willful self was out and about in the sky that blustery night, she took it as a personal affront and at-tacked, from all sides at once, and above and below. She hissed and screeched and wailed at the dragon and his passenger, churning the clouds and the water in the most astonishing tumult. She pushed and shoved and clawed and buffeted the fliers and bellowed in their ears, lobbing lightning bolts all around and dropping great thuds of thunder directly in their path. The dragon flew on as steadily as he could, although even he had considerable difficulty maintaining his course through the mushrooms of updrafts and downdrafts the wind planted in front of him. By the time they got to mid-lake, the owl was feeling airsick and giddy (it's one thing to fly, and another to be flown), as well as terribly frightened. He wished mightily that he had obeyed his first instinct and flown home to the comfort and safety of his beech tree, or that at the very least he had insisted on a parachute or water wings.

But there was no going back now, for back was farther away than forward, and anyway, the dragon was clearly concentrating on getting to the other side of the lake. So he squeezed his owl-eyes tight, clamped his beak shut, and hung on as hard as he could until at last they reached the other side of the lake and the dragon landed with a bump on the shingly shore next to the Water Bird's hangar.

The minute the dragon set foot on earth, the owl opened his eyes, flew into the nearest tree, and shut his eyes again. He stayed there, breathing heavily, clutching his branch, and wondering if he was actually going to be sick. By the time he decided he

414

wasn't and ventured to open his eyes, the dragon had already gone to work.

Thorvaald was glad to see that the guard who had been patrolling the building had taken his lantern and sought shelter indoors, probably thinking that no self-respecting thief or vandal would be out on such a wild night. He flew twice around the aeroplane hangar, studying the construction of the roof and thinking that this wasn't going to be as easy as he had hoped. In fact, now that he was here, he wasn't sure he could do what he had come to do — and if he could, whether it would work out the way he hoped. But there was nothing to do except try.

He flapped his wings and flew high into the air, then headed about a half-mile north, upwind of the hangar. He turned and hovered for a moment or two, judging the strength of the gale at his back and inviting the wind to give him some help. She considered this, decided it might be an amusing game to try, and gave him an extra hard blast. When it came, he rode it as a boat might ride a cresting wave, skidding downward on the wild rush of air. As he reached the edge of the roof, he snatched it with his talons and peeled it off, just as you might peel the hat off your head. The entire roof came off in one piece. The dragon carried it a little distance, then released it. Freed to take off on its own, it sailed across Cockshott Point like a huge sheet of cardboard, turning and tumbling, until it crashed into the ferry's loading dock and splintered into a thousand pieces.

Having unzipped the roof, so to speak, all the dragon had to do was turn and watch, and the wind did the rest. Peering down into the roofless hangar, she saw to her enormous delight that someone had left a light, flimsy aeroplane, which struck her as the perfect toy. She picked it up and turned it over curiously once or twice to see how it worked and what it was made of. Then, because she thought it might make an interesting kite, she tossed it into the air. The Bird didn't stay up long, of course. When it landed hard on the shingle, it was upside down, one wing was broken off, the tail had splintered, the propeller was smashed, and the center float had split open like a pea pod.

When she saw that her new toy had broken into bits, the wind was so annoyed that she blew in all four walls of the hangar, one after the other. Luckily, the guard had taken shelter under a sturdy table when the dragon peeled the roof off. He crawled out of the wreckage of the hangar, very shaken up but without injury. Nobody would ever believe him, of course, if he said that he had seen a small green dragon with leathery wings peel the roof off, just before the wind picked up the Water Bird and began tossing it around. He didn't believe it, either, and went off to the nearest pub for a stiff one.

The wind, who as you know is entirely amoral and has no conscience or any sense of consequence, found a great many toys to play with in the neighborhood of Cockshott Point that night. She blew down the Presbyterian Church steeple in Bowness, snatched the roof off a stable and the school in the town of Windermere, turned over several wagons at the lumber mill, and shoved the ferry onto its loading ramp, seriously damaging the hull. Farther afield, she pulled up any number of trees, flooded fields, and set a house and a haystack afire with lightning bolts. Altogether, she had a very entertaining evening for herself, and when she finally got tired and went home, she could think back on her games with a great deal of pleasure.

As for the dragon and the owl, they waited until the wind left and then flew back across the lake. The owl went straight to the drinks pantry in his beech tree and poured himself a double shot of elderberry wine. The dragon flew on to Briar Bank, where he crawled under the covers of his bed and slept for a whole twelve hours before he woke up, to find that Bailey and Thackeray were having bacon and eggs (borrowed from Mrs. Crook's chickens) for lunch, along with fresh-baked bread, butter, and strawberry jam. Thorvaald had second helpings of everything.

25

IN WHICH WE TIE UP ALL THE LOOSE ENDS — BUT ONE

The days after the storm were filled, as you might expect, with plenty of work for everyone, as people in the Land Between the Lakes repaired the shingles and slates on their houses and barns and sheds, picked up the broken branches, sawed the fallen trees into firewood, swept up the flood debris, and got things back to normal again.

But there was to be no return to normal for the Water Bird, which was damaged beyond repair. Oscar Wyatt went to his new investor to ask for money to rebuild it, but she turned him down flat. She? Yes, indeed. The investor who had taken Mr. Baum's place, believe it or not, was Lady Longford. It was one thing, she said, to invest in a going project that had every chance of success. It was quite another to invest in an aeroplane that had to be rebuilt after every storm.

If you're surprised to learn that it was

Lady Longford who promised money for the hydroplane — in spite of the way all the villagers felt about it — perhaps you might recall some of her earlier actions. When she heard that Miss Potter wanted to buy Castle Farm, she tried to buy it first, and it was only with Mr. Heelis' help that Miss Potter was able to get it. It was also Lady Longford who insisted on closing the footpath across Applebeck Orchard, which caused the villagers no end of grief before it was reopened. So even though she sometimes changes her mind and makes things right again, her ladyship's first impulse is always to cause somebody some sort of trouble.

With Lady Longford out of the picture and Mr. Baum no longer able to provide funds, nothing more was heard about the hydroplane for some time. This did not make Winston Churchill happy, of course, but the First Lord of the Admiralty had other fish to fry and other aeroplanes to look at, and before long he had found one that he liked even better than the Bird. He did not, however, end his association with Oscar Wyatt, who was assigned to teach him to fly. Churchill's wife, Clementine, was much alarmed about this and tried to make him stop. He refused. She prevailed, however, when his teacher flew an aeroplane into the ground and killed himself, which was the end of Oscar Wyatt.

The destruction of the Water Bird might have been mourned by the men who were directly involved with it, but it was a great cause for rejoicing among the denizens of the Land Between the Lakes. They could now do their work with the great silence of the moors and fells ringing in their ears, and with nothing but the soft bleating of sheep and the sweet calls of the birds to keep them company. The men of the village could stop plotting ways to destroy the enterprise, Miss Potter could work in her garden without irritation, Henry Stubbs could pilot his newly-repaired ferry without fear of frightened animals causing the ramshackle boat to turn turtle, and the birds, sheep, badgers, and owls could go about their business without fear of being eaten by a large mechanical monster.

Other people went back to their business, too. Caroline Longford said goodbye to her grandmother and returned to her classes at the Royal Academy, where she continued to excel. Of course, her young heart was broken, for she truly loved Jeremy, or thought she did, which (as Jeremy says) amounts to the same thing. But Caroline was not quite ready to love anybody but herself, and needed a few more years of growing up before she began to think seriously of a husband and children, since these require that a wife and mother allow them to be real people and not just figments of her rich imagination.

Mrs. Lythecoe went forward with her wedding plans with a much happier heart, now that she knew that there wouldn't be any more ugly letters put through her mail slot. She could also look forward to saying a cordial goodbye to "dear, dear Mrs. Thompson," who had served Vicar Sackett so long and faithfully and who was going home to care for her mother. She even began to think that it might be nice to give Mrs. Thompson a proper farewell tea — as long as Mrs. Belcher baked the scones.

Jeremy and Deirdre were going forward with their wedding plans, too, although poor Mrs. Sutton had already begun to be sorry that she allowed Deirdre to marry. Who was going to help her care for the ninth little Sutton, who was going to make his or her appearance at about the time Deirdre moved into Slatestone Cottage? However, everyone in the village wished the young people all the happiness in the world, not least because they all agreed that Jeremy was the very best teacher that Sawrey

School had ever had and they hoped he would stay in that position forever.

And eventually, even poor Mr. Baum recovered from his injuries. One morning he woke up and demanded coffee and *The Times,* just as Dr. Butters had said. The next day he was sitting up in a chair beside his bed, with his broken leg propped on a cushion. As soon as he could, he returned to Lakeshore Manor, with one of Dimity's housemaids to cook for him and make him comfortable. He couldn't afford any more than that, for he had invested almost all of his fortune in the aeroplane and wasn't going to get a shilling out of it. In my opinion, he was the biggest loser of the lot, although he rather asked for it, allowing Oscar Wyatt to talk him into putting all his money into an aeroplane.

As to how Mr. Baum came to tumble down from the top of Oat Cake Crag, the answer was exceedingly simple. He had gone up there to spy on the aeroplane hangar on the other side of the lake. He dropped his telescope, tried to retrieve it before it went over the edge, missed his footing, and fell. There had been no foul play, and no one else — not Oscar Wyatt nor Paddy Pratt nor any other person — had been there with him. The fall that had nearly killed him was entirely accidental.

It was a good thing that the dragon did not aspire to fame and fortune in return for destroying the Water Bird, for he didn't get either. He had done the daring deed at night, in the middle of a tremendous storm, and no one knew that he was responsible. None of the Big Folk, that is. The animals knew about it, though. They learned about it from the Professor, who was only too glad to tell the tale to anyone who would listen — emphasizing, of course, his own role in the night's events and embroidering them just a little. Bosworth Badger wrote the whole story down in the *History,* and it came to be a favorite tale for telling around The Brockery fire and at Briar Bank on a chilly winter's night.

In fact, the owl was so inspired by his participation in the adventure that he decided to use it as the basis for his own motto and emblem, which (as perhaps you will remember) had been suggested to him by Bosworth and Parsley. The Professor rather liked the dragon's family motto, *Alta pete* (Aim at high things), but since that one was taken, he searched through dictionaries and old documents and found another he liked just as much: *Alis aspicit astra,* "Flying, he looks to the stars." Since the owl was both learned in astronomical studies and a superb flier, it seemed to him to fit perfectly. For his emblem, he took his friends' advice: an owl on a branch, a scroll in one claw, a telescope in the other, and a laurel wreath on his head, with the moon, a few stars, and a dragon — yes, a dragon — in the background. He asked Fritz to paint it for him in rich shades of red, blue, and gold, and when it was done, he mounted it proudly above his door.

But the dragon did earn something very important from his night's heroic efforts. He had Bosworth copy the passage recorded in the *History* and took it with him when he flew to the next meeting of the Grand Assembly of Dragons. When it came time for him to make his report, he simply submitted the paragraphs from the *History,* signed and accompanied by a certificate of authenticity by Bosworth. The Clerk of Dragons read the paragraphs aloud to the Assembly, who listened, spellbound, to the entire account. When it was concluded, the Grandest Dragon arose and pronounced that Thorvaald the Remarkable, son of the magnificent Thunnor, son of the splendid Snurrt, son of the celebrated Sniggle, had now been released from his assignment to the census and promoted to second lieutenant in the Dragon Corp.

Which leaves Beatrix, Will, and the Potters, doesn't it?

I don't suppose it will come as any surprise that the letter that Beatrix received from her parents was scorching. But since it said all the things that the Potters had been saying for quite a few years, it was all old news to Beatrix. While she didn't exactly dismiss their objections, she and Will read every sentence aloud together, laughing a little at the vehemence, which really sounded rather silly.

And then they kissed and promised each other not to be dispirited by her parents' opposition, but to love each other and be faithful and true, and live patiently apart until the day when they could at last live together, happily ever after.

HISTORICAL NOTE

The tale of the hydroplane on Lake Windermere in 1911–1912 is a true one, although I have fictionalized certain details — including the dragon. For the curious, here is the true story of Beatrix Potter and the Water Bird.

The Water Bird, which some have called "Britain's first seaplane," began its life in Manchester, England, where it was built as a land plane. It was first flown in July 1911, and was then moved to Lake Windermere, to a hangar on Cockshott Point, where a float and airbags were substituted for the wheeled undercarriage. It made its inaugural seaplane flight on November 25, 1911, and after that, made an astonishing 60 flights on 38 days, its longest 20 miles at an altitude of 800 feet. The plane's chief financial backer was a man named E. W. Wakefield from Kendal; its pilot was Stanley Adams. Early in 1912, a second plane joined the first, and Wakefield was said to have plans for five more, with which he hoped to establish a passenger route between Bowness and Grasmere.

There was a great deal of understandable enthusiasm for the project among local shopkeepers, who felt that aeroplanes would be good for business, and the press was regularly invited to take photos and write stories. The promoters energetically spread the word that the work they were doing had scientific merit and that the aeroplane — and specifically, the hydroplane — would prove useful if England went to war with the Germans. There was a great deal of war-talk in the years before fighting broke out, and the government was actively supporting experiments in flight.

But the local folk and those who loved the scenic beauty of the Lakes were not nearly as enthusiastic about the project. The letter Beatrix Potter begins on page 13 of this novel, expressing her unhappiness about the hydroplane, is an excerpt from one she wrote to Millie Warne on December 13, 1911. Potter spoke for the many who found the hydroplane not only a nuisance (what we today call "noise pollution") but a serious hazard to boating, fishing, and transportation, and she found in this "a cause she could not ignore, for both personal and environmental reasons," as Potter biographer Linda Lear puts it. In January 1912, Potter wrote to *Country Life* magazine, protesting that "a more inappropriate place for experimenting with flying machines could scarcely be chosen," citing the "danger to existing traffic — the traffic of steamers, yachts, row-boats and Windermere Ferry." She was specific about the situation:

We are threatened with the prospect of an aeroplane factory at Cockshott Point, between Bowness Bay and the Ferry Nab, and with the completion of five more machines before next summer. The existing machine flies up and down in the trough of the hills; it turns at either end of the lake and comes back. It flies at a comparatively low level; the nose of its propeller resembles millions of bluebottles, plus a steam threshing machine.

The flying continued daily, although there was a brief respite in February, when Potter wrote to Harold Warne that "the hydrop. seems to be stopped with ice at present."

Beatrix Potter wasn't the only one writing letters. That same month, Canon Rawnsley, a personal friend of the Potters and one of the founders of the National Trust, wrote to *The Times,* saying that "the value of the shores of Windermere as a resort of rest and peace is seriously imperiled." The barrage of letters continued for some weeks, and Potter herself launched a petition that garnered local and London signers. "I find radicals much more willing [to sign] than conservatives," she wrote to Warne. The National Trust formed a committee "to preserve Windermere from being used as an experimental ground for the hydroplane" and lodged protests with the home secretary, who brought Parliament into the act. On March 20, 1912, a meeting of Members of Parliament and "interested parties" was held in the House of Commons, where objections were raised to this rude disturbance of the tranquility of the Lake District. At the end of the meeting, it was decided to ask the home secretary to hold an inquiry and regulate the air traffic under the new Aerial Regulation Act 1911.

Shortly after that, however, the dragon took matters into his own hands. Oh, no — I'm sorry. It wasn't like that at all. It appears to have been a simple windstorm that did the damage. On April 4, 1912, Beatrix wrote to Harold Warne that she was "very pleased to hear that the roof of the hydro hangar has blown in, & smashed two machines." One of the aeroplanes was repaired, but the Water Bird was totally destroyed.

The British Admiralty must have been disappointed in this outcome, for there was serious military interest in the plane. It is not recorded that Winston Churchill ever visited the Cockshott hangar, although he certainly might have. He was keenly interested in flying and in fact took flying lessons himself in 1912–1913, stopping only when his instructor died in a plane crash (as the fictional Oscar Wyatt dies in this book) and his wife, Clementine, put her foot down, grounding him. As First Lord of the Admiralty, Churchill created the Royal Flying Corps in May 1912. It was his personal sense of urgency that got England into the air during the First World War and eventually made the seaplane an important weapon against enemy submarines.

In addition to inserting the dragon into the aeroplane story, I have taken a few other liberties with real-world facts, chiefly with the way Beatrix Potter tells her parents about her engagement. According to Linda Lear, she made that announcement some months later, in the summer of 1912, after which "there ensued another long and bitter contest of wills, not unlike the violent battle between badger and fox that she had described in *Mr. Tod*." If I were Miss Potter, I think I would have chosen to tell them in a letter.

Susan Wittig Albert
Bertram, Texas, September 2010

RESOURCES

Denyer, Susan. *At Home with Beatrix Potter.* New York: Harry N. Abrams, Inc., 2000.

Hervye, Canon G.A.K., and J.A.G. Barnes. *Natural History of the Lake District.* London: Frederick Warne, 1970.

Lear, Linda. *A Life in Nature: The Story of Beatrix Potter.* London: Allen Lane (Penguin UK) and New York: St. Martin's Press, 2007.

Potter, Beatrix. *Beatrix Potter's Letters,* selected and edited by Judy Taylor. London: Frederick Warne, 1989.

Potter, Beatrix. *The Journal of Beatrix Potter, 1881–1897,* new edition, transcribed by Leslie Linder. London: Frederick Warne, 1966.

Potter, Beatrix. *The Tale of Mr. Tod.* London: Frederick Warne, 1912.

Taylor, Judy. *Beatrix Potter: Artist, Storyteller and Countrywoman,* revised edition. London: Frederick Warne, 1996.

RECIPES

OAT CAKES

The oat cake has been the mainstay of Scottish breads for centuries, going back at least as far as the Roman invasion and likely before. It is traditionally made almost entirely of oats, the only cereal grain that thrives in northern Scotland. Oats made up the Scottish staple diet of porridge and oat cakes, a dietary pattern that flourished across the north of England. The oat cake is a flatbread, like a pancake, made from oatmeal and sometimes flour as well, and cooked on a griddle or baked in an oven. (You may also be familiar with its cousin, the Johnnycake, which is made of cornmeal and was often cooked on a board, shovel, or even stones, just as it had been done in Scotland long before.) This version is baked.

1 cup oats or quick-cooking oats
1 cup flour
1/2 teaspoon baking soda
1/2 teaspoon salt
1/2 cup shortening
2–3 tablespoons cold water

Mix the oats, flour, baking soda, and salt. Cut in the shortening with a fork or pastry blender until the mixture resembles fine crumbs. Add the water, 1 tablespoon at a time, until a stiff dough forms. Roll 1/8 inch thick on a lightly floured surface. Cut into 2-inch rounds or squares. Place on an ungreased cookie sheet and bake at 375° until set and barely brown (12–15 minutes). Serve warm or freeze.

POTATO AND SAUSAGE SOUP

Potatoes were grown in every garden and were served at every meal. This modern recipe includes celery, but at Hill Top Farm, it would likely have been made with celeriac, which was grown as a root vegetable and valued for its celery-like taste. Also called celery root or turnip-rooted or knob celery, it contains much less starch than other root vegetables and was an important addition to soups and stews.

1 1/2 pounds mild sausage
1 tablespoon butter
1/2 cup chopped onion
1/2 cup chopped celery
2 cloves garlic, minced
3 cups chicken broth
1 cup water
4 medium white potatoes, peeled and diced
1 cup cold milk
1 1/2 cups yellow cheese, grated
Salt and pepper to taste

In a large, heavy saucepan, brown the sausage and chop into small pieces. Remove the sausage from the pan and drain off the fat. Set aside. Melt the butter in the saucepan. Sauté the onion, celery, and garlic. Add the broth, water, and potatoes. Bring to a boil, reduce heat, and simmer, covered, for about 25 minutes or until the potatoes are tender. Drain. Mash about half the potatoes in the pan. Leave the remaining in chunks. Add the sausage and stir until heated. Just before serving, add the milk, stirring constantly. Add the cheese and stir until melted. Season with salt and pepper.

MATHILDA CROOK'S MOTHER'S SODA BREAD RECIPE

3 cups all-purpose flour
1 tablespoon baking powder
1/3 cup rolled oats
1 teaspoon salt
1 teaspoon baking soda
3 teaspoons dried herbs (a combination of thyme, marjoram, sage, chives, and rosemary)
1 egg, lightly beaten
2 cups buttermilk
1/4 cup butter, melted

Preheat oven to 325°. Grease a 9-by-5-inch loaf pan.

Combine the flour, baking powder, oats, salt, baking soda, and dried herbs. Blend the egg and buttermilk together, and add all at once to the flour mixture. Mix just until moistened. Stir in the melted butter. Pour into the greased pan. Bake for 65–70 minutes, or until a toothpick inserted in the bread comes out clean. Cool on a wire rack. For best flavor, wrap in foil for several hours, or overnight.

PARSLEY'S HONEY CAKE

1/2 cup light brown sugar
3/4 cup butter

3/4 cup honey
2 tablespoons cold water
2 large eggs
1 teaspoon vanilla
1 1/2 cups flour
2 teaspoons baking powder
1/2 teaspoon salt

Heat the sugar, butter, honey, and water in a large pan. When the butter has melted, beat in the eggs and vanilla. Mix together the flour, baking powder, and salt, and add to the sugar and egg mixture in three additions, beating well after each. Put into a greased 8-inch square pan. Bake at 350° for about 40 minutes. Frost while warm.

Honey Frosting

1 tablespoon honey
1 tablespoon cold water
3/4 cup confectioners' sugar

Mix the honey and water, then stir in the sugar. Pour over the warm cake.

Mrs. Jennings' Apple Pudding

When Beatrix Potter bought Hill Top Farm in 1905, there were already a number of apple trees on the place. She wrote to Millie Warne the next fall that she was busy with gardening chores, which included "putting liquid manure on the apple trees." In a letter dated October 6, she drew a picture of herself shoveling manure with a long-handled scoop. "The apples on the old trees prove to be very good cookers," she added. "We have had some for dinner." Miss Potter might have liked them baked in this traditional apple pudding.

Syrup
1 cup brown sugar
1 tablespoon cornstarch
1/4 cup butter
1 cup water

Apple Batter
1 1/3 cup sifted all-purpose flour
2 1/2 teaspoons baking powder
1 teaspoon cinnamon
1/2 teaspoon nutmeg
1/2 teaspoon salt
2/3 cup brown sugar
1/4 cup butter, melted
1/2 cup milk
2 1/2 cups sliced apples mixed with 1/3 cup
   brown sugar

To prepare the syrup: In a saucepan, combine the brown sugar, cornstarch, and butter. Stir in the water; cook over low heat until thickened. Pour the mixture into a lightly buttered 10-by-6-inch baking dish. To prepare the batter: In a bowl, combine the sifted flour, baking powder, cinnamon, nutmeg, salt, and brown sugar. Blend in the melted butter and milk, stirring just until dampened. Stir in the sliced apples mixed with brown sugar. Pour the apple batter over the syrup in the baking dish. Bake at 350° for 30 minutes.

GLOSSARY

Some of the words included in this glossary are dialect forms; others are sufficiently uncommon that a definition may be helpful. My source for dialect is William Rollinson's *The Cumbrian Dictionary of Dialect, Tradition, and Folklore.* For other definitions, I have consulted the *Oxford English Dictionary* (second edition, Oxford University Press, London, 1989).

Allus Always.
Auld Old.
Awt Something, anything.
Beck A small stream.
Betimes Sometimes.
Bodderment Trouble.
Dust, dusta, dusnta Does, do you, don't you.
Goosy Foolish.
How Hill, as in "Holly How," the hill where Badger lives.

Mappen Mayhap, perhaps.

Mebbee Maybe.

Nae No.

Nawt Nothing.

Off-comer A stranger, someone who comes from far away.

Pattens Farm shoes with wooden soles and leather uppers.

Reet Right.

Sae So.

Sartin, sartinly Certain, certainly.

Scotch, as in "Scotch that aeroplane." To damage, crush, destroy something dangerous.

Seed wigs Small, oblong tea cakes, flavored with caraway seeds.

Sumbody Somebody, someone.

Summat Somewhat, something.

Taties Potatoes.

Trippers, daytrippers Tourists, visitors who come for the day.

Verra or varra Very.

Worrit Worried.

Wudna, wudsta Would not, would you.

ABOUT THE AUTHOR

Susan Wittig Albert grew up on a farm in Illinois and earned her Ph.D. at the University of California at Berkeley. A former professor of English and a university administrator and vice president, she is the author of the China Bayles Mysteries, The Cottage Tales of Beatrix Potter, and a new mystery series set in the 1930s: The Darling Dahlias. She and her husband, Bill, also coauthored a series of Victorian-Edwardian mysteries under the name of Robin Paige. The Alberts live near Austin, Texas. Visit their website at www.mysterypartners.com. The Cottage Tales website is www.cottagetales.com.

We hope you have enjoyed this Large Print book. Other Thorndike, Wheeler, Kennebec, and Chivers Press Large Print books are available at your library or directly from the publishers.

For information about current and upcoming titles, please call or write, without obligation, to:

Publisher
Thorndike Press
295 Kennedy Memorial Drive
Waterville, ME 04901
Tel. (800) 223-1244

or visit our Web site at:

http://gale.cengage.com/thorndike

OR

Chivers Large Print
published by AudioGO Ltd
St James House, The Square
Lower Bristol Road
Bath BA2 3SB
England
Tel. +44(0) 800 136919
www.audiogo.co.uk

All our Large Print titles are designed for easy reading, and all our books are made to last.